Niccolò Ammaniti, Andrea
Massimo Carlotto, Sandrone Dazieri,
Giancarlo de Cataldo, Diego De Silva,
Giorgio Faletti, Marcello Fois,
Carlo Lucarelli, Antonio Manzini

CRIMINI

Short stories edited with a Preface by
Giancarlo De Cataldo

Translated from the Italian by
Andrew Brown

BITTER LEMON PRESS
LONDON

Fic
CRI

BITTER LEMON PRESS

First published in the United Kingdom in 2008 by
Bitter Lemon Press, 37 Arundel Gardens, London W11 2LW

www.bitterlemonpress.com

First published in Italian as *Crimini* by
Giulio Einaudi editore s.p.a., Torino, 2005

Bitter Lemon Press gratefully acknowledges
the financial assistance of the Arts Council of England

A CIP record for this book is available
from the British Library

ISBN 978–1–904738–26-8

Typeset by Alma Books Ltd
Printed and bound in the United Kingdom
by Cox & Wyman Ltd, Reading, Berkshire

Contents

Preface

It can be considered as a trademark, or else as an apt (or merely descriptive) synthetic label: either way, the expression "Italian noir" is now undeniably – some may say "dreadfully" – familiar to an increasing number of readers.

But what do we mean by "Italian noir"?

We mean, in my view, a group of authors who use the themes and paradigms of a genre that, in Italy, is pretty minor, if not downright rare. But in just a few years these authors have gained an audience for what is a decidedly original way of narrating the myths, the rituals, the (occasional) splendours and the (frequent) miseries of contemporary life.

These authors, it goes without saying, have all followed their own paths in total independence and without kowtowing to any schools, trends or literary cliques. They vary in their narrative backgrounds, their language and their own highly personal obsessions, which are described sometimes with glum melancholy and sometimes with savage sarcasm, sometimes in the mode of pathos and sometimes in epic style. And only the perception of a community of readers – nothing more, nothing less – has made it possible for this merry, anarchic mixture of such many and varied kinds of writing to be viewed as a "whole". The whole genre of "Italian noir", to be precise.

Such a huge diversity of styles and personalities could not fail to be reflected in this anthology which originated in an idea for television – narrating a "tour round Italy" in terms of noir fiction – and was eventually transformed into a kind of "snapshot" of Italian noir.

So this anthology, like any self-respecting noir, does not only subordinate logical development to emotion but also allows the reader to grasp and distil the basic themes that pervade it only once he or she has read right through to the end.

The first of these themes – the most intense, the one that is present in each of the stories – is corruption. Financial corruption: the desire to turn a quick buck, the spasmodic quest for a "short cut" to the hellish delusions of heavenly satisfaction. But also, subtler and more disquieting, moral corruption, interwoven with the sense of a loss of limits and with the abolition of all moral striving. And underlying this, a propensity to evermore violent criminal action, fuelled by a mystique of the "moment of decision" that finds expression as a sense of indifference towards the consequences of any act, however extreme.

The second theme, which has been present for some time in recent narrative fiction (not only in Italy), is that of the foreigner. These stories swarm with figures from the underworld, with labourers or women of easy virtue, with killers, thieves, tramps, desperadoes and maybe, here and there, a *deus ex machina*, all of them united by the fact they belong to a wave of migration that is perceived either as a threat or else as an unmissable opportunity for an old, tired, jaded country like Italy to renew itself. Immigrants are the new raw material of stories. The authors of Italian noir have been the first to realize this, and they have done so with great flair.

The third theme concerns the obsession with success – individual success, first and foremost, seen as something to be attained at any cost: a corollary of moral corruption and a sense of indifference to the consequences of one's own actions. But also, more specifically, success as fame, celebrity, a launching pad to the upper echelons of showbiz society. Such success is a guarantee of immortality and an antidote to the grey tedium of the humdrum life that awaits the majority, a boring existence that now seems nothing more than a source of pathological depression.

The result is a portrait of contemporary society that is at times chilling but not deprived of a few slender glimmers of hope. The picture is one of an ocean without beacons or landmarks, which you have to navigate by sight, trying not to lose your bearings. Or, if lose them you must, to do so at least with a certain style.

– GDC

6

Crimini

You Are My Treasure Chest

Niccolò Ammaniti and Antonio Manzini

> Sure but you'll have heard the name o' Groppone da Ficulle.
> He was the greatest captain in Tuscia so, an' it was me that
> with a single blow of my axe smote him in half, I did.
>
> *For Love and Gold* (1966)

Seeing him lying there on the sofa with a trickle of dribble smeared down his chin and half a bottle of Pampero rum clutched to his chest, you wouldn't have given him the change for a cup of tea. And yet he was a man of some importance.

He'd been born in 1960 at Città di Castello, to a family of craftsmen in wood. High school in Perugia. A brilliant career as a medical student at the University of Florence. Specialized in plastic surgery at the University of Burlington and then did a Master's in maxillofacial reconstruction with Professor Roland Chateau-Beaubois in Lyon. At the age of thirty-five, he was assistant consultant at the Bambin Gesú hospital in Rome and at forty, consultant at the San Roberto Bellarmino private clinic on the slopes of Monte Mario.

His name was Paolo Bocchi, the highly respected surgeon Paolo Bocchi.

Mr Bocchi was asleep on the sofa in a penthouse from which you could see the mosaics of Santa Maria in Trastevere and, further away, the church of Sant'Andrea della Valle rising up between the yellowing leaves of the plane trees along the banks of the Tiber.

The phone started to ring. It took about three minutes to stir Mr Bocchi's central nervous system, heavily congested as it was with cocaine and rum.

Bocchi slowly swung out one arm, groped around the floor trying to find his cordless phone and picked it up, uttering a guttural diphthong that might have been mistaken for an obscene noun in some Celtic language but was meant to be a simple "Hello?"

The voice at the other end was decidedly brisker: "Mr Bocchi, it's the secretary at San Bellarmino clinic here, I'm just phoning to remind you that at ten-thirty you're doing an additive mastoplastic. If you've got any problems getting here, Doctor Cammarano is happy to take over."

From this monologue Bocchi grasped three ideas:

1) he was supposed to be doing a boob job;
2) the operation wasn't tomorrow but today;
3) that son of a bitch Cammarano was ready and waiting to stuff him.

His reply was swift and to the point: "I'm on my way." He put the phone down and finally opened his eyes. His gaze fell on the elegant little table designed by Gae Aulenti. On it, three white lines were visible, together with a cellophane bag containing more or less two pounds of high-grade cocaine from the eastern Cordillera a hundred miles from La Paz.

With the sinuous winding movement usually found only in a coral snake homing in on its prey, Bocchi crawled over to the glass-topped table and with an adroitly flared nostril snorted one of the three lines.

Now he felt so much better.

He examined himself.

His Ferragamo moccasins were covered in mud, as were his trouser turn-ups. On his Ralph Lauren cotton sweater there were dozens of gorse prickles, and a nettle emerged from his socks. His pockets were full of soil.

"Where the fuck did I end up last night?" he wondered.

He remembered arriving outside the Hotel ES with . . . but at this point his memory ground to a halt, and beyond that everything went blank.

However, his general feeling was that he had spent an extremely pleasant evening.

He staggered out onto the balcony. The sun was shining over the roofs but hadn't yet started to roast the city. Down in the Vicolo del Cinque it was the usual hubbub. Cars hooting, voices shouting, dogs barking. He'd had it up to here with Trastevere. A villa in Saxa Rubra: that was his next objective.

He took off all his clothes and started to swill himself over with the hosepipe he used to water his plants.

From the shape Mr Bocchi's body was in, you could guess that in his younger days he'd played plenty of sport. He had indeed been something of a tennis player – he'd even won the Aureggi tournament at Borgo Sabotino several times over. But now his muscles had lost their tone. The only place they still showed much life was his belly, swollen and oval like a rugby ball. His hair, which he usually liked to wear combed back and encrusted with gel, was full of russet leaf-mould. His narrow eyes, sunken under a forehead as solid and square as a brick, were separated by a nose that he liked to think was imposing, though it was actually nothing but a thick, squashed protuberance.

As he dried himself against the fabric of his parasol, his gaze travelled down the façade of the house opposite until it reached the street corner and the window of the old Quattroni snack bar. Standing there was a guy who at first sight looked like a Swedish tourist. He was blond-haired and wore shorts and Birkenstock sandals; he had a knapsack on his back, and he was pretending to study a map of Rome.

"Bastards!" Now they were even disguising themselves as Scandinavian tourists. "Think you're going to screw me that way?" The guy down in the street wasn't a tourist but a narcotics agent.

They were keeping tabs on him.

Over the last month he'd already identified at least five plainclothes agents spying on him from the Quattroni bar: a pretend housewife laden with shopping bags, a street cleaner, a street bum with three mutts (sniffer dogs, obviously), an electrician pretending to change the bulb in the street lamp, and, quite definitely, Charin, the woman from the Philippines who came to do his cleaning and whom he trusted less than he did an Egyptian Airways Boeing.

He swiftly got dressed, pulling on a cool, crisp woollen suit from Comme des Garçons. He slipped on his Rolex.

Nine thirty-five!

He needed to get to the clinic pronto. He hadn't the slightest idea whether Charin was supposed to be coming in to do the cleaning today. What if she took advantage of his absence to come upstairs with the narcs, sniffer dogs and all?

He couldn't leave the coke at home. He snorted the two lines, carefully gave the glass surface a thorough lick, picked up the cellophane bag, dropped it into his jacket pocket and went out.

11

Where in fuck's name was his Jaguar?

Total blank.

He saw a Multipla cruising along, with a taxi badge. He hailed it.

*

The road along the Tiber was as choked as a toilet drain in Tiburtina railway station. His hands were sweating. He lifted one of them. It looked just as if he'd got Parkinson's.

Behind them was a compact metallic mass, hooting non-stop; a big scooter had been nosing the rear of the taxi like a gadfly ever since Ponte Garibaldi. It was driven by a girl who seemed different enough from the classic cop in civvies to be real. And why didn't she weave between the cars as any decent human being should?

But by now he was having to repress the tremor that had spread from his hands to his shoulders and was starting to attack his neck. There was no putting it off any longer: he needed another dose, just a small one, if he was going to be in any shape to operate.

He bent down and slipped his hand into his pocket. He stuck his proboscis straight into the cellophane bag and inhaled deeply.

He passed out.

*

"Doc? Hey, doctor!"

The surgeon came round when the taxi dropped him off in front of the clinic. He handed fifty euros to the taxi driver and clambered out.

His limbs had grown as stiff as if he'd injected Polyfilla into his veins. His knees and elbows were as rigid as if they'd been encased in aluminium. He tottered into reception. He made his way forward slowly, swaying like Robocop after a gunfight.

To give himself a casual air, he was chewing on a Cohiba Lancero cigar that he'd happened to find in his jacket pocket. He gave a Mussolini-style salute as he said hello to the girls at reception and took the elevator up.

The corridor leading to the operating theatre went on for ever.

Paolo Bocchi made his way along it with his heart thrumming in his ears. There was a bitter taste in his mouth.

I haven't even had a coffee, he said to himself as he crossed the path of a black porter helping an old woman totter along on her Zimmer frame. "Good morning, doctor."

With a forced smile, Bocchi returned his greeting.

Who the fuck is that?

Another spy.

He went into the changing room where he found Sara, his right-hand assistant. "Ah, you made it."

"Sorry, Sir . . . ?"

"Nothing. It's just that . . . with all this traffic . . ."

Even Sara, with whom he'd worked for ten years, had gone over to the other side. Bitch! She even preferred that pansy Cammarano.

He was alone, surrounded by throngs of enemies.

He scrubbed up as the nurse slipped his gown on. "Don't you want to take your jacket off, Mr Bocchi?"

"No fucking way," and he patted his swollen pocket.

They slipped on his gloves, surgical mask and cap.

He took a deep breath and, holding his hands aloft before him, went into the operating theatre.

*

There was a beautiful woman lying naked and anaesthetized on the operating table. She was tall, white and slim.

"Who is she?" Paolo Bocchi asked the anaesthetist.

"Simona Somaini. The actress off the television."

"And what's wrong with her nose?"

During his taxi ride the surgeon's mind, like a sieve, had failed to retain what the clinic secretary had told him.

The operating team looked at him in embarrassment, then Sara leaned towards him, "It's an additive mastoplastic." And she pointed to two huge silicon prostheses lying ready on the trolley.

The actress didn't have big boobs, true, but the ones she did have weren't bad at all.

Perhaps he ought to try and talk her out of it. She was running the risk of swayback with all that weight on her chest.

13

But why should I give a shit?

The surgeon closed his eyes. His hands relaxed and his fingers became as nimble as those of Glenn Gould playing the *Goldberg Variations*.

He put all his anxiety, fear and anguish on a back burner of his mind.

"Scalpel."

Once he felt the steel of the scalpel against the flesh of his fingertips, he once more became the celebrated surgeon, the man who had restored the youthful looks of hordes of featherheaded Roman women. He moved with the grace and agility of Oriella Dorella dancing *Swan Lake*.

With a thrust of his blade he made a long incision under the left breast and started to gouge out the mammary gland.

The theatre assistants and nurses could see that the master had not lost his touch.

Then, just as it had begun, the spell evaporated. His hands went stiff, and the blade of his scalpel came up against a rib. He was sweating, and his sweat ran down into his eyes, blinding him. "Nurse, could you wipe my forehead please?"

"Isn't the incision too wide? The scar will be visible . . ." the assistant ventured.

"No, no . . . It's better like this. It's a big prosthesis."

He looked up at the team, staring into their faces one by one. They knew . . . They knew all about him. And the thing that hurt him most was realizing they were afraid. Afraid he might hurt this woman. He resumed his work, clenching his teeth and yearning more than he'd ever yearned in his whole life for another line of coke.

Suddenly a nurse entered; she came up to him and murmured in his ear: "Mr Bocchi, sir, there are two people who'd like a word."

"What? *Now?* Can't you see I'm in the middle of an operation? Who is it?"

In some embarrassment, the nurse whispered, "It's the police . . . They say it's really urgent."

The room started to sway. He clung to the thigh of the anaesthetized patient so as not to end up measuring his length on the floor.

"Anything wrong, sir?"

He gestured that everything was fine. He turned to the nurse "Tell the police I really can't . . . ! I'm operating, dammit . . ."

Bocchi realized how long he'd been waiting for this moment. At last, it was all over. Now they'd just need to find a nice little clinic for him to go and detox in. He could weave baskets there. The idea rather attracted him.

When confronting the inevitable, it's better to put a brave face on it, his father had always said. Wise words.

But a nasty little voice kept whispering to him: *Where do you really think you're going, chum? Don't forget you've got so much coke on you that you'll be lucky to get off with ten years.*

"Anything wrong, sir? Not feeling so good?" The words of his assistant brought him back to reality.

"Sorry . . . can I have the number five forceps please?" he stammered.

They handed the forceps to him and, barely holding back his tears, he started to probe the connective tissues.

Pull yourself together, you schmuck, try and come up with an idea. Make an effort.

And the idea came.

The surgeon's coke-addled brain plucked it out of thin air: just like that, as if the Coke Fairy herself had kindly and quietly suggested it.

He took a deep breath and asked the assistant to get some thread for stitches from the other operating theatre; he asked the theatre nurse to check that the blood pressure apparatus was working okay; and he sent the other nurse to fetch the patient's medical records.

And for a while, for a single, brief instant, he was alone.

Just himself and the actress.

He picked up the sterile silicon prosthesis and shoved it into his left jacket pocket. Meanwhile, with his right hand, he pulled out the bag of coke and slipped it into Miss Somaini's boob.

Perfect.

The rest of the operation passed quickly and without complications. He made an incision in the other breast, inserted the second prosthesis (the real one), and with a firm hand manoeuvred them both into place underneath the mammary glands.

"Okay then, we're all done here. Sew her up and take her into the recovery room," said the surgeon. And then: "So . . . now let's go and see what those gentlemen want."

Two years later

Under a sky as heavy as a cast-iron skillet, the gates of the Rebibbia prison swung open, and three men came out.

The first was Abdullah-Barah, an Algerian purse-snatcher, a persistent offender; he'd been given six months. The second was Giorgio Serafini; he'd been working for the Association of Italian Authors and Publishers when he'd siphoned off the royalties from the song 'Gioca Jouex' by the well-known DJ, Claudio Cecchetto. The third was a plastic surgeon, and his name was Paolo Bocchi.

The incredible thing about it all was that he hadn't been given two years for possession and supplying of narcotics.

In 1994 Paolo Bocchi had embezzled money that was meant for humanitarian aid to the disabled children of Cambodia. The sum involved came to a total of several thousand million old lire, which he had successively invested in:

1) a penthouse suite in Trastevere;
2) one of the historic cave-dwellings on the island of Pantelleria, given a style makeover by the famed Scintilla Greco interior design company;
3) a 1972 Riva Superacquarama that had sunk in Lake Bracciano;
4) an unspecified quantity of narcotics;
5) and finally a lifetime subscription to the "Blond Tiber" Rowing Club.

When he came out of prison he was clean of drugs. He'd also been cleaned out of all his worldly possessions.

He was flat broke.

*

In those two years, while the surgeon rotted away in a cell he shared with three members of the Chinese mafia, the actress Simona Somaini, with a little help from her breast enlargement, had become the star of various Italian TV dramas.

Her role as Maria Montessori, in the serial of that name in seventy-six episodes, has become the stuff of legend: it kept the whole nation glued to its screens for eight months. Thanks to the little Psaoin TV set, Bocchi did not miss a single one. He stayed glued to the mind-boggling boobies of the educational theorist from Rome, devouring them with his eyes through the cathode tube. But it was no primitive sexual desire that drove him.

Those breasts were his treasure chest, bouncing and jiggling.

Over his prison cot he'd fastened the "Max" calendar on which Miss Somaini was, without too many scruples, showing off her generous décolleté. Bocchi had circled her left boob with a marker pen. In Rebibbia, he was considered to be Somaini's number one fan. All the prisoners passed on to him tons and tons of women's gossip mags in which the actress's love life was closely tracked. The only other reading matter he had allowed himself during his incarceration was Dumas's *The Count of Monte Cristo*.

*

By the time Bocchi came out of jail he'd put on thirty pounds. The endless card games in the cell, the shitty food and the gallons of sake had made him swell out. His skin was the colour of the waxworks at Madame Tussaud's. He'd shaved his grey hair right off. He was wearing the same woollen suit he'd gone into jail with. Now he could barely get into it. All he had left was a bus ticket (courtesy of Ling Huao), 30,000 lire (the lira had not been legal tender for two years), a bag stuffed with women's mags (*Novella 2000* and *Eva 3000*) and an infallible plan for recovering his treasure.

Once he'd got back what was rightfully his he'd be flying off to a tropical paradise where he would spend the rest of his days.

He took the metro and got off at the Circus Maximus. Two years had gone by, but Rome was still the same old shithole.

He headed for San Saba. He arrived at Via Aventina, number 36.

17

The nameplates by the entry phone only gave the internal numbers. He rang number 15.

The voice of a Philippino woman replied, "What you want?"

"I'm a friend of Flavio's . . . Is he home?"

"Flavio who? No Flavio!"

An elegant door porter with the aristocratic bearing of Alec Guinness was observing him with an expression of disgust, as if he were some poor mutt off the streets.

In that gaze, as penetrating as a CAT scan, Paolo Bocchi saw his condition reflected.

A dropout, an outcast, someone who on the social scale came only one step higher than a Senegalese refugee who'd just disembarked at Lampedusa.

He, the surgeon to VIPs, now felt intimidated by a door porter. He'd never have dreamed it.

"Can I be of any help?"

"I'm a friend of Flavio Sartoretti . . ." said Bocchi, keeping it short and simple.

The doorman started to shake his head slowly from side to side. "No."

"No what?"

"No he doesn't live here any more . . ." He turned his back on Bocchi and walked away.

Bocchi, with a gesture that had by now become habitual, clung to the bars of the gate. "So where's he living now?"

The lordly figure lifted his hands skywards and went back into the porter's lodge.

*

Flavio Sartoretti was a comic actor, famous the length and breadth of the land. He was a great mimic, a cabaret artist and an actor in "committed" films, but his career had really taken off when he became a pillar of the programme *Welcome to Sunday* and the indisputable star of the *Maurizio Costanzo Show*.

Flavio Sartoretti and Paolo Bocchi had got to know each other when they frequented Body and Soul, a health and fitness club at Portuense which, behind body peel sessions and Ayurvedic massages, acted as a front for a circle of Russian whores, drug pushers and arms traffickers.

Here the two of them fucked Irina together, snorted anything they could get their hands on and bought a couple of Kalashnikovs so they could go and shoot sheep out near the coast, at Maccarese.

Flavio Sartoretti reached the peak of his popularity thanks to his hilarious take-off of the AS Roma striker Paco Jiménez de la Frontera, bought from River Plate for thirty thousand million lire; he won the Golden Boot in 2001 and was the unrivalled idol of the whole capital.

Then, in 2002, Flavio Sartoretti had dissolved away like a kidney stone bombarded by magnetic fields. And nobody knew what on earth had become of him.

*

After exhaustive investigations, Paolo Bocchi read in a paragraph in the local news rag, the *Gazzettino dell'Agro Pontino*, that his old friend would be appearing that evening at the Festival of Lobster Ravioli at Nettuno.

*

Paolo Bocchi got off the coach just a few minutes before the comedian finished his gig in front of a party of old-timers from the Villa Mimosa retirement home.

Sartoretti wasn't particularly delighted to see his old partner from the good old days, but he agreed to go for a quick meal at the Blue Pagoda, a Chinese restaurant some sixty miles from the Via Pontina. Over their bowls of sweet and sour soup, the two men gazed at each other. Both reflected that the other was really showing his age.

"What the fuck has happened to you?" they asked each other in unison.

Paolo Bocchi told his friend that he'd been spending the last two years in Afghanistan, where he'd joined Médecins Sans Frontières to treat those affected by the horrors of war. Sartoretti stared at him. "Get out of here . . . me too! I went to Angola to cheer up

NICCOLÒ AMMANITI • ANTONIO MANZINI

the kids in the hospitals . . . I reckoned you only live once, and it's important to give a laugh to those that really need it . . ."

They ordered chicken with almonds and squid with bamboo shoots.

As they stuffed their faces, Bocchi decided that the moment had come to pass on to serious matters, "I've got a plan . . . to make a bit of money . . . and I was thinking . . ."

"How much?" Sartoretti interrupted him.

"Ten thousand euros!"

"What's the deal?"

"You need to help me get in touch with Simona Somaini."

"Yeah, I know: the actress," replied Sartoretti, pulling out a ring of squid from the hot broth. "But you know . . . being in Angola, my contacts . . ."

"Stop messing with me! I don't give a monkey's whether you know her or not! Just listen . . . I've spent quite some time studying Somaini's biography. Her life looks just perfect. Professional success for one thing: after the Salerno Prize for *Text Message From The Beyond*, she's been queen of the TV dramas. She's loaded with money. She's going to be presenting the San Remo Music Festival with Samantha de Grenet. 'What's missing in her life?' you may ask. You'd never believe it, but there *is* something missing. A love story that will get the women's-mag readers reaching for their hankies. That affair with Michael Simone, the PR for Excalibur, was a load of bullshit, all dreamed up by the dailies. That business with the playboy . . . Graziano Biglia: a short-lived fling. There's just one thing Simona needs: the football player!" And he pointed to Sartoretti.

"How the hell do I come into this?"

Bocchi nodded with a sly smile, "Oh, you come into it all right, my friend. You transform yourself into Paco Jiménez de la Frontera and you invite her out for dinner!"

At the name of the Argentine centre forward, the comedian almost choked on a sliver of bamboo.

"Forget it," he mumbled. "Not for all the tea in China."

*

After two pots of warm sake, Flavio Sartoretti confided in his friend that on the 25th of March, 2002, at four-thirty p.m., he'd gone to his dentist's, Dr Froreich's in Via Chiana, for a dental X-ray.

While he was sitting in the waiting room, four heavies had come barging in: Salt Beef, the Pit-Bull, Rosario and the Undertaker.

Salt Beef, whose right biceps was tattooed with the She-Wolf of Rome and the twins Romulus and Remus, and whose left biceps was inscribed with the first twelve lines of the *Aeneid*, had grabbed him by the scruff of his neck and flung him into the trunk of a Ford Ka. When they pulled him out, he found himself aboard the Civitavecchia-Olbia steamer.

They'd dragged him by the hair to the foredeck, where Rosario, the group's theologian, had addressed him in these terms:

"The image of Paco Jiménez de la Frontera is not for repro-duction. You don't draw him; above all, you don't take the piss out of him the way you do by trying to copy him. Taking him off like you do is pure blasphemy! And you're gonna to be punished according to Koranic law!" And they tied his ankle to a rope and keelhauled him four times over, in the time-honoured way of buccaneers.

When they pulled him out, more dead than alive, the Undertaker – who on his back had a tattoo of the Rome Orbital Road, including exit roads and petrol stations – politely suggested that his impression of the legendary centre player was not to be repeated.

Paco Jiménez was not amused.

"From now on you're gonna be silent and invisible like the little fart you are," Rosario had advised him.

"Forget about television. Not even as a TV salesman," the Pit-Bull had snarled.

From that day on, Sartoretti's star had waned.

*

"Oh fuck . . . could have done without that . . . But what if it's for 20,000 euros?"

"No way . . . Can't do it. They'll murder me."

"But look, nobody's going to see you. You only have to ask her out to dinner. Then you drop a couple of Rohypnol in her glass. I'll take care of the rest."

The rest consisted of operating on the actress and getting his cocaine back. Then he'd jump onto the next plane and spend the rest of his life relaxing on some coral beach in the Mauritius archipelago, rich and happy.

Bocchi took exactly three hours and twenty-three minutes to convince the comedian.

At 25,000 euros, Sartoretti gave in.

*

Simona Somaini was trying to read the script of *Doctor Cri 2*, the follow-up to the successful TV series that had turned her into the absolute star of the show.

She didn't like it the least little bit. Too technical. All those scientific names: epidural, mammography, cartilages, Saridon – she couldn't get her head round them. There was no love here, no feeling, no great passion. Those were the things her fans wanted. Not stories about abortions, junkies and the handicapped.

She phoned her agent, Elena Paleologo Rossi Strozzi, for the fourth time.

"Ele . . . It's no good! It's like being in a home for the disabled. Spastics, cripples, mongols, junkies . . . Anyway, what's up?"

"Simo, keep your hair on! I've got some fantabulous news! Are you sitting down?"

The actress looked down at herself. She was on her exercise bike. *Ergo* she was sitting down.

"Yes. So . . . what is it? Hollywood?"

"Bigger!"

"Oh my God! The Telethon!"

"Better!"

"Oh, please please tell me! I'm *dying* to know!"

"You've got an invite to dinner . . ."

"Huh . . . ? Well, big deal! I was expecting a bit more than that."

"Don't you want to know who with? Paco Jiménez de la Frontera."

The agent heard the noise of something crashing to the ground, followed by an ominous silence.

"Simo? You still there?"

Somaini crawled across the floor and picked up the cordless phone.

"Don't you ever fuck with me like that again! I won't stand for it!"

"But it's true! In two days' time! Simona, you've made it! This is your big break! I'll take care of the paparazzi . . ."

The actress shot to her feet as if someone had shoved a rocket up her backside.

"What can I wear?" she wailed. "I don't have a thing! *Oh – my – God!*"

"Listen, Simo, tomorrow we start flashing our credit cards, and we shop till we drop!"

"Okay . . . okay . . ." she gasped. And then: "Screw it! I don't have time to get my cheekbones heightened . . ."

*

The plan Bocchi had hatched was pretty complicated.

To begin with he needed to get hold of a really swish car, something that would be worthy of the great Argentine footballer.

The Chinese guys he'd shared a cell with in jail had given him the address of a certain Huy Liang, who without a word gave him the keys to a bottle-green 131 Mirafiori '79.

Then Sartoretti, putting on Paco's hoarse voice, booked a table for two at Regions of Italy: the most exclusive restaurant in the whole capital, run by the temperamental Bulgarian chef, Zoltan Patrovic, a great pal of Somaini's.

Their meticulous plans ran into an unexpected hitch: Jiménez only ever wore Prada.

And Sartoretti, in his one-room studio out in Forte Boccea, only had a Sergio Tacchini acetate jumpsuit and a sequin-studded smoking jacket.

At this juncture, Mbuma Bowanda weighed in with some advice on the right look. Mbuma was a sixty-three-year-old Sudanese pastor whose skin was scarred and scaled by psoriasis. Right now he was sharing a cardboard shelter with Bocchi under the Sistine Bridge. The only thing Mbuma owned was the robe he had worn for his initiation into the priestly life, now jealously stashed away in a Giesse beachwear bag: it was a long tunic in coarse cotton, decorated with imaginary figures based on rock-paintings. Mbuma and Paolo Becchi opined that Sartoretti looked both elegant and casual in it.

"You really sure?" he asked, staring at his reflection in the turbid mirror of the river's surface.

In addition to the African tunic, he wore Bocchi's old Adidas trainers, in preference to a pair of down-at-heel shoes that had floated ashore on the banks of the Tiber. And finally they dyed his hair Barbie blond, with the ammonia nicked from the cleaner at the Bambin Gesú hospital.

Perfect!

*

Elena Paleologo Rossi Strozzi lay sprawled on the sofa, half-buried in a huge pile of shopping. Like a horde of rampaging Visigoths armed with credit cards, they had ransacked the shop windows of half the Via Condotti.

Somaini was walking round and round the living room, naked. Anyone with an ounce of testosterone in his veins would have massacred his whole family just to be there.

She had thighs as long as the Via del Corso, rising to two hemispheres of an architectonic splendour worthy of Renzo Piano. Her waist was slender, and her shapely abdomen curved down to a pubis covered by a downy strip the colour of malt whisky. Her luxuriant, glossy, unruly hair framed a face in which her plum-coloured lips glistened and her black Berber eyes gleamed.

But all of this paled in comparison with those masterpieces of modern surgery, her tits. They were gigantic, sticking out in protuberant splendour from her chest like two juicy watermelons.

Elena Paleologo Rossi Strozzi was healthily heterosexual, but she'd happily have had a fling with her favourite client.

She looked down at herself: as lanky as a middle-distance runner from Ethiopia, as flat as the electrocardiogram of someone who'd just croaked and as tall in stature as a jockey from Newmarket.

She wondered why it was that the Almighty, in His infinite wisdom, distributed His gifts in such a bloody unfair way.

"So, what shall I wear?" Simona asked her agent.

"As little as possible, my treasure!"

*

At 7:42 p.m. precisely, Sartoretti-Jiménez was ready.

He climbed into his 131, and Bocchi and Mbuma pushed him out onto the causeway along the Tiber. He engaged second and headed off.

*

Simona Somaini's penthouse suite was in the prestigious Parioli district, in via Cavalier d'Arpino – and thank God the street sloped downwards.

Sartoretti rang at number 15. The croaking voice of a Philippino maid replied, "Hello?"

"Soy Paco."

"The signora she comes straight down."

The actor's heart leaped halfway up his throat. He walked up and down, telling himself over and over, "You can do it. You can do it!"

*

And in the elevator, Somaini too was telling herself, "You can do it. You can do it!" She took a last glance at herself in the mirror. Not even at the Castrocaro New Faces, New Voices talent show had she dared to bare so much. Under a slender tube of tissue paper she was practically naked. The lift doors opened. She took a deep breath, and her high heels clicked across the atrium, all marble and *trompe l'oeil*.

Signor Caccia, the engineer, was just back from taking his Alaskan Malamute out for his evening piss. His path crossed Somaini's: he skidded, and his bypass nearly blew a fuse.

The actress opened the gate and went out into the street. No sign of Paco. All she could see was a man disguised as a Negro. She wondered if it was carnival time – but it was June! And yet his face bore a marked resemblance to that of Jiménez, despite showing all the symptoms of an attack of typhoid fever. Her memories of him were of a distinctly more attractive and healthier-looking man. And then she was sure he was a natural, not a peroxide blond, without this guy's receding hairline . . .

But this was no time to start creating problems.

The footballer advanced towards her.

"*Olà . . . chica . . .*"

"Ciao, Paco! It's *such* a thrill meeting a Golden Boot champion!" She offered her face for a peck on the cheek. Paco merely shook her hand.

"*Tambien tambien . . . Vamos!*" And he pointed to something on four wheels sitting double-parked out in the street.

Simona's mouth fell open

"*No te gusta?* She a vintage car. Lateest fashion in London . . . You know quanto she cost?"

Simona shook her head.

"*Mas . . . Muy mas!*"

Somaini, in some perplexity, climbed into the 131. She was greeted by a powerful pong of garlic and grease that almost brought up the Danone Slimline she'd eaten a couple of days before.

Paco, with the engine off, allowed the car to roll down the hill. Then, with a masterful gesture, he engaged second. The car spluttered into action and an illuminated Christmas Crib scene shed its light on the dashboard and the leopard-skin seats.

"She is some car, eh, *chichita*?"

*

Paolo Bocchi was riding the Fantic Caballero motorbike that belonged to Sartoretti's brother-in-law, following the 131 like a leech as it sputtered its way down the Viale Bruno Buozzi.

The plot that he'd hatched in the darkness of a prison cell over a period of two years was finally being put into effect.

His treasure chest was right in front of him.

Sartoretti was going to hit the jackpot. The big one.

*

Flavio Sartoretti drove on, feeling increasingly uncomfortable. Never had his sense of being an exile caused him as much grief as now.

It had all been the fault of that bastard footballer's lack of a sense of humour. Because of that, Sartoretti had been relegated to the sidelines of the glittering world of showbiz. In dingy, poky little venues, he had just scraped by on appearances at homemade cake awards, evenings at provincial nightclubs and beauty contests in godforsaken holes up in the hills of Aspromonte.

And now, like some punishment in Dante, he was being forced – all for peanuts! – to play the role of the very man who had brought about his downfall.

Once upon a time, he could have had a woman like Somaini just as easy as gobbling down a club sandwich.

He looked at himself. He was togged up like an African street vendor playing some ridiculous practical joke.

"Who designed your traditional costume, Paco?" asked Somaini. Her voice tore the spider's web of his thoughts to shreds.

"He's a styleest from North Africa. *Muy famoso* . . ." he replied, refraining from turning his head. If he'd seen her tits, he'd have jumped her there and then, in the Piazza Quadrata.

He took a quick glance into his rear mirror.

Bocchi, astride the Caballero, was right on his tail.

*

The Regions of Italy restaurant had been designed by Japanese architect Hiro Itoki as a miniature version of the whole country. Seen from above, the long building had the same shape and size as the Italian peninsula, islands included.

It was subdivided into twenty rooms, corresponding in shape to the different regions and offering all the regional specialities. The tables were named after the main cities. Sartoretti and Ms Somaini were led to Sicily, one of the most exclusive and secluded regions, just five yards away from Calabria.

The restaurant's main advantage was that nobody came bothering you for autographs and photos, since the clientele was handpicked.

They'd booked the table called Syracuse, separated from the other tables by a gigantic marine aquarium in which swam lobsters, groupers and moray eels. They were shown to their places by a waitress wearing traditional Sicilian costume.

The President of the Italian National Olympic Committee, sitting at the Catania table, saw Paco Jiménez de la Frontera come in. Eyeing the tunic he was wearing he called out: "Hey, Paco! What brings you to Lampedusa? Just swum ashore have you?" – and he snickered gleefully at his own joke to his lady friend.

"*Olà chico* . . ." Sartoretti replied curtly.

*

From the head of the Caltanissetta table, Sergio Pariani, the AS Roma goalkeeper, saw the Argentine centre forward taking his place with that nice piece of nookie, Somaini. He spat his first forkful of aubergine *caponata* out onto his plate and flattened himself like an American marine taking cover in the jungles of Vietnam.

"Get down, get down!" he hissed at Rita Baldo. "It's Paco! Fucking hell!"

Hearing this name, the well-known TV news presenter jumped up in her seat, "Where?"

Sergio, on all fours under the table, silenced her, "Shut it! You know that if my wife so much as . . . What if he's seen me?"

"He definitely *has* seen you! But he's pretending he hasn't. He's a real gentleman, not like you!"

The goalie, using the ancient respiratory techniques of Qi-Yi, tried to breathe out the anguish now gripping him. He relaxed his abdominal muscle, thereby lowering his diaphragm, and emitting a strangled wheeze.

"What the hell d'you think you're doing?" the journalist asked him.

"Panic attack! Panic panic panic . . . ! Shall I phone him? What do I do – phone him? I'll phone him! Yes, I'll phone him!"

He picked up his mobile.

*

He was cornered. He'd run out of bullets, and his pocket torch had run out of batteries. Now the only thing left was his pickaxe. Three zombie nurses had him surrounded and were moving in for the kill. He hit one of them, and she promptly disintegrated. But the other two had already sunk their fangs into him.

The phone rang. Paco dropped the joypad of his PlayStation 2 and answered it, "Who the f—?"

"Hey, it's Sergio . . ."

Paco loathed anyone phoning after half-past seven.

"What's up?"

"You ain't seen me!"

Paco was dumbstruck, "What you mean?"

"I mean you ain't seen me. If Luana ever finds out . . ."

"What?! Speak louder, *cabròn*, I can't hear you! Where are you?"

"I'm in Caltanissetta! Can you see me?"

"Er, nooooo." Paco wiped his brow. "The derby, it's in two days, eh . . . ? What you been smoking?"

"Hang on, I'll give you a little wave, that way you'll see me . . . There, see me now?"

Paco took a nibble on a *würstel* he was holding over an electric grill next to the sofa. "Sergio, you're starting to get on my tits!"

"Ah, yes, Somaini . . . Gorgeous, ain't she?"

"Yeah . . ." He hadn't the slightest idea what was going on.

"But d'you get my drift? We're both in Sicily. You know, there's times when life just . . . Anyway, this is the best region . . . I ordered the *caponata*. I can recommend the *pasta alla Norma*."

"Sergio, you're a fucking pain in the butt!"

"Sorry, I didn't want to hassle you. It's just that I saw you were in Sicily and thought I'd give you a spot of advice. But if that's how you're gonna take it . . ."

The two footballers were getting themselves in as much of a tangle as a plateful of spaghetti.

After a quarter of an hour, they'd started to sort out the confusion.

"You're right, it can't be you. I can see you – you ain't got the mobile. So who *is* that guy, then?"

"Let me get this right. I'm in the restaurant – and I ain't in the restaurant."

"Precisely. But he talks like you, he moves like you. Admittedly, his getup's a bit strange, but . . ."

"Okay Sergio. I understand. Thanks. I take care of it."

*

Simona Somaini was feeling tired. She couldn't keep her eyes open.

It was incredible: for two years she'd hardly slept for three hours a night and she never got tired. To be more precise, ever since the operation on her breast she'd been filled with the most incredible energy – a zest for life that meant she could keep going for ever and cope with working hours that would have brought an elephant to its knees.

And yet, this evening, here she was having dinner with Paco Jiménez de la Frontera, and her agent had probably rustled up a whole army of paparazzi waiting for her outside the restaurant – and all she could think of was snuggling down quietly in bed.

She mustn't doze off. Not now. Not this evening. Not with Paco.

*

Whatever could it have been? The chilled Planeta Chardonnay, the Sicilian pizza, the slice of bread and *meuza maritata*? Flavio Sartoretti had no idea. But he'd never felt as well and relaxed since he'd won that TV show back in '99. The only discordant note was having to watch Somaini drooping with exhaustion. She'd stopped listening to him. The three Rohypnol tablets he'd dissolved in her glass when she popped out to the loo were taking their effect.

What a pity. He'd really like to have screwed her later on that evening.

But he had an urgent need to satisfy before the actress lost consciousness completely.

"Simona, listen to me, you know an actor, a great actor, an actor *muy lindo che se llama* Flavio Sar . . ."

All of a sudden he found himself in a different, watery ambience, and in front of him Simona Somaini had been replaced by a grouper that was staring at him in perplexity. He saw Rosario, the Pit-Bull, Salt Beef and the Undertaker, their faces twisted out of shape by the glass walls of the aquarium, waving bye-bye.

Then somebody grabbed him by the hair.

*

Paolo Bocchi, outside the restaurant, kept nervously checking his watch. They'd been inside for a long time, and if everything was going according to plan, Somaini ought to be already out for the count.

Any minute now, Flavio would be emerging with the actress. He climbed into the 131. He gazed at the restaurant entrance. Finally the doors opened. Four Orcs straight out of *Lord of the Rings* were dragging along a soaked and bedraggled heap vaguely resembling Mbuma's tunic.

He swore. Someone had fucked up.

Then he saw something that was just incredible. One of those thugs was folding Sartoretti up like a leaflet and bundling him, against every law of the physics of solid bodies, into the boot of a Ford Ka.

Then all four of them climbed into the car and drove off.

Bocchi dashed out of the 131 and jumped onto the saddle of the Caballero.

He couldn't abandon him like that.

*

"Remember the film *Ben-Hur*, with Charlton Heston?" Rosario asked Flavio Sartoretti, who was lying on the ground of the Circus Maximus chained to an '83 Harley-Davidson Wide Glide.

Sartoretti emitted a wheezing noise that was meant to be a "yes".

Salt Beef revved up the twin-cylinder to four thousand. The exhaust fumes choked the actor.

"Remember the chariot race?"

Sartoretti could see where this was going. It was one of his favourite films, together with *Kramer vs. Kramer*.

"How many times was it they went round?"

Sartoretti whispered, "F-four. Like the f-four t-times . . . with the . . . k-keel . . ."

"Bright boy!" Then Rosario turned to Salt Beef. "Off you go . . ."

Salt Beef produced a burnout and the rear wheel put on a song-and-dance act of smoke and dust. He eased the clutch out, popped the bike into second and shot off on one wheel.

*

From up on the heights of the municipal rose garden, Bocchi saw his friend being dragged round the ancient Roman stadium. Behind the motorbike he writhed like a tuna as he was pulled through the stones, the piles of dog shit and the shards of broken bottles.

The former surgeon hid his face in his hands. As the roar of the Harley-Davidson echoed against the walls of the Domus Augustea, he was overwhelmed by despair.

He'd have to come up with another plan!

Two months later

Those two months were really tough for Paolo Bocchi.

He spent the first fortnight after the plan's failure huddled in his box under the Sistine Bridge listening to the cars whizzing past over his head. He tried and tried, but he simply couldn't come up with any new ideas.

Mbuma would come back late in the evening. He wasn't much comfort, filled as he was with homesickness for the arid wastes of his homeland. Bocchi decided it was time for action.

Sartoretti, in a clinical coma in the Fatebenefratelli Hospice, was no longer of any use.

One morning, while he was earning a few euros by washing the windows of Trony Electrics, he saw, on a TV plasma screen, Simona Somaini giving an interview to the *Life Today* programme. He dropped his washcloth and dashed into the store.

"I'm going to be Dr Cri all over again! It'll be my job to help people in need, just as before. We've tried to stick to reality as much as possible. In short, it's going to be exactly like in a real hospital."

"Any newcomers in the cast?" asked the dapper presenter.

"Of course. In particular, a new director. Michele Morin . . . a real pro . . . and . . ."

The right hemisphere in Bocchi's brain, where memory resides, juddered under a seismic jolt.

Michele Morin . . .

He'd operated on him five years ago.

It had been his masterpiece. One of those operations that ought to end up on the TV news and in the pages of *Nature* but which can never be openly mentioned. For an exorbitant amount of money, he'd signed a confidentiality agreement, in view of the extremely intimate and private nature of the operation. The surgeon had extended Michele Morin's male member to a length of nearly ten inches, where previously it had hardly reached three and a half, even when fully erect. Seven hours – that was how long the operation had lasted.

Michele Morin was at his mercy.

*

Antonella Iozzi was lying naked on the leather sofa of an apartment in the Viale Angelico. Her ash-blond hair was cut short. She was a slender figure; a pair of round, gold-framed spectacles was dangling over her flaccid tits. Her nose curved down between small, sky-blue eyes. She was as still as if she were sitting in the waiting room of a railway station. In front of her, on his short, fat legs, wearing nothing but a kimono, stood the well-known director Michele Morin.

Morin wasn't particularly impressed by the physical charms of his editorial secretary, but Umberto, the chief electrician in the team, had assured him that Antonella gave blowjobs with such sincerity, such total enthusiasm, that everything else paled into insignificance.

As a general rule, before he started filming, Michele Morin would get all the women in the team to give him a blowjob. He did this not out of mere sordid lechery but for two reasons. One was professional: in this way he created a greater sense of complicity with his female collaborators. The other was personal: it meant he could gratify his ten inches.

"Try swallowing this fat trout!" he told her, resorting to colourful metaphor as he drew his erect member from out of his kimono.

Antonella, who was several dioptres short of 20/20 vision, placed her spectacles on her nose and focused. "Jesus! That's a whale not a trout!!" she exclaimed in her Umbrian accent.

The director took her by the hair, like Perseus holding the head of the Medusa, and drew her towards him.

Just at that delicate moment, he heard, thirty yards away, a ring at his door.

"Oh who the fuck can that be?"

But if it was Grazia, the costume designer, things might become quite interesting. He hesitated for a moment, and then the idea of having a threesome won.

"You hang on here! I've got a surprise for you . . ."

*

But when he opened the door, disappointment awaited him.

It was a man.

"Don't even think about it. I'm not buying anything. Anyway, who let you in?" – At the next meeting of the condominium committee, he'd be asking for the head of the concierge on a platter.

"Michele! Don't tell me you don't remember me?"

The director did a quick scan through his famous photographic memory banks, but he was damned if he could put a name to this face. It must be one of the usual third-rate actors down on his luck and begging for a part as an extra.

"No. Sorry . . . I'm busy . . ." And he started to close the door.

But the man slipped an old Ferragamo moccasin into the doorjamb.

"Michele, you sound awfully sure of yourself. So you've got over that little psychological problem of yours then?" And he glanced meaningfully at the member dangling out of the kimono like the clapper of the bells in the cathedral at Orvieto.

Michele pulled his vesture together in irritation. "Get lost! What are you after, anyway?"

"That there" – and he pointed at the director's pubis – "is my masterpiece!"

Morin cast his thoughts back to the past, five years ago, when he'd been at the San Bellarmino clinic and had met . . . what was his name . . .? Bo . . . Bocchi! Paolo Bocchi. They'd been in the surgeon's office as Bocchi sized up his appendage.

"A couple of inches or so: that should have the problem sorted…" Bocchi had said.

"No, sir. I want more than what's strictly necessary."

If this great medical luminary had put himself out to come and see him, perhaps they'd discovered side effects, problems, perhaps a risk of imminent organ rejection.

"Mr Bocchi! I'm so sorry! I didn't recognize you. Come in!" And he took him into his studio and told him to take a seat.

Antonella could wait.

"But tell me, Mr Bocchi, is there anything wrong?"

Bocchi sat down and lit a cigarette.

"You could say there's something wrong, yes."

"Oh, my God . . . Now you've got me worried! What is it?" His hand moved instinctively to his groin.

"Imagine you've made a film . . . a masterpiece . . . let's take, hmmm . . . *Apocalypse Now* for example. You've made this great work, but you can't show it anyone. How would you feel about that?"

Whatever could the surgeon be driving at?

"I'd be gutted . . ."

"My sentiments entirely. That" – and he again pointed at the director's dangler – "that there is my *chef-d'oeuvre*. What do you say to me giving it a bit of an airing in public?"

Michele Morin blanched. "What . . . what do you mean?"

"You know that there's photographic evidence of before and after the operation? I'm pretty sure that several papers would pay through the nose for material of that kind! Especially given that it belongs to a famous director."

An image flashed through Morin's mind. Hundreds of women tittering behind his back. Their sneers would kill him. He saw himself hanging by the neck from a rope. Then a retrospective of his works on the Arts Channel at 2 a.m.

This piece of shit was blackmailing him.

"You can't do it!" he whimpered. "It's against the Hippocratic Oath. You'll ruin me. You signed a confidentiality agreement, and I . . ."

"What'll you do? Get me struck off?" Bocchi replied quite unfazed. "I already am. Jail? Been there. Sue me? Don't have a penny. As you can see, I don't have anything to lose. Whereas you . . . You'll look a right stupid . . . well, a right stupid prick – won't you?"

"I get it. You're a heartless bastard: you take advantage of other people's weaknesses . . ."

"Too right."

There was no way out. That son of a bitch had got him cornered, like a Range Rover stuck in a back street of Rome.

Morin collapsed onto his Louis XVI sofa. He knew he'd lost. "How much do you want?"

Bocchi shook his head.

"No: *what* do you want? That's the question you need to ask."

"Okay. What do you want?"

Bocchi stubbed out his cigarette.

"You're about to start shooting the TV serial *Doctor Cri*. I'm writing the third episode."

Morin didn't understand. "Why?"

"Just because. In this episode, Doctor Cri, poor woman, discovers a lump in her left breast and has it operated on. She's a doctor-turned-patient. From a dramatic point of view, it's flawless. And to operate on her they'll call in a famous surgeon from the States. Me. Accompanied by his Afro-American assistant, Mbuma Bowanda Jr."

Morin wondered if he'd overdone the Xanax the night before.

"But why, Mr Bocchi? You fancy a stint as an actor?"

"No."

"But I can't do it . . . I'm not bullshitting here: the whole network makes the decision. Somaini won't agree. I . . ."

"Look, Morin, I'm not going to bandy words with you. This is how things stand. In two days' time you'll get the script. Either I write the third episode, or you'll be all over the gossip mags. Be seeing you."

Bocchi got up and left the building.

*

SCENE 12 – OPERATING THEATRE INTERIOR DAY

Doctor Cri is lying on the operating table, anaesthetized. The team is anxiously awaiting the arrival of the famous surgeon James Preston.

CLAUDIO: But when's he going to get here?

LINDA: His private jet has already touched down. I can't understand . . .

At this moment the doors of the operating theatre open. Enter James Preston followed by his faithful right-hand man, Mbuma Bowanda Jr. All the team members feel intimidated: before them they have one of the legends of modern medicine. The women cannot believe how very handsome this artist of the scalpel is.

LINDA: Mr Preston! It's a real honour . . .

JAMES PRESTON: First, please all call me John. Second, we're team players, and by God, we're all of us equal here. I want you to give of your best and I know that, for Doctor Cri, you will give me your best.

CLAUDIO: Sir, I would like to be relieved of the obligation of taking part. For me, Doctor Cri is . . .

Preston silences the assistant with a gesture.

JAMES PRESTON: Claudio. Don't back out now. I can use you. This woman . . .

*

"This woman . . . ?" Bocchi looked up from the sheet of paper. "This woman . . . ?" he asked Mbuma, who was toasting homemade bread on the little bonfire they had lit on the riverbank. The African gazed into the distance, towards the Isola Tiberina. The setting sun

37

was casting an orange glow over the rooftops, and the sky was mottled by streaks of purple cloud. Then, in a slow, solemn voice, he rehearsed the lines: "This woman is to be the mother of your children, Claudio, and she will lead your flock to the great river!"

"Great stuff! You're a great writer!" And he carried on scribbling with his pencil stub.

*

On the third floor of the Viale Mazzini an extraordinary meeting had been underway for three and a half hours. Around the long walnut table, laden with bottles of water and plastic goblets, were sitting, in order: Ezio Mosci, head of organization for the RAI network, the director Michele Morin, Francesca Vitocolonna, producer at RAI, the actress Simona Somaini, the agent Elisabetta Paleologo Rossi Strozzi and the head of drama, Ugo Maria Rispoli.

They had just finished reading through the third episode.

Nobody spoke.

It was Mosci who broke the silence.

"Are you sure, Simona, that you want to show your breast? We could have you being operated on for a kidney stone, or a sebaceous cyst . . ."

Simona Somaini was drying her tears. "No! It's so beautiful the way it is . . . At last, a bit of heart, soul, life! It's the most beautiful episode in the series. For an episode of this calibre, I'm more than prepared to show my breast. The breast is a source of problems for so many women . . ."

And, like the professional she was, Elena Paleologo Rosso Strozzi picked up the ball and ran with it. "This is obviously going to heighten my client's cachet!"

"Sure, sure, of course . . ." cut in Ugo Maria Rispoli, sounding annoyed. "That's fine, but the scene in the operating theatre when the doctor's at death's door – isn't it just a bit too messy? All that blood, the defibrillators . . . You need to remember our audience."

"No, sir. They'll all be convinced that our main character is dying. Our viewing figures will skyrocket."

"That's right!" Somaini exclaimed in excitement. "It's a great scene! The blood is spot on. Our audience needs to realize that even Doctor Cri is a normal woman who can die under the knife just like anybody else. They'll identify with us!"

Ugo Maria Rispoli was doubtful.

"Hm. Okay then. Let's just hope we don't get a rocket from the viewers' associations . . ."

"You can rest assured. We won't be showing too much. I want people to be touched, I don't want it to look like an abattoir," interposed the director.

"Morin . . . your fate is hanging from a thread. You screw this one up, and you can kiss goodbye to that mini-series. You know the one: *Italian Heroes*."

There was a sudden chill in the air, as if the air conditioning had been turned up to full blast.

The director passed his hand through his hair and thought: *Okay, I'm risking my ass but at least I'll save my prick.* He looked at Ugo Maria Rispoli and nodded serenely, "Don't worry. Leave it to me!"

"And who did you have in mind to play John and his assistant Mbuma?" asked Francesca Vitocolonna, who was making notes on her palmtop.

"I've got them sorted," said Morin. "Two up-and-coming actors. Classic theatre training."

Nobody could think of anything to say.

"Fine . . . So . . . let's go for it," concluded Ugo Maria Rispoli. He lit a cigar and rose to his feet. "But don't overdo it with those tits. We go out before the watershed!"

*

In studio no. 2 at Formello, the set designers had already rigged up the operating theatre. In the day's schedule, the last scene to be shot would be the long-awaited operation on Doctor Cri.

In changing room no. 12, Paolo Bocchi and Mbuma Bowanda had already been through the costume designer's hands. Bocchi, with his surgeon's green gown, looked at himself in the mirror. The gown was his second skin. He felt at home in it. Mbuma

NICCOLÒ AMMANITI • ANTONIO MANZINI

rather less so. The make-up artist had plastered his face with tons of greasepaint to cover his psoriasis, with the result that his visage had assumed the green hues of a zombie.

"This time we're going to get lucky. I can feel it, Mbuma. We're going to Mauritius. White sandy beaches. Dusky maidens. The sea. Not a tap of work to do all day."

There was a knock at the door.

It was the director's assistant. "So, if you'd like to come down, we're ready and waiting . . ."

Bocchi looked at Mbuma, then nodded. "We're ready too!" He picked up a small packet and slipped it into his trouser pockets.

*

"Give me a frost! This light's too dazzling! . . . down a bit, down a bit!"

It was Marzio De Santis, the director of photography, going round like a water diviner brandishing his light meter. The weary electricians were dragging the quartz lamps and spotlights around, just waiting for this God-awful day to end. They'd shot eighteen scenes.

"Hey, Marzio, when're we gonna be finished? It's six o'clock! I'd like to spend Christmas at home, okay?" grumbled Umberto, the chief electrician.

One of the grips was just finishing setting up the dolly.

"Hey, Umbè!" he shouted. "At least now we can get an eyeful of Somaini . . ." And his hands sketched the actress's generous curves.

"Okay, you guys!" interrupted the assistant director, a young man with pigtail and goatee. "Set's off-limits. Everyone clear off while we're shooting. Somaini doesn't want any interference!"

"Shame!" came the cry of disappointment from every throat.

"Check. Two point eight, and we're ready," said Marzio de Santis to the number one cameraman, who immediately changed the aperture on the camera.

"Are we there yet? I really need to start shooting. Okay, actors!" – Morin was in front of the monitor, next to Antonella Iozzi who was sitting on a stool with her inseparable editing notepad.

In came Somaini wearing a dressing gown. The hairdresser was still smoothing down her hair.

"Hi there, Simona . . . we're ready!"

"Evening, everyone!" the actress greeted the team.

"Evening, Miss Somaini . . ." They treated her with a certain deference and at the same time kept darting glances at her, hoping for a quick flash of bare skin.

"Anybody who's not needed off the set!" Morin slipped on his headphones and adjusted the contrast on the monitor.

In came the main actor, the athletic-looking Fabio Saletti, who hailed from the reality show *Guantanamo*, where eight contestants lived together in chains for four months, in a nine-by-six foot cell: once a week they were tortured.

He strode over to Morin. "What do I have to do?"

The director put his arm round him and led him to the operating table, next to the other actors already waiting to shoot the scene. "So, Fabio, you just put yourself here, easy does it, you stand still and you don't touch a thing, and when you have to say your lines, you say them. Nobody'll bite you."

Morin returned to his monitor, shaking his head. It had been easier directing the swarm of African wasps in his first feature-film, *The Deadly Sting*, than getting that brainless twit Fabio Saletti to say just two lines.

Bocchi and Mbuma made their entrance. The prop-man rushed over to Bocchi. "Who's the surgeon, you or the Negro?"

"I am," replied Bocchi.

"Right then . . ." And he slipped a scalpel into his hand. "I'll just explain how you use this little thing. You hold it with two fingers . . ."

Bocchi stopped him. "I know how it works. Thanks."

Meanwhile Somaini had laid herself down on the operating table, covered herself with the operating sheet and taken off her dressing gown. It looked just as if two ripe watermelons had been placed between her and the sheet.

"Right, we'll start from where Simona is already anaesthetized. From the first scalpel cut . . . is the fake blood ready?"

"Ready!" came the voice of the set designer.

"Good; carry out the whole operation and keep going until I say *cut*. And please, when you're trying to bring her round, I want *real*,

I want *authenticity* – you need to think that she's really dying. And you, Simona darling, please, you need to be trembling like . . ." He couldn't think of an apposite simile. "Anyway, you know . . . you're a great actress. Cameras ready. Clapperboard in view."

"Now everyone quiet, and mobiles off or I'll say *cut*!" yelled Roberto, the sound engineer, who'd had it up to here with this lousy bunch of amateurs.

"Clapperboard in view . . ."

Bocchi went over to the operating table and took out a syringe, which he was holding concealed in the palm of his hand.

How often had he dreamed of this moment! His treasure was there, just a couple of feet away, buried under Somaini's mammary gland. His heart was racing just as it had done the first time he'd ever operated. He tried to calm down. He needed to be precise and swift. He looked at the Sudanese pastor. He too seemed ready.

"I said clapperboard in view!" yelled Morin. Bocchi bent over the operating table and quickly jabbed the syringe under the actress's left breast.

Inside the syringe was a cocktail of lidocaine, mepivacaine and benzodiazepine that would produce a local-regional anaesthesia in the thoracic region, while leaving Somaini awake and fully conscious.

The actress gave a start. "Ouch! What was that?"

"Just a pin in the sheet." Bocchi showed the tip – no more – of the syringe.

"Oh, do be careful!" the actress rejoined irritably.

"Okay, camera!"

"Camera rolling."

"Clapperboard in view."

"12 – 24 first!"

"Aaaaand . . . *Action!*" yelled Morin.

The camera was rolling.

Bocchi brought the scalpel up to the breast. He set it against the flesh. He tried to make an incision. The blade was blunt.

Fuck – it was a fake scalpel! How could he have forgotten?

But the blood, pumped out by the set designer, was issuing in copious streams from the actress's left breast.

Mbuma looked at Bocchi. He'd realized that something had gone wrong.

"Good, good!" murmured Morin in front of the monitor. "Zoom in, zoom in . . . Close-up on the breast," he ordered the cameraman.

Bocchi observed Somaini. Either she was putting on a world-class performance, or . . . Fuck it! All the symptoms were there!

Muscular tremors. Depression of respiratory activity. Narrowed pupils. Blue in the face.

A cocaine overdose!

When he'd given her the injection, the point of the needle had pierced the bag, and the drug had seeped into her bloodstream.

She was dying.

Bocchi looked at the monitor of the electroencephalogram. It was switched off! He punched it, not realizing that it was merely a stage prop.

"Defibrillators!" he yelled at the actress standing next to him.

She passed them over to him. Bocchi grabbed them. "Two hundred and fifty joules! Clear!"

Morin was in seventh heaven. He'd never shot such a realistic scene.

Somaini had stopped breathing. Her mouth was wide open as she laboured to suck in air, but the muscles of her thorax were paralysed. Bocchi placed the two electrodes to her chest. But nothing happened. He lifted them up and realized that the leads weren't attached to anything.

"What the fuck is all this?" he yelled at Fabio Saletti.

"But . . . they're not real!" the actor just managed to stammer.

"Oh, *screw you!*" Bocchi let fly and punched Pretty Boy on the nasal septum.

"Ow! You bastard! My nose!" He bent double while blood drenched his chin.

"Stick to the script! The script!" yelled Morin, rising and gesticulating at his actors.

The sound technician intervened. "We can dub all this. No frigging big deal as far as I'm concerned."

"Quick, Mr Preston! We're losing Dr Cri!" The actress playing the part of the nurse recited her lines.

Mbuma looked round and, with the age-old wisdom of Africa, turned on his heel and fled from the operating theatre.

Bocchi, meanwhile, was trying to perform a cardiac massage, but Somaini's heart was far, far away, on the verge of extinction like a dying star.

Dripping with blood, but still right inside his part, Saletti recited his lines. "Sir, we're going to have to intubate her!"

"But what the fuck do you expect me to intubate her *with*, you idiot? She's dying!"

Antonella Iozzi sat imperturbably keeping an eye on the script. "Michele, that line's not there!"

"Who the hell cares? Keep it rolling! Keep on shooting! It's fantastic!"

Bocchi tore off his surgical mask. "She's dead!" he said resignedly. Then he realized that Mbuma had made himself scarce.

He turned his back on the set and did likewise.

*

Four days later

The sun was already high over the Piazza del Popolo, roasting the throng that had gathered along the pavement. The citizens of Rome had reacted with intense emotion to the death of the great actress of TV drama. They'd been there ever since the crack of dawn to bid her a final farewell. There were groups of TV reporters everywhere. The police had formed a cordon to allow the authorities to reach the Artists' Church. Above the city's historic centre, police and *carabinieri* helicopters were buzzing like flies over a carcass. These were preventive measures against popular unrest and terrorist attacks. The traffic had been diverted. And the actors' union had asked all public buildings to fly the flag at half-mast and restricted traffic access.

The church, packed to overflowing, awaited the coffin in silence. Hundreds of wreaths had been laid at the altar covered in mourning cloth. The full orchestra of the Santa Cecilia Academy was tuning up. Maestro Renzo di Renzo was praying with bowed head. Ten dapper little priests were swinging their censers and filling the aisles with eddies of foul-smelling smoke. Sitting in the front pews were all of Somaini's relatives: they had travelled here in a coach direct from Subiaco, where the family had resided for centuries.

"Who's getting married?" asked Grandma Italia, who suffered from advanced arteriosclerosis. She hadn't understood a single damn thing.

Giovanna Somaini, Simona's elder sister, explained to Grandma for the umpteenth time that her granddaughter had died. Giuliana Somaini had no tears left, and she still couldn't understand how on earth her daughter, the light of her life, had died. Bowed down with grief, she leaned her head on the shoulder of Elena Paleologo Rossi Strozzi, who was wearing a Chanel funeral outfit. Then there were cousins, nephews, brothers-in-law, mothers-in-law and half of Subiaco. In this grief-stricken crowd there was one man with a tense, concentrated expression, staring at the carpet on which they would be laying the bier. This was Paolo Bocchi's last opportunity to take back what belonged to him.

The plan, this time, was of a disquieting simplicity. After the ceremony he was, somehow or other, to gain possession of the funeral car and take it to the pine forest in the Infernetto area near Ostia, where Mbuma, armed with hammer and tongs, was awaiting him to profane the catafalque. From here, the Fiumicino airport and Mauritius were just a hop, skip and a jump away.

The maestro raised his arms, and the orchestra started to perform Barber's poignant *Adagio*.

"Here she comes," murmured the crowd inside. All turned towards the entrance. The long funeral Mercedes was parked just outside it. They opened the door. In the distance, a man started to advance with martial step towards the altar. Paolo Bocchi couldn't understand what was going on.

How could a single man bear the coffin on his shoulders all by himself?

But there was no coffin. He was carrying an urn . . .

That stupid great tart had gone and got herself cremated!

Paolo Bocchi had stoically put up with two years in jail. He had seen a perfect plan fail because of one moronic actor. He had almost managed to get his hands on what rightfully belonged to him; he had fought his way through a severe depression; but when he saw that his sole *raison d'être* had been reduced to nothing, then the old, insane rage that had been pent up for so long inside him exploded like a nuclear bomb. He clambered onto the pew and howled in despair: "My treasure chest! Give me back my treasure chest!"

The crowd stared at him.

Must be a fan, driven to distraction by grief.

"Please calm down . . ." Somaini's brother-in-law took hold of him.

"I fucking will not calm down!" – and he darted out into the central nave. With a Fosbury flop, he cleared two rows of pews and ended up on top of Grandma Italia who, under the weight of this assault, corkscrewed round on herself and crumpled to the ground.

Crack!

Bang went her femur.

"Goddammit!" the old woman swore so loud that she drowned out Barber's *Adagio*.

Bocchi picked himself up. Everyone piled on top of him, like in a rugby scrum. He jabbed his elbow into little Pietro's face, ramming his dental brace into his gums.

"Aaargh!" Young Somaini dropped to the floor in floods of tears.

"You bastard! I'll kill you!" yelled his father. But Bocchi, with a well-aimed kick in his balls, silenced him. A forest of hands reached out to grab him. With a sudden swerve the surgeon pulled the censer from the hands of one of the dapper little priests and started to wield it like a mace, flooring anyone who dared to approach him.

"Stop! Police!" – Sergeant La Rosa drew out his Beretta pistol.

Bocchi, whirling his deadly weapon round and round, marched forward in a cloud of incense, like a horseman of the Apocalypse, heading for the man from the undertaker's. Paolo felled him with a well-aimed blow to the neck, and then rapidly swept up the urn like a running back for the Miami Dolphins and set off at a canter towards the piazza.

At the exit he was greeted by a burst of applause that faded away as soon as he darted to one side and crashed into the tables of the Café Rosati.

Rita Baldo, there with her TV news team, was the only person who deigned to help up the grief-crazed fan as he staggered to his feet from amid the broken glasses of Campari soda and smashed plates of open salmon sandwiches.

Sergeant La Rosa had caught up with him. Racing along, arms extended, he was aiming his pistol at him, "Stop! Stop!"

Bocchi, like a demented ninja, grabbed a glass ashtray, smashed it in two, and lashed out at the sergeant, bashing him on his front teeth.

"You wuckin' wastard . . . ! I'd only 'ust ween to 'er wentist's!" The representative of the forces of law and order fell to his knees.

The surgeon grabbed the pistol from the ground and shot three times into the air. The crowd scattered and started fleeing down the side streets.

*

Marco Civoli, from the special anti-terrorism forces, was hanging with his sniper rifle out of the helicopter hovering over the Piazza del Popolo.

"What's happening?" he yelled to the pilots.

Six hundred feet below, a man was running down the middle of the Via Ferdinando di Savoia towards the Tiber, followed by an angry crowd.

The radio burped and spluttered into life. "Calling all units! Dangerous subject, armed, heading towards Ponte Savoia. Repeat, dangerous. Must be stopped!"

Marco Civoli smiled. He had spent so much time shooting at cardboard cut-outs. This was his big chance.

The helicopter dived swiftly down towards the fugitive.

"Move it so I can nail him!" said Civoli, and loaded his weapon.

*

Bocchi hugged the urn under one arm and carried on running. He chucked the pistol away. He turned round. The crowd was still in hot pursuit. His heart was racing, and he was out of breath. Above him he could hear the whirring blades of the helicopters.

He crossed the causeway along the Tiber, just managing to avoid a Micra, but not a Smart, which crashed straight into him, breaking three ribs. He hauled himself to his feet only to be hit by a Burgman 250. The urn rolled to the kerb. Bocchi had lost all sense of feeling in his right leg but managed to limp over to the container and pick it up.

"Iss mine! Iss mine!" he mumbled, spitting out streams of blood. Everything was a blur. The plane trees, the cars, the wan sky. Then he realized that the low wall along the Tiber causeway, just there in front of him, had an opening from which a ladder led straight down to the river. He reckoned that God had placed it there especially for him. He climbed down it, howling with pain at every rung.

There was an unnatural silence. The only sound in his ears was that of his own breathing.

The sea before him was still and clear, and the seagulls were chasing each other over the watery mirror of the surface.

Mauritius . . . He'd made it!

At last he was there. It had been easy.

He took just one step towards the beach and his chest exploded. He looked down. In the stinking jacket of fresh wool there was a red hole. He stuck a finger into it.

Blood.

He collapsed onto his knees, raising his arms to the sky. The urn tumbled in front of him, and the lid came off. The ashes scattered over the pavement. A red mist veiled his sight. His head fell slowly backwards and then forwards, and he swayed for a while on his knees before falling face down amid the ashes.

"My . . . trea . . . sure . . . chest!" he gasped, and breathed his last.

*

Civoli had scored a bull's eye with his the first shot. The lieutenant pilot gave a thumb's up. The helicopter rose into the sky.

The corpse lay on the riverbank, with the bridge, the people leaning out of their windows to see, the Flying Squad cars, the rooftops, Castel Sant'Angelo, Saint Peter's, the Rome orbital, the sea.

The sea.

The Third Shot

Carlo Lucarelli

Halfway through the night, she got up to take off her bra. Marco had already been moaning in his sleep, so she gently lifted the blankets and slid out of bed; then she slipped her hands up the back of her T-shirt and undid the little hook. But that wasn't it, she knew, and when she found herself with her head back on the pillow, staring straight up at the pulsating reflection of the radio alarm clock on the ceiling, she said to herself, *I know what it is*, almost whispering it aloud, between lips dried and soured by sleep. She eased herself up into a sitting position, paying no heed to Marco who, this time, woke up, and said *what's the matter*, without a question mark, because he'd already gone back to sleep. *Nothing*, she said but without meaning it; she was really thinking, *I know what it is*, and she got up and went into the living room and sat on the sofa, pulling up her bare feet onto the cushion and placing a finger on her cheek so that she could gnaw at it edgily from inside, as if she wanted to make a hole in it.

She knew what it was.

So she went back into the bedroom, took the notebook out of the pocket of her jacket dangling from the back of the chair and went back to bed again where she sat upright, holding the notebook on her belly. But this time she kept her eyes closed.

She still didn't go to sleep, even when she put the notebook on the bedside table, and for a few moments she let her hand rest on it, as if the contact could make her stronger and stop her changing her mind. And all the rest of the night, she felt – just a bit, just a tiny bit – calmer.

*

"What's up, didn't you get much sleep? That Marco must be some stud, hey? Who'd have guessed . . . he looks as if the thought never even crosses his mind . . ."

"Fuck off. The thought crosses his mind all too often, like it does yours. And don't think I didn't get much sleep, 'cos I didn't get any sleep at all, actually. But Marco didn't have a fucking thing to do with it."

She didn't usually talk like this. Or rather, she didn't talk like this to him. He'd known her for ages, ever since she'd been a rookie *carabiniere* freshly arrived in Bologna, with her uniform so neatly ironed that she looked like a cover photo for an official journal entitled *Women in the Police Force*. And even now that the back of her jacket was more wrinkled than the shirt of a taxi driver in summer, after five years with the Flying Squad and a commendation that had gone to her grasping patrol commander even though she was the one who deserved it, a bit of respect, even now, seeing that he ran the office, a bit of respect, well – she always showed him *that*. And so she directed his gaze to the sheet of paper she'd placed on his desk, and to her slender finger with bitten fingernail pinning it down on top of the other papers.

He picked up the sheet of paper and held it out at arm's length, since he didn't want to surrender yet to the passing of time or to the optician he never quite got round to visiting.

Bologna Central Police Station. Office of the Flying Squad. *I, the undersigned, Assistant Lara D'Angelo . . .*

"Well? I've read your report, I've already passed it on to the magistrate."

"It's wrong. I mean . . . it's incomplete."

"What do you mean, 'incomplete'?"

"In the sense that what I wrote didn't actually happen like that."

"What do you mean?"

She felt a great desire to bite the inside of her cheek, to give it a good chew, in fact, since she wanted to think things over, but she was also in a hurry to speak, since she was still afraid that she might say, and still wanted to say, *no, nothing, sorry* and then go away.

But he was the one to speak.

"Let's summarize the facts. On such and such a day, et cetera, et cetera, i.e. the day before yesterday, at 24:32 hours, a member of the public goes and telephones 113 because he's heard shots being fired at number et cetera, via Emilia Ponente. You and Officer Giuliano go there and find the window of a jeweller's shop smashed in and two Albanians on the ground. Dead. There waiting for you is Inspector Garello; he hands over his regulation Beretta, registration number etc. etc., and tells you he fired because, while he was off-duty, returning home from the cinema, he saw these Albanians smashing the windows, and then he told them he was police and ordered them to stop, but one took out a pistol and fired a shot in his direction. Garello, who's no rookie, had dropped down into a firing position and taken aim and then it was bang bang and he blew them away. Am I wrong?"

Lara shook her head and said nothing. She wouldn't have been able to, with her mouth awry and her lips all twisted to one side as she bit into her cheek.

"Signed and sealed by your partner Giuliano too. Then there's the evidence of the member of the public who phoned 113, a certain Signor et cetera. et cetera, a retired *carabiniere*, who informs you that *I distinctly heard three explosions that I immediately identified as shots from a firearm, given my past experience in the Carabinieri. I likewise declare that I heard two louder shots, as if from a larger calibre gun, and one that was not so loud, as if from a smaller calibre.* He also says, *two bangs and a bing*, and you, as is only right and proper, wrote it down. Isn't that right?"

There was a sharp stab of pain in Lara's cheek. She swallowed, and the sickly sweet taste of blood trickled down her throat.

"More or less."

"But you wrote it."

"Yes, but I didn't write everything. I lay awake all night thinking about it. The witness, the *carabiniere*, didn't put it quite like that."

"Bang, bang, bing. It's definitely Garello's weapon, two shots from a 9 mm, and the Albanian's little 6.35, that's right."

"No."

'Two bangs and a bing."

"No, two bangs *and then* a bing."

There, she'd said it. Lara touched her wounded cheek with the tip of her tongue and almost shuddered at the taste, as metallic as when you lick a battery. But the Inspector's face did not look as concerned as it would have done if he'd understood what she was saying.

"The Albanian fires and then Garello fires back," said Lara. "Bing, bang, bang. But the *carabiniere* says bang, bang and then bing."

The Inspector's face did not look concerned; it looked annoyed. More than that: it looked disgusted.

"To begin with," he said, "maybe the *carabiniere*'s wrong. Second, maybe you're wrong. Third" – he touched the tip of his finger and bent it backwards as if he wanted to break it – "let's say that, for the sake of argument – and this is *just* for the sake of argument – Garello had happened to be passing by and had seen a guy smashing the window and had said to him, 'Stop! Police', with his pistol at the ready, and why shouldn't you have your weapon out ready if you've seen two guys like that, one smashing a window – you'd have done the same, wouldn't you?"

Lara nodded, her mouth twisted, but on the other side, on the unbitten cheek.

"And now let's say, for the sake of argument, and *just* for the sake of argument, let's say that the guys there turn around a bit too quickly and one of them pulls out a gun, or even that Garello's got a 6.35 in addition to his service weapon, the sort that you carry with you because you never know, and then – just for the sake of argument, right? – he fires first, as anyone would, and then, to avoid any future hassles, he fires off a shot with what will now look like the dead Albanian's gun."

He leaned against the back of the armchair, his hands resting on its arms. He seemed calm, but he obviously wasn't.

"You do know who Garello is, don't you?"

Lara nodded.

"And are we going to put a colleague like Garello on trial just for two Albanian pricks?"

Lara didn't move. Then she shook her head.

The Inspector smiled. Now he seemed really calm.

"Let's leave well alone. If the magistrate smells a rat here, maximum collaboration please, and if not . . . well, too bad. And stop pulling such horrid faces with that mouth of yours: don't want to spoil those good looks . . . Sooner or later you're going to make a hole in that cheek."

*

Lara would have been a beautiful woman if she hadn't always thought she wasn't beautiful. Too lanky and too skinny, she always said, and in one sense this was quite true. Since she was tall and wore her blond hair cropped short, and especially when she was in uniform (the blue jacket with the white bandolier and those boots she wore in the patrol car, the clothes of a cop and not of a beautiful woman), at first glance everyone did a double take on her. But already at second glance, seeing that she was a bit awkward, with shoulders hunched to conceal an invisible bosom and arms that swung stiffly at her sides, people turned away, demoting her to the category of a gawky beanpole. In reality, Lara was neither quite so lanky nor so skinny. She was slender and athletic, built like a handball player, broad-shouldered, long-legged and with a discreet bosom. And a nice face, with steel-grey but kind eyes, under her cop's beret. Rather good-looking, the Inspector said. Yes, good-looking.

Special officer Giuliano Pasquale was in love with her. He was one of the few who had been lured into looking at her three times. Marco had done the same – but he'd got there first.

"Are you listening to me or not?"

No. Pasquale hardly ever listened to her. Partly because whenever it was his turn to drive, he concentrated fully on looking ahead, because – as he knew – he was absentminded, and if he hadn't kept thinking *slow down, watch the lights, keep an eye open for stop signals*, he'd have sailed blithely across at every junction. On the other hand, whenever she wanted to drive, which she didn't need to do since she was the patrol leader, he just looked at her and didn't hear what she was saying. He really liked the way she moved her mouth when she was speaking, curling her lower lip a little, but more on the right, so that it was only just perceptible. He wanted to kiss her, not sit there listening to her.

"The union, I was saying," she said.

"Which union?"

"Our union. I was saying I could maybe talk to the union about it."

"About Garello you mean? You're crazy. You know who Garello is. And anyway, he's in the union too."

Lara pursed her lips. Pasquale didn't see her do so, since he was driving, but he imagined her face from her silence. He'd seen her doing it so many times. The lower lip over the upper lip. That was what it was; it made her look a bit like a little girl.

"If I'd screwed up," Lara said at one point, "I mean *really* screwed up, would you rat on me?"

"No," said Pasquale too quickly and too loudly. "No," he said again, more softly. "Not even to the union."

"Because you don't rat on a colleague?"

"No. I mean that's not the only reason. Because . . . because I admire you."

Lip on top of lip, and silence. Pasquale ventured to dart her a sideways glance, just a quick one. It wasn't lip on top of lip. Closed mouth and finger in her cheek, devouring herself from within.

Lara was thinking. She was thinking that she admired Garello. Everyone admired him – Chief Inspector Garello. The last time he'd been officially commended had been at the police party, and she'd lost count of all the other times. In the narcotics department, on the wall, there hung a photo showing him in front of a table piled high with confiscated heroin, and the photo wasn't even in his own office, but in the chief's. And in the corridor, in the Flying Squad section, there he was again, half-leaning out of a car window with a captured criminal in handcuffs inside. Garello's face was covered by a balaclava, but everyone knew it was him, because he was the plump one. So she thought *okay*.

"Okay."

"What do you mean, 'okay'?" Every so often Pasquale did listen to her.

"Okay, that's that. End of story. It pisses me off, but I don't give a shit. None of my fucking business."

"Good girl."

"Let me drive, will you?"

Pasquale pulled over, and they swapped places. Just then the car radio went off.

"Calling Car Five, we have a 113."

Pasquale made as if to return to the wheel, but Lara shook her head. She got onto her mobile and called 113. A member of the public had been reporting strange goings-on in the Fruit and Veg Market area. "It'll be some stupid shitty job, but don't you think we should take a look?"

"We're here behind the station. We'll be right there."

Via dei Carracci, left, left, then straight ahead. There was a wide empty space where a social centre had once stood. A few old walls were still left, and a couple of new ones were being put up. It was dark; there was a streetlamp on the other side of the road, but it wasn't on.

"Can't see a thing," said Pasquale.

'There's someone down there," said Lara. "I can see something white."

An instant later, the car windscreen exploded. Or rather, it seemed to Lara that it had exploded, since her side was suddenly completely covered in cracks, a dense web of irregular little pieces, like a glass mosaic. She swerved suddenly, taking the car up onto the pavement, and Pasquale lolled against her, flabby, too flabby, sticky and warm, his head flopping down on her arms gripping the steering wheel, and when she took them away, her colleague's face ended up between her legs, heavy, almost obscene.

Lara saw the holes on the windscreen, three neat little holes in the cracked glass, and she also saw that the sleeve of her jacket was all red; she saw too that Pasquale's back was all red, and then she opened the car door, dived out of the car and ran behind it, scurrying along on all fours on the asphalt, and pulled out her pistol, taking aim into the darkness.

There was nothing there, not even a shadow, not even a rustle.

She waited. Later she would tell her colleagues that she had waited until she was sure there was nobody there, but in reality she waited because she couldn't do anything else, she couldn't stop trembling. And when she did move, it was because the blood on her jacket sleeve had soaked through onto the skin of her arm, where it had congealed and turned cold. She walked round the corner of the car and looked through the open door.

Pasquale was lying with his face on the driver's seat. She tried to lift him up but he was really heavy, and she only managed to turn him onto one side, in an unnatural, twisted posture.

He had one hole in his chest, one under his neck, and there wasn't any face left.

Lara let him fall back, took a quick step backwards and started to vomit.

*

If she'd been a hard woman, or simply if she'd been used to reacting to events in this way, Lara would have asked to return to work with the Flying Squad straight away, even in the shape she was, with the plaster on her nose where it had been scratched by a splinter of glass, and that slight tremble that afflicted her hand every now and again. But Lara wasn't a hard woman, not that hard anyway, and she'd stayed at home for the full three days the doctor had prescribed for shock, and she'd even taken two days' more holiday and gone to the coast with Marco, to stay with Marco's family – they had a boarding house in Rimini. Sitting on the beach covering her bare feet with the cold sand of the winter sea, she thought that she could easily ask to leave the Flying Squad and get a desk job, something nice and quiet. An investigation into the death of special agent Giuliano Pasquale was already being planned by the Flying Squad; they already had one investigative hypothesis, one that the Inspector had given her. He'd told her this was Jari the Albanian's turf, prostitution and drugs, who knows what heist they'd interrupted to make them react like that, but you can be sure, he'd told her, that we're going to get those bastards. She hadn't wanted to know anything else. Not because she didn't care that Giuliano had died, but because she didn't want to think about it, she was repressing it, she hadn't even been to the funeral, and sooner or later she'd burst inside, what with that dead face lying heavily between her legs and shedding blood all over the crotch of her trousers – she'd thrown them away without even trying to wash them. Sooner or later, but not now. Now she was sitting on the sand, covering her toes with a greyish film of sand that she let trickle from her clenched fist, before it was half blown away by the damp, salty breeze.

But she knew that it wasn't like that.

Something (and she knew very well what it was) kept forcing her to think of other possibilities, to think that it was time to take a desk job, go back to college, change jobs. Go steady with Marco, make a home, have a child. Take off her bra when she was making love, because she'd never taken it off, not with Marco or with anyone else. Anything but think of that, and she knew very well what it was, but she didn't want to think about it. She wanted a quiet life. It wasn't for her to sort out. It was none of her fucking business.

But she knew very well that it wasn't like that.

Then she got up. She picked up her gym shoes, pulled her feet out of the sand and walked off along the cement walkway that divided the beach into two.

*

It was the first time that he'd seen her in civvies, without her jacket and her boots, and he thought, well, look at her, she's not as gawky as she seems at first glance. She's actually quite cute is Lara, really rather attractive. And she does have a pair of tits too. She just needs to be treated better. Looked after a bit. Who knows, we might get somewhere with her.

"But where've you been hiding that lovely body, eh? You should get a transfer to the plainclothes unit. Did you know how good you look in civvies? What on earth are you doing here? You've still got another day's leave."

Lara bit the corner of her lip, just inside the mouth. Just a nibble, but it was enough. She didn't know how to begin, and now that the Inspector was looking at her like this, with that idiotic smirk, she felt even more embarrassed. Another woman would have put on a skirt instead of jeans, and a short, figure-hugging pullover not quite covering her flat belly instead of the turtle-neck sweater that had, admittedly, after so many washes, become a bit tighter and showed off her tits, and look what an effect it was already having on the Inspector. But there was one thing she needed to get from him before she could tell him what *she* had to say.

So she controlled her emotions and shrugged, which brought her bosom into relief, hoping that it wouldn't be obvious that she was doing so on purpose.

"It's about Garello," she said.

The Inspector wrinkled his brow and stopped staring at her tits.

"Thing is, I've realized it was a fuck-up, that maybe I got it wrong, and in any event it's none of my fucking business, so . . . I wanted to know if you've told anyone."

"Me? Course not."

"I mean the magistrate, the Police Chief . . ."

"Like I said, no."

"To Garello."

"Not likely. Why should I tell Garello, of all people?"

He'd answered quickly, and in the same tone of voice, but something had flickered in the corner of his eye, a kind of glitter, an instinctive reflex, like a dim, veiled glint.

"No, just . . . maybe to find out how things actually went that evening . . . and I wouldn't want to find myself in an awkward spot when I meet him, if he did know . . ."

Lara knew that glint. Perhaps she wasn't such a hard woman, but she'd got five years' experience of the Flying Squad under her belt, and spending so much time with people who didn't want to tell you the truth had taught her to recognize by sight when someone was lying, whether it was a Senegalese, a junkie, a member of the public – or even an inspector.

"No. I didn't say anything to Garello. Don't worry."

The glint had vanished, but then it doesn't appear every time. Only the first time, and you have to be quick off the mark to notice it then.

Lara sat on the chair in front of the desk. She crossed her legs as if she'd been wearing a miniskirt, but she didn't do it on purpose, she did it without thinking, and she did it so well that the Inspector darted a glance at the blue thigh of her barely faded jeans.

"You did tell Garello."

The Inspector didn't say anything.

'Sir, you did tell Garello."

The Inspector looked away. Then he winced and looked Lara in the eyes.

"Listen, Lara. I've known you for three years now, ever since I came to run the office, and I've always seen you on duty. Good at your work, oh yes, everything right and proper between us, good morning, see you tomorrow, the odd joke. Colleagues, in short, with me as the boss and you the subordinate, but just colleagues, nothing more. With Garello I worked in the Anti-Mafia division in Calabria. When I found myself working with him again up here in Bologna, we saw each other every week, we went out for meals, we did stuff together. We weren't just colleagues, we were friends. It's only natural that when some nosy bitch, good at her job, oh yes, everything right and proper, but a nosy bitch all the same, tells me something that could get him into trouble, well, I go and tell him, like that, just so's he'll be prepared if anything happens. Wouldn't you do the same with Giuliano, if I had something on him?"

Lara nodded, quickly. But this wasn't what she had in mind. She got up.

"Listen," said the Inspector, "you know, I told Garello that you're not a stupid cunt . . . a nosy bitch but not a stupid cunt, anyway, you've done your duty in telling me, that's all we'd need, he realized as much too."

Lara nodded again, feeling scared. She got up and left the office.

*

If Lara had been able to, she would have told the Inspector two things.

The first was that when they'd fired at her and Giuliano, they hadn't fired at random, bang, bang, bang, at the car, one shot here and one shot there, but three sharp shots, one after the other and all aimed at one particular place.

At the passenger seat.

Where she should have been sitting. Logically speaking, anyway, since she was the patrol leader.

Someone who isn't a cop doesn't know this kind of detail. A colleague does. Two drug dealers busy trafficking behind a wall see a patrol: they take a pot shot and run for it. But if someone fires straight at the passenger seat, where there ought to be a nosy bitch who's got some strange ideas into her head, perhaps they're doing it because she's the person they're after. Someone who isn't a cop doesn't know this kind of thing. A colleague does. Garello does.

The second thing was that after the beach, with the sand still between her toes, Lara had climbed into her car and driven to Bologna, to the home of the retired *carabiniere*, at 16, via Emilia Ponente, she remembered the address clearly. She hoped that he'd tell her she was wrong, that he hadn't heard *bang bang bing*, but *bing bang bang*, first the 6.35 and then Garello's 9 mm. And that's what he had told her, yes indeed, the quieter shot and then the two louder ones; it's obvious that you misunderstood me when you took down my testimony.

But he'd said this with that glint in the corner of his eye, and even a half smile, with the corner of his mouth pulled up. She was certain that if she'd asked him if a colleague from the narcotics squad had come to see him, a big guy in civvies, he'd have said no, but his voice would have trembled a little.

The final confirmation was still lacking. The confirmation that Garello knew that she knew. But the Inspector had told her this directly.

And now?

Lara sniffed: she was starting to cry. There were plenty of people she could go and see, there was the Police Chief, there was the magistrate, there was the union, she could have told them what was going through her head, although these were just suspicions she had, accusations, and heaven only knew if they were true, would she have believed them if Giuliano had told her about them, ideas of this kind? And why would somebody like Garello have wanted to kill her? Because she knew that he'd shot the two Albanians, maybe by mistake. But a man like Garello doesn't need to kill a colleague just because he got trigger-happy with two Albanian pricks – what does he risk, disciplinary measures? A trial? He's more likely to finish up in Parliament, on the benches of the Northern League.

Lara started to cry. Because there was a whole load of people she could have told everything to, of course, but it wasn't anything to do with her, she wasn't the sort, she wasn't tough enough and she felt lonely.

So she started to cry silently, her face covered by a stream of tears and her mouth twisted into the grimace she made when chewing her cheeks, until she realized there was somebody calling her name, there in the square, right in front of her car.

It was Garello.

*

"Okay then, you've seen the photos, that's water under the bridge, just like the official commendations, you know I saw you once at that official do last year, I noticed you because you look cute, Lara, my love, the kind of woman who first looks like a beanpole and then a bit gawky, then someone says, forget all that, she's actually cute you know, don't take offence, all right, it's a compliment. Anyway, I was saying, forget the photos, they're history, anyway, look, I'm here now, I've been living in Bologna for two years, working in the narcotics department, and busting my gut, you'd never believe it. I'm not saying this to imply that, well, you're the Flying Squad and we're a bit different, I know that everybody busts a gut if they want to get the job done, but I do loads of stuff, Lara sweetheart, who'd have believed it. Do you know how many drug dealers I've busted here in Bologna? Sixteen. Over three hundred pounds of horse confiscated. Three shoot-outs, including the one the other night. Been wounded twice. I know I'm jinxed, but what d'you expect? I'm telling you all this because you're a colleague, you're experienced too, they took a shot at you, was it the first time?"

"Yes."

"Well, let's hope it's the last. You know what I think, Jari was doing an arms deal with the Slavs, some big shot in the Serbian mafia must have been there, something like that, because otherwise they wouldn't have shot, you were unlucky you two, especially your poor partner, what was his name, Giuliano, but was that his first name or his surname?"

"First name."

"And what was his surname?" asked Garello.

"Pasquale."

Garello stopped the car outside the front entrance, took out his police parking permit from under the sunscreen and placed it in view on the dashboard.

"This way we won't get a ticket," he said. Lara sat there immobile, huddled against the car door as she had been all through the (brief) journey from Piazza Roosevelt to Via Rizzoli, partly because Garello was really fat and partly because she was afraid. No, she wasn't afraid, she was terrified.

"Fancy a coffee?" said Garello. And he climbed out.

Sitting in front of her coffee, Lara felt stupid. Afraid of what? she thought. That he'll kill me, here under Bologna's Two Towers, after picking me up from in front of the police HQ? Come off it, Lara, love . . . Anyway, he was a nice guy. An easy-going local boy, tough as nails, a burly, noisy kind of guy. At one point he'd got up to show her where he'd been wounded the first time and she'd just laughed, seeing him standing there in the middle of the bar, so very fat, hoisting up his vest to the armpit to show her the scar on his side.

"What are you laughing at? They hurt me."

"Sorry."

Garello had a nice smile. He was ugly, too fat, with a busted nose, but he did have a nice smile. And nice hands too, strangely enough given the kind of person he was, strong hands but not stubby, and warm too – Lara had felt them when he placed his hands on hers to look her in the eye.

"Lara, my love, I swear it. They shot first. I'm not a killer, I'm a cop. Do you believe me?"

"Yes," said Lara, but Garello shook his head.

"No, you don't believe me. You had that glimmer in your eyes. If you knew me better, you'd believe me. What are you doing tomorrow evening, Lara, my love? This evening I'm busy. How about we go out for a pizza tomorrow evening? That way we'll get to know each other better."

"I . . . I've got a boyfriend."

"I don't want to get my leg over with you, sweetie, I'm sure you know that much. I want you to be convinced that I'm not a killer. Tomorrow evening? The day after tomorrow's no good, I can't. Either tomorrow or not at all."

"Tomorrow," said Lara, and no sooner had she said this than she wondered why she'd said it. And she was still asking herself the same question a minute later, when she gave an involuntary little smile.

*

They didn't go out to dinner the next evening. Lara wasn't on duty and so she heard the news on the TV. They'd found Jari, a drugs trafficker, suspected of the murder of special agent Giuliano

Pasquale. They'd found him in a small house up in the hills, in Vergato in the Appenines, and there'd been a shoot-out. Lara had seen the images of the stretcher with the sheet over it being loaded into the ambulance, and then the head of the narcotics squad speaking mutely, his voice covered by that of the presenter. Behind him stood Garello, looking serious, his arms folded.

The next day, she popped up to the Flying Squad, on the pretext that she needed to deliver a report, and glanced down the corridor of the narcotics division. It was full of people going to and fro, but Garello wasn't there. The chief took the report from her and she asked him how things were going. Fine, we're sending the whole gang of Albanians down. Bologna's going to be quieter, she said, partly to gain time, and partly so that she could peer down the corridor. Maybe, he said, but I'm not so sure. And the theory that nature abhors a vacuum. Now that Jari's Albanians have left a vacuum, it'll be Rashid's Moroccans who fill it.

Lara went back down. In the elevator, her hands in the pockets of her dark blue jeans, she felt strange and thought that she knew what the problem was.

The problem was not that Garello hadn't phoned her to cancel the date: that was normal, given all that had happened. But he hadn't phoned her the following day either. And that was making her feel strange, a bit angry, a bit sad and a bit stupid.

And the worst thing was that she felt happy when, two days later, he did phone her.

*

Lara knew why she fell in love with somebody. It happened whenever she discovered something that she hadn't been expecting, something hidden beneath the surface, something that dumbfounded her, struck her powerfully, filled her with affection, over and above the physical aspect or the question of personality. With Marco, for example, it had been a kiss. When she'd met him, she'd thought he was her ideal. And he wasn't a cop, and this was a period in which she only ever saw colleagues, both on duty and off duty, and she'd had quite enough of that. Then he was like her, they enjoyed the same things, the same films, the same books, the same music. The fact that he'd been so amazed when he'd found out she was a cop, oh come off it, a girl like you, what do you mean, what kind of a girl am I then? You're like me, do *I* look like a cop? Then, in the car, when she'd been taking him home, that kiss that was meant to be a quick kiss between two people who are starting to take a liking to one another and then who knows, and instead it had become an intense, definite kiss, one that you wouldn't have expected from a man like him, and it hadn't finished there, and as he continued she knew that she was falling in love.

The drawback was the fact that it was never true. After a bit she realized that the thing she had discovered wasn't really there, that she'd probably put it there herself, and she discovered this too late, when she was in it up to here.

But perhaps she always knew already that it wasn't there. Perhaps that was why she didn't commit 100 per cent when she started going out with someone, she never let herself go completely, she always kept something back. When she made love she didn't take off her bra.

For Garello, the thing that had made her fall in love had been his hands. Or rather no, his hands had made her curious. She hadn't been expecting those hands of his to be on hers, his eyes on hers and then that smile. It was the whole thing, she'd been thinking of a murderous cop, or at best some macho character from a film, and instead she'd found this nice, passionate man, at times almost tender. But this had just made her feel curious.

What had made her fall in love had been the compliment. The way he'd said to her, first smiling, then lowering his eyes, looking awkward and then laughing, but just with his eyes: "Your boss says that you're cute, but that's not true. You're beautiful, Lara, darling, and I want you."

*

"Take your bra off, Lara."

"I can't."

"What do you mean you can't, whoever makes love with their bra on? Take it off, Lara, you've got really lovely tits, not too big and not too small, just the size I like."

"Lara laid her hands on Garello's head and gently pushed it down, arching her back to present him, not with her bosom, but with her belly. Garello kissed her round her navel, and with the tip of his tongue licked her skin, the clear skin of a winter blonde, passed the tip of his tongue across her abdominal muscles that were as flat as those of a handball player, and then came back up to the level of her bra."

"Come on, Lara. What's the matter, you got a complex? I've told you you're beautiful, Lara, I want all of you, my darling Lara, all of you, take off your bra, do you want me to do it?"

"No."

"Lara sat down on the bed, turning her back on Garello, who had propped himself on one elbow and was looking at her. She bent one arm backwards and her fingertips reached the metal hook. She undid it, the bra straps slipped down onto her arms, and there they stopped, because she was clutching the material close to her breasts, with her hands, like at the seaside, when she changed position on her towel. She stayed like that for a while, for as long as she could, then she got up off the bed and quickly did her bra up again."

"Sorry."

"Sorry for what? Are you crazy?"

"Sorry, I can't."

"Why not?"

"I don't know. I can't. I've got a boyfriend."

"Come off it!"

"I don't know. I can't. Not like this."

"She picked up her skirt and the short, figure-hugging sweater that revealed her belly and ran out of the room."

"Oh, go fuck yourself, you stupid whore!" Garello shouted after her, without even getting up.

*

For a few nights she dreamed that, while she was swimming in the sea, a great wave came up and swept away the top of her swimming costume. The cold slap of the water on her skin made her quiver with pleasure, but then the wave deposited her on the beach and she started to run between the parasols and the hot sun shone down on her tits and made them swell up until they were more huge and overblown even than Pamela Anderson's. Then she woke up. It wasn't exactly a nightmare, something you woke up from all sweaty and panting: it was a bore, an embarrassment that simply made her feel rather silly.

Garello didn't see her again, except for once when she crossed his path in the parking lot, just for a second, and he darted her a quick, nasty look, like a fierce (but caged) animal. She'd like to have gone over to him to talk, to say something, however meaningless, but he was with a couple of other people and had already got into his car.

Then, one day, the Inspector called her and told her that the head of the narcotics squad wanted to see her.

Lara didn't know any Arabic, nobody in the office knew any, neither the boss nor Garello, who was staring at her impassively. But there was an interpreter. The only thing that Lara managed to make out through the crackling of the interference was her name, clear and distinct, both her first name and her surname.

"It's a mobile call we intercepted, from a North African drugs dealer, one of Rashid's men, who's . . . anyway, never mind that. Our man's talking on the phone to somebody we don't know and, as you've heard, says your name. He says . . . what's he say?"

The interpreter said it in Arabic and then repeated it in Italian.

"She has to die."

"Yes, but not like that, he says it with a question mark, as if he were asking. *She has to die?*"

Lara leaned with her hand on the back of the seat, because, question mark or no question mark, she felt faint. She has to die. "What's this – I have to die? Why?"

"We're asking you. Because that's not all he says, our boy, he says . . . what's he say?"

This time the interpreter said it in Italian, straight away.

"That whore of the Albanians has to die."

Lara sat down.

"Jari's Albanians and Rashid's Moroccans are at each other's throats here in Bologna. If the Albanians take a shine to somebody, the Moroccans have it in for that person and vice versa."

She didn't like the way the head of the narcotics squad was staring at her. Garello was staring at her too, but that was different. There was a repressed hatred, there was any number of things in Garello's stare – but it wasn't the same as the expression in the boss's eyes.

"Listen, Lara, I'm calling you by your first name since you could be my daughter, if you have something to say it's better that you speak out right now. Do you have anything to tell me? Because the way the Moroccans are voicing an interest in you is rather odd. And so is your involvement with the Albanians. You just happen to be passing by with your poor partner, and you get shot at. Why? What had you got mixed up with? Then these others are saying they want you dead . . . Anything you've got to tell me?"

Lara didn't reply. She couldn't have said anything in any case, since she had lost her voice. She felt an intense cold inside her. She was trembling too.

"And then there's this business about Chief Inspector Garello . . ."

"No, sir, I'm sorry . . ."

The boss lifted a hand, and Garello shrugged. "We'd said we wouldn't mention that," he murmured.

"No, because that story's a bit odd too. You see, again it's you and your partner who arrive at the spot when the Inspector is forced to defend himself against the two Albanians, and these Albanians aren't just thieves, they're fucking drug dealers, and who're they working for? For Jari, of course."

"They phoned us . . ." whispered Lara. "The operators . . ."

"And yes, off you go, no problem with that, it's what the report says. But then, what do *you* do? You change your version of events and start accusing the Inspector. Why? Do you know what that's called, Lara? It's called making false accusations. Even if it's true, of course, but we're just mulling over possibilities here, just for the sake of argument. Unless there's something you've got to tell me. *Do* you have anything to tell me, Lara?"

She felt the tears pouring down her cheeks even before her eyes misted over. She didn't even sniff. It was a dry, abrupt kind of crying, just those two tears and a sigh that was half a sob, like that of children.

The boss waited for another few moments.

"Good. Or rather, not good. Now listen. I'll ask for you to be transferred to another city, to a desk job, because another dead cop here is something we can do without. You'll soon be getting notification of the investigation I'm opening into you and poor Giuliano. Meanwhile, just think about this. We're the only ones that can protect you. Just remember that. You don't have anyone else. Just us."

Lara looked up, and her eyes met those of Garello.

He smiled, but only with his eyes.

*

She thought: I'm screwed.

I'm not one of those women cops you see in films, I'm scared, I don't get it and I'm scared, I can talk to husbands who beat up their wives, with hooligans brawling in a disco, I can recognize a junky who's taken an overdose, a stolen car, I've never left a fingerprint at the scene of a crime, not even a shoe print, I can find things, coke hidden in cars, knives stashed away in pockets, I know all U2's albums, all Baricco's novels, I can score amazing goals, but I'm not one of those women, someone who can just turn up and understand everything that's going on. I just write reports. But who to? The suspect now is me.

She thought: I just don't get it.

She thought: and what do I do now?

She took a shower. Then she waited for Marco to get back from his job at the library and told him everything.

And as she told him everything, she gradually stopped crying and realized that even if she wasn't one of those women, little by little, she *was* starting to get it.

*

"Are you crazy, Lara?"

Yes, thought Lara, but she didn't say so. She held the pistol pointed at Garello, one hand over the other, the way they taught at Police Academy.

"Put it away. And take your finger off the trigger, or the gun'll go off even when you don't want it to."

Actually, she'd like to have fired. But she knew that she wouldn't. She'd never taken a shot at anyone.

"Have you ever shot anyone dead, Lara?" whispered Garello. "It's really pretty messy, even if you've got loads of reasons to do it. Believe me."

"Let's go upstairs. Turn round. And no pissing around."

"*No pissing around*, Lara, my love . . . Where do you think you are then – in a film?"

All the time they were going up in the elevator, and then even when she opened the door, Lara was thinking that a strong man like him would easily be able to jump her and grab the pistol out of her hand, but for some reason or another he didn't. Once inside she closed the door and stood there in the hall.

"That's where we went when we almost made love, remember?" Garello pointed to the door at the far end.

"You framed me," said Lara. "Why me? You're working for Rashid."

Garello didn't reply. He gave a self-satisfied smirk. Lara understood straight away. She started to undo the buttons on her shirt and open it at the front, pulling it up out of her jeans. She lifted it with one hand, half turning to show him her back.

"I don't have a mike. If you like, I'll strip naked."

"Great."

"Pig."

"I'm not joking. I don't know what you're after, Lara, but if you want to talk to me, I need to be sure. If not, just shoot me and game over."

Lara pursed her lips. She bit on one lip a little, just there inside, pulling away a painful flap of skin. Then she pressed down on the back of her foot with the heel of a gym shoe, slipped it off, pulled off the ankle sock, then did the same to the other gym shoe with her bare foot. She took off her shirt, first one sleeve and then the other sleeve, passing the gun from one hand to the other. She unbuttoned her jeans, pushed them down and waggled her legs until they fell to the ground. She stood there in her panties and bra.

Garello smiled. He raised his eyebrows.

"Pig," said Lara.

She tugged at the elastic of her panties with her thumb and

pulled them down, before kicking them away. Now only her bra was left.

Garello shook her head.

"You know they make tiny microphones these days. And it looks to me as if that one tit's bigger than the other one."

Lara sucked in her cheek and started nibbling it. She bit so hard that she felt her mouth growing numb. For a moment, tears came to her eyes. Then she slipped off her bra straps, took the cups of her bra in her hand and pulled it down to her belly, her lips twisted in a grimace, as if she'd pulled a muscle, and it hurt her, it hurt her a lot. She brought the hook round onto her belly, undid it and let her bra fall to the ground.

Now she was naked. Apart from the pistol.

"I'm working for Rashid," said Garello. "I've made an agreement with him, against the Albanians. If you'd checked it out, you'd have realized that all the big ops I've been involved in were aimed at getting Jari, while all I did to the Moroccans was confiscate a few bits and pieces of stuff, with Rashid's agreement. But don't worry, no one's ever checked it out."

Lara shifted her weight from one leg to the other. Standing in the middle of the corridor, naked as she was, with her arms out holding the pistol, she was starting to get cold. But she felt as if all the cold was concentrated on her breasts, frozen and quivering stiffly.

"The two Albanians I killed – I took them out because, two days before, they'd blown away one of Rashid's team. They weren't even planning on a break-in, those two, they were big shots. Rashid wanted them dead, but he didn't want to attract too much attention, so I thought of it. I shot them both, I chucked the brick through the window. Nothing like a real cop to get rid of two dealers . . . Only problem: the nosy cop bitch. But why don't we go and sit down over there? It's easier to talk."

Lara nodded. She followed Garello into the living room, still with her pistol pointed. He sat on the sofa. She sat in the armchair. Garello took his pistol out from behind his back and placed it on the little table, gently, as she'd told him to. Lara picked it up, and, as if she couldn't manage two of them, she put hers down and kept Garello's.

"But do you know what? You've got a pair of really nice tits," said Garello. "What a fucking stupid idea it was, trying to kill you, Lara . . . I'd just got my blood up. It happens when you've just bumped someone off, either you get a real downer or else you stay pumped full of adrenalin, and that's the category I fall in. Unfortunately. I made a mistake. I think if I'd done nothing, you wouldn't have shopped me. There was a bit of chemistry between us, wasn't there? What have you come here for, Lara? You don't want to kill me."

"No," said Lara. "I'd come to talk. I wanted to tell you I'd understood the whole situation too. It was all clear in my mind's eye, and it didn't bother me one little bit. I know, it's not fair, I'm sorry about Pasquale, I'd like to see you behind bars, but what do I do, this is the way things have turned out, I've been framed, you set me up with that fake telephone call, you can still kill me whenever you want, so I'd come to ask you to please leave me alone, I wouldn't say anything, what the fuck do you want me to say, they want to get me behind bars, what have I got to lose? I wanted to tell you that I'm happy to let the storm blow over, and that I'm leaving the police force, what's done is done, I'm marrying Marco and I'm going to train the school handball team. I'd come here to tell you all that, then I changed my mind."

Garello frowned. He said nothing, because he'd seen something in Lara's eyes. Not the glint, something else. Something cold.

"Meaning?" he asked.

"Meaning that I've realized that now I'm capable of killing you. I don't know. I think it was the bra. All of a sudden it was just too much."

"Wait, Lara," said Garello, but the shot interrupted him. He was hurled backwards, one arm flailing in the air, the nape of his neck striking the wall, his body pushed back on the sofa, and he remained there, stiffening against the cushion, until his arm fell to his side and he toppled completely sideways and then down onto the carpet.

Lara's ears were ringing. She soon swung into action, even before she had started to think, and she did everything with deliberation. She got dressed, picked up the pistol, looked down the stairs to see if anyone was there and went into the elevator.

If nobody saw her, she'd go home and take a shower, even though she wasn't in the slightest bit dirty. If nobody saw her, she'd chuck Garello's pistol away and then resign her job with the police. If nobody saw her, she'd marry Marco and start to train the school team. She'd have a child. And now, perhaps, she'd make love without her bra on.

If nobody saw her. Otherwise, that very same day the Flying Squad would be here with an arrest warrant and a pair of handcuffs.

But nobody had seen her.

A Series of Misunderstandings

Andrea Camilleri

Prologue

He

Bruno Costa is a technician in a telephone company, one of those who set up new connections or are sent out to apartments to find out what's caused a loss of connectivity.

He's thirty-five – a tall, handsome young man, very likeable. The companies he's worked for view him as a reliable employee, a nice guy.

He isn't tied down to any particular girl, as he thinks the right time still hasn't come. He likes women too much and demands absolute freedom of manoeuvre.

He lives by himself in a small place that he owns in Mondello, a few minutes away from Palermo.

Actually, the apartment belongs to his parents, but five years ago they moved to Barcellona Pozzo di Gotto, the place they come from in the province of Messina, where their married daughter lives – she has two small children of her own. And the grandparents couldn't stand living so far from their grandchildren any longer.

So Bruno has the run of this apartment, which he keeps very clean and almost obsessively tidy.

Bruno doesn't have many friends. In the evenings, if he isn't out for a walk or else at the cinema with a girlfriend, he prefers to stay at home and read a good novel (he's choosy and has innate good taste) or watch a decent film on satellite TV.

Apart from reading, Bruno has a secret hobby: he allows his curiosity free rein. Can that be defined as "a hobby"?

Actually, if Bruno is sent to an apartment to carry out a check, he can't help wondering: who are the people who live here, how do they get on with each other?

And, from the smallest clues, he tries to find answers to his questions.

This curiosity is perfectly harmless because, unlike the devil Asmodeus, who – it is said – lifted the roofs off houses to see into the lives of the people living inside them and turn them upside down, Bruno makes absolutely no attempt to interfere. What he observes in other people's houses merely provides food for thought when he's alone in the evenings, before settling down to read a novel. All things considered, it's a kind of solitary vice.

She

She is Anna Zanchi, thirty or maybe a bit older, blond, a striking woman even if her figure isn't all that attractive, elegant, from a good Milanese family.

She graduated at a very young age in Hungarian language and literature. Why? Ever since her teens she'd daydreamed over the novels of Kormendi and Zilahy. After her degree she spent a year in Budapest to improve her Hungarian.

Then, on her return to Italy, she married a cousin of hers, a brilliant young engineer from a wealthy family, also from Milan. Her husband's work brought them to Palermo. This marriage was one her family had dreamed of. But it lasted less than a year. The husband turned out to be an incorrigible chaser of whores, and Anna rebelled against this daily humiliation.

After the divorce Anna rented a bijou apartment in the centre of Palermo, where she now lives alone, translating from Hungarian; she also acts as a consultant for various publishers. One result of the divorce was that the husband was forced to pay her substantial alimony.

After her bad experience of marriage Anna has stayed resolutely single. She carefully avoids getting involved with anyone, even fleetingly. But this situation has left her feeling empty inside, an emptiness that she masks with indifference and detachment.

For these reasons, Anna often stays at home by herself, only occasionally accepting invitations from one or other of her girlfriends – not that she sees them at all often.

She studies and writes essays on the literature she loves.

She has a secret ambition: to get into academia and end up as a professor.

The First Encounter (Friday)

One day Bruno is sent to check the phone of a customer, Anna Zanchi, who lives on the Corso Vittorio Emanuele. By the time he gets there it's late afternoon: it's his last job of the day.

When the woman comes to open the door to him Bruno is pleasantly surprised. He had been expecting an elderly, querulous woman. But Anna, rather than being a woman of indifferent looks, turns out to be rather exotic.

"Ah! Here at last! You'll have to hurry up. I've got a meeting, I need to go out."

And she leads him into a living and dining room whose walls are covered from top to bottom with books. Bruno, from their spines, recognizes several novels that he has read. This "elective affinity" kicks his hobby into action by spurring his curiosity.

"I've got another two sockets, one in the bedroom and the other in the study," says Anna.

Bruno realizes that the problem doesn't lie with the phone line, but in the actual phone set. It's bust. He could solve the problem in a matter of seconds, but he doesn't. He wants to find out more about this woman.

"So there's another socket in the bedroom, right?"

"Yes."

"And how's the sound from there?"

"Not good."

A broken telephone stays broken, wherever you take it. Elementary.

"May I?" whispers the voice of curiosity.

Anna leads him into the bedroom and watches as he tinkers with the receiver. She cannot conceal her impatience.

"Do you mind getting a move on please?"

Anna's almost imperative tone annoys Bruno. Out of pure spite he replies that, in the best-case scenario, he's going to need a good hour.

"Do you want me to come back another day?" he asks sarcastically.

"Oh no, not that *please!* I've been phoning for three days, and it's taken you all that time to turn up!"

Anna leaves the room, comes into the anteroom, picks up her handbag, takes out a mobile, dials a number, talks to someone, rings off and puts the mobile back in her bag.

Meanwhile, Bruno has been taking a look around. He greatly approves of the extremely tidy bedroom: there's not a trace of any masculine presence here. He even pokes his head into the bathroom next to the bedroom. Here too, no trace of any masculine presence.

"Excuse me, miss, where's the study?"

Anna opens a door for him. The study is small, full of books and papers. The socket is next to the desk. Bruno fiddles with it, looking all around. He can't help commenting:

"What a lot of Hungarian books!"

Anna stares at him in some surprise but says nothing.

When Bruno goes back into the living room Anna follows him, takes a book from a bookshelf and starts to read. Bruno glances surreptitiously up at her, trying to see the book's title, but he can't make it out.

He doesn't see Anna glancing at him from time to time.

"If you really must know," she suddenly says, "I'm reading *The Dying Animal* by Philip Roth."

"I didn't like it that much," says Bruno.

Anna stares at him, completely taken aback. A telephone mechanic who reads Philip Roth? She feels the desire to find out whether his answer was for real or just an empty boast.

"Oh? What of Roth's *do* you like?"

"Hmm . . . *American Pastoral,* for example, or *Sabbath's Theater* . . . Yes."

"Do you fancy a drink?" Anna says on impulse.

"Thanks, that would be really nice. Especially as this is my last job of the day. I'm free after this. Actually, the problem isn't with the line; on Monday I'll bring you a new phone set."

And that's how the evening began.

How the Evening Continued

After they've drunk a little white wine they both realize at the same time that they don't want to say goodbye. Not at all. They have an extraordinary and unexpected desire to get to know each other. They talk on and on. And then:

"Do you need to get home?" asks Anna.

"I live by myself."

"What do you say about getting a couple of takeaway pizzas?"

"Great idea."

They eat. They talk. They feel like bosom pals.

When Bruno leaves, around midnight, he knows almost everything about Anna. And Anna knows almost everything about Bruno. Throughout the evening they have never even touched. When they say goodbye they shake hands a little clumsily.

They've agreed that Bruno will pass by and pick her up tomorrow evening at eight. They're going out for a meal.

1. The events

The Second Evening (Saturday)

But the next day is Saturday. Bruno and Anna quite forgot this when, yesterday evening, they fixed their date. And that's why Bruno phones Anna at around ten in the morning.

"Do you realize it's Saturday today?"

"No? So what?"

"It means that this afternoon I'm free. We could . . ."

"Yes?"

"It means we could meet up earlier. I could . . . call by at yours around six-ish and then we can go out for a meal."

"Okay!"

*

And he doesn't take even a quarter of an hour to get to Anna's – after which, as was inevitable, things suddenly go a lot faster. To their reciprocal and evident satisfaction. Indeed, at around eight-thirty, the need to get out of bed, get dressed and head out for a meal no longer seems so obvious. They talk it over.

"Let's do it this way: we'll go out for a meal and then dash back here," says Bruno. Sensible guy.

They laugh as they take a shower together. Naked. Happy.

*

She has chosen the restaurant. They drive there in Bruno's car. Palermo on a Saturday evening is really swarming, and the restaurant is packed. They only just manage to find a table in front of the counter, right next to the toilets. On the counter, a mobile phone is lying: sometimes it's used by the customers (though they in their turn are almost all equipped with mobiles), and sometimes it's used to take orders. No sooner have Bruno and Anna sat down than the phone rings. It has an irritating, noisy ring tone, impossible to ignore. A waiter picks it up, listens and, brandishing it in the air, starts to wander around between the tables, asking:

"Signor Zanchi? Signor Zanchi wanted on the phone!"

"Must be a relative of yours!" says Bruno with a laugh.

"When whoever it is replies, we'll see who it is," says Anna, turning round to look.

But nobody thinks the call is for them. The waiter returns, speaks briefly into the mobile and places it back on the counter.

Anna and Bruno are enraptured, so enraptured that they don't hear the deafening hubbub of voices and laughter in the restaurant; so enraptured that they don't notice how slow the service is. In fact, while waiting for the first course, they've managed to empty a whole bottle of *prosecco*.

*

They tuck into their first course. They carry on drinking. While they're waiting for the second, a waiter repeats aloud to the customers, as he passes between the tables holding the mobile:

"Signor Zanchi? Signor Zanchi wanted on the phone!"

But Signor Zanchi does not materialize this time either.

"Why don't you answer the next time?" suggests Bruno.

"Me?"

"You take the call and say, 'I'm his cousin, you can talk to me and I'll pass the message on.' That way whoever's calling will feel happier."

"You're crazy!"

*

The third time the phone rings for Signor Zanchi, Anna and Bruno are on their dessert course. This time, when the waiter embarks on his futile odyssey among the tables, he leaves the mobile on the counter. Before Anna can stop him, Bruno jumps up, dashes over, grabs the mobile and puts it to his ear.

"Hello?"

(With a strong Sicilian accent) – "Bruno?"

His own name!

"Yes. Who's this, please?"

"Hey, you fuckin' fucked us up! And this is the third time I've called you! You fuckin' listen to me: you come as arranged in two hours' time. And you better show your face, or else. *Capisce?* End of message. I'm not going to call you again. Right?"

The person at the other end hangs up. Bruno puts the mobile down and hurries back to his seat.

"Well?" asks Anna.

The waiter, back from his futile quest, picks up the phone, hears that the other person has rung off and puts it back down. He is unaware that Bruno got there first.

"Well?" repeats Anna.

By now Bruno is completely plastered. He's almost forgotten his act of bravado.

"Oh yes. That thing. They wanted to remind him to keep some appointment or other. Guess what! That Signor Zanchi has your surname, but his first name's the same as mine: Bruno."

The coincidence makes them laugh till they cry.

*

The room is a kind of office in a small tower. Through the glass walls, a large store of unrecognisable goods can be kept under surveillance.

In the office there are two men, one fat and one thin.

"It's not him," says the fat man, whose name is Tony, putting the receiver back on the phone on the table.

"Whad'ya saying?" asks the thin one, whose name is Michele.

"Didn't sound like Bruno's voice to me," explains the fat man. "I'll cut my balls off if it was him."

"Whad'ya mean?"

"I mean Bruno's sent a pal of his to the restaurant to keep us kickin' our heels. And while we wait for Bruno like we arranged, he's fuckin' legged it. He's conned us. We fuckin' swallowed the bait."

"So what we gonna do?"

"I've had an idea," says the fat guy, dialling a number on the phone.

*

In the restaurant, as Anna and Bruno are drinking a *digestif*, the mobile rings again. The usual waiter answers, listens, then begins his usual round:

"Signor Anselmi wanted on the phone!"

"Over here," says a man who looks like an office clerk and is sitting two tables away from Anna and Bruno.

*

"Giulio! You saw that guy that answered the phone instead of Bruno?" asks fat Tony.

"Yep," replies the man who looks like an office clerk, in the restaurant.

"You know him?"

"Nope."

"He still there?"

"Yep."

"You ever seen him with Bruno?"

"Nope."

"When he leaves the restaurant you trail him. See where he lives."

"Yep, I'd already thought of that," replies the Clerk.

"Then you call me, okay?"

Tony dials another number. The telephone rings in the (filthy) bedroom of a man who's lying on his bed and watching television. The man lifts the receiver from the bedside table.

"Hello?"

"Peppino old pal. Tony here. You get your butt round to Bruno's place. If nobody answers, go in anyway."

"And if there is somebody in, whad'ya want me to do then?"

"Don't you worry your head about that. Won't be nobody at home. When you're in, you call me."

*

Finally, after going round the block several times, Bruno manages to park his car near Anna's home. They climb out, in a hurry to get inside. Anna opens the front door and they go in. The Clerk, who has followed them as per orders, is a meticulous kind of fellow: he first wrote down on a piece of paper the number plate of Bruno's car, now he adds the name of the street and the number of the building. Then he sets off again. As he drives along, he dials a number on his mobile.

*

The mobile rings in Tony's pocket. He's inside a swish car bowling along at top speed towards the airport at Falcone-Borsellino-Punta Raisi.

Michele is at the wheel.

"Hello? It's me," says the Clerk.

"And?"

"I followed him. I know where he lives. Got his car number too. Whad'ya want me to do now?"

"You go to the store. You wait for us there."

*

Anna and Bruno are making love.

*

Peppe has entered Bruno's apartment, forcing the lock. An incredible mess. But the wardrobe is empty, and there's no linen in the drawers. Bruno has obviously cleared off. Peppe picks up his mobile and phones.

*

Tony's mobile rings as they are walking, with Michele, from the car park to the airport.

"Peppe here. Bruno's done a runner. Cleared off somewhere. Whad'ya want me to do now?"

"We're all meeting up at the store."

Tony and Michele enter the airport. Not many people. Not much happening.

"You want my opinion? Bruno's fuckin' screwed us," *says Tony disconsolately.*

"He's got three hours' advantage of us," *says Michele.* "He could be fuckin' anywhere by now."

They go to look at the list of planes departing, but without much conviction.

*

Anna and Bruno are lying asleep in one another's arms.

*

They're all there in the storehouse, Tony and Michele, Giulio the Clerk, and Peppe. It's obvious that the boss is fat Tony and his second-in-command is Michele. The other two are faithful sidekicks.

Tony is reassessing the situation. It's obvious that Bruno has screwed them. First he was late delivering the money he got from the sale of the gear, then he didn't turn up at the last appointment. He told them he'd turn up at this restaurant for a meal, and they checked it out, but he got somebody else to go, to give himself time to make his getaway. The only person who can put them on the trail of Bruno is his friend, the one who answered the phone in the restaurant instead of him. There's no other solution. They'll track Bruno down: they must get the money back. The bosses will never believe they allowed a small-time crook like Bruno to screw them. They'll think they were in on the act. And they'll make them pay. And so . . .

*

The Third Day (Sunday)

Shortly after dawn Bruno gets quietly and carefully out of the bed where Anna is still sleeping soundly, gets dressed without even washing his face, writes a note that he leaves on the kitchen table, exits from the apartment, goes out through the building door that swings shut behind him, heads towards his car, gets in, sets off.

No sooner has Bruno's car left than, from the other side, the Clerk's car appears. The Clerk, of course, immediately notes that Bruno's car is no longer where it had been left the night before. He sees a similar car; he checks the number plate against the one he noted; it's not the same. Scrupulous as ever, he goes round the block one more time. Nothing. So he parks the car.

He goes to the building door. It's locked. He starts to look down the list of names on the interphone. It's a completely stupid thing to do, given that he doesn't know the first thing about Bruno's presumed accomplice, but he does so because you never know. As he stands there looking, a plump woman comes up behind him.

"Can I help you?"

"And you are . . . ?"

"The concierge."

The Clerk feels at a loss, but he makes the most of the opportunity that presents itself. He pretends to be perplexed, hesitant.

"I don't know how to put it, but it's, like, there's this guy . . ."

The concierge, apart from feeling curious, feels it's her duty to help a man who seems so stylishly dressed and respectable.

"If I can be of any help . . ."

And the Clerk makes up a story: the day before, he happened to strike up an acquaintance with a young guy, Mario Zolli, who's in the same line of trade as he is. They discovered that they share a hobby: model trains. So he invited him round to this address. But his name isn't on the interphone . . .

"He's not here," says the concierge.

"Must be my mistake," says the Clerk in such a disconsolate tone of voice that the concierge feels duty bound to ask:

"But what's he like then, your friend?"

This was the question the Clerk was hoping to hear. He describes Bruno, but the concierge shakes her head.

"Nope. Can't help. Don't know him."

And she is telling the truth – after all, she's never seen Bruno. On Friday evening, she did see a young man from the telephone company walking quickly past her office, but she never saw him coming out again. And she didn't even see him yesterday, since on Saturday afternoons the building entrance is locked. And of course she didn't see him at night time, when Anna and Bruno came back. She has no way of linking him to the man being sought by the Clerk. The latter wanders off. The woman enters and slams the building door shut – it needs to stay locked, as it's Sunday.

*

In her kitchen, Anna, drinking a cup of coffee, reads Bruno's note and smiles.

*

Bruno has finished taking a shower back at his place and is tidying up the bathroom, when he hears the phone ring. He goes to answer it. It's Anna, phoning him on her mobile.

"Why did you go away, you idiot? I went to sleep thinking how nice it would be to wake up and find you with me."

Bruno feels awkward.

"Well . . . you know . . . I rather thought that when you woke up you might not be very pleased that . . ."

"But you are *such* an idiot! We missed out on a good opportunity to . . . Anyway, what shall we do today?"

"I thought that, as it's Sunday, and the weather's good . . . we could go and have a meal outside Palermo. What do you say to Cefalú?"

"Great idea! What time will you come and pick me up?"

"Around noon? That suit you?"

*

"And whad'ya want me to do now?" asks the Clerk from inside his car, parked almost right in front of Anna's front door.

"Listen," replies Tony, from his office at the storehouse. "If the car ain't there, and the lady at the door don't know the guy, it can only mean one thing; he went to that fuckin' bitch's place he was at the restaurant with and fucked her. Then he went back home."

"So?"

"So this is what you do, right? You go and get hold of that fuckin' bitch and get her to spill the beans."

"But Tony, I don't even know her name! Can't I wait to do this job till tomorrow? It'll be Monday, the building door'll be unlocked all day, I can get it sorted much easier, no problem."

"Tomorrow's too late."

"So whad'ya want me to do?"

"Do I have to spell everything out to you? What's the apartment block like? Big?"

"No. Four storeys."

"So if there's three apartments on every storey, there's twelve people living there. Go inside with someone coming back home an' knock on all the doors. Keep asking. You get a good view of that lady?"

"Yep."

"Get movin' then. An' don't you fuckin' mess around like you usually do."

*

The Clerk climbs out of his car, and stands behind a newspaper kiosk on the pavement opposite the main door. From here he can keep a lookout. He prepares for a long wait.

*

Bruno is in his car, driving down a road with little traffic on it. So he can zip along. He sings as he drives. It's a way of expressing his joy at the idea of seeing Anna again so soon.

*

Anna has dressed quickly and casually, since she has a ritual that she needs to perform, as she does every morning: go downstairs, cross the road, go over to the newspaper kiosk, buy the papers and return home. So she's now opening the front door.

The Clerk can hardly believe his eyes, especially when he sees Anna walking towards him. He hides behind the kiosk. Then, when Anna returns to the front door and pauses to fish out her key, the Clerk rushes up from behind her and manages to get his foot in the door as she closes it. Anna, as she steps towards the elevator, turns round, sees a stranger entering and smiles at him.

"Hope you don't mind," *he says.*

Anna opens the elevator door and enters. The man follows.

"May I?"

Anna's sole reply is to make room for him, flattening herself against the wall at the back.

"Which floor?" *asks the Clerk with his finger hovering over the buttons.*

"The top floor."

"Me too."

Anna starts to browse the headlines of the papers. When the elevator stops, the Clerk takes his time closing the elevator doors. No sooner has Anna opened her apartment door than the Clerk shoves her in, pushing her between her shoulders, and closes the door. Anna turns round in amazement. The Clerk is pointing a pistol at her. But the scariest thing is the way he smiles.

"One sound from you, and you're dead."

Anna freezes in horror.

"You alone, or somebody with you?"

Anna manages to shake her head.

"Move it."

Anna, as if hypnotized, moves forward. When they enter the living room the Clerk orders Anna to sit in an armchair. The girl obeys. The man forces a table napkin into her mouth. She almost chokes on it.

"Keep quiet. I'm just going to ask you a few little questions. Then I'm outta here."

Anna, who had persuaded herself this man was a mugger, is now confused, surprised and even more terrified. What does this crook want to know about her? Meanwhile, the Clerk has had a brilliant idea; if it's the right one, it will mean he can cut to the chase.

"You know Bruno?"

Anna is completely taken aback by the question, and her eyes open wide. What secrets has Bruno been keeping from her? What kind of circles does he move in?

"Well, do you know him?"

86

Anna nods. The Clerk's smile broadens: he'd guessed right. He can pursue this line a little longer.

"You know where he is?"

Anna hesitates. She doesn't want to betray Bruno. Then she reflects that, if she does find herself in this situation, it's all Bruno's fault. She nods.

The Clerk pulls the napkin out of her mouth. Anna draws a deep breath.

"Where is he?" the Clerk asks again.

"At his place," replies Anna.

The man's backhanded slap is so violent that it almost knocks Anna unconscious. A trickle of blood starts to pour from one lip. The man stuffs the napkin back into her mouth.

"You fuckin' cunt. We already been to his place an' he ain't there. He's cleared off. Now you're gonna tell me where he is. I'm good at finding things out. Okay?"

*

Bruno's car is stuck in the traffic. An accident has happened, and the tailback goes on for ever. He can't go backwards or forwards.

*

Calmly, still smiling, the Clerk takes off his jacket, his tie and his shirt. He stands there with his chest bared. Anna's eyes are still wide open. A tremor runs through her. Then the Clerk takes her by one arm, makes her get up and pulls her along behind him. With her he inspects the apartment. In the study he sees the Hungarian books. This confirms his hunch.

"You wanna know something? Once upon a time Bruno told me he'd been seeing a girl that spoke Hungarian."

When they enter the bedroom the Clerk gives Anna a violent shove and makes her fall back onto the bed.

"Here we're gonna be more comfortable."

The thing that rebels, suddenly, is Anna's body. It acts on its own initiative. She lands a powerful kick on the man's testicles. He bends double. Anna leaps to her feet, manages to tear the gag out of her mouth and tries to start screaming. But the Clerk's fist smashes into her face, dislodging teeth, breaking her nose and knocking her out. She falls back. The man regains his breath, staring at her. And inside himself, he seems to hear Tony's voice.

"Don't you fuckin' mess around like you usually do."

But it's too late. The devastation he has wrought on Anna's face arouses him. He can't control himself. With a sort of fierce bellow, he tears off her blouse and bra. Then, from his trouser pocket, he takes out a pair of surgeon's gloves and slowly puts them on. Then, from his rear pocket, he pulls out a jack knife.

"Now you and me's gonna have a little game of doctors and nurses."

*

Bruno drives round and round Anna's block, he can't find anywhere to park. Eventually he finds a spot, parks the car, gets out, and when he reaches Anna's building door he is just about to ring the interphone when he sees that the door is just ajar. He goes in, takes the elevator and notices that the door to Anna's apartment is wide open. Why? He goes in and calls:

"Anna?"

But nobody replies. The apartment is in perfect order. Feeling more and more perplexed, he goes to the bedroom. Anna is lying on the bed, naked, her body twisted, the sheets soaked in blood. Bruno dashes over, lifts her up, hugs her to him. He cannot think straight. Under Anna's body lies a jack knife. Automatically, Bruno picks it up.

*

At that very moment Signor Cavilli and his wife, who live opposite Anna, come out into the corridor.

"Strange," she says.

"What is?" he asks, as he locks the door.

"Ten minutes ago, when we got back from church, Miss Anna's door was open and it's still open now. I'll go and take a quick look."

"Like it's any of your business," says the husband.

But his wife resolutely goes in.

"Hello? Hello? Miss Anna?"

After a few seconds her scream pierces the air and echoes through the whole apartment block.

"She's been murdered!"

*

2. What Happens Afterwards

Sunday, Late Morning and Afternoon

What *can* happen after that woman's scream, which leaves Bruno rooted to the spot?

But also, how can anyone argue with Signora Cavilli when she sees Anna lying naked, her body twisted, on the bloody bed, and a wild-eyed stranger, also drenched in blood, with Anna's body on his knees and, to complete the picture, holding a jack knife?

Of course, nobody dares to go into that room: there's a dangerous murderer in there. But they all come crowding out onto the landing. If he had any desire to do so, Bruno could make a getaway, but he has no desire to do so; in fact he doesn't even think about it. Stupor has now been succeeded by grief. He is weeping. This is how the police find him; someone has phoned for them. Two policemen disarm him; they struggle to pull him off Anna's body and drag him into the living room.

Then Police Inspector Chimenti arrives, together with Sergeant Villanova and the forensic scientists who start to busy themselves in the bedroom. After the on-the-spot investigation and the first statements, Chimenti and Villanova take Bruno into the living room for further questioning. The first thing Bruno says is:

"It wasn't me. I found her like that. I'd only just got here!"

"By car?" asks Chimenti, an investigator of few words but a good deal of practical sense.

"Yes. I have a sky-blue Suzuki."

"Get your keys out," says Chimenti; then he yells:

"Airoldi!"

An inspector comes running in, and Chimenti gives him the keys, saying, "Just pop out and have a look at this gentleman's car. It's a sky-blue Suzuki, get him to explain where it's parked."

The Sergeant turns to Bruno.

"What's your name? Do you live here? How long had you known the victim?"

Bruno, feeling ever more devastated by events, embarks on a confused explanation. The Sergeant's questions increase his uncertainty.

Airoldi returns and takes Chimenti to one side.

"The car engine's still warm."

But the Sergeant's already feeling pissed off, and now it's his turn to take Chimenti to one side.

"Listen, Inspector, can't we put all this off until tomorrow? It's Sunday, and I'd promised my wife . . . you know?"

Chimenti agrees, as he can't wait for the Sergeant to beat it. He orders Airoldi to have Bruno taken to the police station.

"Shall I handcuff him?"

"Are you joking? Make sure nobody gets a look at his face."

*

Inspector Chimenti sends away the Sergeant and makes the other residents return to their apartments. Now he can begin his investigation. In the anteroom he notes, on the ground, the two newspapers that Anna had bought. He looks at them: they're today's.

"Airoldi! If I remember rightly, there's a newspaper kiosk right by the front door. See if the victim bought the papers there, and if so, what time it was."

Then he goes into the study and sits at the desk. Anna has put all of her personal papers in one of the drawers. Chimenti takes notes. The pathologist comes in.

"I'm off."

"So, Doctor, was she raped?"

"I couldn't say just like that, not without a proper examination. Don't think so."

"What makes you say that?"

"Well, the poor girl . . . on her face and in her hair she had traces of . . . Anyway, I think the murderer masturbated after killing her."

"How did he kill her?"

"He throttled her. With his bare hands."

"And all those wounds?"

"They're superficial wounds. The murderer's a sadist."

"Around what time did she die?"

"Ah, on that question I can be more or less certain: no more than two hours before we arrived."

The doctor goes away, Chimenti takes notes from Anna's papers. Airoldi returns.

"I got to the guy who runs the newspaper kiosk just in time, he was about to close. Yes, the victim bought the papers there, as she did every morning. He said he saw her at around half past ten, eleven."

"Okay. I'll be off. You stay here and when everyone's finished you get over to HQ."

Chimenti walks downstairs. When he reaches ground floor he's stopped by the concierge.

"Inspector, I wanted to tell you that I'd never seen the murderer before. But I just needed a quick look at him when they were taking him away; that was enough for me to recognize him from the description."

"I don't quite follow you. Do you mind running that past me again?"

And the concierge relates to the Inspector how she had met the Clerk that morning, and the questions the latter had asked about Bruno after describing him in perfect detail.

"And you didn't see that man again all morning?"

"No, Inspector."

"Not a word of this to any journalists. Or else."

Hardly has he opened the front door than Chimenti finds himself in front of a swarm of journalists, film crews and photographers.

"Is it true that you've arrested the murderer?"

Chimenti manages to extract himself from the throng without replying. He climbs into his car and is driven off. But the concierge can't resist the temptation of becoming the celebrity of the moment.

*

Chimenti is a scrupulous man, and when he's bringing an investigation to a conclusion he doesn't take any time off. So it's only natural that, after wolfing down a sandwich in a bar, he heads back to HQ. He asks them to bring Bruno to his office.

When he appears, Bruno is even more exhausted but certainly less confused. He realizes that, right now, he's suspect number one and he has no intention of making any gaffes, not so much for his own sake but because he thinks that if the police waste their time with him, they'll give the murderer time to get away. And he hopes that the murderer will be captured so that Anna can be avenged. This much emerges from the first words he exchanges with the Inspector.

He relates how, last Saturday, he made Anna's acquaintance. He also adds that from the registers of the telephone company it will be possible to check the assignment that he was given that day. Not just that: on Saturday morning, when he returned to the company's offices he requested a new telephone for the customer. A phone that he was due to pick up on Monday.

He tells of the mutual attraction that he and Anna quickly developed for each other. He tells of how Anna ordered two pizzas and that she kept a notebook next to the telephone to remember the number of the pizza place. It will just be necessary to check this notebook (which the Inspector has asked to be brought in, together with other papers, by Airoldi) and the truth of what he is saying will be completely confirmed.

He relates how on Saturday afternoon he went over to Anna's. He says, quietly, that they made love. Then, after that, they went out to a restaurant whose name he remembers perfectly well. The waiters will be able to confirm that they were there. But ... wait a moment, Inspector! He rummages around in his jacket pockets and brings out a piece of paper that he hands over to Chimenti.

"I still have the bill."

He continues, saying that they went back to Anna's, where he stayed until the early hours of the morning. Then he went back to his place. Anna was still asleep.

"Why didn't you stay?" asks Chimenti.

"Because I thought it might make her feel awkward . . . in her bathroom there was nothing for me to shave with . . . and I needed a clean change of clothes."

"And why did you go back?"

Bruno replies that, shortly after, Anna had telephoned . . . And at this point he gives a start: Anna's landline telephone was broken, she'll definitely have phoned him from her mobile, and so there must be a trace of that call . . . And that call will demonstrate unequivocally that he didn't spend the whole morning with Anna and that Anna was still alive while he was back at his place . . .

Bruno continues his narration. They'd agreed to get away from Palermo and go to Cefalú; he was held up because of an accident, and when he eventually arrived he found the front door ajar; he went up, saw Anna's apartment wide open, walked in, and . . .

At this point he can't go on. He has forced himself to stay calm, but he can't keep it up any more and bursts out into a cry of despair.

"But apart from you and Anna, who else knew that you'd be going back to the apartment this morning?"

Bruno can barely understand the question and has to have it repeated to him.

"But nobody could have known!"

Chimenti explains to him that, in fact, this can't have been the case. And he tells him what the concierge said. Bruno comes down to earth with a bump: he can't possibly imagine the identity of the man asking for information about him.

*

The game has finished on TV. Chimenti kisses his daughter who is doing her homework and kisses his wife.

"I might be a bit late home this evening. I'll let you know."

He goes to HQ where Airoldi is waiting for him. Airoldi brings him up to date. He's questioned all the residents, and they are all in agreement: Anna was a serious, pleasant, nice woman. No one feels able to say whether she had lovers or a lover. The most widespread opinion among the residents is that the man was a thief whom Anna surprised when she came back from buying the papers. A thief who took advantage of a pretty woman and then savagely murdered her. Of course, say the residents, it must have been one of those immigrants who roam around at will and do as they please. A few of the neighbours said the police would do well to check up on Anna's ex-husband, a man who (especially when she was first living in this apartment) used to come round and start quarrelling with her.

"Not necessarily," says Chimenti pensively.

"What?"

"It's not necessarily the case that she didn't have other lovers. She only needed to be careful, and nobody in the apartment block would have noticed. Look at what happened with Costa: nobody ever saw him going into Anna's apartment. Yet he came back on Saturday afternoon, he went out with her, they returned Saturday night, and then he went out on Sunday morning, round midday . . . That man who went to ask the concierge about Bruno . . . couldn't he be a jealous ex-lover?"

Airoldi shrugs.

"Come with me."

They leave the HQ, take Chimenti's car and go to the restaurant where they're laying the tables for the evening. The manager recognizes the receipt as having been issued the evening before. And then there's a waiter who remembers the two of them very clearly. Once he's back in his car, Chimenti consults Anna's notebook, dials the number of the pizza place and gets their address.

At the pizzeria they clearly remember the two pizzas that were ordered on Saturday evening.

"How come?"

"The lady was a regular customer of ours. She always ordered one pizza. On Friday she ordered two. And I thought to myself: what's up? Inspector, please, I need to know: did the poor girl eat that pizza with her murderer?"

Chimenti shrugs. And then he says, to Airoldi:

"Fancy a pizza?"

"Why not?"

And of course, as they eat, they talk over the case. Neither of them seems to believe in Bruno's guilt.

"His car engine was still warm when you got me to check," says Airoldi. "If you want my opinion, Bruno really did go back to his place yesterday morning and then he got back just in time to find himself up to his neck in it."

"Tomorrow morning we might have definitive confirmation," says Chimenti.

"How?"

"Bruno says that Anna phoned him from her mobile, the one we've taken back to HQ. If she did make that phone call, it'll come out of the calls tabulated. We'll also get the length of the conversation."

"Why don't we go and check straight away?"

"Because today's Sunday – or had you forgotten?"

After their pizza Chimenti and Airoldi go to Bruno's place. Chimenti has got hold of the keys. They go in, they look around and cannot help but admire the tidiness of the apartment.

*

The next morning, at around ten, while Bruno is repeating to the Sergeant, ever more wearily, what he has already told the Inspector, Chimenti receives the confirmation. From Anna's mobile it is clear that she called Bruno's number at around half past nine on Sunday morning. It was a short conversation. At this point, after Chimenti and the Sergeant have discussed the matter together, Bruno is allowed to go, once he's signed his statement. Of course, there are journalists who want the Inspector to give them the latest on the case (which has been splashed all over the papers), but nobody has photographed Bruno, nobody knows that he was the person detained. But just as he is allowing Bruno to leave, Chimenti notices that Bruno isn't feeling too good.

"What are you going to do now?"

"I'm going to pick up my car and then I'm going home."

"Listen, I'll get Airoldi to drive you in my car, at least as far as where your car is parked."

As they are making their way to the internal car park in the police building, Bruno hears a female voice calling him:

"Bruno!"

He stops, surprised. He doesn't recognize the woman in uniform who has called to him and is now walking over.

"Hi, Airoldi. Bruno! Don't you recognize me?"

"Grazia!" says Bruno after staring at her for several seconds.

Grazia gives him a hug. She's pleased to see him again.

"But it's been at least fifteen years since I last saw you! What are you doing in this neck of the woods?"

Bruno feels intensely awkward. Airoldi intervenes.

"I'll explain to you later. Shall we go?"

Grazia watches in some consternation as they get into Chimenti's car and drive away.

*

Bruno opens the door to his apartment, goes straight to the bedroom and climbs into bed still fully dressed. He is wracked by convulsive tremors.

*

Grazia is having it all explained to her by Airoldi. That is how we find out that she and Bruno had been going out together when they were fifteen. Then they lost touch.

*

In the Following Days

In the following days, interest in Anna Zanchi's murder wanes, now that almost everyone is convinced that the murderer is a thief, an immigrant from some country outside the European Union: he was caught in the act and gave way to his animal instincts. Even Chimenti's investigation has reached a dead end. Anna's ex-husband has a cast-iron alibi for that Sunday morning.

For Bruno, things have been going rather differently. He has been struck down by a violent fever that has kept him in bed for three days – obviously a consequence of all the stress. Grazia has lovingly tended to him – she has come to see him between police shifts. Bruno has no desire to read the papers, nor any desire to watch television: he is desperately trying to forget what has happened. He doesn't even know that Anna's body has been returned to her family and that the funeral has taken place in Milan.

*

One achingly beautiful evening Grazia persuades Bruno to go out with her. Bruno has lost weight, he is pale and seems dazed by the Palermo traffic and all the people walking by.

"Let's go home."

"No, please, another five minutes."

Eventually they go home. Bruno collapses into an armchair. He is deadbeat. Grazia tidies up and then switches on the television to watch – she puts the sound on very low – the news. They've got to the last items. Grazia doesn't notice that Bruno is behind her, absently watching the news too.

All of a sudden the presenter says, as the photo of an unknown man appears on the screen:

"The Italian mysteriously killed yesterday in Paris has been identified. He was a Sicilian tourist, from Palermo: Bruno Zanchi, aged . . ."

*

But Bruno has stopped listening. A sudden, terrifying surge of memory is sweeping through his mind. He sees the waiter from the restaurant, wandering among the tables calling for Signor Zanchi, and himself jokingly asking Anna whether it's a relative of hers, then him going to pick up the mobile and the voice saying, in a thick Sicilian accent, "Bruno?"

Bruno Zanchi!

Grazia hears a noise and turns round. Bruno is falling to his knees in a faint.

*

Grazia does not leave, since as soon as Bruno comes round, he appears to be in a strange state of elation. Now his innate curiosity is driving him on to act, to find out. He tells Grazia about his stupid practical joke that Saturday evening when he passed himself off as Bruno Zanchi on the mobile.

"And what does that mean?" asks Grazia.

But for Bruno there certainly *is* a meaning. He formulates a hypothesis that he has come up with. It's not altogether precise, but it is logical. Zanchi must have been involved in some dodgy business;

his accomplices, not trusting him, sent a certain man to keep an eye on him in the restaurant where he went to eat. So this man goes to the restaurant, but he doesn't know Zanchi, he's only been given a description of him. And great is his surprise when he sees a man going to answer the mobile – a man who doesn't in the least resemble Zanchi's description.

He decides to follow him and thus becomes convinced that the place where Anna lives is Bruno's. The next day he returns, but he doesn't find Bruno, he finds Anna who cannot answer his questions. He tortures her and kills her.

"Tomorrow morning I'll mention it to Chimenti," concludes Grazia.

"No. Don't."

"Why?"

"It's something that I need to do myself. Tomorrow morning I'm going back to work. You simply need to tell me when Zanchi arrived in Paris."

Grazia can finally return home. She senses that – miraculously – Bruno has got over it.

*

Bruno returns to work. He's been on sick leave, and his colleagues do indeed find that he looks rather drained but only physically. The positive side of the whole business is that none of those who work with him links him to the murder. They do know that, on Friday afternoon, Bruno had gone to Anna's apartment and that he was due to return there on the following Monday with the new phone; they know that he had to make a statement at police HQ, but they don't know anything else and so their questions to him are limited to a superficial curiosity.

"What was she like? Was she as beautiful as all the papers say she was?"

Bruno replies evasively and says he didn't get to see much of this customer. His boss phones him and tells him that the external jobs for the day have already been assigned. He should turn up tomorrow; he can resume his normal timetable then.

But Bruno doesn't leave the building. He goes down into a kind of Kafkaesque basement and arrives in front of a door with a sign, in block capitals, stating that entry is strictly forbidden to all unauthorized personnel.

Next to the door is a desk with two telephones and various papers. Behind the desk is a man in uniform.

"I'd like to speak to Umberto Dominici."

"You can't go in."

"All right. But he could come out for a minute."

"What's your name?"

Bruno gives his full name; the man reluctantly dials a number and says a few brief words.

Shortly afterwards, the door opens and Umberto appears. He is one of Bruno's few friends – one who, when Bruno was in a bad shape, phoned him several times. They arrange to meet up in the evening; they'll go out for a meal together.

*

And Bruno takes Umberto to the same restaurant, just as crowded as usual, where he had been with Anna. Bruno is wearing dark glasses. "My eyes are sore," he says. As they are eating their first course, a waiter starts to circulate among the tables holding the usual mobile:

"Signor Dominici? Signor Umberto Dominici?"

"It's for you," says Bruno.

"For me? But nobody knows I'm here!"

"You can still answer."

Umberto raises his hand, and the waiter passes him the mobile.

"Hello? Who's speaking?"

"I'm Grazia, a friend of Bruno's. Is he with you?"

"Yes. Do you want me to pass him over to you?"

"Yes."

Umberto, bewildered, passes the mobile over to Bruno.

"Was I good?" she asks.

"You were terrific."

"See you tomorrow?"

"Sure thing."

Bruno hands the mobile back to the waiter.

"Would you mind explaining what's going on to me?"

And Bruno starts to tell him all about himself and Anna. And eventually Umberto asks him the logical question:

"Why've you told me all this?"

"Because you have to help me. Have you seen that the only phone they have here is a mobile? Well, you're the right man for the job."

"What job?"

"I'd like you to find out where the three phone calls for Bruno Zanchi came from on that Saturday evening."

"But why don't you go and talk to the police?"

"I'll go to them when I've found out."

"You know that if they find out what I've done, I'll lose my job?"

*

It takes Bruno another half an hour to overcome Umberto's resistance. Eventually the latter says:

"I'll need to have the mobile."

"No problem."

Bruno simply waits for the most convenient moment. All of a sudden he gets up, and as he walks past the counter he quickly picks up the mobile, turns it off, puts it in his pocket and continues on his way to the toilets. Then he comes back and sits next to his friend, saying:

"Sorted. I'll ask for the bill straight away."

*

Grazia, in uniform, is talking to the concierge of Anna's building. She's asking her to describe the man who, on that morning, had come to ask her if Bruno lived there.

"But he called him something else, Inspector."

"Never mind that; describe him to me."

The concierge gives quite an exhaustive description of him. And she concludes:

"He looked just like a clerk."

Grazia takes her leave, walks round the corner and climbs into Bruno's car, which sets off. They go to Bruno's place. They talk. Grazia reveals to him that she has found out that Zanchi had stayed in a Paris hotel on Saturday night. And so, when they attempted to reach him at the restaurant, he'd already left Palermo.

The telephone rings. It's Umberto.

"I'm in luck. The calls were all made from a phone that belongs to Antonio Caruso, who runs a big import business for various products in Via . . . By the way, there were four telephone calls, not three as you said. Write the number down."

"It all fits together like a glove," says Bruno to Grazia. "The fourth telephone call was the one he made to his accomplice telling him to follow me – this was the guy who then went asking the concierge about me."

"Don't you think the time has come to go and talk to Chimenti?"

"Not yet."

The next day, from all the telephones that he finds in the homes to which his work has taken him, Bruno dials the number of Tony (Antonio) Caruso and as soon as he hears the voice replying with a strong Palermitan accent that he now remembers perfectly, "Tony Caruso, imports. Who's speaking?" he replies, in an equally strong accent, "Bruno! You fuckin' fucked us up! And this is the third time I've called you!"

And he hangs up.

Only the sixth phone call, at sunset, is different from the rest.

"Don't leave the office. If you've told the others about my telephone calls, you've made a big mistake. You can fix it. When I phone you this evening at eight, try to make sure you're alone. Best if you don't try any funny business."

*

Bruno calmly telephones from home at eight o'clock on the dot. Tony answers.

"You alone?"

"Yes," says Tony.

And that is true.

"Listen," continues Bruno briskly, "I know that you had Bruno Zanchi murdered in Paris and the woman who was here with me."

"That was . . ."

"An accident? But it's all the same to me. At this moment in time I'm in a position to have you all arrested."

"So whad'ya want?"

"Let's cut a deal."

"What kindova deal?"

"You hand over to me the man that killed the woman, the one that looks like a clerk . . ."

Tony cannot repress an exclamation that Bruno notices. "Screw him!"

"Yeah, too right. He's the only one I'm after. The Clerk. He's dropped you in the shit."

"And in exchange?"

"I won't turn you in. I'll forget all about you."

A silence. Tony is thinking the offer over.

"I'll telephone you tomorrow morning at eight. Think it over," says Bruno curtly.

He hangs up just in time. Grazia is opening the front door.

*

Bruno's mood has changed so much that Grazia stares at him with wide-open eyes. He doesn't feel like eating at home, so he takes Grazia out to a pizzeria. When they return home, Bruno embraces her passionately. And Grazia is delighted to change roles: she is no longer Bruno's nurse, but the woman in his life.

*

"I have to start work early tomorrow," says Grazia as she gets dressed.

But when she goes to her car it won't start. She tries and tries again. Nothing doing. She calls Bruno on the interphone, and he comes down and tries in turn. Nothing doing. Then Bruno tells her to take his car and gives her his keys. Grazia gives him hers.

*

The following morning, at eight, Bruno phones Tony. And Tony tells him that he's inclined to let him have the Clerk. On one condition: Bruno must kill him. The Clerk knows too much, he mustn't fall into the hands of the police. Bruno agrees. And he arranges to meet at eleven in the evening, in a certain street in Isola delle Femmine, just outside Palermo, on the coast. Then he goes down to see a mechanic friend of his whose garage is practically next door and gives him the keys to Grazia's car.

"I want it ready for this evening at eight."

*

While Bruno goes from house to house for his work, in his company office Tony has called a meeting of his associates. Only the Clerk is missing. Tony gives them the details of Bruno's request but doesn't tell them that he's accepted. And he concludes:

"I say send the Clerk. He's gonna fuck us all. The reason we're all in this fuckin' mess is 'cos he couldn't keep his fuckin' hands off that girl. I'd send him. He doesn't leave us with any choice."

"Whad'ya mean?"

"What I mean is that we're gonna be there at Isola delle Femmine too. Let's wait till the man Bruno bumps off the Clerk and then we do Bruno in too. Whad'ya reckon?"

They all gaze at each other. Then one of them asks:

"Where's the Clerk?"

"In Baghera, at home."

"Call him. Now."

And this is the sentence of death.

Before he phones, Tony sets out his plan.

"I tell the Clerk we've discovered where Bruno's accomplice is. And we need to eliminate him. We fix a meeting with that bastard at Via dei Saraceni in Isola delle Femmine. Okay? The rest of us go to Isola too, but we bump off Bruno as soon as he's fixed the Clerk."

*

Bruno is driving to Isola delle Femmine. The road is empty, and so is the countryside – it's out of season. He's driving Grazia's car – he's told her he won't be able to see her this evening. It's nearly eleven o'clock. He drives down the little road, the Clerk is already there, half-concealed in a bush in front of a low wall. The Clerk watches the car go by, but he doesn't recognize it, since it's Grazia's. The car disappears at the end of the little street.

Shortly afterwards the car reappears, headlights blazing. It just takes a minute. The car accelerates, slams into the bush, crushes the Clerk against the wall; the front bumper of the car pins him there. The Clerk, eyes wide open, tries absurdly to push the car away from him with his hands. He's groaning with pain; his legs must be broken, only the car is holding him upright.

Bruno very calmly opens the car door and gets out.

"And now I'm going to kill you," he says to the Clerk.

And he lifts the monkey wrench that he's holding. But somebody grabs him from behind and disarms him. Bruno struggles, but the man behind him is agile and manages to get him down on the ground. It's Airoldi. Not far off is Inspector Chimenti. While Chimenti, Airoldi and the others wrench the Clerk away from Bruno, Grazia helps him up off the ground. Bruno is helpless, drained.

"Was it you that alerted them?"

"Yes. They've been bugging your phone for two days. This evening they arrested all the others. They'd been planning to kill you after you'd . . ."

Bruno pulls away from her brusquely and starts to walk off alone. The night rapidly swallows him up.

Death of an Informer

Massimo Carlotto

Inspector Giulio Campagna felt ridiculous in this flowery shirt, with ripped jeans and down-at-heel gym shoes. He'd never liked having to wear a disguise, but on this particular day he needed to look like one of the horde of foreigners desperate to keep body and soul together that thronged Padua railway station. Together with two other colleagues from the Flying Squad he was waiting for the arrival of a drug mule who was due to replenish a Bolivian gang's cocaine supply. He avoided crossing the paths of any transport police in case he was recognized; those smart alecs might easily give him a wink and thus balls up the whole operation. You couldn't rule out the possibility that the Bolivians had sent a couple of stooges to keep an eye on the situation. The Inspector leaned against one of the columns propping up the roof of the platform and checked the arrivals board. The Eurostar from Milan, destination Venice, was only five minutes late. The other two cops were hovering in the underground passageway, watching the stairs that led up to the two exits. The mule stood no chance of getting by unobserved. Providing, of course, that the information was correct. To recognize him, the Inspector had only a description to go on, but it was pretty detailed. Especially when it came to physical appearance.

The passengers got off the train and streamed down the platform. There were more of them than the Inspector had expected. For a brief moment he feared that the mule might slip between his fingers. Then, all of a sudden, he saw him walking by. Or rather, he saw *her*. Because she was a woman. A beautiful woman. "Nice bit of skirt," he thought, observing her attentively. About twenty-five, tall, black hair cut in a bob, long legs, a nice behind and a shapely bosom, she walked with the elegance of a model. But that wasn't her real profession. In reality, she earned her living by working as a bar hostess in a nightclub in Varesotto. She got pawed and screwed by fifty-something industrialists whom she selected with some care and supplemented her income by transporting cocaine for Bolivian gangs. As far as Campagna knew, she was French; she must have met the Bolivians in some nightclub when she was working in Toulon. The Bolivians were pretty good at setting up trafficking networks, and they enjoyed a certain notoriety, which enabled them to avoid being conned by their clients; but they still hadn't learned how not to get noticed. They threw money around in the nightclubs and kept expensive whores, using them to test out the quality of their coke. The cops always turned up eventually and started poking their noses in.

The French woman was swinging an elegant crocodile-skin handbag in one hand, and in the other a small travelling bag. The cop reflected that they wouldn't need to look far for the coke.

The mule climbed up the steps, followed by the Inspector, who pointed her out to his colleagues with a rapid jut of his chin. One of the two made an appreciative gesture. They didn't get to tail such a beautiful girl every day.

The bar hostess climbed into a taxi. The fourth cop in the squad started up his car and picked up the others. The girl had asked to be driven to the other side of town, to a new block of two-storey villas, built in the style of old country cottages. The Inspector nostalgically remembered that, once upon a time, there had been nothing in this district but fields and ditches full of frogs, which his grandma frequently used to spice up her favourite risottos. The town had changed radically over the last few years, and he wasn't entirely sure that it had changed for the better. Too many foreigners. And too many lowlifes among them. The Inspector preferred the underworld of the Veneto – so much simpler.

The bar hostess rang a doorbell and gave her own name – Lise – when asked by a voice from the entry phone.

The door clicked open, and at that moment she found herself surrounded by the cops. She immediately realized what was happening. She turned pale, but she had no time to react. Campagna's hand was clamped over her mouth while the others rushed inside. The Inspector took her by one arm and pushed her up the stairs. They found two olive-skinned men, faces to the wall.

Lise looked at them, then turned to Campagna. "I want to cooperate," she said in a firm voice. "The coke's here, in the bag."

The Inspector gave a furtive glance down Lise's cleavage. She caught his glance and smiled at him. The message was clear: she was ready to do anything that would make things easier for her.

The following day, in the offices of the Flying Squad, Campagna was reading the news item about the operation against the Bolivians when his mobile went off.

He immediately recognized the number on the display panel. He didn't bother to reply. He knew that there would be just five rings before the mobile fell silent. Every informer had his own number of rings to alert the Inspector whenever he needed to see him urgently. Five rings meant it was Giancarlo Ortis. Campagna folded his newspaper, took his pistol out of his desk drawer, tucked it into his shoulder holster and went out of the office.

The traffic at this time of the morning was running smoothly. He crossed the Prato della Valle, took a shortcut down the Brenta embankment and after twenty minutes or so reached Abano Terme. Ortis was waiting for him in the bar of a big hotel full of German and Dutch visitors drawn by the curative powers of the old spa's waters. He recognized a couple of gigolos scouring the local hotels for custom. They earned three hundred euros in return for whispering sweet little nothings into the ears of elderly foreign women out for one last fling. Ortis was drinking an aperitif. Campagna ordered a tomato juice with a pinch of pepper. The informer was a little man of about forty-five. As usual, he was wearing a well-cut suit. His shirt was open at the neck to show off a heavy gold chain – the kind of mannerism you expect from a crook of the old school. Ortis had picked up quite a few prison sentences for drug trafficking. Now he ran a pizzeria on the outskirts of Padua, along with his wife, an ex-prostitute whom Ortis had rescued from a gang of pimps. Campagna had him under his thumb, thanks to some business with coke that could have got him put away for a good ten years. That would have been ten years too many at his age. Ortis knew that if you were going to get through jail in reasonable shape, you needed to be young and sturdy or else a big shot in the underworld. Otherwise, the others just took advantage of you. Especially the young men from North Africa. And jail had changed in recent years. Ortis wasn't best pleased at having turned into a squealer, but he'd been forced to choose between freedom and life behind bars.

"Thanks for the tip-off," said Campagna. "The Bolivians have shut up shop."

"And the French woman – easy on the eye, don't you think?"

"Nice tits," commented the Inspector. "And she's not stupid, not by a long chalk. She'd spilled the beans even before we reached HQ. The whole lot. She'll be off the hook in no time."

"I've got a bit of a problem," said Ortis, changing tone.

"Let's hear it."

"A Croatian's turned up, looking for my wife."

"Nothing strange in that. Your wife's Croatian," Campagna interrupted.

"They come from the same part of the world. But this man's an ex-soldier. One of the bad guys . . . Know what I'm getting at?"

"Ethnic cleansing? Nasty stuff like that?"

"Exactly. He asked Naza if he could rent an apartment in Jesolo. With a garage. He said he'd need it for a couple of months."

"What did Naza do?"

"My wife took her time. She wanted to turn him down, but he scared the hell out of her."

"So what's any of this got to do with me?"

"I don't think he wants the apartment for a holiday. Our ex-soldier's got something else in mind."

Campagna scooped up a handful of peanuts from the bowl on the counter and started to pop them into his mouth one by one. Ortis could be right. The Croatians were pretty active in the North-East of Italy. Gangs of thieves or drug peddlers, often ex-soldiers, or even members of the Croatian mafia, were crossing the borders with impunity. They were well armed and dangerous.

"What's this guy's name?"

Ortis reached for a piece of paper in the inside pocket of his jacket and placed it on the counter.

Campagna picked it up. "I'll see what I can do."

Ortis shook his head. This wasn't enough. "He's coming back tomorrow, and he wants an answer."

The cop gave an eloquent shrug, "You can handle it, Ortis. Make something up! Tell Naza to take her time."

"Naza's minded to do him the favour. She's afraid. She's still got parents and a sister back home."

Campagna wiped his face with his hand. "That'll make you accomplices, especially if they're up to no good."

"You can cover us."

"Ortis, don't talk such fucking crap. If I don't get my bosses' agreement, there's nothing I can do. And at this moment in time I don't have a single thing to go on. Do what I say. Otherwise you risk ending up in deep shit."

*

Back at HQ, the Inspector sat down at his computer and typed in the Croatian's name, Josip Persen. Within a matter of minutes he'd found out that he was forty-nine years old and had long been the head of the Ultras in Zagreb, where he'd acquired quite a reputation for acts of violence and vandalism. Then, on the outbreak of the civil war, he'd enlisted in a paramilitary corps linked to an extreme right-wing party. He'd been accused of war crimes but had managed to get himself acquitted. Campagna printed out the information and went into the office of Giorgio Veronesi, the Superintendent. His conscience impelled him to explain it all to his boss who, as he had imagined, told him to wait until he had something concrete to go on. It couldn't be ruled out that Persen really did want to enjoy a couple of months' holiday in Jesolo.

"Even scum like him go on holiday every now and then," said Veronesi.

The Superintendent knew perfectly well that this was total bullshit. When scum from the underworld go on holiday, they don't seek out compatriots to rent an apartment from. Campagna remained silent. He merely stared at his boss. On this particular day he had no desire to argue. Veronesi was a fine cop, but he'd never placed any trust in informers, especially not in Ortis. On more than one occasion he'd told him that he was nothing but a sly old bastard who passed on information of no great value just to keep himself out of the slammer. The Superintendent lowered his eyes to the bumf scattered across his desk. Campagna mentally told him to go and fuck himself.

A few hours later he returned home. He found his mother in the kitchen, busy getting the dinner ready. He kissed her on the cheek and then lifted the lids of a couple of the pots bubbling away on the stove to see what was cooking.

"You'll get me fat," he commented with feigned indignation.

"A few extra pounds wouldn't do you any harm. You're as thin as a rake."

Campagna patted his flat tummy. "Where's Ilaria?" he asked.

"Playing with Granddad."

Campagna went into the corridor and opened the door to his daughter's bedroom. The moment she saw him she ran up and hugged him.

His father greeted him with a brief wave. He was too busy building a robot out of Lego bricks.

"Mummy phoned," Ilaria informed him. "She said she's coming home next week."

"Let's hope so," muttered Granddad. "That way I can go back to the Old Folk's Home for a bit of peace and quiet."

Campagna smiled. His father was always moaning, but he couldn't wait for Gaia, Campagna's wife, to be away at work so that he could spend all his time with his only granddaughter.

He went into his bedroom to get changed and phoned Gaia.

"So you're going to be away for another week," he growled into the receiver.

"Grandma and Granddad can look after Ilaria," she replied serenely. "And you can fuck one of your junkie whores without anyone giving a damn."

"Screw you, Gaia. Don't start bullshitting me again."

She didn't reply but merely hung up. His wife had never forgiven him for having been accused of forcing his attentions, almost one year ago, on a woman dealer pushing ecstasy. She was a thirty-something from a good family, her father was a big cheese at the university, and she'd told how she'd managed to escape arrest thanks to a quick blowjob in the disco car park. The internal inquiry had cleared him, but Gaia had believed the drug pusher's story. She knew her husband too well.

Gaia was a landscape architect. She was good at her job and in demand pretty much everywhere. This time she was working on a municipal park in Tuscany. Ever since the business with the drug pusher, she'd been looking for jobs further and further from home. Campagna knew they'd eventually separate, but he was worried about their daughter. And about himself. He had no desire for the single life.

He returned to the kitchen with a pensive expression that did not pass unobserved by his mother. "You don't lift a finger to try and sort things out," she rebuked him.

"Oh come on, Mum, give it a rest, eh?"

"Marriages don't just trundle along all by themselves. You need to work on them."

"Too right," thought Campagna to himself. "And where does anyone get the necessary energy from?"

*

The following day he knocked at the door of the Anti-Mafia Bureau. He mentioned Josip Persen's name and asked if they knew of any recent movements among members of the Croatian underworld.

One of the men in the office burst out laughing. "Movements? They're managing to get lorry-loads of weapons through, right under our noses, every other day. But this Persen isn't one of them."

But Campagna was uneasy. He knew Ortis well, and he knew that he was a seasoned old con whose nose for what was happening in the underworld rarely betrayed him.

That evening, before leaving HQ, he knocked on the door of Police Sergeant Amelia di Natale.

"Fancy going out for a pizza?" he asked.

She took off her glasses and stared at him. Amelia was a cutey; she was separated from a police chief who'd asked for, and obtained, a transfer, and she'd never made a secret of the fact that she fancied Campagna.

"You mean you're inviting me out?"

"Just a pizza. I need to check a place out."

She snorted. "And there was I thinking my boat had come in," she said, picking up her handbag. "But you're paying."

*

Ortis's place was crowded. The two cops had chosen a table from which they could keep an eye on the entrance and the door to the kitchen. The informer pretended not to recognize him when he came over to their table to take their order, recommending a pizza with buffalo mozzarella. But when two guys had come in and walked with an air of determination to the kitchen he'd managed to meet the eyes of the Inspector and signal that the Croatian was back.

Campagna sized them up with the trained eye of a cop. Josip must be the older of the two. The other couldn't be more than thirty-five. They both had crew cuts. The young one had long sideburns and an earring. They looked like tough customers. At that moment, the Inspector felt sure that Ortis had got it right. These two had no intention of taking a quiet holiday by the seaside.

Amelia had quickly realized that her colleague was taking an interest in these two guys, but she said nothing. None of her business. She was only here because two people together draw less attention to themselves. Campagna looked like a cop. And if he'd been sitting at a table all by himself, he wouldn't have fooled anyone.

Josip and his sidekick emerged from the kitchen a few minutes later. They looked ratty and obviously hadn't yet got what they wanted.

Campagna waited for the entrance door to swing shut behind them and followed them out of the pizzeria. He came back a few seconds later.

"Manage to get the car number?" asked his colleague.

"No. There was a dark Mercedes waiting for them with its engine running."

"Too bad," commented Amelia.

The Inspector shrugged. "Maybe it's no big deal. You know, this isn't really a proper investigation . . ."

"One nagging little hunch and a whole load of doubts," his colleague said jokingly.

"Precisely."

"Just the type of initiative that doesn't go down too well with the boss. Veronesi's all right, but his horizon's pretty limited."

"You mean he's a dickhead."

While he was driving Amelia home his mobile phone rang five times. She immediately knew what it was about. "Oh. That means I can't even ask you up for a drink," she said, heaving a sigh of disappointment.

*

Ortis was waiting for him in a supermarket car park. It was completely empty at this hour of the night.

"Who's the other guy?" asked Campagna.

"Never seen him before," replied the informer. "But he's Croatian too. He gave his name as Zoran."

"I saw them coming out, and they didn't look too happy."

"They were totally pissed off. Naza said she was still thinking about it, and Josip didn't take it well. He's coming back later today."

"And Naza's going to say okay. But she'll make it clear that if there's anything to be made on the deal, you're ready to get really cracking."

"I don't think that's a good idea."

"Use your head, Ortis. These guys are up to something, they're in a hurry and they don't have anyone else to turn to. Otherwise they wouldn't be so persistent."

"I don't like it. Too risky. Not enough in it."

The cop's voice became harsh. "You're earning your freedom. You owe me big time, and the debt's never going to be paid off. Just get that into your thick skull."

*

"You had no authorization!" hissed Veronesi. "You should have talked it over with me first."

"I did, but you wouldn't listen."

"I'm your boss. You need to show a bit of respect."

"Okay, okay . . . I haven't done anything except give the Croatians a bit of rope to hang themselves with. Naza's going to rent out the apartment and we'll keep an eye on it."

"We who? We don't have anything to go on."

"I got a good look at them. They're a couple of crooks. I just have this gut feeling. After all, I've been a cop for quite a few years now."

"Like the Chief could care less about your gut feeling."

"*You* know you can trust me. Just listen."

"Giulio, you're wrong. And that's *that* – at least until you can bring me something concrete."

Campagna shook his head. Veronesi was a pain in the backside when he insisted on playing the bureaucrat, come hell or high water. He went back to his desk. He did a computer search on Zoran but found nothing.

That evening he met up with Ortis again. The informer was tense and preoccupied.

"I'm seeing you more often than I'm seeing my own daughter," commented the cop.

"They've changed their minds. Now they don't want the apartment. Josip has said they'll use the pizzeria storeroom."

Campagna listened more attentively. "When?"

"I don't know," he replied. "They'll show up again when the time's ripe."

"What else did they say?"

"Nothing. Just that they'll pay us for the bother."

"How much?"

"Not a lot."

"Don't make me lose my temper."

"Five thousand."

"So, at the end of the day, you've even managed to get paid for your trouble," the cop exclaimed. "The minute you hear anything from them, call me."

*

Campagna poked his head in through Amelia's door. "I need a bit of help."

"Another pizza in that rundown joint?"

"I have to find those two guys we saw the other evening. They're Croatians, and they might be staying in some local hotel."

Amelia looked at him askance. "Does Veronesi know this?"

"No. And he wouldn't agree."

Amelia raised her eyes heavenwards.

They gave up after two hours of going from one hotel to another. Josip and Zoran hadn't checked into any of them.

"They've got an apartment," said Amelia.

"In that case, why do they need Ortis's storeroom?"

*

The informer surfaced again two days later. They met in the hotel in Abano Terme. Ortis was looking glummer and glummer. And that morning he hadn't shaved.

"What's happened?" asked Campagna.

"They came last night, straight after I'd closed," he replied. "They unloaded a few crates from a van, and Zoran shut himself away inside the storeroom. They wouldn't even let me in to get some more beer when the bar ran low. Then, this morning, another lorry arrived and the crates disappeared."

"Why didn't you call me?"

"I was afraid. If anything happens, those guys are going to know that it was me that squealed."

"Did you get the vehicle numbers?"

Ortis shook his head.

"And the money?"

"They left an envelope for me in the storeroom."

"What do you think was in those crates?"

"They were pretty heavy. I'd swear it was weapons."

Campagna finished his tomato juice. "Okay, now listen. The next time, you call me. I just want to follow the cargo. If you don't, I'll pop over to the magistrate and tell him all about that business with the coke. And you'll be fucked."

*

On his way back to Padua his mobile rang. It was HQ. The Superintendent wanted to speak to him.

Veronesi wasn't alone. He had three men with him that Campagna had never seen before. They looked like cops, and Campagna would have bet on them being *carabinieri*. In fact they were from Customs and Excise.

The boss went straight to the point. "You're starting to stick your nose into a Customs operation. And these colleagues have come to ask us to break off any contact with Ortis."

"But the informer's one of mine," protested the Inspector.

"Not any longer," replied one of the three. "From today he's one of ours."

"He trusts me."

"He'll trust us too," replied another.

Campagna gazed at the Superintendent, seeking help. "Why can't we work together? I keep up my contacts with Ortis and pass on the information to Customs."

"Things don't work like that. You know they don't," said the Superintendent curtly.

"Can I at least know what the operation's all about?"

"When it's all over we'll be organizing the usual press conference," replied the one who hadn't spoken up until now.

Veronesi showed his colleagues from Customs out. Then he gave Campagna hell. He threatened him with disciplinary measures, but the Inspector knew it wouldn't go that far. He too was stung at the way the Customs guys had snaffled the case away from him. Even if he hadn't authorized it.

*

Over the following few days, Ortis rang several times. But Campagna didn't reply. He couldn't. And it made him feel sore that he couldn't. Not that he really cared all that much about Ortis; still he was convinced that a good cop should never betray the trust of an informer.

He talked to Amelia about it. She merely shrugged. "I've never had anything to do with them. But if I were you, I wouldn't bother my head so much over this one. Informers are just vermin. They sell themselves for money or just to keep out of the slammer."

"You think the same way Veronesi does. But you're both wrong. Without that vermin, there's a whole load of cases we wouldn't be able to solve. They're our daily bread, and it's difficult to find good ones," he replied, vexed.

*

For a whole month, nothing happened. He had stopped thinking about Ortis, and Veronesi had actually forgiven him. With Gaia, on the other hand, he'd had several rows. The fault lay with an architect who phoned rather too frequently, even in the evenings when Campagna was at home. Ilaria had sensed the tenseness in the atmosphere and had become tetchy and sulky. Campagna and Gaia had mutually agreed to give themselves a cooling-off period before fixing a timetable for separating without traumatizing their daughter too much.

One Saturday afternoon Campagna happened to be in a supermarket with his wife and daughter. He was wearily pushing along a trolley full of food and bottles of detergent. Ilaria was running up and down the aisles, returning with her arms laden with sweets. The mobile rang, and Campagna hoped it was HQ. He couldn't take much more of this weekly shopping ritual. It was Amelia. It was her day on duty.

"Perhaps it's best if you come and join me."

"Perhaps?"

"Nobody quite knows as yet whose pigeon this is, even if it was our lot that found the bodies."

"Whose bodies?"

"Ortis and his wife."

*

Two ladies had stumbled across the corpses. They were both in their forties, and every morning they went jogging along the canal banks to keep themselves in shape. They also went to the gym three times a week. They wore jumpsuits and gym shoes in the latest style. They were as wrinkled as prunes, and their coiffure, crafted by expensive hair technicians, was held in place by designer headbands. Their nails were immaculately manicured; they were both separated from their husbands and in hectic pursuit of a good match. In five minutes they had managed to tell Amelia all of this. But she was good at getting other people to tell her their life stories.

117

When they clocked the bodies, the most with-it of the two had phoned 113 for the emergency services. Campagna was observing the work of the forensic scientists. They were taking photos and fingerprints. But his expert eye had already sized up the scene. The position of the bodies and the two spent cartridges found next to them said it all. They'd been driven here at gunpoint and then forced to kneel, before being given the classic shot in the back of the neck.

"An execution," said Veronesi, who had suddenly materialized at his side.

"Yup," replied Campagna laconically.

"I've already talked to the big shots," the Superintendent continued, pointing to a magistrate who was talking to the police doctor. "As soon as they've finished taking the prints, we're all off to Customs and Excise; from what they tell me, the boys there are about to get going. These murders have moved things up a notch."

Campagna gripped him by the shoulder. "You should have listened to me," he hissed. "These two would never have died, and we'd have had the Croatians screwed."

"Oh, don't bust my balls!" shouted Veronesi. "And get your fucking hand off my shoulder!"

Everyone turned round to look. Campagna lit a cigarette.

*

The special squads from Customs and Excise swung into action that same night. On the Mestre flyover they stopped a heavy goods vehicle in which, under a load of mattresses, were concealed several crates full of Kalashnikovs and explosives meant for the Mafiosi of Calabria. At the same time, they raided three apartments, arresting a dozen or so people. The next morning, during a press conference, various officials, surrounded by agents whose faces were swathed in balaclavas, explained how they had handled the operation. After a long and patient undercover investigation the Customs Police had managed to break up a gang of Croatians specializing in arms trafficking. Josip Persen was the undisputed leader, but he'd managed to get away, together with Zoran Runjanin and another three accomplices. As for Ortis and his wife, nobody breathed so much as a word about them. "No surprise there then," thought Campagna as he watched the local TV news.

What did surprise him, however, was the fact that one of the three Customs and Excise officers whom he'd met in Veronesi's office came knocking at his door.

"The file's still not ready," Campagna told him.

"I've come to have a talk with you," the man replied. Then he held out his hand. "Staff Sergeant Ernesto Fiore."

The Inspector asked him to take a seat. The Customs officer had the svelte physique and attitude of the special squads. "I was the one maintaining contact with Ortis . . ." he explained. "I just wanted to tell you that I was really careful. It wasn't me that blew his cover."

"So who was it?"

"No idea. Perhaps he gave the game away himself. Or perhaps he started playing a dangerous game. Ortis always did want to make a bit of money, any way he could."

"Do you know who actually did the job?"

"Yes. One of those arrested has started to spill the beans. It was Josip who fired the shot, and with him there was Zoran, Mate Mihanovi and another two men, we only have their names."

"The group that was on the run."

"The hitmen in the gang. They were all ex-paras, well-trained."

Campagna tried to find the right words for a question that had been churning round in his head ever since the start of this conversation. "It's really good of you to call by like this; thank you, and . . ."

The Customs officer lifted a hand to interrupt him. "The reason I came round to see you is quite simple. I didn't want you to think I wasn't up to managing the informer."

"I never thought that."

"I'm glad to hear it."

The Customs officer shook his hand and turned to the door, but then another thought crossed his mind. "I shouldn't be telling you this, but we're pretty certain Josip's group hasn't left the area."

The Inspector suddenly listened hard. "How come?"

"The guy who's collaborating with us has told us they're also on the run from the Croatian mafia. They crossed them a while ago – and it's turned into a death sentence. So it's out of the question that they've gone back over the border."

"But the Croatian mafia has pretty solid bases on this side of the border too."

"According to the guy who's turning state's evidence, they're only passing through. They want to make a bit of money before transferring operations to Canada."

"But now they've been left penniless . . ."

"From our calculations, they've just got enough to hide out for a couple of weeks. Then they'll have to get money somehow or other. It's an expensive business, hiding out."

The Customs officer smiled and left. Campagna smiled too. The message had been quite clear.

While he thought over what he'd just learned, Veronesi phoned him. The Superintendent informed him that Naza Sabic's sister had arrived to identify the body and transfer it to Croatia.

"I'll wait for you here in the morgue," he said.

"Do I really have to come in person?"

"Which bit of 'I'll wait for you here in the morgue' don't you understand?"

Mara Sabic was an attractive woman of about thirty-five. Not too tall, but a nice figure, with a delicate face and a shy smile.

He held out his hand as he introduced himself. "I'm Inspector Campagna."

"Mara Sabic."

"I'm really sorry about what happened to your sister."

"She'd got out of Croatia because she wanted to save her own life," she replied in good Italian. "Instead, she ended up being killed by other Croatians."

"Where did you learn to speak such good Italian?"

"I'm a nurse. During the war, I worked in a hospital run by the Italian Red Cross."

An official accompanied them to the place where her sister's body was being kept. Mara was stoical and dignified. She gently stroked Naza's face and said, "Yes. She's my sister."

Campagna helped her to fill out the necessary paperwork for the body to be transferred. When this was done he asked, gently but insistently, if he could buy her a coffee. In reality, he wanted to question her, but he didn't feel up to taking her back to HQ. He took the photo of Josip, Zoran and their mate from his jacket pocket. "Do you know them?"

She nodded. "All three of them. They're from my part of the world."

"What are they like?"

"They used to be crazy about football. They've since become crazy about politics. Nationalists. Ugly customers. They've hurt such a lot of people."

"And why was it they turned to your sister?"

"Back home, a lot of people knew she had links with the underworld, and she wasn't all that fond of cops."

Campagna took the photos and put them back in his pocket. "Let's hope we nail them soon. As soon as there's any news, I'll let you know."

Mara shook her head firmly. "I'm not going back to Croatia."

"Why's that?"

"I want to help the police to arrest the men who murdered my sister."

"I can understand you're angry and upset, but it's not possible for you to help in the investigations. I can assure you that I'll do everything in my power. Trust me."

"Fair enough. I'll go it alone."

Campagna lost his temper. "Okay, do what you want." He paid for the coffee and walked away from the bar. She followed him with her eyes.

*

Two days later, Campagna was woken right in the middle of the night. It was Amelia again.

"What's happened?" the Inspector asked, glancing at his watch.

"We've rounded up a few prostitutes. There's one without ID who claims she knows you."

He got up while his wife grumbled about the lousy profession he'd chosen. For a moment, Campagna was tempted to argue back, but he let it go.

"Starting tomorrow, I'll sleep on the sofa, that way I won't bother you."

"It's your colleagues who cause the bother. I bet it was that Di Natale woman."

"Just think of your architect and forget all about Amelia. She only ever phones on business, nothing else."

An hour later, in a foul temper, he entered the cellblock at HQ, sipping coffee from a plastic cup. As usual after a round-up, there was total chaos. Amelia, exhausted after her long shift, was trying to sort everything out. When she saw the Inspector she pointed to a cell.

"Mara!" exclaimed Campagna in surprise, as he gazed at her short skirt and thick make-up. "Only just got here and already on the job?"

She hurled a few shrill insults at him in Croatian. Losing his temper, the Inspector called a colleague over to release her from the cell. Then he took her by one arm and led her to his office. Mara seemed indignant.

"Now we're going to draw up a nice little extradition order for you and send you back home," he hissed.

Mara snorted. "I'm not a whore. I'd gone looking for somebody."

"Dressed like that?"

"I didn't want to get noticed."

"But then you went and got yourself caught in a raid."

"Please, you have to believe me."

"So who was it you were looking for?"

"If I tell you, you won't send me back – okay?"

"That depends. Try and convince me you weren't hooking."

"Zoran's ex-fiancée – she's working the streets round here. I'm sure that he asked her for help."

Campagna was taken aback at this information. "And why didn't you tell me when we met in the morgue?"

"You didn't want any help from me."

The cop stared at her for a moment. "All right," he said. "Now I do. What's her name?"

"I don't know. She was from another town. But I remember her clearly."

The Inspector left the room and returned with various albums full of mug shots. Mara started to leaf through them, gazing attentively at each face. Day was breaking by the time she saw the right photo. "Here. That's her!"

The Inspector found himself looking at a pale blond Slav woman with a round face and dark eyes. Her name was Dinka Zadro. He immediately phoned his colleagues in the Vice Squad; they told him she'd moved to Mestre a few months ago.

Campagna went to talk to Veronesi, then came back and told Mara not to leave HQ. He'd be back soon.

*

Amelia drove fast. At her side sat the Superintendent, who was on his mobile, explaining the situation to a deputy chief superintendent in Mestre. Campagna, on the back seat, was phoning his wife.

"I can't get Ilaria from school. I'm busy," he said in a low voice so as not to be overheard by his boss.

He listened to Gaia's protests for a while. Then, since he wasn't able to say what he wanted, he rang off.

"She does it on purpose," he thought. "She knows Veronesi won't stand for family rows while we're on duty."

Actually, the Superintendent did mutter darkly, but both Campagna and Amelia pretended they hadn't heard.

The car left the motorway, hit the flyover and came into Mestre. The house where Dinka Zadro lived stood in a side street off the Via Piave, near the railway station. When they reached the right neighbourhood, they found their colleagues from Mestre already in position.

"There's someone in the house," he was informed by a plain-clothes officer. "But it's not the woman. We picked her up as she was heading for home after work."

Dinka was sitting in a car with a policewoman keeping an eye on her. Campagna opened the door.

"Who's in the house? Zoran?" he asked.

She burst into tears and nodded.

"Is he alone?"

"I don't know."

The Inspector joined his colleagues, who were getting ready to break in. "It's definitely Zoran. He might be alone."

"We're not ruling anything out," retorted Veronesi. "These guys are armed and dangerous."

A white-haired official with a vast fund of experience to draw on pointed out that the longer they waited, the greater the danger that the people in the house would become aware of their presence. "And then," he added, "we'll find ourselves facing a siege, and that's a real pain in the butt – all those negotiations, new risks . . ."

They split into two groups and prepared to break in. Campagna and Amelia went in through the main entrance first, followed by the others. The door wasn't reinforced, and it was easy to smash it in.

"Police!" yelled Campagna as he went in. He found himself facing Zoran, who was just loading the magazine into a Skorpion submachine gun. The barrel was pointed at the ceiling.

"Drop it!" he shouted, his finger already pulling the trigger. Two shots to the chest – and the Croatian was dead even before he hit the ground.

"He forced me to do it," the Inspector said to justify himself. "He refused to surrender."

Veronesi took the Skorpion from Zoran's hands and cocked it.

"You did the right thing. He'd have shot you dead," he said flatly.

Amelia placed her arm under his and led him out of the apartment. "Could you use a coffee?"

The Inspector shook his head. "That's the second man I've killed. The first was when I was still in the Flying Squad."

"The mugger. I remember. He'd taken a shot at you."

"I know. But it still makes me feel shitty."

"You're right to feel like that. You were a bit too quick on the draw for my taste."

Campagna gazed straight into her eyes. She smiled.

"Don't worry," she said gently. "In the report, I'll say he had you in his sights."

Just then, Veronesi came out and motioned to him to go back inside. In one room his colleagues had found some interesting material. Campagna went past Zoran's body without deigning to glance at it.

On the kitchen table, the contents of a sports bag had been tipped out. Arms, ammunition, balaclavas, two-way radios . . . but what had really attracted the attention of the cops was two pairs of handcuffs together with chains, padlocks, chloroform, syringes and sedatives. All the equipment for a kidnapping. Veronesi ordered two men to go and get the girl. Dinka started shouting and bawling when she saw her ex-fiancée's body. The police got her to sit down in front of the objects found in the bag, offered her a glass of water and then started to grill her. They needed to take advantage of the psychological disarray caused by the sight of her friend Zoran's body. She reacted exactly the way they had expected, and when the right time had come, Amelia sent them all away, sat opposite the girl, offered her a cigarette and calmly started to question her. Dinka talked. She told her everything she knew. It wasn't a lot but enough to get the cops worried.

"She doesn't know where Josip and the others are hiding out," Amelia told them. "Zoran had told her they were planning to kidnap an industrialist from the Venice area."

"An ambush?" Campagna burst out. "But these guys are all in hiding, and they don't have the necessary support to carry out a major operation."

"Actually, it's not the usual kind of kidnapping," Amelia explained. 'They want to capture an industrialist who's laundering money for the Croatian mafia."

"That way nobody will dream of squealing on him," commented the Inspector. "Did she tell you who it is?"

"Sorry, but no. Zoran always kept his mouth shut about that."

*

Campagna, Veronesi and Amelia returned to Pavia. Their colleagues in Mestre would carry on questioning Dinka in the hope that she'd remember something useful. The cops knew that, sometimes, all you needed to solve a whole case was one single detail.

"Back to the admin," commented the Superintendent. "Anti-Mafia and Customs can fight over the investigation."

Campagna cleared his throat. "Maybe there're still a few things we can do over the next twenty-four hours."

Veronesi turned round. "Giulio, I just know you're up to something. What the fuck's going on in that head of yours?"

"This gang we're dealing with has one characteristic: its members all come from the same district. Zoran had taken refuge there with his ex-fiancée. I'm willing to bet that this is the trail we need to follow if we're going to uncover Josip and his mates."

"But there's absolutely no way we can do a blanket search of all the towns and villages where all the Croatians in the Veneto come from. We don't have the time."

"True," replied the Inspector. "But we do have Mara, Naza Sabic's sister. She knows the fugitives and could give us a hand in building up a picture of their contacts in the area."

Veronesi smiled with satisfaction. "Okay. You and Amelia can follow this one up. And if you get any results, we pass everything on to our colleagues. Right?"

Mara had been put back in a high-security cell.

"She tried to escape," one of the cops explained.

"I got tired of waiting!" said the woman in self-justification. "I wanted to go to a hotel to get changed. I'm still all tarted up."

Campagna and Amelia took her to the hotel. Mara came into the entrance hall wearing a two-piece suit of rather old-fashioned cut and without a trace of make-up.

"That's more like it," commented the Inspector.

"I'm hungry," said Amelia. "I'm really starving."

Lunch had finished a while ago, and the two women had to content themselves with a sandwich. Campagna wasn't hungry. He hoped his tomato juice would eradicate the whiff of cordite that still clung to his throat.

"Zoran's dead," he said wearily. Then he felt the need to justify himself and added: "He forced me to shoot."

Mara continued to nibble at her ham sandwich. "I'm sorry for his mother. She's a nice woman. But he was a pig. He felt pity for nobody. Not even for Naza, even though he'd known her ever since they were kids."

At the thought of her sister, she burst into tears. Amelia stroked her hair tenderly. "We know it was Josip who pulled the trigger," she explained. "We have to catch him. Otherwise your sister will never receive justice."

"We need your help," added Campagna. "We need to check if there are any friends or relatives of the fugitives in these parts."

"You know everyone from back home," intervened Amelia. "Just by making a few phone calls to friends and acquaintances – any excuse will do – you might be able to discover something."

Mara looked her straight in the eyes. "But then I'll never be able to go home. Their relatives will take their revenge."

The two cops exchanged glances. They hadn't really thought about this side of things.

"You're right," admitted Campagna. "Let's leave it."

Mara thought things over in silence. "If Josip got away with it, I'd never forgive myself," she said firmly. "So I'll stay here. I'm a good nurse, if the truth be told, and I'm always sure of finding a job here."

"Don't make your mind up too quickly," said Amelia. "We're cops, and your help will come in useful for us. But you're risking your whole future."

"I'm doing it for Naza," she insisted with some vehemence, 'she was my only sister."

When they got back to HQ, Campagna was summoned to Veronesi's office. Two officials were waiting to ask him about the shooting. The Inspector had been expecting this – it was all part of the procedure. The two men were polite but needling. Veronesi stood up for him, the way a real chief always does for his men. Amelia was summoned too. She told them that the Inspector hadn't had any choice. It was him or Zoran.

Mara spent the afternoon and the evening on the phone. She talked to a great many people, including the parish priest and one of her old school friends who now worked in the local registry office.

At the end of all this time she had come up with just one name. Antun De Zajc. He'd moved to San Donà di Piave, in the province of Venice, in 1980. He was fifty-five, a wine salesman.

Campagna and Amelia were too tired to start investigating the Croatian now. They decided to postpone things until the following morning. Amelia went with Mara back to the hotel, while the Inspector stopped off at a bar on his way home. He needed time to think. It's not every day that you kill a man. He ordered a glass of prosecco. Then another. His stomach was empty, and he stuffed himself with nibbles so as not to get tipsy. He forced himself to remember every second and every movement he had made during the raid. There was no doubt about it. He'd screwed up. Zoran would in all probability have given himself up. He promised himself that, the next time, he wouldn't be the first to go in. He drank his third and last glass of wine as a toast to the Croatian. He looked at his watch. It was really late. He had no desire to go home, but there was nowhere else for him to go.

Ilaria had been in bed for a while, but his wife was waiting up for him, watching an old film on video – De Sica's *Bicycle Thieves*. Gaia knew it off by heart, but whenever she felt low she'd go and dig it out.

"You and I need to have a talk," she said curtly. "I had to leave a meeting with a client so I could pick up Ilaria from school."

"And I shot a Croatian fugitive who was pointing a submachine gun at me. Blew him away with two bullets."

Gaia went pale and said nothing.

"Any comments?" he asked her provocatively.

"Could you sleep on the sofa . . . ? If you don't mind . . ."

*

Antun de Zajc's criminal record was as pure as the driven snow. The police in San Donà di Piave viewed him as a fine, upstanding citizen. Campagna hoped with all his heart that he wasn't. Otherwise they'd never find out where to look for Josip and his gang.

"Need a hand?" Veronesi had asked. He replied that he didn't, and now he was driving along the motorway with Amelia, keeping a careful eye open so as not to go past the right exit.

"What exactly does this Antun do?" Amelia asked.

"He's a wine salesman. Specializes in discount shops. He imports the stuff from Croatia for the local wine stores."

"A scam, right?"

"No, all legal. Generally speaking, Croatian wines aren't bad . . ."

He realized that Amelia was gazing at him. "What?"

"Things not going too well with Gaia, are they?"

"Bloody awful."

"Separating?"

"Got no choice."

"Sorry. Well, not really. Perhaps this is a good opportunity for you to hop into bed with me. I'm tired of flirting."

"I don't like it when women are so direct."

"I had to tell you, Giulio."

"There wasn't any need. I'd already got the message."

"So what's the problem? Don't you fancy me?"

The phone rang just at that moment. It was HQ. End of conversation.

*

Antun owned a villa and a store in the village. And an old farmhouse in need of repair, about six miles from the town centre. According to the information from the local police, the place had been uninhabited for years and was surrounded by soybean plantations.

"Just the place to hold a hostage," commented Campagna.

"Not necessarily," retorted Amelia. "These country areas seem empty, but the locals always know everything."

"Maybe they just mind their own business? It wouldn't be the first time."

He was referring to the case of a serial killer who'd tortured and killed several young women in a farmhouse just like this one. The neighbours had always thought something strange was going on, but they'd decided to talk only when the *carabinieri* had come knocking on their doors.

Campagna halted on a small bridge over an irrigation canal. Beyond it there were no more trees to protect the road, which ran almost straight to the farmhouse.

"If we go any further, they'll see us," said the Inspector. "Assuming they're actually there."

"We could try to be a courting couple looking for somewhere quiet."

"They're not stupid, that lot. They fought in the war, they've learned not to trust appearances."

129

"I really don't want to have to leg it all the way there. It must be nearly a couple of miles."

"I don't see any alternative. Even if we wait for dark."

"So we've got plenty of time to find a volunteer."

Just then, Campagna's mobile went off. It was Veronesi. "The Anti-Mafia's just phoned. They say that since yesterday evening, rumours of a kidnapping have been going round, even though the family's denying it. Somebody called Alfio Rossato. Owns a textile factory. Seems they picked him up while he was opening the gate to his villa. The woman next door saw it all, but she's ninety-two and her story's a bit mixed up."

"And what's the family saying?"

"They're saying Rossato's abroad on business but his mobile's switched off."

"Looks like the little old lady was right."

"It does indeed. Where are you two?"

"San Donà. We're just checking out an abandoned farmhouse, property of Antun De Zajc. Could be just the place to keep a kidnap victim."

"I'll warn Anti-Mafia and send reinforcements."

Campagna reversed the car and parked it a short distance away. Then the two cops got out of the car and continued to keep an eye on the farmhouse from the shelter of the trees.

*

Campagna had been right when he'd said that the Croatians were veterans of the Civil War and knew what they were doing. In fact, Josip had ordered Mate to watch the little bridge, the only place from which the farmhouse could be observed without one being spotted. Mate had been in position ever since dawn and had observed every movement made by Campagna and Amelia through his binoculars. Every so often he reported to Josip via the two-way radio. Mate was in no doubt that they were cops, and the boss decided to evacuate the hideout with the hostage. Before he rang off, he gave Mate one last order.

The two cops saw a white van leaving the farm and heading towards them.

"What do we do?" asked Amelia in alarm.

"We let them go by, then we follow them and we just hope Veronesi and our colleagues in San Donà manage to rustle up a roadblock in time."

They ran back into the car. Campagna reversed back into the bushes to avoid being spotted and they waited for the vehicle to pass. Amelia was on her mobile, talking to the Superintendent, and they both had their eyes glued to the entrance to the bridge. They were quite unaware of the man creeping up on them from the side, gripping a Kalashnikov. He opened fire from about ten yards. A long hail of bullets smashed into the right wing of the car. Amelia took a direct hit. And, shielding her colleague with her body, she saved his life. Campagna opened the door, threw himself to the ground and rolled through the bushes, trying to find shelter. Mate halted to reload. He fired off another burst to cover the arrival of the van. The rear door opened, the killer jumped in, and the driver stepped on the accelerator. Campagna got a grip on himself. He loaded his Beretta and started to run. Cutting across the fields, he could try to reach a hairpin bend where the van would be forced to slow down. He didn't have any clear plan. He just knew that he had fifteen 9mm bullets in his magazine. He skidded on the grass and wasted precious seconds. The van took the curve while he was still thirty-odd yards away. He halted, took aim holding his pistol in both hands and started to fire at the driver's cabin. He didn't want to risk hitting the hostage. He'd fired off all his rounds in a few seconds, but he had the impression he'd hit the man sitting next to the driver. He thought he'd seen him start to writhe. And he was certain it was Josip. Their eyes had met for a fraction of a second.

He went back to the car. He closed Amelia's eyes and then embraced her. He was weeping.

*

By the time Veronesi arrived, the area was swarming with cops. Campagna was sitting at the foot of a tree smoking a cigarette and staring out at the countryside. The Superintendent drew aside the sheet covering Amelia's body and stood gazing at it for a few minutes. Then he started shaking with emotion.

"I can't believe Amelia's dead," muttered Campagna.

"You allowed yourselves to get spotted," Veronesi replied harshly. "I'd told you to stay under cover."

The Inspector shook his head. "That lot are behaving like a small army. They were already keeping the place under surveillance when we arrived. They reacted with speed and precision."

"And they killed poor Amelia."

"I might have got one of them, actually."

"You sure of that?"

Campagna shrugged. "You know how it works. You take aim and you fire. You think you've seen things, but you don't know if you really have."

"No. I don't know that. You're the crack shot here," replied Veronesi. "Still I hope you got him."

An agent from the Anti-Mafia unit came over and informed them that they'd found clear evidence of a hostage sequestered in the house.

The van was found an hour later in a country lane that crossed the main road to Trieste. In the cabin they'd found traces of blood. For Campagna this was clear proof that he'd hit Josip.

"They've taken off for Mestre," said Veronesi. "They commandeered a van from two Belgian tourists who saw them heading in that direction."

"But the border's in completely the opposite direction," the Inspector pointed out.

"They've still got the hostage," said the man from Anti-Mafia. "They still think the deal's on."

Campagna waited for the man from Anti-Mafia to leave. "I'm going after Josip," he said.

Veronesi stared at him. "Look at the shape you're in. You go home."

"No. I want to be in on it too."

"You've got too involved. I don't want you here. You'll screw things up."

A squad car arrived with Antun De Zajc in it. He was snivelling and raising his handcuffed wrists to the sky in search of divine aid. He was yelling that he knew nothing about the kidnapping and had done Josip Persen a favour only because he was the cousin of his brother-in-law.

"D'you believe him?" asked the Inspector.

"He could hardly have been unaware that Josip was a nasty piece of work. We'll bang him up for being an accessory to kidnap and murder. Then we'll see what happens."

Once the forensic team had finished taking prints and the police doctor had completed his inspection, Amelia's body was loaded into a police mortuary van. Campagna had to bite his knuckles so as not to start bawling again.

A car took him back to Padua. Throughout the journey he sat in silence, thinking. By the time he set foot inside HQ, his mind was pretty much made up. He made his way to the weapons store, where he picked up a couple of pistol magazines, and then went to get his car. He phoned Customs and Excise on his mobile, leaving his number and asking for Staff Sergeant Fiore to call him.

The Customs officer phoned ten minutes later.

"I need a favour."

"I've already done you one," retorted Fiore. "You go through the official channels, okay?"

"I can't. The Croatians murdered my colleague right in front of my eyes, and my lot have taken me off the case."

"So I heard. Sorry, but I can't do anything for you. Especially if you're going to start acting outside the rules."

"Let's do it like this. You listen to my request and then decide whether or not to say yes."

"All right. That much I can do."

"If I were wounded and needed to hide out in the area between Mestre and Padua, who could I get to treat me?"

Fiore sighed. "If you were a wounded 'Croatian', my advice would be: try the Chinese. Croatian and Chinese gangsters are as thick as thieves with each other, and the Chinks have got a couple of apartments rigged up for emergency surgery."

"Thanks."

"What for? You're not wounded. You're not even Croatian."

*

The Chinese community had for years been surrounded by an impenetrable wall of silence, but then the new generation, born in Italy, had started to move away from the old traditions and become more independent. And they'd committed a series of blunders that had drawn the attention of the forces of law and order. In the small towns abandoned by the Mafia of the Brenta region – a Mafia sold off to the state like a bankrupt firm by its head, Felice Maniero – gangs of Chinese kids had arrived and were demanding protection money. Indeed, Campagna, informed by a furrier, had managed to nick one of them who'd then preferred to become a stool pigeon rather than have his family find out – they'd have sent him home to his mum and dad's back in China. The Inspector contented himself with little dribs and drabs while waiting for the lad to make his way up in some organization or another. Then he'd have more interesting information to hand on.

But this time he was going to squeeze him until the pips squeaked. He absolutely had to find out where Josip was being treated. Unless he'd bitten the dust in the meantime. But something told him the Croatian was still alive and getting ready to beat it with the ransom money.

He found Hu Wenzhou in the usual small square where the Chinese kids who hoped to become big shots in the world of crime habitually gathered. He made sure Hu Wenzhou saw him and then waited for him in a nearby street. Hu arrived on a moped. He was driving slowly and jumped into Campagna's car when he was sure nobody would spot him. Campagna explained what it was he wanted to find out. The boy couldn't tell him anything. He had no idea where such a clinic might be. Then the Inspector told him he'd better talk to somebody who did know. Hu was scared, but the cop turned up the pressure. He climbed back onto his moped, shaking his head.

Campagna waited for more than hour then spotted a car with four Chinese on board. The one in the front passenger seat climbed out and came up to the window. He was in his sixties, with a discreet paunch and an air of authority.

"I know one of your doctors is treating a Croatian who got wounded in a shoot-out," said Campagna. "I was the one that fired the shot. I don't have anything against you, but I need to find him. Otherwise I'll make sure that you lot start to feel the heat."

The Chinese guy didn't reply but went back to his car and spoke over his mobile phone for a few minutes. Then he came back and told the Inspector that, yes, the Croatian was a nasty piece of work and they'd be glad to help the police. But they couldn't give their doctor's address, let alone get involved with the arrest. They knew Josip's friends would be coming by to pick him up at a certain time, and the cop could wait for them at a certain road junction they'd need to cross. He gave a precise description of the model and colour of the car. The cop asked him why he was so certain they'd be using this car, and the Chinese replied, with a smile, that he himself had procured it for them.

*

Campagna took up his position two hours early. He wanted to make sure he got them. His mobile rang. He looked at the display and saw it was Veronesi's number. He decided to answer.

The Superintendent came straight to the point, "You didn't go home like I told you. Instead, you went to get more ordnance from the armoury. I'd like to know exactly what you're planning to do with thirty rounds."

"Nothing. Don't worry."

The Superintendent's voice went up a tone, "Oh, but I *am* worried, Giulio. Really worried. You're going to do something really stupid. You're going to throw away your career by playing Dirty Harry. You've got a wife and daughter. You could at least think of them."

Campagna didn't reply.

"Giulio, tell me where you are. I'll come over and we can have a nice little chat."

The Inspector cut the call short and switched off his mobile. This conversation was pointless. He had no idea what was going to happen. In particular, he didn't have a plan. He wanted to get Amelia's murderers. That was all. Then he'd face up to the consequences. He thought that maybe he'd already thrown away his career by disobeying an express order from his chief. So, in that case, he might just as well play the game out to the final whistle. He checked his pistol for the umpteenth time and resigned himself to waiting. He was certain that he'd have three of the Croatians to confront. Josip and another two. The fourth would be staying behind to guard the hostage. He could manage. Yes, he could manage all right.

*

No more than three hundred yards away, an old Chinese doctor was bandaging Josip Persen's shoulder and side. The Croatian had taken two bullets. It was his good luck that their impact had been deadened as they went through the metal side of the van. Otherwise he'd have been a dead man. Josip started to groan. The effects of the anaesthetic were wearing off. He asked the doctor, in Croatian and English, for another injection.

"It is not right time for another shot of morphine," replied the Chinese, in Italian. "It could be dangerous."

"What the fuck do you care?" spat out Josip.

The doctor shrugged and gave him a jab. Josip sighed with satisfaction at the idea of being able to sink back into unconsciousness. He'd suffered quite enough for one day.

*

In his office, Veronesi had gathered a group of men he could rely on.

"You all know Campagna, and I know you admire him as a man and as a colleague. He's after the Croatians, and he's armed to the teeth. I'd like you to help me find him. Obviously this is an unofficial operation, and if any one doesn't feel up to it, don't feel obliged."

Nobody said a word. Veronesi smiled. "Okay, let's get cracking."

*

Mate and another member of the gang called Jure parked near the clandestine clinic that was on the first floor of an apartment block on the southern outskirts of Padua, inhabited almost exclusively by Chinese. Their boss was out for the count, and to move him they were obliged to use a wheelchair provided by the doctor, who accepted the money, thanking them with a discreet nod.

The two Croatians carefully deposited Josip on the rear seat of the car, loaded the wheelchair into the boot and set off at a moderate speed, not just to avoid jolting the wounded man but so as not to draw the attention of the cops.

Campagna saw the car crossing the junction a few minutes later. He recognized the driver as the man who had killed Amelia, and for a few seconds he sat there frozen, unable to turn the ignition key because his hands were trembling so much. Then, cursing himself, he calmed down a bit and swung into action, following the Croatian car's tail lights.

When they crossed the Tencarola Bridge and took the road to the Euganean Hills, Campagna realized that the gang's new hideout must be one of the countless little cottages scattered round the area. A vast empty landscape, thickly wooded, criss-crossed by country lanes that made it possible to move around quickly and discreetly. But he knew the area well – and definitely better than they did. They weren't going to get away from him. Every so often he glanced at the passenger seat, where his pistol and mobile lay. These were the only alternatives still left to see the game through to its end.

The Inspector was so intent on tailing the car that he completely forgot all about his rear mirror. Otherwise he'd have realized that he was being closely followed by the car of Police Inspector Alberto Marangoni, who'd been waiting on the bridge at Tencarola, one of the roads leading out of town. Marangoni was in continuous contact with Veronesi. All the other cars were catching up behind.

*

The Croatians turned left, heading for the old abbey at Praglia. The road was completely deserted, and Campagna was obliged to fall back. After a few miles the car turned into a dirt road that climbed up towards the top of a hill. This was the moment that Campagna had been fearing. Now it was starting to become really difficult to avoid being noticed, even if the endless bends in the road and the thick vegetation kept him concealed. The Croatians probably felt safe since they never bothered to check whether anyone was following them. They drove in through a gateway at the side of the road and carried on for another hundred yards or so until they reached a house that was completely shrouded in darkness. The Inspector turned off his headlights, got out of the car and walked down the path. He gripped the pistol in both hands, ready to shoot. A rectangle of light pierced the darkness when someone opened the door to admit Mate and Jure, who were carrying Josip in their arms. Then night fell over the house again.

Campagna didn't know what to do. He wondered whether to wait for dawn, but he'd never manage to get into the house and take them by surprise all by himself. Unless he intended to get himself shot. A hail of bullets from a Kalashnikov. Like the hail of bullets that had ripped their way through Amelia's body. The idea forced him to start thinking with a minimum of lucidity.

"What the fuck am I doing here?" he said to himself through gritted teeth.

He went back to his car, picked up his mobile and dialled a number. He spun round on hearing another mobile go off a few yards away. He reached for his holster, but Veronesi's voice stopped him.

"I bet you were just phoning me to give me the position of the fugitives," said the Superintendent. Other colleagues emerged from the darkness around him.

"You're right," admitted the Inspector. "But how did you . . . ?"

"Forget it," Veronesi interrupted him. "Welcome back into the fold. This way we can wrap up what might otherwise have turned into a rather nasty business. For everyone involved . . ."

Campagna was flabbergasted. And he was touched that his director and colleagues had turned up to cover him yet again. He wanted to find the right words to thank them properly, but he couldn't think of anything.

Shortly before dawn the reinforcements arrived. By first light they'd worked out the layout of the house and had the raid planned.

"You in on this?" Veronesi asked him.

"D'you trust me?"

"I just hope you won't start shooting left, right and centre like a bleeding idiot."

*

They went in through the main door and the garage entrance. The Croatians, still asleep, were taken by surprise. Josip would never wake up: he had died during the night, and none of his partners had even realized. Even the hostage, bound hand and foot, was asleep at the time of the attack. His joy at being freed evaporated when he was handcuffed by agents of the Anti-Mafia.

"Where are you taking me?" he asked anxiously.

"To a really nice cell."

"But I haven't done anything!"

"Shut your face, you fucking piece of Mafia scum. A colleague of mine got herself shot dead to save your skin."

Campagna gave Amelia's murderer a kick in the balls. Then he whacked him hard across the nose with the barrel of his pistol.

"Okay, that'll do," ordered Veronesi quietly.

*

At Amelia's funeral there were a lot of people. Even the mayor, wearing his sash, and the Interior Minister. Campagna was in the front row, next to Amelia's parents who'd come up from the south. It was tough for him, having to say goodbye to Amelia.

In the following days, the Inspector helped Mara Sabic to find work in an area where the Croatian underworld wasn't much in evidence. She was taken on by a private clinic in the Marches. After that, he never heard from her again.

*

The body of the young Hu Wenzhou was found in a disused kiln just outside Padua. They'd slit his throat. Campagna heard the news when he came back from a holiday. He'd gone for a seaside break in Sicily with his daughter. Gaia had preferred a trip to France with her architect. He shut himself away in his office with the file on the case. Then he went to see Veronesi.

"I want to be switched to the Chinese section," he said. He sounded serious.

"You been out in the sun too much? Nobody wants to go there."

The Inspector placed the file on the investigation into Hu's murder on the desk. "I think it's my fault he died."

The Superintendent leafed through a few pages to find out what this was all about. "He was the informer who put you in contact with their *numero uno*?"

"Yeah."

"You can't possibly get your own back for every informer they bump off."

"That's not the reason. This kid was seventeen, and they cut his throat just because he'd passed on a message. We can't let them get away with this kind of thing."

"If that's it, the Chinese gangs do far worse. And we manage to uncover maybe a half of what they get up to."

"Precisely. I got a good look at the boss who negotiated with me. It's a lead. I can start there and work my way up until I've sussed out how the whole organization works and what they're up to."

"Okay. You can take care of the Chinese."

*

Late at night, in a Chinese restaurant, a few men were gathered round a table. They were talking business as they ate and drank. Outside, lurking in a van, Campagna and another cop were observing the entrance through a telephoto lens.

"It's nearly three a.m.," protested his colleague. "When the fuck do these guys go to bed?"

The Inspector didn't reply. He continued to keep the restaurant under surveillance. Just then the door opened, and four Chinese came out. Among them was the fat guy who'd passed him the information about Josip.

Campagna gave a satisfied smile. The Chinese said goodbye, and the man climbed into his Toyota. No sooner had he engaged first gear than he was surrounded by plain-clothes cops. He held up his hands and came quietly. He showed his ID and allowed himself to be frisked without any fuss. Campagna climbed out of the van and started to search the car. From under the seat he pulled out a bag filled with greyish powder.

"I'll bet this is Burmese heroine," said Campagna.

The Chinese guy turned pale. He started to shake his head. "It not mine, it not mine," he protested.

Campagna spoke right into the man's ear. "I know," he murmured. "It's a present. Compliments of Hu Wenzhou."

What's Missing

Marcello Fois

"Oh dear," thought Marchini as he hung up.

Inspector Curreli, who was stacking up a pile of dossiers on his desk, waited for a while to hear what it was all about. In vain. With a jut of his chin, he asked Marchesini who'd been on the phone. "Well?" he said, seeing that his assistant was reluctant to speak.

"A murder," the latter replied all at once. "It was De Pisis. An old woman killed in Via Gaudenzi, not far from here."

Outside the window, behind the Inspector, purple clouds were scudding along.

"It was De Pisis," repeated Marchesini as if to underline the fact that, if the Prosecutor General in person had taken the trouble to phone, it must be something important.

Meanwhile a dolphin-shaped cloud was hovering almost at the height of the building opposite – but this must be an optical illusion. Shit, thought Marchini.

Curreli, who was just about to leave, stopped in the middle of the office. "Penny for your thoughts," he said.

Marchini's eyes abandoned the cloud at the point where it was becoming so shapeless that it would have required too much effort to identify it. "That was . . ."

". . . Yes, that was De Pisis on the phone, I got that much. Talk about stupid . . . Let's get going, okay?" said Curreli curtly, reaching for his coat.

"It's just that the victim appears to be a certain Elena Marcucci . . ."

At this news, Curreli shrugged and started to walk away . . .

"Crescioni's grandma . . . The engineer . . ." Marchini concluded.

Curreli halted, thunderstruck. "Crescioni?" he repeated. "The one standing for Mayor?"

Marchini nodded. Yes, that was the man. "Precossi's already there, just by chance, he says . . ."

Shit, shit, shit, thought Curreli. The deputy prosecutor "just by chance" happening to get there before the police. Just by chance. That said it all.

*

Since for Curreli there was no such thing as chance and never had been; since, in fact, Eraldo Precossi, the deputy prosecutor coordinating the investigations into the death of Elena Marcucci, had swung into action before the members of the team, indeed even before Signor Stefano Crescioni, the victim's grandson, who was standing for Mayor in the next municipal elections; and since there was nothing that pissed him, Giacomo Curreli, Police Inspector, off more than something that ought to have been a matter of chance but had every sign of being a stitch-up . . . In short, all these "sinces" were making Curreli seethe like a pressure cooker.

Marchini refrained, of course, from asking him what was on his mind and pulled his jacket from the back of his chair, as if to say that he needed to get a move on and join Precossi at the scene of the crime, before *just by chance* he did something irreparable.

In short, this was how it had happened: incredibly, Precossi just happened to be near Via Gaudenzi, just at the time a murder was being committed, and he'd gone up to take a look . . . The Deputy Prosecutor had felt duty-bound to warn the Prosecutor General, who, in turn, had decided it would be a good idea first of all to entrust him with the investigation and secondly to alert Signor Crescioni. Signor Crescioni had arrived straight away, abandoning a party he was throwing for supporters of his mayoral candidacy, and had spent a good minute standing silently in front of the corpse of his poor grandma lying supine on her back (a tremor in his lips had silenced the buzz of the tenants who had gathered on the landing). In this way useful time had been frittered away just to enable a brief discussion between Precossi and Crescioni and for an excited chinwag over the phone to take place between Deputy

Precossi and Prosecutor General De Pisis, in which the same De Pisis had officially entrusted Precossi with the task of coordinating the investigations into the death of Elena Marcucci; hence it had been decided that the moment had arrived, just as a matter of courtesy, to phone the relevant department. Which, as it happened, was Curreli's.

*

And now, we're back where we started . . .

Marchini receives the phone call and says: oh dear . . . Then he says to Curreli that there's been a murder, and they need to get a move on to the scene of the crime, since Precossi, who may be a magistrate but isn't exactly the brightest of the bunch, is already there.

*

In fact, by the time Curreli and Marchini arrived on the third storey of the apartment block at 3, Ippolito Gaudenzi, scientist (1729-1792), Precossi had already investigated, listened, defined, said goodbye, concluded. He had even had one suspect arrested – a painter who was so guilty that the word "suspect" was being used merely as a formality.

*

Curreli looked around: the room had been turned topsy-turvy. Precossi looked as if he wanted to tie things up as quickly as possible. Listening to him, you'd have said that things were pretty much sorted; he just needed to talk to the residents who were standing around on the landing. Precossi was one of those people who believed in activity for activity's sake, and indeed he kept coming in and out of the apartment. Now, for example, a few minutes after the arrival of Curreli, he had gone out without any obvious reason.

"Tell them to clear the landing," said Curreli to Marchini in a neutral tone, following Precossi with his eyes. "When the forensic guys arrive, they won't even be able to get in here!"

Marchini had a moment's hesitation, as always when he had to do something unpleasant. Curreli, seeing his uncertainty, decided to get in first. "Nothing to see here!" he yelled as he advanced towards the landing.

Marchini, taking a couple of steps backward, made a vague gesture with his arm to encourage people to obey the Inspector. The small group backed off a little.

"This is the kind of thing that really makes me lose my rag," commented Curreli, loud enough to make himself heard. "Somebody's made a right mess of this apartment. And that's not the worst of it," he said, looking down the shadowy hallway. "Not one son of a bitch bothered to stop them. Nobody heard or saw a thing, and now here they all are, rolling up to enjoy the show. They only get in our way when we're trying to do our job!"

Marchini assented, albeit discreetly: for one thing he'd never managed to get used to Curreli's tirades, and for another, Precossi was coming back.

Elena Marcucci, the manageress of the apartment block, was lying in the hallway. From a summary examination of the position of her body, it appeared that she had tried to flee from her murderer. Without success, obviously, since now she looked like a tailor's dummy lying spread-eagled on the floor with her legs half-splayed and her hands clutching her throat.

"Her home help found her just after she came back from shopping. She always did the shopping in the afternoon, while the manageress was resting. She phoned us straight away," Precossi reported.

"She phoned *you*," Curreli corrected him.

"Strangled?" suggested Marchini.

"No doubt about it," confirmed Precossi.

Curreli pulled a face as if to say maybe, maybe not. "Let's wait for the forensic team, shall we?"

Precossi looked at him unflinchingly. "When you're all done here there's going to be a briefing in De Pisis' office," he announced curtly. He went off without awaiting a reply.

Marchini looked at Curreli . . . For a fraction of a second he had feared the worst; he knew that words such as "briefing" made him lose his rag. "D'you you think it's going to rain?" he asked, just to take his mind off things.

"Know what, Marchini? Just shut the fuck up!" was the reply.

*

Curreli arrived late for the briefing.

De Pisis and Precossi told him to take a seat. "It's for the murder on the Via Gaudenzi," announced De Pisis. Curreli sat down. "Elena Marcucci," he added.

De Pisis adjusted his tie. "Yes. Seems an open and shut case to me . . ."

Precossi intervened before Curreli could reply. "We're holding a man, so let's try and bring things to a rapid conclusion."

"A rapid conclusion?" asked Curreli.

"A rapid conclusion," replied De Pisis.

"Is there something I'm not quite getting?" asked Curreli provocatively.

De Pisis cleared his throat. "No," he grated.

Precossi looked like somebody who'd just been forced to cancel a night out with his girlfriend. "Elena Marcucci is, or was, Stefano Crescioni's grandmother, on his mother's side."

Curreli couldn't repress a chuckle, as happened every time that he was forced to observe how certain deputies could be so ridiculously pernickety. Without asking any questions he waited, counting up to ten in his head.

When he got to five De Pisis asked: "You do know, don't you, which Crescioni we're referring to?"

"The one who's standing for Mayor," said Curreli simply.

This very simplicity of tone made De Pisis narrow his eyes and forced Precossi to shift in his seat.

"Precisely," the latter confirmed. "And that says it all, don't you think?"

"Not in my view," Curreli's voice was as flat as that of a simultaneous interpreter.

De Pisis sat up imperceptibly on his chair. Precossi furrowed his eyebrows as if someone had been shining a dazzling light into his eyes.

"The investigations are still under way, the conclusions of the forensic team are still to come out, the report of the path lab will be ready tomorrow . . ." Curreli would like to have given an official ring to his words.

"But we have a suspect, the tenant from the apartment opposite."
Precossi didn't know Curreli well enough not to egg him on.

"He denies everything."

De Pisis shrugged. "As if a suspect denying everything didn't
happen every day."

Curreli didn't turn a hair. "With the evidence at our disposal
there's no way he isn't going down."

"Maybe we can leave this to the examining judge. What do
you say?" The sarcastic tone was quite familiar. "There are
the statements made by the tenants and by Crescioni, and the
suspect . . ." Precossi beseechingly tried to catch De Pisis' eye.

"Fabio Porzio."

"That's the one. Fabio Porzio didn't get on with Marcucci, who,
among other things, owned his apartment and for years had been
trying to evict him . . ."

*

"I was working. When I work I play loud music, and the front
door is open, so if somebody comes I don't have to stop my work."
Porzio looked worn out.

"Were you alone?" It could hardly be said that Curreli was
putting the pressure on him.

Porzio looked at the Inspector without replying.

"Were you alone?" repeated Curreli, and this time he didn't
seem quite so accommodating.

"Yes," said Porzio, but he took a few seconds more than he
should have.

"Sure about that? We have evidence that you were with someone.
A woman, if we're to believe the lady who lives in the apartment
under yours. A woman that you quarrelled with . . ."

"She's wrong." It looked like Porzio had no intention of
cooperating.

"Fine, so you were working . . . What happened then?"

"Perhaps she heard the music, I do keep it on a bit too loud . . . I
was working, then I went to get an aspirin from the bathroom, and
when I came back I saw him."

"You're sure he came in?"

"Must have done . . . anyway I'm sure I caught a glimpse of him, he had his back to me, but I recognized him . . . That's how it must have happened."

Marchini intervened at this point, "So, in your view, Stefano Crescioni was in the building on the afternoon his grandmother died."

Porzio nodded. Marchini stared at him insistently. "That's not how it looks to us," he said, seeing that Curreli was letting him get on with it. "Crescioni has provided us with an alibi for that afternoon."

Porzio's gaze fell. "But he *was* there," he said.

"If Crescioni was there as you say, it's a shame there wasn't anyone else with you who could confirm that," the Inspector's words hinted at a barely disguised hope.

Porzio did not reply.

"That really complicates matters. Especially in view of the fact that you had several good motives for bearing a grudge against Elena Marcucci."

"She was a really difficult woman, and now they're passing her off as a saint, but in the building nobody could stand her . . . Not even her grandson could stand her."

"And yet you can confirm that you never sold or gave one of your drawings to Signora Marcucci?"

"What? One of my drawings – to *her*? You crazy? I hadn't even finished it, it was a sketch I was working on."

*

Curreli put on a face that Marchini didn't really like; he knew him well enough to understand where that expression might lead. The question seemed simple: the murder of Elena Marcucci was clearly the logical conclusion to a deeply rooted enmity. On this matter the statements made by the tenants had been unanimous: Marcucci had done everything in her power to evict Porzio. He was a strange guy, he hung out with people who must have seemed to the old woman like a bunch of total weirdos – and, indulging in artistic licence, he brought a different girl home every evening. And then there was always that loud music and his habit of not closing the door to his apartment.

Now the point was that, according to Crescioni's statement, the old woman and Porzio had met and had a violent quarrel – the grandmother had even telephoned her grandson to tell him all about it, saying that Porzio had nonetheless tried to worm his way into her good books by giving her a drawing. More than a drawing, actually, a sketch: something that, in the artist's intentions, was meant to represent a siren or something of the kind. It certainly did show the figure of a woman, scantily clad and surrounded by waves in blue and turquoise chalk. She, the old woman, wasn't the kind of person to be swayed by a gift of this kind . . . And perhaps, more than a gift, she had taken this offer as a provocation, since Porzio generally called her an ugly old witch. Anyway, whether she had been given a drawing as a gift or not, Elena Marcucci had felt threatened and feared for her own safety. Porzio, for his part, completely denied it: he'd never bumped into the old woman, and he hadn't given her a drawing. Just imagine – an unfinished work, a study for the *Dancing Naiad* – was he likely to do such a crazy thing? Chalk and acrylic on board, Porzio had added; he'd sketched it out that very afternoon: the layout had been good but the final result was clumsy, and he'd finally decided it all needed to be redone . . .

But the *Dancing Naiad*, however clumsy and unfinished it might be, did exist and was there at the scene of the crime, on a side table not too far away from the body.

*

Think it all over calmly: according to Porzio, Crescioni was at his grandmother's home on the afternoon of the murder, but this circumstance had not been confirmed by any of the tenants. According to Crescioni, Porzio had given the old woman a drawing, but Porzio denied this. Porzio's alibi had not been confirmed because there was no trace of the woman who was supposedly with him that afternoon, and Porzio resolutely refused to cooperate. As for Crescioni's alibi . . .

*

Marchini was driving slowly, and the images of a starchy-looking Stafano Crescioni plastered to the walls filed past the car windows.

"On the posters he seems younger. Look at all that hair! Is it a photo from his First Communion . . . ?" Curreli wondered aloud.

Marchini continued to drive without commenting, but a laugh shook his belly.

"It's important, you know, looking young. What do you do if you're going to run for Mayor? Get some plastic surgery of course! Because without a pretty face you can't possibly have the right ideas, in fact you must be a crook . . . Makes me sick. I know so many of those bastards, they have a pretty face but . . ."

Marchini kept the car moving along slowly as he waited for this outpouring of emotion to dry up. He knew that, once the Inspector had started, it was no use trying to stop him.

"Lombroso . . . We've returned to the days of the physiognomist Lombroso, except that at least in those days they deluded themselves that they could recognize crooks from their faces. These days, if a guy's got a pretty face, it means he must be honest."

Marchini braked suddenly to avoid a man on a moped who'd cut him up. This was enough to reduce Curreli to silence. "Sorry," said Marchini, accelerating again. "But you have to agree, it's a tricky situation. That guy Porzio doesn't exactly inspire confidence."

"See what I mean?" objected Curreli. "You're saying exactly the same thing! Why shouldn't Porzio inspire confidence? Because he's an artist, because he doesn't shave every day, because he went to the G8 thing in Genoa last July?"

"No, that's got nothing to do with it . . . It's just that he looks like someone with something to hide."

"Like most of the people I know. Let me give you an example: what if I told you that all cops are corrupt, fascists, goons?"

"Well, I'd reply that there are police chiefs who've handed in their resignations rather than give in to pressure, and you find all sorts in a police force."

"Meaning?"

"Well, meaning that you need to distinguish."

"Meaning?"

"Meaning that Porzio isn't automatically guilty."

". . . And neither is Crescioni."

"Okay, and neither is Crescioni . . . but what do we know about him? Only as much as he's condescended to tell us."

"He went to the police of his own free will; there are elections on, and he's standing."

"I understand *that* bit all right: and so?"

"And so . . . what do you want me to say . . . ? We've arrived . . . This the right place?" said Marchini tentatively parking in front of the gate of Crescioni's big house.

*

De Pisis was sweating copiously, Precossi wore a vaguely helpless expression. Curreli was standing waiting for the storm to break: how had he permitted himself to disturb Signor Crescioni at his own home? How had he dared to take an initiative of this gravity without consulting them? Crescioni, thank Heaven, had not exactly protested, but he had phoned Police HQ to tell them he had nothing to do with it, a fact that had been quickly confirmed, as had as the assurance that he would not be disturbed again. This was why De Pisis had called Curreli in. Curreli listened calmly and replied that he'd wanted to clear up a few things, such as ascertaining what relations had been like between Crescioni and Marcucci. So, what had they been like then? From what Crescioni said they were idyllic. And so? So the neighbours had testified that they were not as idyllic as all that. Ah, no? And what would this imply? Well, that somebody wasn't telling the truth. Oh come now, please, don't be ridiculous. You're just wasting time! Anyway, Signor Crescioni had been given a formal apology by Police HQ and also by the Prosecutor General. And there was nothing else to be added, except that any other personal initiative on the part of Curreli would not be tolerated.

*

The Inspector emerged from De Pisis' office with an air of apparent tranquillity. Marchini was waiting for him in his office. He didn't ask any questions, but it was easy to see what he wanted to know. Curreli, in his corner, kept his mouth shut. He ostentatiously plunged into the study of dossiers that were of no interest to him at all.

"You know, I didn't say a thing," muttered Curreli at one point.

Marchini half-pirouetted round, as if taken completely by surprise at the Inspector's words.

"Yes," continued Curreli, as if Marchini had replied. "However much it may surprise you, I just stood there meek and mild as they dumped all over me. You should have seen De Pisis' face."

"I did see it, actually," murmured Marchini. "He called me in this morning before you arrived."

"Oh, really? And what did he tell you? To keep me on a leash?"

"More or less."

"And then?"

"And then what?"

"What do you intend to do?"

"Why?"

"Because I don't have any intention of stopping now, even if this is the last case I ever work on."

*

Think it all through in good order. Marcucci had been killed early in the afternoon. Strangled. The apartment had been turned upside down, as if the murderer had been looking for something. They couldn't officially investigate Crescioni. Porzio was digging his own grave. And then there was that drawing . . .

*

If it was the rule that you needed to keep ahead of events, Curreli was following it to the letter. So, half an hour before Ginetti from the forensic team could deliver the results of the analysis of the drawing found in the victim's home, he was standing in front of Curreli. Ginetti said that Precossi was waiting for these results: he wanted to be the first to see them, and it was causing him a lot of worry. Curreli reminded Ginetti that on previous occasions he'd covered for him without asking for anything in return. When Ginetti came out of Curreli's office he left the file on the table . . .

*

"What interests me is not what's there, but what's missing . . ."

Marchini gave a sidelong look at Curreli. "Precossi will be pissed off."

Curreli carried on regardless. "Porzio's fingerprints would be on the drawing – I was already sure of that. But there are another person's fingerprints on it too. By the way, have you had this checked?"

"I'm waiting for a reply."

"And then there's that scratch on the colouring. Ginetti says that it's too regular, it doesn't seem to have been made by the artist . . ."

Marchini was listening in silence.

"What's missing then?"

Marchini waited a few seconds.

"The old woman's fingerprints are missing," replied Curreli.

Marchini's eyes widened. "D'you mean that Marcucci never even saw the drawing?"

"Or else she never touched it – but that's not the point: if Crescioni is right and the old woman accepted it in spite of her fraught relations with Porzio, her prints ought to be on it."

Marchini was about to add that this didn't mean that Porzio hadn't put it in her apartment when the old woman was already dead, but the telephone rang, so he kept his thoughts to himself. "Yes . . . ? I'm listening . . . You sure . . . ? Wait while I get something to write with . . . Yes, I got it . . ." Marchini finished jotting down a name and hung up. "Serena Vacchi," he announced. "The other prints on the drawing belong to Serena Vacchi, and she's got a police record."

"Check everything. Then let's go and hear what she has to tell us."

*

When you looked at her closely she wasn't such a great beauty. She was one of those rather glitzy women who attract your attention when you first notice them but seem rather coarse when you focus on particulars. Her lips, for instance, were filled with collagen, and her skin was starting to betray a few too many wrinkles round her eyes.

"Was it Fabio who told you I was here?" Serena Vacchi asked the question with the air of someone who didn't like having to give answers.

"No," replied Curreli harshly. "We found out just by asking around. So?"

Serena Vacchi didn't miss a beat; with a gesture that she tried to make seductive, she lifted the blond-tinted hair from the nape of her neck. "It's no secret to anyone that I pose for a few artists. Anything wrong with that?" she asked aggressively, looking at Marchini.

"That's not what we're here for," clarified Curreli; this woman irritated him, perhaps because she continued to answer his questions without looking at him.

The woman, still turned towards Marchini, tossed her chin so that her hair fell back on her shoulders.

"What the Inspector wants to know is whether you were in Porzio's studio on the day of the crime," explained Marchini, as if he wished to get out of an awkward situation.

"I wouldn't know," said Serena, trying to assume a tone of detachment.

There followed several seconds of silence. Then Curreli planted himself squarely in front of her, so that she couldn't avoid looking at him. "But do you only pose for Fabio Porzio?" he hissed.

Serena Vacchi flinched and pursed her artificial lips, as if trying to repress an answer that would cost her dear: the two idiots standing in front of her were police officers, after all. "Who do you think I am?" she asked.

"Two arrests for soliciting, one for pushing drugs, various little things like that," enumerated Curreli.

"Learned your lines, haven't you? But that was all a long time ago. I haven't been on the game for five years."

"Maybe not on the streets." This remark rose instinctively to Marchini's lips.

Serena Vacchi seemed to take this particularly hard. She'd persuaded herself that she had nothing to fear from Marchini. For a moment she seemed on the point of giving in, then she got a grip on herself and managed the ghost of a smile. "You know, you just can't count on anything these days. Whatever happened to good cop, bad cop?"

Curreli was starting to get tired of all this. "No, today we decided that we'd both be good cops. So: were you or were you not at Porzio's the day of Elena Marcucci's murder?"

Serena Vacchio looked them straight in the eye. "If Fabio has said I wasn't there, then obviously I wasn't."

*

"In my opinion, they're covering for one another," mumbled Marchini, who had bitten into a white-hot rice croquette.

Curreli shook his head, swallowed the morsel of sandwich that he was chewing and looked for yet another paper serviette. "Not very well," he said. "She could keep him out of jail, and yet she isn't doing so. No, not very well," he repeated.

"Maybe she's telling the truth: she has a police record, she doesn't want any hassle. Maybe she'd like to help him, but she really wasn't at Porzio's."

"If you carry on like that, I'm going to lose my temper. She most definitely *was* there! Might you have been just a little bit swayed by those lovely eyes of hers?"

"Who, me?"

"Yeah, you. Maybe now you're going to tell me that she's a beautiful woman."

"Well . . . she's quite easy on the eye."

"Course she is. She's fake from head to foot, let me tell you, and she's at least forty."

"She's thirty. I saw her file." Marchini's tone of voice was slightly piqued.

"Thirty?" said Curreli with exaggerated surprise, reaching for another paper serviette.

"You're always talking about Lombroso, but then you judge from appearances too."

"I don't judge from appearances, and that's exactly why I think that Serena Vacchi's lying. I look people right in the eye, and she tried to avoid my gaze."

"Sounds like you don't like her."

"True, I don't like her, any more than I like that tailor's dummy Crescioni and all those like him. They get on my tits, all of them, the way they try to make you believe . . . The way they want to seem different from what they really are. Maybe it's just me, but that's the way I see it . . ."

"Nothing wrong in wanting to seem different . . . If someone's not happy about the way they are . . ."

"I'm not just referring to physical appearance. Do try and listen, Marchini, just once in a while."

"I still don't think there's anything wrong with it."

"If it gets in the way of democracy, there *is* something wrong with it. A whole lot wrong."

"And there I was thinking you weren't interested in politics, Inspector. What's democracy got to do with it?"

"Well, what we call democracy has fake lips, peroxide hair and all the rest of it. It's a fake: it isn't what it seems to be . . . or what they'd like us to believe it is."

Marchini decided against his third rice croquette. "And what would that be?" he asked, immediately regretting his question.

"I don't know, I still don't know, but my kind of democracy doesn't have either the time or the money to get itself a boob job. Clear?"

Marchini started, "You telling me Vacchi's had a boob job?"

Curreli looked at him: he already had an answer on his lips, but Marchini wouldn't have understood.

*

Anyway, Serena Vacchi had been there, at Porzio's, and she had seen the drawing and maybe touched it too. Porzio had put it to one side to dry. The afternoon had started off with her posing for him as usual, and then . . . in brief . . . Porzio and Vacchi had withdrawn to the bedroom . . . Anything wrong with that? No, she didn't know how that drawing had ended up in the old woman's apartment, but Porzio had got up to get a drink, maybe to go to the toilet, then he'd come back into the bedroom . . . After five minutes, or ten at most. He'd said: somebody's been in! She, Vacchi, had been scared, she'd thought it might be a Peeping Tom . . . "That fucking way you never shut your door!" she'd yelled as she got dressed. And she'd left. Fabio loved her, she'd said he wasn't just out to protect her, not with her history. When the story of the old woman's death came out, she'd thought of going to the police, but you know what the cops are like. And what are the cops like? We've seen what they're like in Genoa and Naples! Now don't let's talk crap, there are cops and cops . . .

*

"So: exit Porzio and enter Vacchi," Precossi summed up.

"Looks like it," reflected Curreli. "Even though I don't see why Serena Vacchi would have killed Marcucci."

"Because she's a crook, she has a rather full police record, and she thought she'd make a bit of pocket money by robbing an old woman who lives all by herself."

"Yes, but the times don't add up. If Porzio and Vacchi were screwing until four in the afternoon, and the home help came back around three-fifty, Vacchi would have to have killed the old woman with the home help in the house, but she didn't. The home help found her employer dead."

"Only if the two of them are telling the truth."

"If they haven't been, they're a couple of idiots, given that Vacchi punched her bus ticket at ten past four."

"So Porzio comes back on the scene; she says he was away for ten minutes at around three-thirty, he could have gone to the old woman's, killed her, put the drawing there and then . . ."

". . . Turned everything upside down. He'd have had to be as quick as greased lightning, given that he was naked and holding a drawing – maybe he was covering his privates with it. Oh yes, Marcucci would have let him in like that without a moment's hesitation . . . Come off it!"

Precossi was starting to get really pissed off. "To begin with, I'd prefer it if you'd speak with a bit more respect; and secondly, I hope this line of argument isn't leading where I think you want it to lead . . ."

"And where do you think I want it to lead?"

"Well . . . to Crescioni," mumbled Precossi.

At first Curreli nodded, but then he shook his head. "I'd be happy for it to lead to Crescioni's bank account. From what they say, his electoral campaign has cost a mint: manifestos, TV broadcasts . . ." he explained, handing a printout to Precossi.

Precossi looked at the sheet, then looked at Curreli as if he had a gun pointed at him. "You don't realize . . ." he said hoarsely, almost choking. "You . . . you . . ."

"Don't bother trying to find the right words. I know perfectly well that you don't exactly like me."

"No, I don't like you," confirmed Precossi, getting a grip on himself with impressive speed.

"I'm not exactly a big fan of yours either."

"But there are people who think you're great at your job . . . Not me, I can't stand your innate tendency to prejudge people."

Curreli uttered a nervous, edgy laugh. "Innate," he repeated, as if to himself.

"There's just the two of us here, so let's get it off our chests now and then forget all about it: times have changed, Signor Curreli, and you Communists can't do what you like any more," continued Precossi.

"We *what?*" Precossi's claim had caught Curreli off guard.

Precossi didn't reply.

"And why am I supposed to be a Communist, just because I don't agree with you? And anyway, since when, exactly, has it been an offence to be called a Communist? What kind of fucking country have we ended up in, then? And here are *you* telling me that I'm sticking my nose into politics and then you stop me carrying out an investigation into Crescioni."

"Don't say things you might regret. I'm not stopping you doing anything. And I'd appreciate it if you could moderate your language . . ."

"Okay then: sign this paper for me. Because otherwise I'm going to be forced to think that you're trying to stop me from carrying out an investigation into Signor Crescioni's property . . ."

"You're completely crazy. I'm having you transferred somewhere where you'll spend the rest of your career hunting down chicken thieves."

"That was all I needed to know," was Curreli's only reply as he picked up the signed piece of paper.

*

Marchini could hardly believe Curreli had actually done it – asked Precossi to sign an authorization for an investigation into Crescioni's property. And he wasn't surprised to learn that Precossi had taken it badly. Crescioni was his champion, he represented something more than a simple local entrepreneur. But Curreli knew what he was doing . . .

*

. . . And so, when Marchini came into the office as pale as death saying that Crescioni wanted to talk to him and that he was waiting for him in the antechamber, Curreli didn't turn a hair. Marchini couldn't believe it: he realized that Curreli had contrived the whole thing simply to bring about this result. To get Signor Crescioni into his office – which was exactly what was now happening. So he looked at the Inspector the way you look at a trapeze artist who's just done a quadruple salto sixty feet up, without a net . . .

*

"Bit nippy today," said Crescioni airily. He slipped off his gloves to offer a hand to Curreli.

Curreli shook his hand. "I was expecting a visit from you," he said.

"I wouldn't like you to have the impression that I'm here to clear my name, I simply wanted to ask you what you have against me."

"Against you? Nothing. Why should I have anything against you? You represent the bright future of this city and a large amount of investments"

"And that's just the point. How has anyone dared, how does anyone even dare to suspect . . . ?"

". . . It's my job, suspecting people. Anyway, if you don't have anything to hide, I don't see the problem."

"It's not easy to embark on an election campaign these days."

"Of course. You need a lot of money."

Crescioni flinched at the word "money" as if it were an insult. But he put a brave face on it. "Of course. Why deny it? It's . . . it's extremely expensive, running an election campaign."

"So, a lot of money," repeated Curreli. "But in politics, aren't principles and ideas enough?" he asked with slow deliberation.

"Yes," spluttered Crescioni. "And pigs can fly."

"Oh, they can fly all right. They're high flyers."

"I'm not going to sit here while you . . . I'm a citizen with a spotless record . . . If you were to stop wasting your time and mine, you might have more time to track down my poor grandmother's murderer!"

"From what people are saying, you've been having serious financial problems over these last few months," commented Curreli, ignoring this last remark.

Crescioni stared at him for a while, as if thinking what to say in reply. But all he said, finally, was: "I'm starting to realize that I was mistaken in thinking you were someone I could do business with." Before taking his leave, he started to look round. "I thought I had my gloves," he said.

Curreli remained sitting behind his desk, with the most deadpan expression he could muster.

"Anyway, let me tell you that I'm not going to let you start sticking your nose into my life. I had no motive for killing my grandmother."

"Who knows what I might find out? Maybe your grandmother was a guarantor for you, maybe, I can't say, if we have a look through your accounts we might find a motive; you know, you remind me of a schoolmate of mine, we used to say that he'd be quite capable of killing his grandmother just to get what he wanted."

"You do know that your career ends right here, don't you?" Crescioni's voice had risen a good octave. "You do know that you and I will be seeing each other again, don't you?"

"Of course we'll be seeing each other again," agreed Curreli impassively.

*

And they would indeed be seeing each other again – in court. Crescioni just happened "by chance" to have left a pair of pair of gloves in the office of Inspector Curreli. And "luckily" Curreli had discovered, on the seam of the right glove, a tiny, almost imperceptible, turquoise stain, which the forensic team identified as a mixture of chalk and acrylic, from the drawing of a *Dancing Naiad* found next to the body of Elena Marcucci.

The Boy Who Was Kidnapped by the Christmas Fairy (A Noir Fairytale)

Giancarlo De Cataldo

I

In Italy, the Christmas Fairy comes round on the eve of 6 January (Epiphany – hence her name, *La Befana*). She leaves presents in the stockings of good children; children who have been not so good get a piece of coal (or maybe some black sweeties).

The Christmas Fairy who, at 12.35 p.m. on 5 January, carries off Carlo isn't really a true Christmas Fairy but a tall girl with red hair by the name of Adriana.

She is thirty-five years old and has traces of a beauty that is perilously evaporating as she spirals down a path that, to begin with, strikes her as too steep to be true. But when you set out with the hope of making it on the stage and then find that all you really know about is tarot and cocaine, you can't be too choosy. One more step downwards, and you'll be sharing your bed for timed periods with overeager and overhasty men: an experience that she knows well and has no wish to repeat. This is the reason why she's accepted Giangilberto's proposal.

"You lure the kid along with some excuse or other, you give him a bit of a ride, maybe you take him off for a snack or to see a film, and then, around four or half-four in the afternoon, you take him home, ring the interphone and clear off."

"Are you crazy? You want me to end up in jail?"

But who's talking of jail? You just take it nice and easy, it's a trick on his Mum, an old friend of mine – that's what Giangilberto said. He has the gift of making the most improbable things appear perfectly spontaneous and natural. Adriana knows that he's sleeping with this Mum, whose name is Laura. As he does with so many

163

other women. And it no longer bothers her all that much. First: because Giangilberto is certainly not the man of her life. Second: because the man of her life is someone she stopped looking for a while back. Half a day as a babysitter isn't asking much. She quite likes children: for one thing, they don't put on an act, like adults. And after all, the punchline of the story lies in the sum of 5,000 euros: quite enough to stop her asking herself too many indiscreet questions.

And thus it is that the self-styled Christmas Fairy skilfully pilots the kid along the narrow alley crowded with tourists that links the Piazza Navona with the Corso Rinascimento. It's called the Corsia Agonale, she tells him, dragging him along by the arm; she explains that, once upon a time, the chariots would come trundling along this way for the races, like in *Ben-Hur* . . .

"You have seen *Ben-Hur*, haven't you?"

"No," replies the boy, whose name is Carlo.

"But you're ten years old, for God's sake – every boy of ten ought to see *Ben-Hur!*"

"Mum never has time to take me to the cinema."

"What about your friends?" asks the Christmas Fairy.

"I don't have any friends," Carlo shrugs, in a quiet, neutral tone, as if this were something perfectly natural.

And while the Christmas Fairy, a little disconcerted by his reply, goes round the monumental edifice of the Italian Senate, pointing out the old 2CV parked in flagrant violation of every possible and imaginable parking regulation, Laura, the mother in question, is in the middle of a conversation on her mobile with the villain of our story: Giangilberto.

He is a sports columnist and an expert in horse breeding and horseracing, and he claims to be phoning from his paper. He's sorry, no, more, he's gutted, but he has to inform her that he's taken too much time off already. All his holiday leave is cancelled, and in short, not to mince his words, he's stuck in the office. And so, a lunch of Mediterranean sushi at the Caffè Riccioli has had to be cancelled too, and it won't be possible for him to get to the cinema in the afternoon; maybe a residual hope of a candlelit dinner, so long as the babysitter is available on the night before Epiphany, and . . .

"Never mind," murmurs Laura.

Giangilberto is profuse in excuses. But Laura has stopped listening to him. Out of the corner of her eye she's looking for her son, whom she fleetingly saw slipping off between the Japanese tourists enraptured by the mummy covered in a veil of gold and the booths for target shooting; he's decided to take an interest, she seems to realize, in a tall woman dressed up as the Christmas Fairy, with a horrible red sneer – an attempt at a smile that would have terrified children of less unusual character than Carlo. While holding the mobile in one hand, Laura tries to light a cigarette with the other. The holiday is about to reach its deafening paroxysm all around her, while awareness of the umpteenth day she is spending alone gnaws at her innards.

"So I'll get back to you as soon as I know anything . . ."

"That's fine, that's fine."

"And . . . darling?"

"What now?"

"I'm sorry . . ."

Laura puts the mobile back into her handbag and finally manages to light her cigarette. She mechanically resumes looking around. At her third glance, she realizes that something is not right. Carlo has vanished.

II

As the New Year had dawned, in a sordid gambling den of the Mandrione district, the alluring and seductive figure that answers to the name of Giangilberto had lost 50,000 euros at poker with a crook from the Tufello who goes by the name of the Turk.

"You've got a week. Then I'm comin' for your balls."

His bank account is drained dry, and he's being cold-shouldered by the loan sharks who've learned to mistrust his gift of the gab and, in any case, have no idea what he can offer in exchange. Giangilberto has been brooding on extreme solutions, such as getting his hands on a pistol and killing the Turk, or else himself; on middle-range solutions, such as fleeing abroad; and on desperate solutions, such as reporting certain illicit activities on the part of the above-mentioned Turk which have by complete chance come to his attention and getting a judge to grant him police protection. Then, all of a sudden, he has realized that the solution to all his problems is right here, within reach: Laura. She will be the one to get him out of this mess. Their up-and-down affair has lasted about a year. Up until now he's shown her his good side, as a card-carrying member of the Fourth Estate. Single, with the hollow features of a hard-baked old gypsy, and a pigtail to conceal the inevitable baldness, unbelievable blue eyes that encourage you to trust him, and a certain allure, as we've already said, he has a long experience of smoky clubs and cabaret theatres, hence his habit of being able to hold collective attention. But he can also be serious, persuasive and straightforward. Laura fell into his web on their second meeting: he manages to bed her even if she is a bit clinging and, in her close personal dealings, neurotic and easily scared. If it hadn't been for this wimpy boy she has to tow around after her, he could easily imagine settling down with her, at least for a year or two, while there's still juice in the old girl, before she starts to show her age. Giangilberto hates women who show their age. He hates committing too. They see each other two or three evenings a week, and he sometimes stays at her place for the weekend (on one condition: they have to dump Carlo off on one of his aunts), but when Laura starts venturing down the paths of sentiment, of the "we've been together for a year now, maybe it's time to tie the knot . . ." kind, there inevitably crops up an unexpected job somewhere in Europe or Milan (these are synonyms, in his virtual world, held together as it is by a closely-knitted mesh of big, medium and small fibs) – you know the kind of thing: a champion racing driver to interview or a drugs scandal at Longchamp . . . And on his return, when the dust has settled, Laura is yearning for passion and tenderness, poor girl, and everything is soon running like the trains in Mussolini's time again. In the meanwhile, he's treated himself to a fling with a harem of unassuming womenfolk, such as the size zero Adriana, all of whom he asks: (a) to brighten up afternoons and evenings that would otherwise be devoured by anxiety; (b) to disappear quickly once the task assigned to them has been completed. All things considered, he wouldn't have all that much to complain about, if it weren't for that bastard the Turk. Anyway, with Laura he has managed to keep himself, so to speak, morally pristine. His innate ability as a navigator of turbid waters has allowed him to grasp intuitively that, sooner or later, that peevish but compliant woman will turn out to be of considerable use. And the moment has now arrived.

Laura manages the branch of a bank on the outskirts of town. Laura will procure the 50,000 euros that will enable him to save his skin. And a little on the side, let's say another fifty, to pay off his collaborators (that little whore Adriana and the Slav) and put something aside for a rainy day. He doesn't have anything personal against Laura and that snotty-nosed little brat of a son, but when it's a life-and-death matter, you can't give in to your scruples.

Thus it is that now, sitting at a table in the elegant Tre Scalini restaurant, Giangilberto observes his prey tottering and almost falling, then regaining her balance, darting anxious glances in every direction, heading resolutely off to the fountain only to come disappointed at the outcome of her expedition, uncertain as to what to do, already worried but not yet in full hysterical flow. Without a word, he passes his secure mobile to the Slav.

The Slav presses the green button. Laura rummages furiously in her handbag, grabs her mobile and almost screams "Yes?" The Slav clears his throat and recites the agreed message. Laura turns pale, looks around again, then, finding it difficult to breathe, seeks the support of a streetlamp. The mummy considerately abandons its pedestal and goes over to her, for she seems to have lost her colour, her sense of balance, her energy and perhaps her life. But Laura gets a grip on herself and shakes her head decisively; she doesn't need any help, everything is absolutely fine, she doesn't need a thing.

The Slav, sipping a Coke, shakes his head.

"Poor woman. You're a heartless bastard, Italian."

"She's putting it all on, I know her well. She doesn't give a damn about what happens to her kid. Let me tell you: it's not what you think it is . . ."

"I don't think. And you're paying."

"Phone at 4 p.m. on the dot. You know what you have to say. Then disappear. You can keep the mobile, but best not use it for a while. And remember: it's all just a joke!"

"Joke? No joke," hisses the Slav, rising to his feet. "This is kidnapping. I don't know you, I haven't seen you, I haven't listened to you. And some more cash would be useful!"

"Cool it. You'll get it tomorrow, that's what we agreed, wasn't it?"

"Tomorrow," sneers the Slav and draws his finger across his throat. "Or else . . ."

Giangilberto pays the bill. The crowd continues to ebb and flow in great billows around the piazza. Laura is sitting on the edge of the Four Rivers fountain, her head in her hands. Giangilberto seizes the mobile and starts to count under his breath. When he gets to "seven" the mobile starts to vibrate.

III

Carlo spends a morning poring over the scratched bodywork of the 2CV. Old cars fascinate him. He knows everything about the way they work, he's learned it during long hours spent surfing on the Web. When he comes across one of these old models in the street, he stares at it enraptured, until a less than kindly hand yanks him away. The Christmas Fairy is following his awestruck movements with a smile.

"Do you like it?"

"One day I want one like this. Or maybe a Ferrari."

"They're really not the same!"

"No . . . But does this one go all right?"

"I'll say!" the Christmas Fairy proclaims with pride. "She's been round the world twice and goes better than a Ferrari!"

"So one day she'll take me to India!"

"Why India in particular?"

"I don't know, it's just . . ."

Carlo is almost about to confess that his passion for India derives from the time he saw a TV documentary on that great river the Ganges, where people go to immerse themselves – everyone, grown-ups, the elderly, children – at least once in their lives. The narrator said that its waters wash away all of life's little problems. And since there are a whole heap of little problems in his life, and in fact, when he thinks about it, you could count the things that are *not* problems on the fingers of one hand . . . But then he decides to say nothing. Perhaps, if he tells her, the Christmas Fairy will start laughing, make fun of him or even insult him. Nobody ever treats him seriously, everyone makes fun of him when he speaks, and lots of people insult him. For that reason he has learned to say little – just the indispensable minimum. And so they all think he's dumb. This isn't true, but let them carry on thinking so. At least they'll leave him in peace.

"Up you get, shake a leg, climb in!" exhorts the Christmas Fairy a little tetchily, "I can't wait to change out of these rags!"

With a sigh, Carlo gets in.

IV

"Giangilberto? Something's happened . . . something terrible . . . they've taken little Carlo . . ."

"Taken? What? But who . . . ? How? But are you sure . . . ?"

"They've kidnapped him, fuck it. They've taken my son!"

"But who?"

"I don't know. Someone phoned, a foreign voice. He told me not to call the police . . ."

"Don't even think of it, Laura. I'll call them . . ."

"Stop, don't do anything, it's my son, damn it all, my little Carlo! He told me to go home and wait, I . . ."

"Where are you?"

"Where do you think I am? Piazza Navona . . ."

"Okay, just listen to me, go home right now, as the man said . . . I'm on my way, all right? Go home and wait for me . . . chin up, you'll see we'll sort it all out!"

V

Without her rags and without any make-up, the Christmas Fairy reveals herself to be a girl, no, a woman – tall, soft, with attractive if rather hazy eyes and cold-chapped lips. About thirty-five, like his mother, she has short red hair and a nice neat little nose.

"Hi there," she says, holding out a warm, tapering hand, "I'm Adriana."

"Carlo," he mutters, barely touching her hand.

"Disappointed?"

Carlo admires her smile, regretting the stupidity of the question. One of the many mysteries of his young life is the number of people he meets who put stupid questions and make stupid observations to him. Not so much for the questions per se, but because all of them are convinced they are always the acme of intelligence. In this way they make you feel like an idiot, and yet *they* are the real idiots . . .

"Why disappointed?" he replies eventually. "I know that you're not the real Christmas Fairy. Actually, I know that the Christmas Fairy doesn't exist!"

"And how long have you known that?"

"Since last year."

"I bet an older school friend of yours told you . . . some nasty boy . . ."

"No. It was . . . well, Mum gave me my Christmas stocking. You know, the one full of little chocolates and sweeties . . . there were also chocolate coins and chocolate cigars . . ."

"Yummmm! Bet you scoffed the lot!"

"Yes . . . but Mum accidentally left the supermarket receipt inside. And I don't think the Christmas Fairy shops at the supermarket, does she?"

Adriana is tempted to say something witty in reply, but, for one thing, she can't think of anything, and, for another, a curious sense of pity tinged with sadness makes her spine tingle.

"Wait for me here. I won't be long," she says, slipping out of the vehicle.

But the boy follows her. With a sigh, she leans out over the river and chucks the bundle containing the Christmas Fairy's costume over the parapet.

"Look! It hit that guy fishing!" observes Carlo with a chuckle.

VI

On the bank of the river, wrapped in a heavy fur greatcoat that makes him look even more massive than Mother Nature has already fashioned him, a very tall man with very blond hair is fishing with a long homemade fishing rod, trying to pull a mullet for supper from the muddy waters of the Tiber, praying to his ancient gods that he won't fetch up yet another revolting sewer rat. His name is Vitas, and he comes from Lithuania, a cold and faraway country that, for a while, was simply poor and then, after all the invasions and pillaging, desperately poor.

When the projectile falling from above strikes him, the Lithuanian curses in a sonorous voice. They're shooting at me is his first thought. Racist Italian bastards, are they afraid I might catch the last fish in their shitty river? But he suddenly realizes that he's quite unharmed. And he decides that he's just the victim of some stupid kid acting on a dare. Meanwhile, the fishing rod has already slipped out of his hands and is floating away quickly, already beyond reach, dragged along by the current, lured by the capricious whirlpools amid the river waters. Goodbye fishing rod, and goodbye mullet! At the same moment, Mamma Irina, who seemed sunk deep in her canine lethargy but was merely keeping watch as usual, plunges into the water with a muffled growl.

"Where you going, you stupid dog!" yells Vitas.

But Irina, waterproof and immune due to long training to the delights of the river, is already re-emerging, holding in her jaws a parcel that, with a hopeful expression, she drops at the man's feet.

"Clothes. Shit. If I catches that bastard, I'll tear him to pieces!"

Mamma Irina sniffs the bundle, barks, then, her tail in the air, points her snout upwards.

"You say you find him for me, eh? Well, I'm happy you try, old girl!"

The mutt heads off towards the steps that lead to the Tiber-side expressway. Vitas grabs the bundle and follows, yelling at her – in vain – to slow down.

VII

The engine splutters and refuses to start.

"You know, we're going to have to give up on that idea of going to India," Adriana says, attempting to joke.

"We can take the bus," the boy innocently observes. "I've got two tickets!"

Adriana tries the ignition again: once, twice, three times. She's furious.

"You'll flood the engine that way," murmurs Carlo.

"And what do you know about it?"

"I like engines. When I grow up I'm going to be a mechanic, perhaps. Underneath where I live there's a mechanic. He explained to me that it all depends on the gas and the spark. When it makes that noise, it won't spark, but if you tread on the pedal the gas carries on filling a tube and then you can smell a big stink and the car won't start. That's called 'flooding the engine' . . ."

Adriana sighs with disappointment. For the first time since she picked up this strange kid, she's starting to think that maybe the task is beyond her. Maybe she's not going to be able to spend all those hours with him. Adriana needs to go for a pee, look for a taxi, then a restaurant, and then take the boy home, though dammit, she doesn't know where that is . . . and he, Carlo, is staring at her with an expression of bovine trust, and if she could only have a quick snort of coke, then yes, everything would seem so much simpler . . .

"So, shall we take the bus?"

They get out of the 2CV. Carlo leans on the parapet, Adriana loses the keys, they slip out of her hand. She swears in an undertone and bends over to pick them up, but again they slip away – but what *is* this, the way objects rebel against you, God damn it, and when she finally manages to straighten up, she finds herself face to snout with a big dog, enveloped in its powerful wild animal odour, absorbed in its big, round, good-natured eyes, and the keys finally, for the third time, end up under the 2CV, and then there echoes a deep, ironic and kindly voice.

"You have bad habit of losing things!"

The man is more than a man. A giant. With long hair that falls, unkempt, onto the collar of a ridiculous greatcoat from another age. A blond giant, and rather a handsome one, Adriana can't help noting, handsome like an actor of bygone days, a brawny colossus who gives you the impression he could crush you without even breaking into a sweat. But with a curious note of bashful tenderness in the depths of his face, which is broad-cheeked and melancholy, noble and droll, clean-shaven and, yes, ancient . . .

"I . . . I don't know what you're talking about," she says defensively, feeling herself blushing.

"The parcel," smiles the man, pointing to the dog. "Mamma Irina says it's yours. And Mamma Irina don't make mistake!"

The parcel is the bundle with the Christmas Fairy costume. It's in the creature's paws: it's wagging its tail as if it were expecting some kind of reward and sticking its great snout right up to the point of Adriana's boot, seeming to find its smell attractive, or maybe she's being nice to the man, and, in the canine system of values, this is a ticket to its affections . . .

"You can . . . you can keep it if you like," she mutters hastily. Then she digs a hand into her pocket and brings out a wrinkled banknote and hands it to the giant. "And please, accept this . . ."

But the giant pays no heed to her. His attention is focused on Carlo, who has come closer, filled with curiosity for the dog, but is hesitating to bend down over the creature.

"You can stroke. She's good dog!"

Then Carlo holds out his clenched fist to the dog's snout, and Mamma Irina sniffs it, then stretches out on her back and docilely offers herself with her rigid teats sticking up from her white, taut belly.

"What's her name?"

"Mamma Irina."

"Does she have puppies?" inquiries Carlo, stroking the animal's belly so that she utters a little growl of pleasure.

"Every time she meets right dog!" laughs the giant.

"What breed is she?"

"*Bof*, I don't know." The giant scratches his long hair. "Part wolf, part Hungarian hound . . . I just say Mamma Irina is from the Mamma Irina breed!"

"Will you give me a puppy?"

"You need to wait four months, next time in spring . . . then he has to grow, he needs to stay at least fifty days with Mamma Irina . . . then, if you really want one, you come back to Vitas and I give you puppy . . ."

"Who is Vitas?" asks Carlo, who in reality has realized who Vitas is, but he likes the rounded sound of that final "s" and wants to hear it again.

"I am Vitas!" shouts the giant, slapping himself full in the chest and laughing uproariously.

"You'll really give me a puppy?" insists the lad.

And at this point the giant looks up and focuses on Adriana and slyly adds:

"If your Mum says yes!"

"Mum says no," says Carlo regretfully, "she says that dogs make a mess and a smell, and then she goes out to work and there's nobody to take a puppy out to do its business . . ."

"But I bet that when she sees Irina's puppies, Mum will change her mind!"

Adriana realizes that the giant has taken her for the boy's mother, but she doesn't say anything to correct this impression. Let him carry on thinking that. So long as he beats it. But the guy continues to ignore the banknote that she is offering him.

"So, shall we go and get something to eat, Carlo?"

The boy reluctantly pulls himself away from the dog.

"Ciao," says Vitas.

Neither of the two Italians replies. Mamma Irina grumbles, her tail starts to wag.

VIII

One hundred thousand euros! All in unmarked notes! By five o'clock! With a curt gesture, Laura pushes away the glass of whisky that Giangilberto has considerately offered her.

"It must be a mistake," he mutters, trying to get rid of the stain that is spreading on the lapel of the cashmere that she has given him for Christmas, "you . . . I mean, we don't have that kind of money!"

Laura, with a tiger's roar, flings herself onto the white leather sofa of the minuscule living room in her tiny apartment where she lives as a single mother.

"But don't you understand? That man knows everything!"

"You mean the guy who phoned? Everything about what?"

"Everything about the bank, you idiot! He knows where I work, he knows I have access to the safe . . . and he knows that if I want to see my son again, I'll have to . . ."

"What guarantees has he given you that Carlo . . . ?"

"None at all, of course! I just have to go there, that's all. He said . . . he said that I have to leave the money in two shopping bags outside the English Cemetery at Testaccio . . . and then go home. He promised that little Carlo will be there waiting for me . . ."

Giangilberto puts his arm round her shoulder in a tender embrace.

"It was wrong of you not to let me talk to him."

"What do you mean?"

Giangilberto sighs.

"I mean we ought to call the police. Run the risk . . ."

"He's not your son! And you hate him . . . yes, you hate him!"

God save us from scenes of hysteria, even if they are all part of the plan. Giangilberto puts on a worried smile. He adopts a reassuring, protective tone of voice.

"I'm sorry. It's just that you're not thinking straight . . ."

"Listen," snaps Laura. "Do me a favour. Just go away, okay? I don't want to see you. I don't want you getting under my feet. Clear off!"

Giangilberto rises up in all his compassionate virility.

"No, I'm not leaving you. Go on, let it all out if it helps you to feel better. But I'm not leaving you. My place is here with you!"

"I don't want you!"

"That's not true. When that man took little Carlo you thought of me straight away. And you phoned me. I'm the only person who knows about it, apart from you. I'm the only person that's close to you, Laura. You trust me. And you're right to do so. Because I'm not going to leave you. I'm going to stay by your side. And whatever needs to be done, we'll do it together!"

Laura stares at him as if she were seeing him for the first time. Giangilberto, the loyal companion, the solid rock on which she can rely in moments of danger. She has misjudged him. A fleeting encounter, a quick fling, or her last desperate chance not to drown in loneliness, given the rose-tinted past now behind her and the difficult youngster she still has to bring up. Gradually, Laura finds herself slipping into his arms. Giangilberto whispers sweet little nothings into her ear. And an errant smile spreads over his handsome, worldly-wise face: of course you'll get him back, your little scamp of a son. The plan is perfect, nobody's going to get hurt, I've thought of everything. The Turk's going to get paid. And when it's all over, if you manage not to get fired from the bank, we'll end up in bed together again. Yes, everything's going to be just fine!

IX

Fritto misto for starters. Macaroni *all'amatriciana*. Breast of veal oven-roasted with fried potatoes, and then vanilla and chocolate ice cream. Carlo's voraciousness is stupefying. It's at least as great as his adaptability, thinks Adriana as she listlessly picks at a piece of grilled cheese with its side order of undressed salad. The lad is chubby and pasty-faced, dressed with an excessive care that betrays a certain feminine element in his flabby make-up. Adriana feels so sorry for him. He's decided to trust me because he has nobody else, she thinks, nobody else in the whole world. Just like me. I attach myself to a guy like Giangilberto, and I already know he's going to screw me.

"This is nice," laughs Carlo with his mouth full. "Mum never cooks, she never has time. At home we eat frozen stuff: crepes, pizza . . . And school dinners are revolting!"

"What's all this about you not having any friends?"

"I don't. Nobody wants to play with me. They never ask me round to their house."

"Well, why not take the initiative and throw a big party at yours!"

"Mum won't let me."

"Is there anything your Mum *will* let you do?" she says, losing her temper. She is starting, quite naturally, to side with Carlo. This woman, Laura . . . she doesn't know her, but she already feels she hates her.

"Peace and quiet. Mum always wants peace and quiet," replies Carlo, the corners of his mouth dripping with ice cream, after thinking it over for a while.

"And Dad?"

Carlo turns serious. This is a topic he doesn't like to talk about. Given any choice, he'd rather not reply.

"I don't have a dad," he murmurs drily.

Adriana yields to the impulse to take his hand in hers. Carlo withdraws it. He almost looks as if he's going to start crying. Then he fixes his brimming eyes on her.

"I read a lot," he proclaims proudly.

"Fairytales?" she asks with relief, now that the moment of awkwardness following her indiscreet question seems to have passed.

"Science books. And travel. I like travel books . . ."

"Yes, I get it: India . . ."

"But Mexico too, it's where the Mayan pyramids are. Did you know that there were two million Maya and eighty Spaniards, and the Spaniards eventually killed all the Maya?"

"That's so sad!"

"And the American Indians? You know that there were millions and millions of them and that the cowboys exterminated them all?"

Adriana feels an unexpected sense of annoyance. She thinks it's been provoked by the waiter, who's been hovering round the table for a while and is giving every sign of trying to flirt with her, so she sends him off with a curt request for a *caffè americano*. But the sensation persists. Adriana realizes that she feels somehow as if she's being observed. She turns round. There's a man smiling at her. She immediately recognizes him, and he must have recognized her heavens know when, and the man raises his glass and gives her a broad wink, and Adriana would like to sink into the ground or be a thousand miles away or vanish into thin air, as if by magic.

"The bill!" she shrieks, but the man has already risen to his feet and is coming over towards her.

X

Vitas takes up his clarinet and, for the last few passers-by who are hurrying to their lunches, improvises a melting rendition of "St James Infirmary". But into his filthy ragged hat not a penny falls. The Italians walk past, uncaring, tight-lipped. Vitas directs his last solo at the restaurant windows, on the other side of the street, and then puts his instrument down. Mamma Irina, tail hanging and ears erect, disapproves with a muffled rumble.

"Anyway, what is so special about that woman? She is not young, she is skinny, she has boy who seems strange, she is jumpy . . . but she has nice eyes . . . eyes that have suffered but can also laugh . . . and how long is it since we spend time with a woman that laughs, eh, Mamma Irina? And then: what are we doing with our lives? Today we are here – and tomorrow? Jail or a knife in the guts . . . Ah, tomorrow . . . what do you think, Mamma Irina . . ."

Mamma Irina wags her tail, rolls over onto her back and lies there waiting expectantly. Vitas takes a cigar butt from his jacket pocket. He lights it and settles down, patiently, to wait.

XI.

His name is Gerardo, he sells cars. He's rich and vulgar: virtues that often go perfectly well together. From the moment they recognized one another he hasn't stopped cracking jokes at the old man sitting next to him, an ugly old fellow who can't stop shaking – an obvious case of Parkinson's. Adriana knows she's the object of the conversation and doesn't need much imagination to guess its general tenor. But she casts her mind back. The Ylenia Escort Agency. The price tariff still in *lire*, though they were switching over to the euro. This Gerardo had engaged her services for a weekend in Positano simply so he could throw her into bed with another vulgarian, a Milanese with whom he was hoping to conclude a business deal. The Milanese had turned out to be a queer.

"Since we're here . . ." Gerardo had interrupted, slamming the door of the hotel room behind them, "and since you're costing me a fair bit . . ."

Won't she ever be able to draw a line under all of that? The bill is still not here. Gerardo gets up and comes towards her, smoothing down his jacket. He holds out a greasy hand. Adriana reluctantly takes it and shakes it weakly, just to be polite and not to cause a scene in front of Carlo, who is observing with his faraway, somewhat vacant expression. But she too, as she lets him shake her hand, must have the same dumb expression on her face.

"Your son?"

"No, a friend's. I'm looking after him for a couple of hours . . ."

"So," he murmurs insinuatingly, "you haven't changed career . . ."

Then, without waiting to be invited, he sits down and hands a banknote across to Carlo.

"Up you get, little fellow, go and buy yourself an ice cream."

"I've already had an ice cream," protests Carlo, rather taken aback.

"All right, a Coke then . . . whatever you want, I and Miss Adriana need to have a little talk . . ."

"I have absolutely nothing to say to you!" exclaims Adriana; then she angrily tugs the waiter by his sleeve and reminds him she's still waiting for the bill.

But Carlo, opportunistically, has clutched at the banknote and is now heading towards the video game machine next to the cashier's.

"Look, the little guy's wiser than you . . ." sneers Gerardo, taking one of her hands, which she promptly withdraws.

"Might I inquire what you want from me?"

"You still working at the Agency?"

"No."

"Set up on your own?"

"Mind your own damn business."

"Oh, I was just wondering . . . maybe, with the kid's mother . . . two girls, you know how it is . . ."

"Gerry, I'm in a hurry. Can you just tell me what you're after?"

"A work of charity," sighs Gerardo in an unexpectedly humane tone of voice.

"Meaning?"

With an absentminded gesture and a new sigh, he points to the old man whose head dodders as he noisily slurps a little cup of coffee.

"My father . . . poor old devil, he's almost gone . . ."

"So? I'm not a nurse!"

"I'd really like . . . before he dies . . . to give him a nice little surprise . . ."

"But what's that got to do with me?"

"Well, you'd need to . . . anyway, just listen: Dad's in the clinic, or rather an old folks' home . . . you know what it's like . . . and with all the things I have to sort out . . . today I've wangled half an afternoon off for him . . . and so, when I saw you . . . I said to myself, I said . . . maybe Adriana will . . . it's really, really simple . . . we go back to my place . . . the kid we can leave on his PlayStation, by the way, he seems a bit of a halfwit to me, if you want my opinion . . . and you . . . you put on a little show . . . for my dear old Papa . . ."

"A . . . little show?"

"Yeah, that's right, you show it him one last time, poor old fellow, just a flash, what more do you think he wants in the shape he's in now!"

"You mean I'd have to strip . . ."

"Atsarright!"

"And . . . ?"

"And then, if you like, you and I . . ."

Ever allusive, Gerardo gives her another broad wink and leers at her, and Adriana can identify traces of parsley caught in his shining white teeth, and a wave of nausea overwhelms her, and before she can utter any kind of an answer the waiter at last appears with the bill, and Adriana thinks, I'll keep a grip on myself, I'll keep a grip and I'll pay, I'll pay and I'll go, and she rummages around in her handbag for her purse, but Gerardo has beaten her to it, and the waiter is already walking off with his credit card.

"Please. My treat . . . and for this little business proposal, if it suits you all right, there'll be another five hundred . . ."

Then Adriana suddenly rises to her feet, knocking the table over, and everyone in the restaurant stares at her, everyone except for Carlo who is absorbed in his videogame, and the old man, whose head won't stop doddering, everyone else stares at her while she rushes after the waiter, who in the meantime has passed the bill and the credit card to the cashier, and flings two fifty-euro notes at the uncomprehending woman behind the cash register, yelling, "Keep the change!" and like a Fury grabs Carlo who protests, "But I'm setting a new record here!", and, still yelling, *let's go, let's go, bastard, swine* in an instant she is outside this cursed restaurant, outside, in the damp, windy afternoon, outside, and if she could only get outside her present and her past, and outside her entire wretched life . . .

XII

Gerardo isn't the type of guy to give up easily. He's not the kind of guy many people can say "no" to. Just imagine – a stupid little whore like Adriana! And so, clutching his credit card, he waves a reassuring hand at the old man, rushes out into the street and in a few strides has caught up with her.

"Look, I can bump the figure up to a thousand!"

She obstinately refuses even to reply to him and carries on her way, with the little brat next to her, and finally Gerardo loses his temper.

"You fucking whore, where d'ya think you're going?"

And when he reaches out to grab her by the arm, a tremendous blow comes crashing down on his spine, and a hand of steel grabs him by the throat, and an irresistible force obliges him to make a grotesque about-turn, and Gerardo finds himself in front of a blond colossus, a kind of film extra from *Cinecittà*, a beast straight from *Gladiator*, the two-legged one, that is, and in tow there's another beast, a four-legged one this time, a mangy great mutt of a dog, all teeth and snarl . . .

"Maybe you are bothering the lady!"

And Gerardo, who has learned from life when to beat a retreat, holds out his arms in a submissive gesture and tries to make himself as small as possible and in a querulous tone murmurs:

"Sorry, must be some mistake . . ."

Vitas observes Adriana, who is wiping a tear of rage from her eye, and Carlo, who, looking a bit scared, is huddling up to her side. She nods, and the Lithuanian releases his pressure. Gerardo dusts himself down and walks a few steps away, but once he is on the threshold of the restaurant he spits and shouts:

"You could've told me you'd got yourself a pimp, you filthy little whore!"

And then he darts into the restaurant to take refuge.

Once again Vitas seeks Adriana's eyes. And she, with a shrug, signals that it's better if he lets the matter drop.

Then Vitas goes up to Adriana and holds out his hand.

"I am Vitas," he repeats with pride.

"So I'd gathered," sighs Adriana and, with another shrug, she murmurs "Adriana" and returns his handshake.

"A nice name," comments the giant, holding her hand in his a little longer than strictly necessary.

Adriana leaves her hand in his. She has lowered her eyes and feels herself blushing again. It's not just because he's saved her from that horny little bastard. It's because there is something in his tone of voice that she hasn't heard for heaven knows how long. The tone of voice, a sensation of warmth that envelops her and makes her feel like a little girl again or, maybe, like a girl that someone loves. She thinks back over her life and is forced to admit that nobody has ever held out a hand to her quite this way before. Nobody has ever spoken to her with such gentleness. Finally she quietly removes her hand from his. Best not to start getting dangerous ideas. It's no time for daydreaming.

"I have to go," she says, forcing herself to assume a resolute air, but she merely needs to sense the disappointment in his gaze to lower her eyes again.

Meanwhile, Mamma Irina starts barking furiously. She and Carlo are playing tag together. First the dog chases Carlo, then the boy suddenly stops, and the animal darts to one side and transforms herself into the prey. The two of them swap roles with the carefree abandon of a couple who have been together for ages.

"It's like they are old friends!" notes the Lithuanian, with an optimistic glint in his eye.

"I have to go," Adriana repeats.

"So let's go," concludes Vitas with a note of firmness in his voice.

XIII

The main problem with Italians, the Slav is reflecting, as he parks the old souped-up Mercedes right in front of a "Keep Clear" sign in the Vicolo del Bologna, is that they all imagine they're so damn clever. But they're not. Or, to be more precise, not all of them. That Giangilberto, for example. With his half-baked plan and the lies he throws around . . . And yet he thinks he's something of a crime genius when he's actually just an idiot. Because only an idiot could come up with the idea of engaging a professional of the Slav's calibre and imagine he's going to swallow the old betrayed-husband-who-wants-to-scare-the-shit-out-of-his-unfaithful-wife routine and then pay him off with 5,000 lousy euros. And on top of all that he thinks he can get him to make a phone call that, just by itself, means "kidnapping and extortion" and brings with it some fifteen years in jail. No, Giangilberto is a stupid fucker. And choosing the Slav is the worst mistake he could have made. You don't emerge from a war with an honourable career as a sniper behind you, you don't cock snooks at the military police of half the world and the UN Blue Helmets, you don't get to Italy in the engine compartment of an articulated lorry laden with heroin and you don't become the Slav in this shitty country unless you've got real balls! The Slav lights up a cigarette and treats himself to a complacent smile. He just needed a couple of phone calls and a quick chat with the right person, down in Maimon's bar, now acting as his HQ, to size up the situation in all its details. And having sized things up, the result was staring him in the face: why be happy with 5,000, when you can get at least twenty times as much? The Slav stubs out his cigarette and smiles as he pats the pistol that's there where it should be, in the inside pocket of his jacket. Trastevere is a desert that will come to life only as the shadows of evening start to fall. The ideal scene for doing everything in the best possible way, nice and calmly. The Slav hates having to rush, hates having to improvise. The Slav likes to do everything properly, nice and calmly. He's never in a hurry. He lights up another cigarette and waits.

XIV

"You sure about this?" murmurs Laura, when Giangilberto parks outside the bank.

"I've told you," he whispers affectionately, taking her hand in a protective gesture, "I'm with you, and I'm not leaving you!"

"All right . . . I'll get going . . ."

"Off you go, sweetheart, take care . . . don't get panicky. You just go down for a routine audit, make contact, exchange a few cheerful words with the employees and then come out . . . and you do it all as calm as you can, no hurry . . . got it?"

But Laura has already climbed out of the car, and Giangilberto has to lean out of the car window to attract her attention.

"You were forgetting this!"

Laura retraces her steps, takes the computer bag and slings it across her shoulder. The bag is empty. It's just there to confer a semblance of normality on the manageress' unexpected visit. And, obviously, it's also somewhere to put the money.

As she crosses the road, Laura reflects that the next audit isn't supposed to take place until the end of the month. Perhaps, if she mortgages or sells her house, she'll manage to get the cash back and make up the shortfall. Or perhaps she'll lose it all, but at least she'll have Carlo back. But she also thinks, in one dirty little corner of her mind, how different and wonderful her life would have been if that unwanted kid had never got in the way.

XV

At the end of the Testaccio bridge there's a little, run-down bar. So run-down that nobody raises any objections when the gigantic Lithuanian gets a table set up for him outside and takes out his clarinet and improvises a piece that even the manager, a pot-bellied Roman with a greasy apron, finds to his liking. So much so that he presents himself after a few minutes with a coffee, a chocolate ice cream for Carlo and a bowl of scraps for Mamma Irina, which the dog, with Vitas' permission, wolfs down in no time under the amused gaze of the locals.

"You play well," says Adriana.

Vitas shrugs.

"I used to make enough to live on with this. But now . . ."

"You just can't get by," she says with a touch of bitterness.

"No, it's more and more difficult. You Italians are changing. First you always laughing, now you all pissed off. Pissed off, yes, and you move about so quickly, always in a hurry. It's like being in Russia, sometimes . . ."

"Are you Russian?" asks Carlo.

"Partly. But I come from Lithuania . . ."

And Vitas talks about his distant native land. The men there are tall and broad as trees and the women are blond and slender or redheaded and strong, like Adriana – he adds.

"I'm not strong," she murmurs in a sudden upsurge of sincerity.

But Vitas hasn't heard, or pretends he hasn't, and resumes his story. He tells of wild boars and frozen forests. Of Russians who were bosses and were thrown out overnight, and half-Russians, like himself, who are now considered by everyone to be bastards.

"So I say: Vitas, what are you doing in your own country if everyone tells you that you are a foreigner in your own land? And so I come away. Alone. Then one day I meet this stupid dog with her big nose and her big heart, another, what's it called, 'orphelin' like me . . ."

"Orphan," corrects Carlo, who has asked for, and obtained, his second ice cream.

"Orphan like me," resumes Vitas, "and that's when the road gets less difficult! And since then we are wandering round. Here today, and tomorrow, who knows? But maybe one day Vitas and Mamma Irina they find place to live, and their lady and mistress . . ."

There it is. A short, dreamy moment. Vitas said these last words gazing straight into Adriana's eyes, and she has been overwhelmed by a great desire to weep and even to cast herself upon the mighty chest of this colossus, and Carlo, who has noted the awkwardness, scratches Mamma Irina behind her ears until an intense quiver of pleasure runs right down her body, and Adriana shakes off her fantasizing and tries to say, one more time, that it's time to go, and Carlo, who doesn't really want to go anywhere, looks Vitas right in the face and tells him that he knows a great deal about Lithuania.

"Ah yes, little man? What do you know, for example?"

"I know that in Lithuania you're very good at basketball."

"True. But how do you know that?"

"Internet," the boy laughs. "It says that the Lithuanian national team has also won I don't know how many championships . . ."

"True, true!"

"Do you play basketball?"

"Yes. In the reserves," laughs Vitas, "I'm not tall enough!"

Then it's Adriana's turn to laugh.

"It's true!" protests the giant. "We have to be minimum six feet two, six feet four. I am only six feet. A dwarf, you see? And you, Carlo, you play?"

"I'd like to!"

"So why don't you?"

"Mum doesn't have time to take me," the lad sighs.

Vitas knots his brows in a feigned frown.

"You, Missy, why don't you find time to take your son to sport? If he continues to eat ice creams . . ."

"She's not my Mum," Carlo finally points out.

And it's as if the spell has been broken. Vitas suddenly scowls, and a few questions start going round in his ex-cop's head. Adriana feels duty-bound to inform him that she's simply doing a favour for a friend. Carlo takes Adriana's hand and emphasizes that he's having a great time with her. Mamma Irina smells the change of climate and allows herself a muffled growl. When the manager pops up and makes what he thinks is a rather witty joke, nobody replies.

"Now I really do have to go," states Adriana.

Everyone gets up in silence.

XVI

The worst is behind us, thinks Giangilberto, when Laura, exhausted, pale, giving off a strange odour – a mixture of stress and fear, ill-concealed by the faint scent of the perfume she likes to wear – flings the bag full of money onto the back seat and sits down next to him.

"You've done a grand job," he says to her gently.

And if she were feeling just a little less fuddled, a little less anxious, she wouldn't find it difficult to detect the note of smugness concealed in this apparently reassuring remark. Because what Giangilberto really means is: I've done a grand job. I'm still the number one. I'm one who'll always keep his head above water. I'm Giangilberto the unique, the inimitable, the Artful Dodger, the one who has a solution to every problem, the one who, when you think he's all washed up, well, it's at just that moment that you need to be afraid of him, as he'll be working away in the shadows, and when he comes out into the light again, then everyone's going to have to start looking out!

But Laura has other ideas. Now Laura believes in this reliable man who's risking everything for her and her boy. Laura feels an immense sense of gratitude. And at the same time, anxiety gnaws at her.

"Let's go! Now!"

Giangilberto obediently pulls away from the kerb, and only when she realizes that the road taken does not correspond with the planned route does a doubt assail her.

"But where are you going? The man said Testaccio . . ."

"And that," says Giangilberto, appeasing her with his wheedling tones, "is exactly where I'm going. But I'm leaving you at home. There's no need for both of us to be there . . ."

"But that man said it has to be me that takes the money!"

"What difference does it make to him whether I go or you go? He just wants his money . . . Hear me out. You can trust me!"

"And if . . . if anything happens to Carlo . . ."

"Nothing's going to happen to him, you can trust me, I tell you! You have to trust people, Laura! Everything's going to be just fine . . ."

And Laura, who deep down wants to hear exactly these words, that everything's going to be fine, and that someone is taking care of her, someone she can rely on, a friend, a companion and not just a lover, Laura lets herself go as she sits there, and a flood of tears wells up inside her, and yes, she's fine, she's fine, but let's get a move on, please, she sobs, now, I can't take any more . . .

XVII

When he sees the trio plus dog emerging from the far end of the street, the Slav spits out his cigarette butt and squats down inside his Mercedes. Damn: the blond giant and the beast weren't in the plan. Where can that stupid little goose have picked *them* up from? What the hell's happening? For a moment he's tempted to confront them openly, face to face, here in the middle of the street, which remains obstinately deserted. Force them to hand over the kid, put the big bastard and the whore out of action and then vanish . . . But that giant is decidedly a tad intimidating, he has the physique of a bodyguard, and the animal – well, who knows how he might react? The Slav controls his feelings. Calm down, calm down, stay cool . . . Just now the woman in the bank will be withdrawing the dough. That prick Giangilberto will be enjoying his triumph in anticipation. Let's leave everything to sort itself out, let's work out an alternative plan. It was the same in time of war, when you were occupying a house and managed to take out two or three Moslem brats, and then they'd spot you and you had to beat a tactical retreat. Then anything could turn out to be of use: a house, a courtyard, a little tower or some ruin you could fall back on. You always need a fallback position, a Plan B. It is in your ability to foresee the various possible scenarios that the secret of success lies. Leave things to happen. They'll come along, and then we'll see. Take them by surprise. Maybe the redhead is out to get the giant into bed. Let's see. Then, unexpectedly, under the doorway, they split. The giant says goodbye and gives the boy a hug; the boy hugs the dog in turn. The woman and the hostage enter the building, the newcomers go their separate way. The Slav waits a couple of minutes, then grasps his pistol and gets going. It was only a false alarm, after all that.

XVIII

"Why didn't Vitas come with us?"

Carlo looks round in disappointment. He's in a small, untidy room, with odd pictures that he can't make sense of hanging on the walls, a tiny sofa and doilies like his Mum's scattered pell-mell on the little table on which a small TV set stands. Adriana snorts. It's already been so difficult to say "no" to him, and now the kid's starting up too . . . But, God willing, in a short, very short time, it'll all be over . . .

"Because we're going back to your Mum's now," she replies hastily, glancing urgently at her watch.

"They could have come with us, him and Mamma Irina."

"Well . . . maybe your Mum might not have wanted that."

"Why?"

"Well, just imagine, your Mum suddenly sees us turning up with a foreigner and a dog in tow as well . . . Your Mum's not very fond of dogs, is she? And then she gave you to me to look after! I'm her friend, aren't I?"

"You're not a friend of Mum's," protests Carlo, who is now sitting on the sofa, arms folded, a withdrawn, glum expression on his face, almost on the verge of bursting into tears.

Adriana sits down next to him and tries to break through his reserve with a hug. But Carlo pushes her away.

"You're not a friend of Mum's. I've never seen you at home."

"We met at work."

"Mum doesn't have any work friends. Actually, come to think of it, Mum doesn't have any friends at all . . ."

"Oh, have it your own way!" Adriana exclaims, suddenly getting to her feet. "Now let me tell you want we're going to do. I'm just popping to the loo for a minute, then we're going downstairs, picking up a taxi, and I'm taking you home to your Mum's. Does that programme suit you?"

"No."

"What do you mean, 'no'?"

"You're not a friend of Mum's, but you are a friend of mine. I'm fine here. I don't want to go home!"

Adriana smiles – a smile of pity and dismay. What kind of life must this poor kid have, if he prefers a stranger, a street bum and a dog to his safe, everyday existence?

"Listen, if I don't take you back, your Mum will start to get worried . . ."

"Mum always says that if it weren't for me, her life would have been much better . . . and anyway, you only need to phone her, don't you? Go on, phone her, tell her I'm staying here with you . . ."

Adriana puts her head in her hands. Of all possible surprises, this is the most unreasonable, the most . . . Then there's a knock at the door. And a man's voice, a voice she doesn't seem to recognize, calling her name.

"Adriana! Open up, Adriana, I'm a friend of Giangilberto's . . ."

And Adriana, with a sigh of resignation, goes to open the door. The man standing in front of her is a skinny, pale guy, and his left cheek is embroidered with a ghastly scar that has been patched together any old how. His smile is even scarier than the pistol in his hand.

"*Pusti deckica ili si jedna mrtva kurva!*" he growls, shouldering her roughly aside.

XIX

Vitas slowly heads back up towards the road along the Tiber, accompanied by the prudent low growl of Mamma Irina. As he walks along, the man turns gently to his dog.

"You say we should have gone up? But she said 'no'. Still, it's true, when a woman says 'no' she often means 'yes' . . . You say I should have stayed, right? But now I know where she lives . . . let's go back tomorrow . . . But you're still growling, Mamma Irina! You are saying: why wait until tomorrow when you can do it today? So tell me: what am I supposed to do?"

Simple. Go back. Vitas sighs and does an about-turn. He'll wait outside, or he'll try to get into the house where the woman, he knows, he has sensed, will not say "no" to him . . . For a short moment his mind lights up with forgotten scenes: a house – no more beds of cardboard under bridges . . . and a woman, perhaps a child of his own, a job, why not dream . . . ? He has strong arms and he's bright enough too, he just needs to believe in himself, stop hitting the bottle for a while, and then . . . And then the Mercedes almost crashes into him with a squeal of brakes before heading off with a crunch of tyres, followed by Mamma Irina's furious barking. And Vitas cannot believe his eyes, and starts to run after the car; ahead of it there's a traffic light, but the car drives straight through at red and speeds off along the Tiber, but there's been time for another look, no, Vitas isn't wrong, the one behind is Carlo, his hands against the window, his face pale and tense, and now he whistles to Mamma Irina and starts running fast, something has happened, perhaps something serious . . .

XX

In the living room of the big apartment that has been provided for him to rent by the journalists' union, Giangilberto, whistling, extracts the wads of banknotes from the computer bag with religious care and lines them up in order on the table. One last glance at his masterpiece, then a telephone call to Laura.

"Hi sweetheart, I've taken delivery. Now I absolutely have to call by at the paper, or I'll get fired. You'll see: everything's going to be fine!"

Laura manages to stay in control while he's talking; then she bursts into tears. She's in Carlo's room, among his toys and various belongings. She has never loved her son so desperately. All her wicked thoughts have been wiped out by sorrow and fear. He'll be back. And Giangilberto will help him to get over this unpleasantness. They'll settle down. She'll give Carlo a father. It's the right thing to do. Just so long as he comes back, oh God, just so long as he comes back.

Giangilberto puts half of the sum of money to one side. The Turk will be paid straight away, if only to get the whole business sorted once and for all. There'll be a meeting with Adriana and the Slav tomorrow. Now it's time for a double malt whisky and a quick browse through the racing tips. If everything runs smoothly, within half an hour the kid will be home. He'll tell an incredible tale all about the Christmas Fairy and delicious meals, and his Mum won't understand a word. He'll help him get over the shock. Laura has hinted at selling the house. We'll see. The "secure" mobile phone rings. Giangilberto lunges forward to pick it up.

"Hi there, Italian!"

It's the Slav. He wants reassurance.

"Everything sorted," he says slowly, clearly and resentfully. "See you tomorrow."

"Hey, what's the hurry? More haste less speed, Italian. Haven't they told you? And haven't they told you to be polite when you talk to friends?"

"Screw you, Slav, you're no friend of mine. I said everything's sorted, what more do you want?"

"I've got the kid."

"What?"

"You heard me, you dickhead. Did you think you were gonna rip me off with your charity handout? I've got the kid. See you at Testaccio in half an hour. You know where. Bring the hundred thousand, and I'll bring you the kid. And don't phone me back. Ciao, my friend!"

GIANCARLO DE CATALDO

XXI

When the silhouettes of Vitas and Mamma Irina appear in the doorway, Adriana is at the foot of the sofa. The dog is barking loudly, the man rushes forward to her, suddenly, he's standing over her, he gently lifts her up, her face is a mask of blood, one eye is swollen and her nose seems to have been dislodged from its natural position. Vitas manages to lift her up, holding her under her arms, and as he drags her into the bathroom he murmurs words of comfort in his incomprehensible language. In front of the mirror, she vomits up a lump of blood and mucus, she tries to wriggle free, but Vitas plunges her head under the water until she stops, shaking her head furiously, and he realizes that she is starting to emerge from her daze, and then he dries her vigorously with a towel, and finally takes her in his arms without using the least force and lays her down on her bed.

"Maybe nose is broken, maybe not, but anyway, nothing serious," he tells her, with half a smile, but then his expression suddenly turns hard and serious, and Adriana shudders at the tone of voice in which he adds, "But now you tell me what this story all about!"

Before Adriana can explain, the landline phone rings. Vitas answers, at the other end they put the receiver down. It's Giangilberto. The man's voice has only one possible meaning for him: it's an accomplice of the Slav, that much is clear. That stupid bitch has got herself screwed. Or the two have been in cahoots ever since it all started. And he's walked straight into it like the idiot he is. But he's not going to get away with it. The Slav's dreaming if he thinks he's screwed him. Giangilberto has a pistol, and he knows how to use it. You don't start playing games of this sort if you can't play the game fully tooled up, should the case arise.

Meanwhile, Adriana has told the Lithuanian everything. And now she subsides into an uncontrollable flood of tears.

"Tears no use," he reproaches her severely. "If you no stop, I give you slap on face, okay?"

And Adriana, intimidated by his threat, manages to control herself. Vitas sniffs and shakes his great head.

"I don't know if you stupid or pretending . . . You understand yes or no: this is kidnapping?"

"But he told me: you keep the kid for a couple of hours and then you take him back home . . ."

"And who's he that you believe him?"

"A . . ."

"Your man?"

"No . . . a, I've told you . . ."

"Like that one outside restaurant? One like him?"

Adriana doesn't reply. Vitas snorts with rage.

"When all this finishes, you and I have little talk. You need someone who look after you. You by yourself: nothing but disaster!"

But now there's a more serious problem. Finding the boy. Vitas patiently gets her to go over her description of the man. He talked like a foreigner, says Adriana. Stocky guy. With a scar on the left cheek and a pistol.

"Maybe a thousand like him . . . maybe ten thousand . . . we need something else . . . He spoke foreign, but how? Like me? Or different?"

Then Adriana remembers something.

"*Mrtva* . . . damn, a word like that . . . yes, I remember it clearly . . . *mrtva kurvà*."

"*Mrtva kurvà* . . . you sure?"

"You know what it means? Is it your language?"

"No. It's Croat."

"And how much Croat do you know?"

"When you knock around, you get to know a few things, Missy."

"And what does it mean?"

"Something not nice. Better I don't tell you."

"But I want to know."

"It means that you are a dead whore. Sorry, but you did ask . . . Anyway," Vitas says abruptly, "there are not many Croats in Rome. Perhaps this is good trail to follow, perhaps I know where to go . . ."

Vitas gives a whistle. Mamma Irina comes down off the sofa, where she had been perched wrapped around a blue scarf and, with warlike resolve, takes up position next to her master. Vitas remembers having seen the scarf round Carlo's neck and picks it up. Might come in handy.

"Now I go, and you stay here, clear?"

"I'm coming with you," says Adriana decisively.

Vitas looks her up and down, then he nods. A gleam of joy flickers in his eyes. But he sounds serious and threatening when he admonishes her:

"Yes, you can come, but you don't mess me around, okay?"

XXII

Outside the English Cemetery it's freezing, and there's a stream of passers-by hurrying to get the last Christmas Fairy presents in the Via Marmorata right nearby, and small crowds of foreigners chattering together, dark, excited. We're too hospitable with these damn foreigners, thinks Giangilberto, teeth chattering, feet stamping on the cobbles, his right hand tightly wrapped round the pistol grip, we're too kind, that's the problem with us Italians, we welcome them with open arms and then they stab us in the back, you bastard Slav. Then the mobile phone rings.

"Hi, Italian!"

"Fuck off! And get your butt over here, I'm bloody freezing!"

"But when you going to learn manners, eh? I said hello nicely to you, you say hello nicely to me!"

"Hello, Slav!"

"Oh, that is so nice. Sorry if I make you go to Testaccio, but I've changed my mind . . ."

"What do you mean, 'changed your mind'?"

"You know that old factory that's now a theatre?"

"India. It's called the India Theatre. Course I know it!"

"Good. I wait for you outside. Testaccio – too much traffic. Too many people. And you come quick, I'm not gonna wait for ever!"

Giangilberto slips the mobile back into his pocket and heads grimly off. The Slav detaches himself from the small group of country-folk in town for the day, nods farewell and heads to his car. The Italian's alone, that's good. But he's armed, he can tell from the way he behaves, the way he looks round. That's bad. He's even stupider than he'd imagined. He could have got through with the minimum of harm, and instead he insists on playing tough. Too bad for him. And for the boy.

XXIII

Vitas has managed to nick, from its parking place along the Tiber, a big-cylinder saloon car with a "*Corps Diplomatique*" number plate. He pulled a long piece of wire from one of the pockets of his huge greatcoat and forced the lock with derisory ease. Then he leaned his great body against a black box placed under the steering wheel, shifting it out of its position with a couple of quick, expert movements. It emitted a low buzz like the death rattle of an electrical circuit shorting, then silence.

"Now antitheft device dead," he explained. Then, with the same piece of wire, he started the engine. "So, you coming?"

Adriana obeyed, while Mamma Irina snuggled down docilely on the rear seat. Now Vitas is driving confidently through the darkness, maintaining a constant high speed but respecting the traffic signals.

"You never know, we must be careful. Anyway, nobody stops a *Corps Diplomatique*, at least so long as it's not alarmed!"

Adriana cautiously asks him if he'd stolen things in Lithuania.

"Me steal?" splutters Vitas. "What you getting at? I was Lithuanian cop. But from Russian police. So when Lithuania become independent, I was thrown out . . . like a dirty animal . . . luckily, before that, I caught many thieves, learned many tricks!"

As they drive on, he explains to her that there's a place where the "clever" ex-Yugoslavs tend to gather. A bar "at the end of the world", which he hopes he can find as he's been there once and his sense of direction is "fantastic". Adriana cannot help but admire his confidence, but she wonders whether they aren't all making a big mistake.

"We should have asked Giangilberto; he would surely . . ."

"He is certainly accomplice of Yugoslav! You are talking big rubbish! Who do you think sent Yugoslav to your place? Your friend Giangilberto! Who else?"

"I don't think so, Vitas. He . . . he needs money, agreed, but he's not a bad sort. He'd never hurt the boy. But that man, now he's a real beast . . ."

"Oho! You are defending your Giangilberto! After what he does to you, you still in love with him?"

"I'm not in love with anyone!"

"It's never too late!"

But this parody of a comic brawl between lovers comes to an abrupt end. Vitas leaves the main road – perhaps the Via Salaria? The Via Ardeatina? Is this still Rome? Has she ever really known this blessed city? It needed a refugee street bum to show her these exciting places – and he starts to drive down a series of winding little streets, barely lit by streetlamps whose glass has been systematically shattered and only one in five of which works, the rest is darkness, darkness and tall tenement blocks placed at equal distances from one another, with colonnades bearing the signs of closed-down businesses, gardens that have been picked bare and groups of youths kicking a ball around or revving up heavy motorbikes.

"Look," observes Vitas with a certain bitter irony, "look, this is Italy too. But very like Russia or Bulgaria when the Wall was still there . . . yes, here I can sniff the air of home!"

"We've already gone past," she replies timidly.

Vitas brakes suddenly, and Mamma Irina, forced out of her lethargic calm by the jolting vehicle, protests with a muffled growl.

"You're right!" the Lithuanian says with something like despair in his voice. "I recognize this place . . . Maimonides' Bar is nearby, only I don't remember . . ."

"Perhaps there, where the lights are?" Adriana hazards hopefully.

"Let's try," concedes Vitas after a moment's reflection. "Perhaps you are right again!"

XXIV

The Slav gets out of the Mercedes and goes towards Giangilberto with a mocking sneer all over his face. A dog howls at the moon as it sails between two layers of passing clouds. It's a clear, frosty night. The outline of the gasometer dominates the lunar desert of an abandoned construction site.

"Hi, Italian! Have you brought you know what?"

"Where's the boy?"

"In a safe place."

"Bring him to me here, and you'll get the money."

"First you show me the money, and then we'll go and get him!"

Giangilberto slips the computer bag off his shoulder.

"It's here."

Giangilberto advances slowly towards the Slav, who shakes his head.

"Stop there, Italian. Throw the bag and take two steps back . . . That's right! Bravo!"

The bag is now at the feet of the Slav, who, in order to pick it up, is obliged to bend down. He does so quickly, but his vigilance slackens. Giangilberto leaps forward, one hand in his pocket to get his pistol out; he leaps forward and runs at the Slav. But the Slav is a professional: just a swerve of his hips, and Giangilberto misses his target. The Slav's right hand comes chopping down on the nape of his neck. Giangilberto is on the ground, his pistol slips from his grasp. The Slav picks it up, sniffs and snorts, as if feeling embittered.

"Tell me, Italian, whatever am I going to do with you?"

Giangilberto tries to get back on his feet. The Slav pushes him back down with a kick.

"Maybe we can come to some agreement?" hazards Giangilberto.

The Slav spits and checks over the pistol, which is glinting in the moonlight.

"Oh, a Beretta . . . nice piece of work, Italian! Ah, and it's loaded too!"

"At home there's more money . . . come on, Slav, don't be a Goddamn fool! We're friends!"

"Really? We're friends now? But didn't you say you were no friend of mine? Oh dear! I must have misunderstood . . . anyway, sorry, but you were right. I don't have friends. So long, Italian!"

The Slav bends over Giangilberto and fires.

XXV

Maimonides' Bar looks like a Lego building cobbled together by an absentminded boy, with only a handwritten sign to identify it

– in fact it's just a shack of rickety planks stuck out in the middle of this deserted, nondescript, nameless zone on the outskirts of town. Adriana is barricaded in the car, with Mamma Irina protecting her and keeping at bay, with a great grinding of her sharp teeth, the ugly mugs who come up to peer at her between rounds of beer. Adriana lights a cigarette and swears that, if she gets out of this adventure in one piece, if she manages to get Carlo back to his Mum, she's going to change her way of life once and for all. She'll get together with Vitas. They'll find a decent job. They'll have kids. They'll build up a proper home. And she'll conceal nothing of her past, not even the scariest, most sordid things. And she'll find a way of getting Vitas a proper residence permit. Perhaps, if necessary, she'll marry him. And for the first time after so many years Adriana whispers prayers to a God who has always been a stranger to her. She prays that he will help her find the boy and the right path from which she has strayed. That he will make her a better woman.

"Get in the back," orders Vitas, hurriedly climbing into the car.

With him there's a short, skinny guy; Vitas introduces him as Mirko. Mirko bows with a half-smile that reveals a mouth full of rotten gappy teeth. Adriana slips into the back seat, Vitas starts up the engine with the usual wire, Mirko, sitting next to him, points to a rough path leading across the fields. Mamma Irina lays her head on Adriana's legs, and Adriana strokes it gently.

"Pretty woman you've got, Russian," says Mirko.

"I am not Russian, and you keep her out of this," hisses Vitas harshly.

"Just making conversation," says Mirko placatingly.

"Shut up and watch the road," orders Vitas.

Mirko shrugs and starts to hum softly. The path ends on the slopes of a low hill, which the saloon car has to struggle up. But they need to keep going. On the other side there's a railway, and over the railway a bridge, and around the bridge a group of houses shrouded in darkness.

"It's there," proclaims Mirko.

Vitas cuts the headlights and advances with the engine just turning over to the group of houses. Then he turns to look at Mirko.

"There are a hundred houses here. Which is right one?"

"Don't remember. The Slav has a store in there. You find it!"

Vitas clenches his fists, and the veins on his neck swell dangerously. Mirko laughs his wild laugh.

"Maybe, if your lady is nice to me, I'll remember better . . ."

Vitas lands a straight upper cut on his chin. Mirko is knocked back against the car window and starts to whimper. Mamma Irina barks.

"Everybody out!" orders Vitas.

"He'll nick the car!" protests Adriana.

"It's part of the terms. He gives me the Slav, I give him the car. It's an agreement. Come on, let's go!"

They jump out, and Mirko is already off with his bruised chin and his brand-new stolen car.

"But how are we going to find him now?" protests Adriana.

Vitas ferrets around in his overcoat, takes out Carlo's scarf and waves it under Mamma Irina's nose.

"The boy, Irina. We need to find him, okay?"

Mamma Irina seems to nod, sniffs the air, then heads off resolutely, her tail wagging frantically.

XXVI

How much time has gone by? Laura switches off her phone. She feels grim and despondent. At the newspaper office, all they've been able to tell her is that Giangilberto hasn't been in for a week. He's not answering his mobile. An idea she refuses to formulate slowly starts to go round in her mind. Laura picks up the telephone and dials 113 for the emergency services. The phone rings for several moments before anyone answers. But as soon as the cop starts to speak, she hangs up. The thought of Carlo stops her from squealing. She'll wait a bit longer. In the kitchen she pours twenty drops of tranquillizer into a cup of water and knocks the mixture back in one gulp. Then she drags herself into her son's room, picks up a cuddly bear and stretches out on his little bed, in the darkness, her eyes wide open.

XXVII

The houses are half-destroyed shacks, practically deserted, with the exception of a small group of street bums who are warming themselves by a fire of tyres as they pass round a bottle of cheap wine. Adriana huddles up to Vitas, who is busy kicking away the rats that scuttle away, their sleep disturbed by the placid gait of Mamma Irina. The dog has picked up a trail and won't let go. Now they are standing in front of wooden door, sealed shut by two crossed planks. Mamma Irina barks and wags her tail, and refuses to go any further forward.

"You stay behind," whispers Vitas, "the Slav is dangerous. In his country he used to shoot people, what do you call it – a sniper . . . I'll go in . . ."

It takes two robust kicks to crack open the planks, and on the third kick the door gives way with a crash. Mamma Irina catapults herself inside. Vitas follows her. Nobody attacks him, nobody takes a shot at him. Vitas feels along the wall with his fingers until he finds a switch. A dim light reveals the interior. Quite tidy, indeed rather elegant, in comparison with the rest. There are crates of spirits, television sets, stereos, video cameras and PCs. The Slav acts as a fence, or so it appears. Mamma Irina scratches against a kind of trapdoor on the floor. Vitas lifts it up and lowers himself down into it.

"Adriana! I have found him!"

Adriana peers down past the trapdoor. Vitas lifts the boy up and passes him to her. Then he clambers back up again. Carlo is asleep. He is pale and his breathing is barely perceptible.

"Perhaps he has been given drug . . . now quick, let's take him away from here!"

And out they go. Vitas with Carlo on his shoulders, no weight to speak of for a giant like him, and Adriana and Mamma Irina running alongside, only just managing to keep up with him, come on, come on, they can't take the path back across the fields, they can't take the risk of returning to the bar where the Slav keeps court, there's only one possibility, get onto the bridge and cross the railway, get down on the other side, then find a car and finally take the boy home. The night air has a good effect on Carlo, who, with a tremulous moan, wakes up, and the first face he sees is Adriana's, with her smile, and then, from the shoulders of the giant, Mamma Irina with her wagging tail, and Carlo thinks it's all been a dream, half nice and half nasty, but now everything's over, and his hand clutches Vitas's great body tightly, and the Lithuanian tells him, be brave, young fellow, after this adventure you are now a man, and just as they reach the middle of the bridge a figure emerges from the darkness ahead of them. A man with a computer bag slung across his neck and a pistol in his hand. The Slav.

"Well, well, what a nice little family!"

It all happens in a flash, as Adriana will later remember. Mamma Irina barks and hurtles forward. The Slav loses his balance and fires a shot, too high to cause any concern. Vitas places Carlo down on the surface of the bridge and yells to her: "Take him, take the boy, move it!" She sweeps up Carlo, who is still groggy, and drags him towards the other side of the bridge, towards freedom. The Slav gathers his wits, and with a kick sends Mamma Irina flying; but Vitas is already on top of him, two hundred pounds and more of weight crashing down onto his thorax and knocking him back against the parapet of the bridge, and Mamma Irina returns to the attack. But the Slav isn't a man to give up easily. Another kick catches Vitas in his lower belly, and he bends double with a roar of pain. Mamma Irina is knocked away with a swipe, a mighty slap that leaves her stunned, and now Vitas is without allies and the Slav is on top of him, and with another kick he seizes him by the neck, and Vitas seems beaten, incapable of reacting, and the Slav picks him up under his arms and drags him towards the bridge, props him against the parapet, and pushes, hoping to lift him up and over. And he'd manage to do so, but Adriana has grabbed him from behind, her fingernails sinking into his neck, her feet kicking him in the calves, like some savage and fierce creature that takes the Slav by surprise, and now Adriana is clinging to the strap of the bag that the Slav is still wearing slung round his neck, and she winds it round his neck, and pulls, and pulls even tighter, and the Slav is forced to loosen his grip on Vitas, and turns towards her, and sends her reeling with a slap, Adriana falls, but Vitas has gained precious seconds, Vitas clutches at the Slav for all his life's worth, the Slav is disorientated, loses his balance, Vitas puts everything he's got into it, the Slav topples over the parapet of the bridge, and would fall if Vitas didn't grasp the strap of the bag, the Slav tries to cling on with all his strength, and Vitas, trying to help him, pulls and pulls, the Slav grabs at the belt with one hand, but the strap inexorably gives way, and with a howl he lets go and tumbles it must be thirty, forty, fifty feet, and Vitas is left holding the bag, he turns round in a daze, trying to get his breath back after the fight. Adriana is lying on the ground, laughing and crying, and trembling all over, and Mamma Irina is whimpering softly, and Carlo is stroking her.

"Let's hope there's nothing broken!" the boy says quietly and then, more seriously, trying not to burst into tears, "Can you *please* take me home?"

XXVIII

It all finishes with Carlo going back home at one a.m., escorted by the Christmas Fairy who leaves him on the landing with one last kiss and a bag with broken handles containing 100,000 euros. It all finishes with Laura's laments and her promise to become a better mother. It all finishes with Carlo's crazy insistence on relating his incredible adventure and on getting a puppy dog all of his own, and the certainty that when he goes back to school after the holidays those bullies are going to have to deal with a different boy, a cool guy that you don't mess around with. And it all finishes with two human beings walking hand in hand towards the future, down a moon-kissed street of old Rome and a wise dog, still a bit bruised from her last battle, trotting along and wagging her tail beside them.

Teresa's Lair

Diego De Silva

The woman is on her way home. It's early in the afternoon. She's just been out to get something she needed, maybe washing-up liquid, or mincemeat (as she walks along the last stretch of the pavement even she wouldn't be able to say which of these it was, and she doesn't have any desire to look at her shopping list to remind herself); in fact she has neither coat nor bag, just the change she counted out clutched in her left hand, together with the keys.

When she arrives at the front door she realizes that its lock is broken. So she leans sideways against the door and pushes it open with her shoulder.

In the entrance hall there's the clapped-out bike that belongs to the people who live on the mezzanine, chained to the handrail of the stairs leading to the lift. Every time she sees it, she's overcome by an irrepressible feeling; she'd really like to pretend she didn't have this feeling, but the blood rushes to her face because of the indignation she feels at the barefaced cheek of those people. She sniffs and gives a quick glance into the mailbox, for no particular reason, just in case. Then the main door slams shut. With such force that it nearly comes off its hinges. She jumps, her heart hits the pedal and turns into something else that goes along at its own rhythm. She shuts her eyes tight and then slowly reopens them. "Again," she says between clenched teeth. She puts her hands on her hips and turns to look at the front door as it groans on its hinges. What vexes her more than anything else is the thought of the notice the property manager put up on the notice board a while ago: "Polite notice. Please shut the front door gently. Do not bang it!" With official signature and stamp. But why don't you fix the spring then, you lazy so-and-so, instead of wagging your finger at others? Tell those lousy hippies to shift that bike of theirs instead! This is an apartment block, not a garage. Get it?

*

She hears someone shouting from the elevator: "Miss Teresa!"

She hadn't been expecting to hear anyone utter her name, and it has the same effect on her as if someone had just snapped their fingers in her face.

"Did I frighten you?" asks the young man as he leans out of the elevator.

She shrugs, tosses her head a little to rearrange her hair and chuckles inside herself at her helpless vanity and the way she simpers whenever a man recognizes her or merely registers her existence, just to ask her what time it is, for example – and even if it's just the son of the lady upstairs, someone she's known since he was a little boy.

"No, it annoyed me," she replies as she reaches the elevator. She steps in, pretending she's feeling a bit tired. The young man closes the elevator gates with a sympathetic expression on his face.

"Third floor, isn't it?" he asks, his finger hovering over the button.

"Yes, that's right. Thanks," says Teresa.

The elevator starts to go up.

"I'd really like to know what we pay him to do. He's useless," she continues.

"The property manager, you mean?"

"Of course. The front door's been broken for two months."

"You're right. He's a moron," he says to please her. But he clearly shares her opinion.

"He even looks like a moron," adds Teresa, flaring her nostrils. And finally she bursts out laughing.

The young man imitates her with gusto.

Now Teresa looks at him a little less mistrustfully. Young Marco has turned into a handsome young man. He has a thin face, one that expresses what he's thinking. God knows what his job is. She'd like to know, but she never asks the people she meets this kind of question. What do you do in life, when are you getting married, when do you finish college? What if they don't have a job? What if they don't have enough money to get married or anyone to get married to? What are you going to do – embarrass them? People don't always think of things like that. Or they do think of them and still insist on asking.

"Sorry, young man. It's just that I had a bit of a turn," she says, placing her hand on her heart.

"No problem. How're things, anyway? It's been a while since I saw you."

"Oh, you know . . . I'm not getting any younger, as you can see."

Marco raises his eyebrows sympathetically. Her modesty is misplaced. Teresa has turned sixty, but it's obvious that she was once beautiful. She has a look of wry amusement, a feigned tolerance towards everything around her. She doesn't have much money, that's obvious, but her whole person has a certain dignity. She's one of those people naturally capable of making you feel accepted. You feel at ease with her right from the start.

"How's your Mum?" continues Teresa.

Marco shrugs.

"It's her legs, as usual. She hardly goes out any more."

"Ah, yes, I haven't seen her for quite a while, actually. But you give her a hand, I suppose?"

"Of course!" he replies, forcing himself to endure her condescension. And he gives a little snort.

The elevator arrives at her floor. Teresa opens the gates and steps out.

"Say hello to her for me."

"I'm on my way there. It's the first thing I'll do."

"Take care, Marco."

And as she says these words, she has a sudden strong desire to give him a kiss.

"You too, Miss Teresa, see you soon," he says. He pulls the outer door shut and closes the gates.

*

Marco is just putting the key into the lock when, from the other side of the door, he hears the voice of a man talking to his mother. He stiffens, withdraws his hand, and stays there listening.

205

The man is asking about him. He wants to know what time he gets back, what hours he keeps, whether he's still working for the same company, where his room is. Questions of a disquieting vagueness, uttered with a reticence that might mark him out as a policeman or a crook.

Marco's mother replies in curt, disjointed phrases. She feels frightened but, at the same time, annoyed at the way this man has forced himself into her home. Now it's her turn to ask what they want from her son, what he's done, why on earth they should be looking for him. And by the way: is the gentleman she's talking to really the person he claims to be? It's not actually all that difficult to get yourself fake ID.

Marco takes a couple of steps back and stares at the door of his home. He makes out, one word at a time, a whole sentence uttered by his mother. She has to raise her voice in order to impose her authority ("No, you're not going into my son's room without a proper search warrant. Don't even try: if you do, I'll make trouble for you."). He looks towards the stairs that lead to the floors above, as if he wants to make sure no strangers are there or might suddenly turn up. He's quick on his feet, he moves with the practised agility of someone who's found himself in similar situations in the past. He's no longer the affable, reassuring person who just now was sharing the elevator with the lady from the floor below. He grips the handrail and looks down. A moment later he pulls his head back in alarm. Then he flattens himself against the wall.

In the entry to the apartment block there's a man standing in front of the mailboxes.

Now Marco is breathing rapidly, as if he'd just been running. But this is merely to give him time to run through his options. In fact, his mind is soon made up. He goes down to the floor below and knocks on the door of the apartment immediately under his.

Shortly afterwards, Teresa replies from behind the door.

"Who is it?"

"It's me, Miss Teresa – Marco."

"Marco?" she replies. And she opens straight away.

She doesn't have time to ask him the reason for his visit – he's already slipped in and closed the door behind him.

"What's happened?" she asks, more surprised than alarmed.

"Nothing. Sorry, just a bit of a tricky situation," replies Marco.

"But what's the matter, who's out there?" asks Teresa. And she tries to brush him aside so that she can reopen the door.

Marco bars her way with his hands.

Teresa steps back, and her face flushes with consternation.

Marco waves his hands in the air, signalling that no, there's nothing dramatic going on.

"I'm really sorry: there's somebody there I don't want to see."

She looks at him in bewilderment.

"A woman," lies Marco on the spur of the moment.

Teresa doesn't open her mouth. Then he spins out his lie, speaking in low, urgent tones.

"Do me a favour and have a look through the peephole to see if she's there."

And as he says so he moves away from the door, instinctively convinced that this is the right thing to do if he is to lend credibility to the story of the spurned mistress.

Teresa lifts the cover of the peephole and looks at the distorted image of the landing outside.

"There's nobody there," she says, turning back. But her voice clearly bears not the slightest trace of conviction.

"I'm really, really sorry to be causing you bother like this," he continues, but his performance is becoming less and less persuasive. "Could you do me another favour? Do you have a window that looks out over the street?"

Teresa stares at him with a mixture of fear and suspicion.

"What's happening, Marco?" she asks, as if this second question of his had removed any doubt she might have had about her visitor having something to hide.

"Nothing's happening, I've already told you, it's a woman that's bugging me," he retorts with impatience; and without waiting for her to give him permission, he goes into the kitchen, as if he already knew where to find what he's looking for.

Teresa follows him in. Initially, his ability to find his way around surprises her. Then she realizes that the rooms in their respective apartments are laid out the same way.

Marco stops a little more than a yard away from the window and carefully leans forward to look down, keeping a cautious eye on the distance between himself and the windowpane.

He suddenly pulls back. Outside the front door there's a dark Alfa Romeo, double-parked; and, with his back leaning against the door on the driver's side, stands the man he saw a minute or two ago from the stairs.

Teresa, framed in the door, is gazing at him.

"What have you done?" she asks him.

Marco turns round. The muscles of his face slacken, like a mask dropping. His voice takes on an anguished, remorseful tone.

"Don't shout, please."

"Oh my God," she says, looking at him with a different expression.

Marco takes a step towards her. Teresa instinctively protects herself with her hands. Marco's lips twist into a painful grimace; he is touched by her childish gesture.

"I'm not going to hurt you."

Teresa tries to flee towards the door. Marco leaps after her and grabs her from behind in the little corridor that leads to the entrance, forcing her to bend forward. Teresa falls onto one knee. Marco pulls her towards him, putting his arms round her to prevent her from falling. Teresa utters a shrill cry of fear. Marco opens his eyes wide, horrified at what he is doing. He puts his hand over her mouth and speaks into her ear.

"Miss Teresa, please just listen to me. I won't do anything to you, I promise. I'll let you go if you promise you won't start yelling. Please. D'you promise? Nod your head, and I'll let you go."

Teresa, her eyes filled with tears, swallows her cry of pain and nods. Then Marco relaxes his grip, gradually, to make sure she'll keep her word. Teresa remains on all fours, panting. She doesn't yell, and she doesn't turn back towards her kidnapper.

Marco sits on the ground, his back leaning against the wall. He bends his knees, drops his arms, listens to her breathing as it grows slower. Teresa stares at him with defiance.

"I'm sorry, I didn't mean that to happen," he says.

Teresa wipes her nose with her sleeve.

Just then, from the floor above, they hear the door of Marco's apartment opening and closing. The man who had been questioning his mother is coming out. They hear him walk across the landing and start to go downstairs.

Marco stiffens. He stays there listening until he hears the steps come to a halt right on the landing outside Teresa's apartment.

He gets to his feet. He looks at Teresa and puts his finger to his lips; then he goes to stand at the door. He doesn't look through the spy hole. He slips his right hand under his belt and draws out a pistol.

Teresa covers her mouth with three fingers.

Still standing over her, he again signals her to be silent with his forefinger. Then he holds in his breath, gripping the pistol in both hands, its barrel pointing upwards, as if sardonically pretending to be begging for mercy.

After a few moments' silence, the steps outside on the landing resume. The man is going away.

Marco heaves a sigh of relief. He wipes his forehead with the sleeve of the arm holding the weapon. Then his eyes turn to Teresa.

"Please," he says awkwardly, "don't look at me like that."

"And how do you expect me to look at you, you crook?"

"I'm not a crook."

"Oh, really? What are you, then?"

"Listen: I'm sorry I've ended up in your home, but there was nowhere else for me to go. You're the last person I'd want to get involved in this business, believe you me."

Teresa sniffs.

"I'm expecting my son this evening."

Marco files away the information and breathes out noisily through his nostrils. So: another problem for him to face. He'll tackle it later.

"Where's your television?" he asks.

Teresa looks towards the kitchen.

Marco slips his pistol back in his trousers and holds out a hand to help her get up. She rejects his offer and pulls herself to her feet by herself, clumsily grabbing hold of the wall. Marco politely steps to one side. Then he follows her into the kitchen.

Teresa settles down on a chair. Her befuddled gaze seems to be registering things only belatedly. Marco switches on the little

TV set positioned not far from the stove, nervously channel-hops, fiddles with the remote and consults the TV menu. He snorts. Switches the telly off. Runs his fingers through his hair. His eyes stare intently into the air, as if running through the possibilities at his disposal one more time. He breathes in and breathes out. Beads of sweat stand out on his forehead. He goes back to check the street, keeping a safe distance from the window. The double-parked car has gone. But the fact doesn't seem to reassure him. Indeed, he assumes an even more hunted look than before.

"Please, Marco, just go away," says Teresa all of a sudden. "Go back home, don't get me involved in this business."

"Me, go home? You're joking."

"I won't say a thing, I swear it."

"I can't go home, Miss Teresa. It's the worst place I could go to. Get it? They're looking for me. Plus I don't want to get my mother involved. She doesn't know anything, and it's better she doesn't. It's the best way to protect her."

"But why should I come into it? What have I done to you?" she says with a plaintive edge to her voice.

"You haven't done anything to me, Miss Teresa. It just happened. I'm really sorry, but we don't have any alternatives. Neither of us."

Teresa would like to hurt him, pounce on him, since right now he embodies the destiny that will not leave her in peace and has brought her yet more pain. She starts to wring her skirt and to weep with frustration.

"Miss Teresa, I'm really jumpy, I don't want to lose my temper with you. Please stop it, stop it now."

Teresa suppresses her tears. And it's as if, all at once, her face becomes brighter, even cheeky. Younger.

"What do you think you're going to do? Kill me?"

Marco stares at her as if she'd just sworn aloud in church.

"What – are you joking? I'm not a murderer."

"You do happen to have a pistol," Teresa points out drily.

A deep wrinkle, like a wound, flickers across Marco's face. He has to think before replying.

"It's not my fault if there's a war on out there."

Teresa opens her eyes wide in consternation. As if she now doubted his sanity.

"War?"

"Yes, war. War isn't just planes dropping bombs and armies invading the lands of other people. War is you too."

Teresa's nostrils flare. She answers through clenched teeth, and with clenched fists.

"What do you know about me? What do you know about the life I lead?"

"I know, I know," says Marco tolerantly.

Teresa turns red with rage. This is my home, she thinks.

"You ought to go. Vincenzo's coming, I've told you."

"Yes. I heard you."

"And what will you do when he comes?"

"He won't come."

"What do you mean?"

"I mean that you're going to call him now and tell him not to come."

Teresa turns pale as she sees the only possibility in which she had placed any hope vanish into thin air.

"I don't know where he is just now. He'll be on his way."

"Well, he'll have his mobile with him, won't he?"

"No, he doesn't have one."

Marco shakes his head.

"Now you're not even trying to understand. I don't have any intention of doing any harm to anyone, not to you, and even less to Vincenzo. If you allow him to come here, you'll get him into real trouble. You follow me? Come on, phone him, stop wasting time."

Teresa lifts up the receiver of the telephone standing on a small cabinet next to the door. She dials a number with some hesitation, as if she found it difficult to remember it.

Marco looks out of the window again. Shortly afterwards, Teresa hangs up.

"He's not answering."

"What do you mean, not answering?"

"I can't get through."

"Okay, try again. What time's he arriving?"

"I was expecting him for supper."

"Fine. So you've got plenty of time."

Teresa sighs.

Marco pulls out the mobile and takes out the battery and the SIM card.

"Do you have any scissors?" he asks.

Teresa nods towards the cutlery drawer.

Marco opens it and finds a pair of scissors with plastic handles. He cuts the card through the middle and drops the two pieces next to the sink. He takes the wallet out of the back pocket of his trousers, pulls out another card, inserts it into the mobile, switches it on and dials a number. In the silence of the kitchen, they can hear the ringing at the other end. Marco counts the rings. He seems very tense, tormented by a suspicion that he will soon discover is justified. When there is still no answer at the fifth ring, he snaps the mobile shut and grinds his teeth.

"Shit," he says.

Teresa frowns. She doesn't like swear words.

Marco switches off the phone, takes out the SIM card and cuts this one in half too. He looks around, not knowing what to do. He checks his watch and switches the television back on. The early evening TV news is broadcasting details of an investigation that has led to the successive capture of members of a terrorist group responsible for one murder and two previous hold-ups. Marco sits down, hypnotized by the sequences. Images flash by: two people under arrest being led in handcuffs to the police car. Marco's face twists into a melancholy grimace. Teresa huddles back into her chair, appalled.

"Jesus, Mary and Joseph!" she involuntarily exclaims.

"Just you be quiet," snaps Marco, switching off the television once the news programme has ended. "Phone your son again."

Teresa hesitates.

"You going to waste even more time? All right then, give me his number and I'll do it," says Marco, rising to his feet and going over to the phone.

"No, no, I'll do it," she says with a note of despair in her voice.

"Just you listen to me. I've had enough. I don't want any more problems. So come on, give me that fucking number!"

He's like a cork about to shoot out of a bottle.

Teresa gazes at Marco with a woeful expression. She covers her face with her hands and starts to cry.

"What's the matter?"

Marco puts down the receiver. This time he doesn't order her to calm down.

Teresa points to the roll of kitchen towel hanging from the wall next to the fridge. Marco tears off a sheet and passes it to her.

"It's not true you were expecting Vincenzo. Is that it?"

Teresa blows her nose, folds the sheet of kitchen towel and slips it into the sleeve of her cardigan.

"It's been six months since I saw him. He last phoned me one month and twenty-one days ago."

Marco sits next to her with a new sense of respect. Teresa stares into space. She lets the words come out with the sense of relief of someone who has kept the pain bottled up for too long inside her.

"It's the apartment he's after. But how can I give it to him?"

She pulls the sheet of kitchen towel out of her sleeve and dries her face.

"But what do you care? Anyway, now you know the life I have to lead. You needn't worry, they won't come looking for you here. Nobody ever comes here."

"I'm sorry."

"You're sorry," she says with a note of sarcasm.

"Yes, I'm sorry," he repeats.

Teresa gazes at him as if he reminded her of somebody else.

*

Marco spends the rest of the day thinking, jotting down notes in a notebook, switching the television on and off, looking out into the street. Trivial occupations, to which he dedicates himself attentively, as if devising some plan of action. Only when he hears his mother's steps over his head does he change his expression and swallow, even if his mouth is dry.

Teresa has wrapped herself in a kind of weariness that allows her to view her kidnapper with lucid resignation. She has even stopped asking him for permission to go to the toilet, and he has stopped keeping such a close eye on her.

They are sitting at the table when the evening TV news opens with the news of the arrest of another member of the group to which Marco belongs.

Teresa has just taken out of the oven some pasta heated up from the day before.

"This recurrent problem," says the newscaster, repeating the words of a written declaration issued by those carrying out the investigation, "will soon be finally eliminated."

Marco's shoulders sag dejectedly. Teresa lays her knife and fork crossways on her plate.

"So what are you going to do now?"

"I don't know," says Marco disconsolately.

"Try and tell me what's happened, I might be able to give you a hand."

"I don't think so, actually."

"Am I so very stupid?"

"No, it's not that. It's really complicated to talk about."

"And you don't want to talk about it to a woman like me, right?"

Marco doesn't know what to say. This, perhaps, is why he reacts with impatience.

"Do you know anything about politics, by any chance?"

"No. I don't understand the first thing about it."

"Well, there you are. What's the point of us talking?"

Teresa relapses into a helpless silence. A silence that reflects on Marco as if it were a rebuke for his presumption. Yes, basically he's chosen the easy way out.

"Let's put it this way," he continues, feeling that it's his duty to add a few words. "I'm tired of it all. They're taking away our rights, our hopes and even the few things we've managed to achieve . . ."

All of a sudden he stops, realizing that his words are floating about on a sea of inconclusiveness. Teresa gazes at him with a kind of compassion.

"I'm tired too. But not because of that . . ."

Marco loses his temper.

"Oh, no please, not that! I know perfectly well where you're going with this, but it's too easy to feel you're in the right that way. You value one thing above everything else and judge from on high, without ever coming down to earth, without ever really understanding things."

"Why do you say that? What do *you* do? Don't you value one thing above everything else?"

"Exactly. We're alike, you and me. Why are you looking at me like that? Perhaps, deep down, you're thinking that I'm partly right?"

"No, it's just that I don't understand you."

"I've already told you it's better if I don't try to explain myself."

"If we can't understand each other, there's no point."

Teresa gets up. She asks if she can go to bed. Marco follows her. He waits outside the bathroom while she gets ready and outside the bedroom while she gets undressed. Then he settles down next to her, in an old armchair.

*

"What's happened?" asks Teresa, waking with a start. She pulls herself upright, fumbles for the light switch on the bedside table, switches it on.

"Please keep quiet," Marco tells her.

Marco is on his feet, his pistol in his trembling hands, his mouth twisted into a grimace of repressed rage, his eyes focused on the ceiling. From the floor above come the sounds of a search being carried out, and his mother's voice, protesting in vain.

They're in his room now. First the desk. Then the wardrobe. They're ruthlessly rummaging through his drawer. His things are being chucked around, turned topsy-turvy, closely examined, thrown aside or else confiscated, one by one. Voices interrupting one another. Something breaking. The veiled threats ("And so you don't know anything? Is that what you're saying? Never a single suspicion, never anything strange – is that it?")

Marco snarls. He aims the pistol indiscriminately at the ceiling, as if trying to aim at an object that keeps moving over it.

Teresa, without moving from her bed, talks to him.

"Calm down, Marco, stop messing around."

He looks at her. He senses a new note in her voice.

"Put the pistol down. You can't do anything."

It's the right thing to say – the thing he needed to hear. He sits down again, and the hand holding the gun sinks on to the arm of the chair.

The search finishes. There's a sound of heels clattering down the stairs. Then he hears his mother starting to tidy the mess they have left in the apartment, weeping and calling on the saints. She sounds like a little girl. Marco clenches his fist, brings it to his mouth, gnaws on it.

Teresa pulls the blankets aside and starts to get out of bed.

"Would you like me to go up to her?"

He turns round, unable to believe his ears.

"What did you say?"

"If you like, I can go up to your mother and ask her if she needs anything."

Marco gives a faint, unhappy smile.

"You don't trust me, do you?" she asks.

Marco snorts.

"If you were in my shoes, would you trust anyone?"

"No, you're right," she replies after a few seconds.

She lies down again, pulls the blankets up, switches off the light.

*

God knows how much time goes by before the sounds from upstairs have ceased. When Marco opens his eyes, day is breaking.

Teresa's bed is empty. Marco grabs his pistol (it had slipped under the armchair) and springs to his feet. He could kick himself as he looks round for Teresa. How ever could he have been so stupid? Why didn't he tie her up? Why didn't he lock her into one of the rooms?

He looks into the bathroom. She isn't there. He dashes into the kitchen. He flips on the light. The electricity's off. He opens the door to the cubby-hole next to him. He points the pistol inside, into the darkness. Nothing.

He hears a noise coming from the entrance. He moves forward, holding the pistol in both hands, aiming at where a man's chest would be. In the gloom he recognizes the outline of Teresa, fumbling around in the opening of the electricity meter.

"Get away from there!" he orders.

"What?" she says, turning round.

Marco comes right up to her and pushes her roughly away from the meter. Teresa bangs her shoulder against the wall.

"What are you up to?" asks Marco accusingly.

"The electricity. The fuse has blown."

With a gesture of exasperation, Marco grabs the lever of the electricity meter and yanks it up, as if he wished to show that Teresa is lying. But the light comes on straight away. Marco blinks.

"It's always doing that," says Teresa, rubbing her shoulder.

Marco looks at her blearily.

She waits.

"How long have you been up?" asks Marco.

The pistol between his hands seems so out of place now.

"Quarter of an hour, twenty minutes," she replies as if telling him today is Monday

"You're joking," he says.

"If you say so."

Marco doesn't know what to say.

She lets another few moments go by.

"Can I make some coffee?"

Marco feels awkward and embarrassed. So she turns her back on him and heads off into the kitchen. He follows her limply. Teresa opens the door of the wall cupboard over the sink, takes out the coffee maker, the coffee jar and the sugar. Marco sits down while Teresa puts the coffee into the machine and lights the stove.

"Did I hurt you just now?" he asks, feeling guilty, after a while.

"No," says Teresa.

"I'm sorry, I thought . . ."

". . . that I'd slipped off while you were asleep and was maybe already at the police station telling them you were here."

"Yes, that's right."

Teresa raises the lid of the coffee maker and lets it fall back.

"Why didn't you?" he continues.

Teresa shrugs. Perhaps she could tell him that it doesn't matter either way, given that she hasn't actually gone to the police station. Or that she didn't want to be alone. Or that it's none of his business. But the truth is that, quite simply, she doesn't feel like answering. So she doesn't.

The coffee maker starts to blow off steam.

*

Marco leaves his pistol out in the open for the rest of the day. Teresa does the housework, taking care not to bother him while he is thinking or otherwise engaged. At around midday she gets something for them to eat, lays places for them both (Marco barely touches his food), washes the dishes, goes to lie down and has a little nap for an hour or so. She gets up and busies herself in the kitchen. The TV set, its volume very low, is on. Marco places his arms across the table and places his head on his arms. In his right hand, lying open as he sleeps, lies the remote control.

Teresa tiptoes over to him, takes the remote out of his hand and switches off the television. Then she goes back to her room, puts on her outdoor clothes and waits for him to wake up. When she hears him moving, she goes back into the kitchen.

"I have to go to the pharmacy," she says.

"What for?"

"I have to pick up some prescription medicine. I've run out."

Marco is at a loss how to react.

"Look," she says. And she passes the doctor's prescription over to him.

Marco takes it, but he doesn't read it. He fills his lungs with air, then breathes out through his nose. He hands the prescription back to her. Teresa, clutching the handle of her handbag, waits for him to give her permission.

Why shouldn't he trust her? She has earned his trust.

"Of course."

Teresa heads off. Marco stays where he is, staring at the refrigerator.

"Marco?" It's Teresa, calling him from the door of her apartment.

He turns round.

"I'll be straight back, don't worry."

Marco nods. It sounds so definitive to him – the sound of the lock clicking as the door is opened and closed.

He brings his hands up to his face and wipes them down his forehead and then his chin, as if he were washing his face without water. Then he runs them through his hair. He glances over his notes. He gets up. He goes into Teresa's room, places the pistol on the bedside table, stretches out on the bed and drowses off.

The doorbell wakes him with a start. It has already rung twice.

He jumps out of bed, picks up his pistol and steps into the corridor. The doorbell rings again, at length. He blinks. Half of him is disappointed, the other half quite understands. If Teresa has betrayed him, he won't hold it against her. Not really. He grips the pistol in both hands, points the barrel at the floor. He prepares himself. Maybe he'll die. In a few minutes. In the apartment belonging to the woman who lives downstairs from him.

*

When Teresa, her hands filled with two supermarket bags, emerges from the elevator and sees the two strangers standing at her door, she has the impression she's dancing – her legs are trembling so much. But it lasts for just a moment: she takes a deep breath and then goes into action.

The men gaze at her as she approaches them.

"What do you want?" asks Teresa.

"Do you live here?"

"Yes, I live here. But what are you doing outside my apartment?" she replies, staggering slightly under the weight of her shopping bags.

The eyes of the two men meet.

"Police, madam. We'd just like to ask you a few questions."

"Me? Why? Have I done something?"

"No, not at all. We're just gathering information."

"Ask away," says Teresa, putting her bags down.

The cop seems a bit confused.

"Has anything strange happened over the last few days?"

"What are you getting at?" she says, staring at the two strangers as if they were lepers.

"In this apartment block, I mean," the man adds, a bit at a loss. "Have you seen or heard anything? Strange movements, people you haven't seen before?"

"Listen. You're starting to get me worried. What exactly are you talking about?"

The other cop looks at his colleague and shakes his head, as if to say: "We're wasting our time."

Behind the door of her apartment, Marco listens intently to the dialogue. Teresa's play-acting fills him with anxiety, but he is also touched by it. He's on the edge of the abyss. If he doesn't fall into it, he'll have her to thank.

"That's fine. Sorry to bother you," says the cop.

"But may I ask what this is all about?" asks Teresa as they turn to go.

"Nothing, nothing at all," says the other guy, "we're just checking things out here. Don't worry."

And they go.

Teresa picks up her bags, puts them down on the doormat, takes her keys out of her handbag, opens the door, picks up her bags, pushes the door open with her foot, enters and shuts the door behind her. And all the tension of the performance she has just put on suddenly overwhelms her, so that she feels faint. She slithers to the floor, half closes her eyes and opens her mouth, filled with a sudden need for air.

Marco jumps out from behind the corridor wall and springs towards her. He lays his hands on her shoulders and speaks to her in a voice swollen with gratitude.

"Miss Teresa. Miss Teresa."

Teresa gasps out a few words.

"It's nothing, it'll go, don't worry."

"But I am worried."

Quite spontaneously he takes her hand and squeezes it.

She smiles. She feels happy.

"It's all my fault. I'm sorry," says Marco.

Teresa seems to be breathing with great difficulty.

"Please help me to my room."

Marco helps her to get to her feet, accompanies her to her bed and helps her to lie down with all the delicacy of which he is capable. He folds the pillow in two and arranges it behind her head. Then he gently lifts her legs onto the bed, holding them by the ankles.

"That way the blood can get to your head. You'll soon be feeling better."

She stops him with a gesture.

"Could you get my medicine out of the bag please?"

Marco lowers her legs.

"Of course."

He dashes to the entrance, picks Teresa's bag up off the floor, takes out the box wrapped in paper from the pharmacy and quickly comes back into the bedroom.

"What do I need to do?"

"Eleven drops in half a glass of water."

Marco dashes to the kitchen, gets the water, returns, sits next to her, holds the glass to her and helps her to sit upright as she drinks it.

Teresa falls back onto the pillow, and the colour slowly returns to her face. After a while Marco starts to talk to her.

"Do you know the risk you've just taken? Do you know the mess you've got yourself into? Why did you do it?"

Teresa is really rather surprised at the natural way the words emerge from her mouth.

"Because I was terrified they might kill you. You won't allow yourself to be taken without putting up a fight with that pistol of yours. That I know."

Marco doesn't know what to say. His eyes are shining. He takes her hand in his and covers it with his other hand. She speaks to him with her eyes closed.

"Don't go."

"Of course I won't."

"Stay here. I'll look after you."

Marco is touched. He smiles at her.

"But you know I can't stay here for ever. And there are other people I need to meet up with."

She turns her head away and nods, swallowing. Marco squeezes her hand more firmly.

"Sooner or later they're going to come here. I need to act quickly."

Teresa breathes out through her nose.

"But I can't go, unless you help me."

A few seconds go by, during which the odd way she is moving her lips seems to indicate that Teresa has been waiting for this request.

She pulls her hand away from Marco, who has been nestling it within his own hands, and sits up.

"Tell me what I need to do."

*

Late in the afternoon Teresa goes out again. She has another bag, bigger than the one she usually uses. When she steps out of the front door, she looks up and down the street cautiously. She walks at a regular pace, despite the agitation she is feeling. She reaches the bus stop and waits.

She gets off at her stop. A short walk, then she goes into the shop she has to enter.

The front wall is completely crammed with television screens of every size, all playing the same channel. There's one that's so big it resembles a cinema screen. Teresa reads the price list, scandalized at the prices: then she stares in enchantment at the monitor, ravished by the quality of the image. Even the sound seems wonderful to her. It is so crystalline, so clean and full, that it is almost disturbing.

The display cases in the middle of the shop are full of mobile phones. Further on is the computer section. Teresa takes a note out of her overcoat pocket and advances to the counter. The assistant smiles at her, filled with curiosity.

"Good evening. What can I do for you?"

"Good evening, I'd like a laptop."

"Ah. Of course. Is it for a present?"

"Oh yes, it is, actually."

"Do you know what you're looking for, or shall I show you a few models?"

"No, I've got it all written down just here, I don't really understand," says Teresa. And she hands the note over to him.

The assistant reads it and nods several times.

"Ah yes, of course. If you can just wait here for me for a minute, I'll go and fetch one from the storeroom."

And off he goes.

Teresa, in the meantime, wanders round the shop. It really is a high-tech Mecca. As she walks over to the household appliances section, she catches sight of a niche with a two-seat leather sofa, surrounded by stereo apparatuses in various price ranges. On the sofa there's a pair of headphones with an antenna. Teresa reflects for a moment and then sits down. She puts on the headphones, half-closes her eyes and leans back in the sofa, enveloped in a few bars of classical music.

After a while, she feels someone tapping her on the shoulder. She opens her eyes. The assistant is looking at her from just inches away. Under one arm, he is holding a box still sealed shut. Teresa takes off the headphones.

"I'm sorry."

"Don't worry, that's always happening! Whenever I lose sight of a customer, I come looking for them here."

They go back to the till. The assistant opens the box containing the computer, gives Teresa a few brief details about the guarantee conditions, stamps the receipt, closes the box again and places it into a plastic bag.

"Here, this is just the modem you need to connect to the Internet. I'll put it in with the guarantee."

Teresa hands over the credit card she was holding ready with the slip of paper.

"Ah, prepaid," says the assistant. "Convenient, isn't it? I wanted to get one for my wife."

Just then, a slight blush passes across Teresa's face.

The assistant deals with the payment, passes her the bag, holding it by the handles, and politely bids her goodbye.

Teresa comes out of the shop and looks to either side. She crosses the road. She goes into a bar and orders a decaf. Then she goes to the toilet. She takes the box out of the bag and the computer out of the box. She puts the computer and the modem for Internet connections into her shoulder bag. She puts the box back into the plastic bag. She comes out of the toilet and leaves the bar. She goes to the exit. The bus soon arrives. Teresa gets on, takes a seat, her shoulder bag slung over her shoulder and the shop bag with the box under her arm. She gets off a stop earlier than the usual one. She locates the nearest trashcan, walks over to it, lifts the lid and throws in the plastic bag with the box. She walks back home.

*

At the front door, there's a woman waiting for her. She is returning home too, carrying a shopping bag. She saw Teresa coming along and is holding the door open for her with her foot. Teresa is momentarily taken aback when she sees her, but she hurries up and goes in before her, thanking her.

"How are you?" asks Teresa.

The woman can barely suppress her tears.

"Terrible."

"What's happened?"

"I really don't know. They've turned my apartment upside down."

"Yes, I heard them."

"I bet you did. Everyone in the whole block heard them."

Teresa clutches the handles of her bag tightly, to ward off her unease at having to lie.

"I'm so sorry."

"Thanks. That's really kind."

They go up. Before saying goodbye, Teresa insists that the woman mustn't hesitate to ask if there's anything she should need.

When she goes back in, she finds Marco in the kitchen, planted in front of the TV as usual.

"All okay?" he says, glad to see her.

"Yes. All sorted."

"You remembered to throw away the box first, right?"

"Of course."

Marco opens the shoulder bag and takes out the computer. A new, bright expression, full of hope, illuminates his face.

Teresa also takes out the credit card.

"Here you are."

"Thanks. That's really kind."

Teresa smiles on hearing the same words that his mother had uttered just now in the same tone of voice.

Marco starts to fiddle with the computer and quickly configures it. Teresa observes him as if she were watching an alchemist at his experiments. Marco takes his key ring from his pocket and selects from this a pen-drive. He inserts it into one of the ports of the computer and opens a text file, which he starts to read avidly. Teresa sits down, taking care not to make any noise, as if fearing she might cause some interference. Marco notices this and smiles. He scratches his chin, reflects, closes the file, and nods as he runs the cursor down the lines of files. He stops. He focuses on the monitor as if he had found the information he was seeking. He types in a command using the fingers of both hands. He picks up the modem that came with the computer for connection to the Internet. He opens his wallet, takes out another SIM card and shoves it into the modem. He attaches the modem to the computer. He proceeds to "settings" and is soon connected. He sends an email (a single word) to an address that he has copied from the file he has just read. Then he unplugs the modem. He folds his fingers together, puts his hands on his head and looks at Teresa, sitting in front of him. She waits a while before speaking.

"What have you done then?"

"Nothing special. Now I'm waiting for news. I'm going to ask you for just one more favour, and then that'll be it."

"And then you're going?"

"Yes, and then I'm going," says Marco a little uncomfortably.

"I saw your mother."

Marco's jaw drops as if a screw had come loose.

"When?"

"Just now. At the front door."

"How is she?"

"I said that if there's anything she needs, I'm always here for her."

Marco pulls a melancholy face as he registers the way Teresa has warded off the question. And, following a natural impulse, probably addressed to his mother, he holds out one hand and strokes her cheek. But Teresa accepts his gesture and looks pleased.

"Will you promise me something?"

"Yes."

"Don't say anything to her. Whatever happens."

"Why? What's going to happen, Marco?"

"Nothing. It's just that I'd prefer it if she didn't know that I'd been here."

"Fine."

"Promise?"

"Promise."

"Thank you."

Marco looks at his watch and then at the computer.

"Marco."

"What?"

"What's going to happen?"

Marco is still wondering what to say when there is a ring at the door. He stares at Teresa with a scared expression on his face, as if he wanted her to tell him what to do.

"Stay calm," says Teresa. "Go into the bedroom."

Marco picks up the computer, the notebook and the various electronic bits and pieces and does as Teresa says. She tidies her hair a little and goes to the door. She takes a deep breath and then lifts the flap of the peephole and looks out.

She turns round to Marco, who peers round the bedroom door and mouths the question, "Who is it?" She puts her finger to her lips. She opens the door.

From the way she looks at Marco's mother, it's as if she has been expecting her. She seems more haggard than when she saw her in the elevator. Her hair is tied back, she's wearing very shabby indoor clothes, and the shadows under her eyes are much darker than they had been before.

"Good evening. I'm sorry, but do you mind if I come in?"

"Of course not. Please, make yourself at home."

She receives her in the kitchen, where, just a moment ago, her son had been. This thought fills Teresa with a sense of guilt, which, however, she takes good care to conceal. Behind the door of the bedroom, Marco bites on the forefinger of his right hand, as when a doctor warns you he's just about to touch you at the point where it hurts, and you prepare yourself for the imminent pain. His mother sits down, barely suppressing a desire to start crying – for which she quickly apologizes.

"Don't worry, it's all right," says Teresa, touching her arm reassuringly.

"You know, I haven't told anyone about it. It's all so strange . . . that's why I've called round."

"You've done the right thing. No need to worry about it."

Marco's mother sniffles.

"You can't imagine what it's like to go home and be too frightened to switch on the television. If I hear the music at the start of the news programme, my heart starts beating so fast that I don't know how I manage not to faint."

Teresa would like to say something vaguely appropriate, but all Marco's mother seems to need is a friendly ear, so she says nothing.

"I can't believe what they're saying."

She licks her upper lip and carefully utters the next words.

"Politics: but what kind of politics? If you've never really talked about it at home, do you ever really know what it means? Not even once, not even a single word."

"I'm so sorry," whispers Teresa.

"I'm afraid," says Marco's mother, lowering her voice, as if she were finally coming to the real point. "Why won't he come home? If he hasn't done anything, and I know he hasn't done anything, why doesn't he call? What's happened to him?"

At that very moment, a noise from the bathroom, like an object falling to the ground, interrupts the dialogue between the two women, who simultaneously turn in that direction and then stare at each other.

Teresa blushes. She doesn't have the slightest idea what to say.

Marco's mother suddenly gets up, looking awkward.

"I'm dreadfully sorry, I really didn't know, please forgive me . . ."

And she hurries to the door.

Then Teresa gets up in turn and follows after her, starting to realize the nature of the misunderstanding.

"Ah, no, not at all . . ."

"It's entirely my fault, I came down without warning . . ." Marco's mother places her hand over Teresa's mouth to stop her speaking. Then she goes out and hurries upstairs.

Teresa gazes after her as she flees. She's flabbergasted. She closes the door and stands for a few seconds in the entrance hall. She could easily burst out laughing, if the situation were not so tragic.

Marco is now sitting in the armchair, the computer is on his knees, turned on, and his hands are riffling through his hair.

"I broke the little round mirror."

Teresa makes no comment.

"But only the handle."

Teresa utters a low snort.

"I'm sorry," he continues, "but I had to stuff toilet paper into my ears. If she'd stayed any longer I'd have come into the kitchen."

"Don't worry, she was feeling better by the time she left."

Marco sketches a faint smile, then changes the subject, as if following an order of priority.

"Tomorrow morning. At quarter past ten. It's the last favour I'll be asking you."

Teresa sits on the bed and listens to him attentively.

*

The next morning, Teresa leaves her home very early. She doesn't take public transport, because it's a nice day and the place she's heading for is not far away. She stops at a newspaper kiosk and buys a magazine devoted to undersea fishing.

At a quarter past ten, she goes into a stationery shop called Mail Corner, where you can also telephone or transfer money over the Internet. Inside there are a certain number of black men and women telephoning, surfing the net or queuing up to transfer money. Teresa fixes her gaze on an assistant with a blond goatee and goes over to him, displaying the cover of the magazine prominently. She asks him to photocopy an article two columns long published in the centre pages.

*

When she returns home, Marco looks in distinctly better shape. He must have taken a shower, since he gives off a fresh smell and has wet hair. Teresa registers this novelty as the sign of his imminent departure and doesn't speak for fear of bursting into tears. She takes off her overcoat, drapes it over the back of a kitchen chair, takes the magazine out of her bag and hands it over to him. Marco takes it from her and opens it. Between the pages there's an envelope. He tears it open. Inside it there's an aeroplane ticket and an identity card. Teresa goes to the window and looks out. She remains there while Marco slips the ticket into his pocket and the document into his wallet.

In the ensuing silence, Marco chooses the words he needs to say to her. It's really difficult.

"I have to go."

Teresa continues to keep her back turned to him, motionless in the window frame.

"Thank you for everything you've done, I won't forget it."

He goes over. Teresa cannot bring herself to turn round. Marco places his hands on her shoulders. She stiffens. She's holding her breath.

Marco enfolds her in his arms, without asking her to turn round. He hugs her tightly, gives her one kiss on her cheek and another on her hair. Then, without waiting a second longer, he goes.

Teresa remains at the window until she can see him coming out through the front door, crossing the street and calmly walking away along the pavement. Only then does she move and starts to wander round her apartment.

Her apartment, suddenly so empty.

*

Marco walks quickly without looking into people's faces, as he had seen a famous actor do in an old film. He arrives at the metro stop and walks down the stairs. He rummages in his pockets when he comes to the automatic ticket machine. He doesn't have any change. He goes towards the newspaper kiosk, a littler further on.

"I don't sell them," says the woman in the kiosk. And she nods in the direction of the ticket office.

Marco turns round, locates the window halfway down the corridor. But its shutter is lowered.

"It's closed!" he observes.

"And what do you expect me to do about it?" she replies.

Marco glances at his watch.

"Fuck you," he mutters between gritted teeth.

And he starts walking quickly towards the trains.

*

Teresa, her arms folded, gazes at the cupboards in the kitchen. She walks round the table. She gazes at the ceiling.

*

There are empty seats in the compartment. Marco sits down in one and peers over at the newspaper of the passenger sitting next to him. The latter notices and moves his paper further away, like a schoolboy who dislikes people cribbing off him. Marco rewards him with a grimace, lowers his eyes to the floor and loses himself in his own thoughts. After a while, someone taps him on the shoulder.

"Ticket please."

Marco looks up at the ticket inspector in perplexity. He gets up, pretends to be rummaging in his jacket and trousers. The inspector waits, but his expression is that of a man who has seen the same performance hundreds of times.

"Oh dear, I'm terribly sorry," concludes Marco after a while. "I can't seem to find it."

"I'm afraid you're in breach of the regulations. Would you mind getting off the train, please?"

"Getting off?"

"Yes, getting off, off the train: what's the matter, is that a problem for you?"

Not much of a problem, thinks Marco to himself, shrugging his shoulders. No need to get into a flap. Plenty of time.

At the next stop, the inspector requests Marco to follow him to an empty bench. He takes out his notebook and starts to fill in a report. Meanwhile, the train empties and sets off again.

"ID please."

Marco hands him the identity card. The man takes it and starts to copy the details onto his form.

Among the people who have just got off the train and are making their way along the platform towards the escalator, a young man with a receding hairline looks in Marco's direction. He seems visibly concerned. Marco does not notice him, intent as he is on following the inspector's procedure. The man comes over. Marco sees him only at the last minute, and his face falls.

"Hi, Marco! What's up, anything I can do to help?" he asks.

The inspector immediately looks up from his notebook and stares Marco in the face.

"What's this? Marco? I thought your name was Antonio?"

A brief but pregnant pause ensues, during which Marco's lie falls irremediably to pieces. He could make something up, maybe say that it's his second name, or that he's been mistaken for someone else: any kind of excuse, even the most stupid – but he can't think of one. He stands there, nailed to his lie, unable to invent a way round it, like a kid whose mother is holding out to him the porn magazine he left in the bathroom just now. He stares at the inspector and his acquaintance, who is unaware of the mess he's just landed him in. Then he suddenly turns tail and dashes off towards the escalator.

The inspector yells at him to stop and then adds something else, which Marco does not understand. He just keeps on running and running: he leaps up the steps three at a time, while people scatter in alarm before him.

*

Teresa, in the bedroom, folds back the blankets and strokes the pillow. She opens and closes the curtains. She sits in the armchair and gets up again.

*

Marco suddenly stops, panting like an asthmatic. At the top of the escalator a cop is already waiting, his pistol drawn. Marco pulls out his own pistol and backs down the stairs. A woman screams. The cop yells at Marco to throw down his weapon, and at the same time, with his other hand, he takes from his belt a bulky telephone and puts it to his ear. Marco continues to move backwards as the sweat pours from his forehead. Behind him, people have flattened themselves against the walls of the escalator, which nobody has thought to stop. "God Almighty," says someone. Is it possible that it might end like this? All because of a metro ticket? He turns round and runs down the steps. If a train arrives straight away, he might yet make it.

DIEGO DE SILVA

He has hardly dashed into one of the two exits that lead to the platforms when, from the opposite side of the tracks, another cop appears, also armed. Marco barely notices him, runs round the corner and dashes down the platform. There is an unnatural silence now.

The cops arrive after a few seconds, running along together. They locate Marco, who has flattened himself into a corner at the far end. They start to advance slowly towards him. Marco grips his pistol and takes aim at them. They do the same.

"Don't do anything stupid. Give yourself up!" one of the two cops advises him in reasonable tones.

Marco trembles. All of this over a ticket. A ticket costing a single fucking euro.

*

Teresa drags herself to the entrance hall, takes the keys to the apartment, opens the door, and goes out. Slowly she climbs the stairs and comes to a halt outside Marco's apartment. She waits for a few moments, then rings the bell. Marco's mother opens up straight away.

"Miss Teresa."

She does not reply.

"What's happened?" the mother asks, moving to one side to ask her in.

Teresa shakes her head, thereby making it clear that if she opens her mouth, she'll burst into tears.

The phone rings. Marco's mother says sorry and goes off to answer it.

*

"I'm not telling you again. Throw the pistol down, *now!*"

Marco hesitates. The whistle of the arriving train forces him to turn for a moment. And that is why he shoots. He would have allowed himself to be arrested, perhaps, if that deafening sound hadn't made him set the trigger on automatic. A hesitant, clumsy shot that doesn't hit anything, like an absolute beginner taking a swipe at a football. But it's enough for the cops.

As the train comes to halt amid a shrill squeal of brakes, Marco is flung backwards as if he had just touched the live rails.

When he lands on the ground, his pistol still in his hand, his eyes assume an expression of melancholy resignation, like the eyes of someone who has just realized he's fallen prey to a hoax.

*

Teresa hears the voice of Marco's mother speaking on the phone in the next room. It must be someone from the family, to judge from the tone of voice she's using. She remains standing in the entrance hall for a while, then goes into the only other room she can see, halfway down the corridor that corresponds to her own. She goes in. Marco's room. His mother must have tidied it up recently, it's so clean and fresh.

Teresa looks around. The bed. The window. The wardrobe. A poster of actor Alberto Sordi, dressed like a traffic cop, with his forefinger raised and wearing an expression like *Il Duce*. A desk with a few books and a photo in a frame. Teresa picks it up to get a closer look.

Marco, a few years earlier, with more hair and a beard, is peeing against a tree. He's holding his hands in front of him, and his face is turned to the photographer as if he's telling him to not even think about taking the photo. A really funny photo. But Teresa doesn't laugh. She places the photo back on the desk and sits on the bed.

From the other room, Marco's mother is still speaking on the phone.

"I don't know anything," Teresa hears her saying between sobs. "I still don't know anything."

Teresa stretches out on the bed, lying on her side. She draws up her legs, leans her head on the pillow, and stares at a corner of the window.

The Last Gag

Sandrone Dazieri

1

This time I've really let myself in for it. The cabaret evening is giving me stage fright even before the curtain has risen. And after that, things just get worse.

The first to come out on stage is a sixty-year-old comic, who since at least the age of forty has been cracking the same jokes about mothers-in-law and honeymooning couples. He calls himself "Giorrrgio", with a trilled "r", and his face is so haggard I'm afraid he may not make it to the end of the show. The audience is thin on the ground, only half the number that usually comes to the Pink Crocodile on normal evenings. And the few people who *are* here look as if they wish they were somewhere else.

Giorrrgio finishes and exits, and the applause is so lukewarm that I can hear the cloakroom attendant masticating his chewing gum in the background. Enter Woodpecker, who plays the drunken conjuror, something that not even veteran comic Gino Bramieri did as a young man. The audience is barely paying attention, and Woodpecker tries to perk things up by firing off a few "fucks" at inopportune moments. The audience hubbub diminishes, but not much, and the noise soon rises again when Woodpecker pretends to pull a rabbit out of the flies of his trousers. *Oh My God*, I think.

Mauro, my barman, comes over to me between serving one customer and the next.

"Charming evening, eh?" he says.

I glare at him.

"It gets even better," he adds and wanders off.

I realize what he means when the following act comes on. He's dressed as a cook. Damn. This was all I needed.

I'm like a cat on hot bricks, but the audience is finally showing signs of life: they chortle when the guy spits on the plate, and the laughter becomes slightly louder when he pretends to wipe the steak over the floor to punish a pain-in-the-butt customer.

Then he starts to overdo it. He flings a fistful of flour at the first rows in the audience and catches a woman in a fur coat who utters an audible curse before running off towards the exit. Any halfway decent comedian would come up with a joke, something sharp and effective, but he just stands there looking taken aback and loses his rhythm. His whole act slows down, and the audience relapses into its boredom.

The cook ends his routine by pouring spaghetti all over his head. He just manages to entice a moderate laugh out of them. He says, "And you'd better all pay up, or else I'll come and piss in your fridges at home." Applause. The cook exits, giving a high-five to Pippo & Budino, the stars of the evening. I don't hang around to find out what they have in store, but get up off my stool and slip into the dressing room.

Maybe "dressing room" is too fancy a term. Seeing that cabaret nights are a new thing with me, I've had a room rigged up in the back, with a curtain separating it from the loos. When I go in, Giorrrgio is bending over the only washbasin in service. "If you have to throw up, please go outside," I tell him.

He turns round. He's removed his foundation cream, and is as yellow as a piece of leftover chicken. "Did you enjoy it, sir?" he asks, looking sheepish.

I stopped him just in time; the washbasin is still clean. "Sure I did," I lie.

The cook is removing his flour-stained clothes. I go over to shake him by the hand, without really knowing quite why. "Well done," I tell him.

"Thanks! Would you like my autograph?"

"Er . . . maybe later."

The voice of Anna, whose stage name is Dragonfly, can be heard in the background. "Careful, he's the man that pays us!" Dragonfly is the singer with the sore throat who bursts out onto the stage at random moments. At present she's waiting for her last entry, drinking a disposable cup full of red wine. She pretends it's Coca-Cola, as if the smell of the wine were imperceptible, or as if any one else cared two hoots about her vices. I know her by sight. Once upon a time she was cute, she did a bit of work on telly, but now she seems like a stand-in for a tenor. It's impossible to say whether she drinks because she's ruined her figure, or whether she's ruined her figure by drinking. However, in her extra-large shape, she manages to get a laugh or two. The kind of laughs that freaks get.

The expression on the cook's face changes. "Ah, sorry, really sorry, sir . . ." Seen from up close he must be twenty-five at most. He has the stocky body of a stevedore.

"No need for formality, my young friend."

"I got in a bit of a tangle, but I finished well, don't you think?" he anxiously inquires.

"Yeah, really well," I try to think of something to say. "That finale with the spaghetti – just great!"

"Isn't it! And the joke about the fridge? Just popped into my head."

"Ah, it wasn't one you'd rehearsed? You've obviously got loads of material," I slap him on the shoulder, then turn to the others. "I just wanted to say hello to you lot. Break a leg and all that."

As I hurry out towards the exit, I see that the cook is staring at me. "Sorry, really sorry, sir . . ." he says. "But now I remember where I've seen you before. Damn it, did you know I'm practically a disciple of yours . . . ?"

He starts walking towards me. I run for it.

2

It's the first Friday for a year that I haven't stayed behind to shut up shop. The boys seem perplexed as they watch me going away. I don't stay to explain, but I think that some of them understand anyway. Mauro, for one, certainly does – he waves me bye-bye with his little hand. Meanwhile, on stage, a quartet of undernourished dancers are jumping about in the tutus of classical ballerinas. I'm not missing anything much, to judge from the yawns in the stalls.

A murk of rain, fog and smog, I take it all in as I jump into my car and drive as far as the Navigli canal area. Then I triple-park and go back to walk along the canals, breathing in the dank odour from the dark water. I have no desire to go home, and I do what people usually do in these situations – I wander round other nightclubs. I drink a couple of tonic waters and chat listlessly for a while, then pop into the Golden Tree in Darsena. It belongs to Bruto, an old friend of mine, but we open and close at the same times, and it seems like a lifetime since I last dropped by to see what he's been getting up to. More than anything else, we keep in touch with each other over the phone, and once every hundred years I go to his place to watch AC Milan playing on his forty-inch screen.

The place hasn't changed. It still looks like an old tavern, tarted up with pink marble and brightly coloured plastic tables and a circle of customers more numerous than mine. I gaze with envy at the throng of people queuing up to drink at the oak counter. At the Golden Tree too there's a show tonight – but here it actually works. On a small dais in the corner, with a threadbare set, two old cabaret artists are singing gangland songs with guitar and kazoo. They've been doing the rounds since the times of that bandit Vallanzasca, but there's life in the old acts yet, and they still bring the punters in. I try to avoid the familiar faces as I elbow my way through the crowd around the bar. Ex-colleagues (or so-called ex-colleagues) especially. As well as a few journalists here to cover the show and a couple of agents. Someone recognizes me all the same, and a couple of them yell "Minestrone!" after me. I pretend I haven't heard.

Bruto comes over to the counter to do the honours of the house. He was a sports rep before he got fed up with footballers and decided, like me, to buy a slice of the action in Milan's drinking holes. He's sixty, wears his grey hair in a pigtail and has the face of someone who can afford to take two months' holiday on a beauty farm every year.

He throws an arm round my shoulders and yells into my ear, "How did the experiment go?"

"You mean the cold fusion?"

"Any use for making ice cream?"

"Not really. In plain and simple terms, I won't be trying it again."

"If you ask me, you're starting to feel nostalgic."

I look at him. "Don't say it. Not even as a joke. I only agreed because the guys from the agency are friends of mine, and I wanted to give them a hand. But once is enough for the next ten years."

"If you change your mind, I'll organize an evening performance for you. There's plenty of folks who'd like to see old Sammy back in action again."

"That was in another life, Bruno, and I don't miss it."

"Really?"

"Pretty much."

"Let me buy you a drink then." He calls over the barmaid. She's an attractive woman, about thirty-five, face looking a bit drawn and tired round the edges. "Serve this old celebrity with all the respect he deserves."

"Straight away," she replies. She has a nice voice, husky caused by smoking too many cigarettes. I have a weakness for husky voices.

Bruto wanders off, the girl smiles at me. "What'll you have?"

"A Coke."

She opens a bottle.

"You're an old celebrity in what?"

"Sport. The hundred metres, five minutes flat."

She looks at me dubiously.

"I'm joking. I used to be on stage, once upon a time."

Now she looks at me more attentively. "So that's where I've seen you before. But you used to have a beard, right? Sammy Donati."

"What a good memory you have."

"Ooh, you're famous! *And I'll put it in the minestrone!*"

She does a good imitation. It sends a shiver down my spine. I lift up my hand. "Let's change the subject."

"You were good."

"There were plenty of people that didn't share your opinion."

"Pah! Critics!" She slices the lemon. "Sammy your real name?"

"Nope. Just my stage name. Not all that original. My birth certificate says Samuele."

I see her looking thoughtful as she passes a table napkin to a girl who's spilt her sparkling wine over her spangled skirt. If you want to know where things are happening in showbiz, look for the places where the girls are showing the most thigh. This one is hanging on the arm of a theatre manager from the higher strata of the trade: four-star hotels and national TV networks. He's dyed his hair and pretends he doesn't know me. Once upon a time I'd have chucked my glass at his face.

The barmaid turns to me, "So it's important, then, the stage name?"

"Less than it used to be, but yes, I'd say it is. Why? You fancy becoming an actress too?"

"Not me – it's my son. He's fantastic. He'll need to get a stage name."

"How old is he?"

"Twelve."

"I'd never have guessed you had a boy that old."

She smiles again. "Thanks." She gives me my glass, adorned with a Chinese parasol. "His name's Alberto. He's already been on *Junior Fame Academy*. Maybe you've seen him. On the telly."

I suppress a shudder. *Junior Fame Academy* is a circus for precocious brats. There's always the six-year-old Chinese trapeze artist and the ten-year-old crooner. "Don't think so."

"He told jokes. You should have seen the audience laughing. They weren't putting it on either."

"A budding genius!" I say with more irony than I'd intended. Me and my big mouth.

She stiffens. "If you don't believe me, come and see him." She rummages under the counter and thrusts a piece of paper into my hand. "Next Thursday."

I sit there like a total dope holding the flyer while she heads off to serve Gio*rrr*gio. So he's turned up too. The Golden Tree really is a sanctuary for all sinners.

The flyer is the typical cheap-looking mimeographed affair of the kind I used to publicize my own talents when I started out. There's an ad for the local social club in Bovisa, with an evening devoted to *New Cabaret Acts*. I stick it in my pocket. The barmaid has buttonholed Gio*rrr*gio, who's chattering away, delighted that someone's paying him attention. I force myself between them. She looks at me coldly, and Gio*rrr*gio even more so. I shove Gio*rrr*gio discreetly out of the way with a nudge of the hips and smile at the barmaid.

"What's your name?"

"Lisa."

"Listen, Lisa, I didn't mean to offend you just now. If your son is as on the ball as you say, he'll certainly go far."

"It's like I said. He . . ." she says, all ready to fly off the handle again.

"Fine," I interrupt, "I was just worried in case you might be storing up disappointments. The showbiz world is a ruthless place. They're sharks out there. Always ready to bite. I know. I've been there."

Eventually her smile returns. "You know about getting bitten, then?"

"When we can be alone together for a while, I'll show you the scars. But we need to talk it over with a bit of peace and quiet. Not in this den of thieves where you have to serve all those winos. Somewhere else."

"Such as?"

"Such as why don't we have dinner?"

A moment's suspense. My cheeks are hurting, I'm smiling so much.

"You'll tell me about the old times?" she asks me.

"I'll tell you about the new times too."

"Evenings I'm always here, except Thursdays when I go to my son's cabaret."

"That's nearly a week away. Too long. So what I suggest is we do lunch. By the light of the sun I'm not so handsome, but I'll take the risk."

She hesitates. "Okay. Sunday?"

"I'll call by to pick you up with a big bunch of orchids."

We swap mobile phone numbers, then she returns to distribute drinks to those that thirst.

I lift up my eyes and look at myself in the mirror to congratulate myself. Reflected in the mirror behind me is the face of Caterina.

3

I sit there for a while staring at her, surprised. To my amazement, for a few seconds I don't have the usual sinking feeling in the pit of my stomach. Then along it comes, the same as ever. Even if it's been three years since I last saw her, even if she looks skinnier and rather run down. Even if I decided all that time ago that I hate her and would like to see her dead.

By the time I've recovered from my stupefaction, Caterina has already disappeared towards the exit, after making the typical gesture of one person telling another one where to get off. The person in question is Bruto, who comes over to me shaking his head. Without quite knowing why, I sidestep him and run outside.

Caterina has vanished. I look for her in all the surrounding streets, and it takes me a while to track her down. She's walking along the towpath, zigzagging like a drunk. I'm on the water's edge, I run to the first bridge, then come back along the other bank towards her. I meet her outside a fortune-teller's booth. She almost bumps into me.

"Caterina . . ."

She stares at me as if she doesn't know who I am. Now that I look at her more closely, she seems even more haggard. She has a nasty bruise over her eye, the sign of a bang that's starting to turn yellow.

She looks at me as if I were a stranger. "Sammy? What you doing here?"

"I was in the club, I followed you. What's happened?"

She walks straight past me. "None of your fucking business."

She carries on walking quickly. I think I ought to just let her go, but I catch up with her.

"Get lost!" she shouts.

I've never seen her looking like this. She isn't like this in my dreams. In fact, when I dream about her, she's usually on her knees, weeping and asking me to forgive me. "Caterina," I say now, "you're behaving like a candidate for the funny farm. What's the matter, who's been hitting you?"

She lifts her hand to touch the bruise, then breathes heavily with her mouth open and seems to calm down a bit. "That was an accident. I have to go."

"Caterina . . ."

She closes her eyes for a minute. "Have you seen Luca?"

The question is so unexpected that I'm left speechless. "Me?"

She shakes her head. "Drop it. I was talking rubbish. Ciao." She

242

walks off a short distance. Then she turns back. "Sorry, Sammy. Can you lend me some money?"

"Money?"

"Whatever you can manage, even just fifty euros. I . . . came out without my ATM card . . ." She bites her lips. "I could do with some cash. I'll give it back the next time I see you."

Again, I just can't think straight. I take two fifty-euro banknotes out of my pocket and give them to her. She grabs them. "Thanks. I'll call you."

I watch as she walks away and suddenly notice how cold it is. I left my jacket in the club. I go back. The party's almost over: the last regulars are the only people left, and the shutter is half pulled down. Lisa has vanished, Bruto is sitting on a stool, smoking a prime stinker with the singing duo.

"I was thinking you'd gone off to beddy-byes," he says.

"I bumped into someone I wasn't expecting to see." The two musicians say goodbye and leave; I take one of their seats. "Caterina."

Bruto raises his eyebrows. "Well, well. What a surprise!"

"I only managed to talk to her for a few seconds. She looked awful. She was looking for Luca, she asked me if I'd seen him. Just imagine."

"Poor gal. And Luca! Poor guy. Or total dickhead, depending on your point of view."

"Is there something I ought to know?"

He gazes at the tip of his cigar. "What interest is it to you?"

"I don't even know if it is. But it's three in the morning, I've had a shitty evening, and perhaps I'm not thinking very straight. I've never seen Caterina looking like that. Never."

"Luca's a dopehead, Sammy. So's she. Maybe not quite so much as him."

My head starts spinning. "Mind if I help myself?"

"Be my guest."

I walk round the counter and look yearningly at the bottles. You never stop being an alcoholic. You just stop drinking. I help myself to a tonic water, pretending there's some vodka inside it; then I prop myself up on my elbows next to Bruto.

"Cute barmaid," he says.

"I want to hear the rest of the story."

"There's nothing to say – and if you dropped by to see me every now and again, you'd know that. Luca's doing drugs."

"Heroin?"

"You kidding? That's *so* last year. Nah: coke. It screws you up just as nicely, and there's more of it going round. When I shut up for the night, I always find loads of the stuff next to the washbasins in the loos. Before long I'm going to start handing it out as small change."

"I can't believe it. Not Luca. He didn't even use to smoke pot. And Caterina . . . She used to look after her health."

"Times change. People change too. You'll have noticed that Luca hasn't worked for quite a while . . ."

"I don't hang out in those circles any more, I don't even go to the cinema. I chuck away the entertainments pages in the papers. All part of the therapy."

"Anyway, he's up shit creek. Without a paddle." He taps the ash from his cigar. "And with Caterina, it's a disaster. They fight, they kiss and make up, they start all over again. He disappears from home, then, when he's run through his money, he goes back to her. Last week Luca was here having a drink and she came in and started giving him hell. They looked like two junkies at death's door. They *are* two junkies."

"How long's all this been going on?"

"Him being a dopehead? A good year, I'd say, but he was starting to go off the rails before that. Happy?"

"Don't talk crap."

"Sure?"

"I really don't give a shit about it, Bruto. Not a fucking shit. They're part of my past life. It's over."

"Good thing for you it is."

"Too damn right."

I decide not to think any more about it. I don't think about it as I'm returning home, I don't think about it as I get into bed, and I don't think about it as I count the hours and wait for sleep to come. It doesn't. I've just got off when the telephone rings. It's Bruto. He tells me that Caterina's been arrested. The cops are saying she's bumped off Luca.

4

Three journalists phone me to get my reaction, I tell them all to get lost. They persist; a gang of them camps out in front of my house, so I clamber over the wall of my backyard and flee. They write that I'm distraught with grief, they write that I've gone crazy, they write that I don't give a flying fuck. They rummage round in my past; they publish old photos, and the TV people put on clips from my old shows. I can't watch them, but I'm starting to see in the eyes of passers-by an expression that I really hoped I'd seen the last of. *But look, isn't that . . . ?*

No, it isn't, I'm not. Not any more. Once upon a time I'd have paid good money to get all this attention, but now I don't even show my face at the club in case I get harassed by a nosy paparazzo. Mauro chucks out two who'd been lying in wait.

The only people I can't avoid are the cops. They call me in to make a statement or whatever the fucking thing's called. Two days have gone by, and I know a bit more. Luca got his head smashed in; then, when he was dead, he was dragged into his car and taken to the countryside outside the San Giovanni district and burned along with the whole vehicle. When he was found he was still smouldering. They identified him from the car number plate and his dental records. It's him all right: no disappearing tricks to escape his creditors. When they burned him he'd already been dead for quite a while. A few days.

The cop questioning me, or rather, listening to me the way you would listen to a useful witness, is a Sicilian, about fifty-five. With moustaches yellowed by nicotine. His name's Ferolli, and the sign on his door explains that he's director of the Flying Squad. In the police HQ at Via Fatebenefratelli, he has an office that looks as if it belonged to the deputy-head of some school out in the sticks: dark, dirty, with Inter football banners hanging on the wall between the photo of the Italian President and the national flag. He behaves in an almost civil manner, even if he doesn't do anything to put me at my ease. He asks me about my past with Luca and then about my meeting with Caterina on the evening of the murder.

I tell him what I know. It's not much. My information about Luca is as old as the Ark, apart from what Bruto has told me. Ferolli asks me if I resented Luca and his success.

I'd been expecting this question, and my reply is quite sincere. "Yes. I did resent it for a while. It's only human, if you ask me."

"Of course," he says in a conciliatory tone. "Signor Melis never tried to get back in touch with you?"

"Yes."

"When?"

"Two years ago. He left me messages on my answerphone."

"And you . . . ?"

"I never got back to him. I didn't even listen to the messages through to the end. Once he even came to my club, but I got them to tell him I wasn't there. He went away."

"What do you think were his reasons for trying to see you?"

"I think he wanted to make up. But now I'm not so sure."

"Meaning?"

I looked thoughtful. "I think he was looking for help. Things weren't going so well for him, work-wise."

"And you could have helped him."

"No."

He ends up by asking me about my movements during the week before they found Luca. It's not difficult for me to reconstruct them: I was at the club, day and night. Ferolli listens, takes notes, then sweeps his hand through what's left of his hair.

"Seems to me we're done."

"What? Already?"

"What were you expecting us to do? Shine a bright light in your eyes and slap you about with a wet cloth?" He stares at me. "But if you do have anything to tell me, go ahead."

"No. Sorry."

He continues to stare at me. "You can say anything at all here, we'll consider it as confidential. Even a confession."

I'm so dumbfounded that I'm left speechless.

He smiles: his teeth are as yellow as his moustache. "Don't worry. Just joking. Typical cop's joke. We're not inclined to think it was you."

I swallow hard. "Me?"

"Doesn't it seem like a plausible motive to you – professional jealousy?"

"I run a club."

"You didn't always. But actually, yes, it's been quite a while since your last job." Ferolli finishes taking notes, then he gets a uniformed cop to type it all out. I read it through: it's what I said, but in bureaucratese:

I never met the victim at any date later than . . .

He proffers me his hand, and I shake it. "Signor Ferolli, do you really think it was Caterina?"

He shakes his head, looking non-committal. "Take care, Donati."

I emerge from his office feeling like I'd just passed an exam. A well-dressed man with dark jowls is standing out in the corridor. A cop in civvies, I think.

"Signor Donati?"

"Have you guys changed your mind? Am I under arrest?"

He raises his eyebrows, looking really surprised. "I hope not. I'm Mirko Bastoni. I'm a solicitor."

"Oh, is this how it works? You lie in wait for clients? I don't need a solicitor, see."

"I'm defending Signora Moretti."

"Caterina."

"Yes. I'd be really glad to have a quick chat with you. Can I buy you a coffee at the bar?"

"Why, if you don't mind me asking?"

He smiles. A weary smile that immediately makes me like him. "I need your help."

5

When I leave Bastoni it's almost noon. My head's in a muddle, and I'm not in the best of tempers for my first date with a girl I fancy. But opportunity knocks only once, and I book the table at the Zen sushi bar next to the Piazza Duomo. Lisa arrives on time, but wants to sit at the bar with the Japanese salarymen, so I agree, to please her. The bar is a long spiral that winds its way round the middle of the club; in the middle are the cooks who prepare the food in public. The plates of sushi go round and round on a little conveyor belt, and you take the one you want. Lisa is fascinated. From the way she struggles with her chopsticks, it's clear that she isn't very used to this kind of food. I give her a hand, and this really helps to breaks the ice.

"You didn't bring me those orchids," she says at one moment. She's been talking a bit about her son, but it wasn't as bad as I'd feared. Parents are all the same, even if they usually want their offspring to be engineers and not stars of the stage.

"What's that? Oh, sorry. You're right, but with everything that's been happening . . ." I take a sip of my green tea. "I'm not a hundred per cent today, you'll have to forgive me."

"You mean the business about Luca Melis?"

"Yeah."

"It's a shame. Were you friends?"

"We had been friends. In another life."

"The life you still need to tell me about. You promised, remember? Your old wounds."

"D'you really want to hear?"

"You betcha. I promise I won't sell your story to the papers."

She gazes at me. I think *why not?* Sometimes you have to get things off your chest if you don't want to explode. "Okay. Let's start in the year of Our Lord 1990."

*

The idea for *Lunch from Hell* had come to me while I was watching an old film in which Tognazzi played the cook and shared roles with Gassman; at the end, the customers were contentedly eating a minestrone in which everything within reach had ended up. I'd thought it might be a sketch that could be repeated as it was, in the Brutos style, but the idea had started to grow. I felt I'd got hold of something good, even if Luca, to begin with, wasn't convinced. Too much like a curtain-raiser, in his view. But I was filled with the divine spark of creation, and I quickly persuaded him it would be good.

He and I had been working together for a good couple of years, trying to get people to buy our idea of a comedy duo – a pretty classic idea, as classic as they come, actually. He was pinched and skinny and I was thickset and square-jawed; he was posh, I was a coarse, ignorant guy. We'd tried out a heap of names, starting with

"The Two Noodleheads" and "Luca & Sammy, cheesy & hammy", without taking much of a liking to any of them. And nobody had taken much of a liking to us either. We had the determination, the intelligence and the physique, but we always lacked that little *je ne sais quoi* that makes all the difference. We lacked our own "voice." Even when we came up with something that "worked" on stage, we always looked like a poor copy of somebody else. And who wants a poor copy when they can have the original? And who remembers the copy anyway? That's the main thing.

Still, we got work. Mime school, dance school, every day we ploughed our way through the papers in search of new gags. All offers of work were gratefully accepted, even if the pay was minimal. Even if we worked for free, actually, so long as it gave us a chance to get ourselves known. We so much wanted to make it, to emerge from the mass of those doomed to failure, that our longing to be a success made us ill.

Or rather, made *me* ill.

I started waking up at night with breathing difficulties. It was like having a ten-ton weight pressing down on my chest. A weight on which was written, in block capitals, the words: YOU'RE A FAILURE. The future appeared to me as a long grey tunnel of grimy one-room studios, final reminders, clapped-out autos, pizza by the slice and girls who dumped me because they'd got sick of a guy who was only happy when he was on stage and didn't have enough money to afford a holiday. Or worse. Real grinding poverty. The night shelter.

Unlike me, Luca always kept his cool. He never got angry, not even when a theatre manager stood us up at the last minute. If we got jeers and catcalls, his ears never burned like mine, he was never jealous of the little squirts who managed to wangle TV contracts. Not that he was an optimistic old fart: he just had an absolute faith in his own capabilities and was convinced that he'd get there sooner or later. Without him, I'd have chucked it all in, I reckon.

Or maybe not. Deep down, there wasn't anything else I could do. My work experience outside of showbiz was limited to a few months as a sales rep for cash registers – something really close to my personal idea of a hell on earth. And once you hit thirty it's a bit late to go back to college and get qualifications for a desk job.

But just then we got something good going. Starting out from the initial premise of a dust-up between the cook and the waiter in a greasy spoon, we developed an hour-long show. The old repertoire could go to hell, and the old gags too. Everything scripted, not much improvisation, two completely new characters. The cook was to show a pathological hatred for the customers, who never showed any appreciation for his efforts; and the waiter, a man of great elegance, was to be his victim. We wrote the first draft in a week, practically without getting any sleep. And, believe it or not, it worked.

More than that: it was a perfect comic mechanism, it was "the right stuff."

We started to take it on tour. Evening after evening, changing things that didn't work as and when necessary. More or less overnight, the Cook stopped being just a stroppy lout and started to incarnate the wisdom of ordinary folk, like a stock figure from the Commedia dell'Arte. He proffered his judgements on the world and expressed the common sense of the man in the street. He took the piss out of fashion, technology, computers. The Waiter transformed himself from a victim figure into a sort of English butler, waxing lyrical on poetry and literature, making friends with the important customers by plying them with gossip about politicians and football players and managing to put the Cook in his place with his sharp retorts.

Lunch from Hell had been born. The show started to appear in places where previously they wouldn't even have let us in to empty the ashtrays: the Circolone in Legnano, the Bolgia Umana in Jannacci, then the Ca' Bianca – and in those days, performing at the Ca' Bianca really meant something – and then the Zelig. By this time we'd signed on an agent, name of Marcello, and the agent had ensured we got to take the show around and gave us our first appearances on TV. Just local channels, you know, but the programmes weren't bad. Kids watched them, and so did the big theatre managers, the ones who were looking for people to put on prime-time national TV. We started to get recognized in the streets, the money started coming in. And I knew, for the first time, what it meant to have backed a winner – and even to be riding it across the finishing line. I could feel it, just as, to begin with, I'd felt the spectre of failure and poverty.

Then Luca had come up with the idea of letting the public in on the act.

It had come to him after a particularly successful episode on a private TV channel, with the audience chorusing our classic lines, of the "And I'll put it in the minestrone!" type. That evening we'd got a guy up out of the audience and forced him to play the role of the customer. Whatever he asked for became the pretext for me to start insulting him and threatening to chuck something at him. The audience was helpless with laughter.

Luca told me his idea while he was taking his make-up off in the TV dressing room. He used to wear a load of greasepaint to make himself look even more pale and pinched. "What if we always did it?" he'd said.

"What?"

"Take a volunteer from the audience and give him a hard time. If there's someone well known in the audience, even better."

"Dunno about that. Seems to me it breaks the rhythm up."

"No, I don't think so. A whole load of new stuff came out. We can use it."

"But it relies too heavily on improvisation. Half the gags we'd scripted we didn't even get to use."

"Did it go down well with the audience, yes or no?"

"Yes . . ." I admitted reluctantly. "But it's a risk. If we pick on someone who turns out to be a wet blanket, the whole thing will just flop."

"Maybe you're right." But he wasn't convinced.

In fact, we talked about it over the following evenings, and we even included Caterina in our discussions. Caterina was my girlfriend and the third, unofficial, member of the duo. We always rehearsed in front of her, and her judgement was fundamental. If there was something she didn't like, we could be certain it would never work. Luca and I trusted her so much that we cut everything that didn't make her laugh.

And laugh she did. She was fantastic. On difficult evenings we'd put her in the front row, to give me courage. I'd picked her up just after a show, and it was her laugh that attracted me. And I'd discovered that she was intelligent, as well as beautiful – though her beauty was of an idiosyncratic kind, with nothing flashy about it. She had the body of an athlete, licked into shape by years of gymnastics. She worked as an interpreter and hostess at the Milan Trade Fair.

To my great disappointment, Caterina sided with Luca.

"I think it's a really great idea," she said.

I glared at her. We were at my place, which was actually not a one-room studio in a block of cheap lets, but a posh three-room apartment at Porta Genova, with a really lovely courtyard garden into which I could flick cigarette ends.

"Don't take it personally, Sammy," she continued. "It adds an extra pinch of salt. People identify with the guy who's the victim of your gags, and if he doesn't work out, you can always just leave him standing around looking like a complete nerd and go ahead with the script. That'll get a laugh too."

I didn't like it, I really didn't like it. Even if I couldn't quite put my finger on why. But I was too used to trusting in her judgement. "Two against one," I said. "All right, let's give it a go."

Caterina was right, as always. The guest we chose from the audience added a new dynamic to the performance. We were no longer a duo, but a trio that changed from one performance to another. We ended our appearances on local TV using this basic scheme, and we repeated it on the evenings we went live. At the Golden Gnat awards in Bologna, we got one of the jury members up on stage and turned him inside out like a sock. Result: we won. Then we also won the Grand Prize at the Saint-Vincent, and so many offers came flooding in that we started to say no. We could allow ourselves the luxury of taking breaks and being a bit choosy. We even took risks, like saying goodbye to TV for a while and going off on tour round the theatres of northern Italy. We repeated half the shows – they'd sold out. It was a complete success, and even the papers took notice: rave reviews, interviews . . .

The only problem was me. I was going through hell.

Now that the performance took the shape of a trio, people were gradually starting to laugh at my gags a little less. The outbursts of general hilarity had died down, the applause that had been so loud I had to pause had started to become less frequent. The show was working better than ever before, but the centre of attention had shifted. Luca, appearing in the role of the Waiter, had become the defender of the fall guy we dragged up from the audience. And people sided with him. They longed for the gag that would put the Cook in his place: only then could they allow themselves to release a really big, liberating belly laugh. Luca drank it all in. Not that he'd just been there as my stooge beforehand, but his role was definitely subtler, almost too serious at times to provoke the audience to hilarity. Now he only had to pull a face, and he robbed me of my laugh. And his asides with the customer had become the centrepiece of the show.

I felt torn apart. On the one hand I was now enjoying the success I'd always craved, but on the other, I was jealous, horribly jealous – of Luca.

Our work started to be affected by it. I began to quarrel with him more and more often. We quarrelled at rehearsals, we quarrelled before we went onstage, we quarrelled afterwards. During the show I tried to divert attention from him. I'd shout my lines so people couldn't hear him. I camped up my role.

I fantasized about leaving him, but I wasn't ready, and the idea of what might happen without *Lunch from Hell* frightened me. I had a load of ideas for a solo show, and I worked on them in secret, but none of them was as good as the Cook-Waiter duo. I knew this, and I kept telling myself as much at moments of calm. *Wait Sammy. Wait.*

You're great.

But it didn't work. To say that this was why I started drinking wouldn't be true. I always drank as much. Those who've worked their way up through the clubs can be divided into two categories, the heavy drinkers and the teetotallers. There's no in-between. I was a heavy drinker, but to begin with I was sensible. I drank after the show, after the rehearsals, after the studio sessions and the preparations. Now I started to drink before them.

On more than one occasion I turned up on stage plastered. The audience never noticed. Basically, the Cook was a brute, and if he tripped up over his words, if he floundered, it was all in character. But Luca was obliged to think on his feet to cover the times I fluffed my lines. He'd give me my cue, wait in vain for me to reply, then turn towards the audience requesting help in his "English Lord" tone of voice – which I had started to hate. Then he'd turn to me and feed me my lines, quite openly. The audience roared.

My relations with Caterina had also started to turn sour. At the worst times, I accused her of being on Luca's side and plotting against me. She put up with it for as long as she could, then she packed her bags and went back home. I started to sleep alone more and more frequently. I also started to say no and to skip engagements, just out of a desire to place Luca in difficulties. It was a suicidal tactic, and I knew it, but I couldn't stop myself.

Marcello, my agent, invited me to lunch after a week during which my tantrums had been particularly irksome. He listened to the tale of my gripes and my frustrations – good agents must have the patience of a saint. Then he dropped his bombshell. "I'm going to make you an offer you can't refuse."

They wanted us on RAI. Channel One.

"Cabaret is the latest thing," he said. "And they've realized they're falling behind the competition. They want to do a daily stint devoted to cookery. There's going to be a female presenter" – he told me her name – "and you're going to be the comic entr'acte between one guest and the next. They're counting on audience figures of at least five million per episode, maybe more. They want you to sign for two months, renewable. Of course you'll have to clean up your act a bit, but I don't think you'll need to bust a gut to do that."

Then he told me how much. It was a lot of money. But even if it had just been peanuts, it wouldn't have changed anything. Loads of people would be watching me. I'd become a member of their family, a daily habit. "I'm in," I said. "But it's got to be the old format. No customer."

Marcello agreed. The entr'actes were too short to include three people. He'd negotiate with Luca to get him to accept – I had the impression he'd already brought him up to speed. That left just one formality: the audition. The managers of the channel wanted to see us do a dummy run, within the time the broadcast required. I unhesitatingly accepted. I felt I had the world in the palm of my hands. I was wrong.

6

I've been talking for practically a whole hour. Lisa has polished off six little plates of fish and is now tucking into a tart that looks like a miniature version of the huge confections made by Disney's Grandma Duck.

"So how did it go?"

I draw a deep breath. The memory still smarts. Seven years have gone by, and I still feel it in the pit of my stomach. "Badly. I'd sworn to myself that I wouldn't drink, but I'd already hit the bottle in the dressing room. I was convinced I hadn't overdone it, but by the time I came onstage to introduce myself, I was barely able to stand. It was as if I was looking at everything through a haze, it was all blurry . . ."

"What a nightmare."

"Yeah. I tried to get a grip, but I'd lost it. My head was empty. I was giggling. I was wobbling on my legs. A painful sight."

Lisa takes my hand. "You poor guy."

"I'd deserved it, completely deserved it." I enfold her fingers in mine. "After a while the director came to make me get off the stage. I resisted: he took me by the arm and I lashed out at his face. I happened to be holding a bottle of olive oil. I broke his nose. Sammy the comedian's final rousing performance."

"But not Luca's," said Lisa.

"No. The rest is history. Luca signed up with RAI and did a solo programme, with a certain success. And he carried on, with the wind in his sails, while I was now finding it difficult to even wangle a performance in provincial theatres. News gets round, as with the director whose nose I broke. After a while nobody wanted me any more. I stayed at home, watching Luca on TV and hating myself. And Caterina. She paired up with him after the business with the audition. I don't know if things had already been developing between them, and I don't want to know." I drop my chopsticks, I haven't used them much. But in any case, I'm not really hungry. "Eventually things went better for me. I joined Alcoholics Anonymous and opened a bar. AA's just like in the films: there are sessions with people sitting in a circle and saying, 'Hi, my name's So-and-so and I'm an alcoholic.' I attended for five years, and I've never drunk since. I spend all day surrounded by bottles of booze, and I resist the temptation." I smile. "Sorry. I've been boring you stiff."

Lisa strokes my face. "Not at all. You tell a good story."

"You can thank the Actor's Studio for that. I deserve an Oscar."
I lean forward and kiss her.

Then we kiss again as we go along the street to the Golden
Tree. I try to convince her to call in sick, but no way. We agree to
meet after closing time. And I need to work, basically. Even if it's
not my usual work.

7

Bastoni, the solicitor, had made a convincing case, or maybe I
just wanted to be convinced at any price. He'd offered me that
coffee he'd mentioned, then he'd talked to me about Caterina.
She was in a bad way. She'd been taken to the hospital ward in
the San Vittore prison, and was being weaned off her habit with
the help of psychotropic drugs. She was scared and confused.
"Given the state she was in," Bastoni said, "if we asked for a
verdict of diminished responsibility, I'd stand a good chance of
getting it for her. And I could even play the 'legitimate defence'
card." He'd explained to me that Luca had been knocking her
about recently. I'd already deduced as much from the marks on
her face.

But Caterina insisted she was innocent. The solicitor couldn't
make head or tail of it. "She can't reconstruct her movements, she
has only the vaguest idea of what she was doing before, during
and after the murder of Signor Melis. Then there's the fact that
traces of the victim's blood have been found at her home and,
according to the path lab, this is compatible with the date of the
murder. Maybe Signor Melis happened to cut his finger that day,
but Signora Moretti can't explain the blood."

"Caterina came looking for Luca at the club the other night.
But Luca had already been dead for a fair while, hadn't he? Why
would she have done that if she'd killed him?"

"Given the state she was in, my client could quite well have
repressed any memory of the murder. This happens more often
than you'd think, especially in cases like this. And then we need
to take into consideration the hypothesis that she put on an act to
create an alibi for herself."

"She wasn't lying, I saw her. I spoke to her."

"Your opinion will be duly noted, but . . ." The solicitor shrugged eloquently.

"So she's had it?" I asked.

"Not necessarily. The murder weapon hasn't been found, and nobody can work out where Signor Melis's body was kept before it was burned. Three days elapsed between the murder and the blaze, and Signora Moretti can't possibly have kept it in the car that was in the underground car park at her home."

"In the wood where it was burned?"

"No. It's a place where couples hang out together, and people go to smoke a quiet joint. They'd have seen it earlier. And why hide the body in a wood only to go and burn it later? Risky, don't you think?"

"True." I just wasn't getting any of this.

"Furthermore, the police are checking for possible leads in the drug-pushing world, even if they don't nurse much hope."

"Why?"

"Signor Melis still had enough money to pay his suppliers, and he definitely did pay them – he was still doing coke. And usually, if it's a supplier who bumps you off – and this rarely happens – he burns you straight away, he doesn't keep you at home like a tailor's dummy. But you never can tell."

He gave me other details. A printout of phone calls – not much use given that Luca never used his mobile for fear of getting cancer; questions asked of the neighbours; results of the autopsy. In all of this, Caterina remained the only possible guilty person. The neighbours had heard them having a hell of a row on the day of the murder. And the bruises on Caterina's face and body (apart from the ones she already had) went back to that very same day.

It was one big mess.

As I tried to absorb all this information, my gaze wandered round the bar. Apart from Bastoni and myself, there were only four uniformed cops laughing and joking as they chewed on their sandwiches. Perhaps they had been the ones who'd found Luca's corpse. I wondered how it affected you, living with violence and death day in, day out. How it marked you.

"What can I do? I've already told people what I knew."

Bastoni stirred his coffee. "I'll be frank. Signora Moretti doesn't have many options. With the cards I hold, to try pleading innocent would be pretty much like committing suicide."

"I'd gathered that much."

"I need to know more about Signor Melis, especially what he was doing on the days leading up to his murder. If he had enemies that we don't know about. That kind of thing."

"The police are investigating . . ."

"The police have everything they need to put Signora Moretti away. And the judge is going to agree with them. I'm afraid an extra investigation won't be required. In this case it's the defence – i.e. me – that needs to get moving."

"How?"

"It's here that you come into the picture. My client tells me you and she are close friends, she's often mentioned your name."

"Really?"

"Yes. And I read in the papers about who you are and what you used to do with the late Signor Melis. You're the only person who can help me. You know the showbiz world, and you know all of Signor Melis's friends, even those who used to be his friends."

"Hang on a minute . . . there are private detectives for that kind of thing."

"We have a few people like that too, they occasionally help us out. The new statutes on the law books make allowance for it. To tell you the truth, we only use one – the Pellaccia practice isn't all that big – but he isn't the best at his job. He's a total bungler, to be perfectly honest with you." He winked at me. "And in the showbiz world he wouldn't be able to move around as well as you. I'm not asking you to give anyone the third degree, just to ask around a bit, discreetly. It's all grist to the mill. If Signora Moretti is innocent, Signor Melis must have met up with someone before the murder. It would be really useful to know who, but I'd be satisfied with less. Gossip doing the rounds, vague suspicions . . ."

"And if Caterina really is guilty?"

"If this is the conclusion you reach, Signor Donati, let me know. I'll try to convince my client to change her line of defence."

"It's quite a responsibility."

"Someone has to assume it."

"Me?"

258

"Why not? You surely don't want my client to suffer, do you? I don't think so. I'll be checking any info you give me. I'm not a complete beginner at this game."

"And what if the real murderer decided that my intrusion isn't welcome? I have my own back to cover."

"If you feel you're in any danger, let me know. Of course, I can't force you . . ." He pulled out of his briefcase a bunch of keys from which a length of twisted leather was hanging. "It so happens I've got Signora Moretti's keys with me. As I told you, the house has already been searched, but seeing that the body was found elsewhere, it hasn't been sealed off. You could maybe have a look round. You might just notice something that the police wouldn't, or couldn't, see."

I dropped the keys into my pocket. Bastoni finally took a sip of his coffee. "Ugh. It's cold."

8

This is one crazy story, I think as I call by at my club. We're closed in the early afternoon, so I limit myself to checking the accounts and the stock list. But my heart's not in it. Caterina's keys are burning a hole in my pocket. I make my mind up and leave.

Caterina and Luca had been living in a street just off the Trade Fair in Milan, an area where people with money to burn live. I went there just the once, when Luca bought the apartment, a couple of months before he and I went our separate ways. *For ever,* I say to myself. Not that I'd ever thought of going back to work with him, but death has one nasty drawback: it makes everything definitive. I find the apartment block, I unlock the front door and go up to his apartment. Of course there are the neighbours on the landing, an elderly couple, staring at me with curiosity. The old guy asks me if I'm from the police, and I tell him the little story I've made up for the occasion.

"I've come to get some things for Caterina."

They believe me, I'm still capable of putting on an act, and they try to peer in when I open the door. I quickly close it behind me.

Inside it's chaos. And it stinks. For a moment I think it must be the stench of Luca's body – a crazy idea, given what the solicitor has told me, but before I quell my revulsion I almost throw up. I take a deep breath through my mouth, and the attack of nausea passes. I advance amid the chaos.

The stench comes from the usual refuse, scattered everywhere. I guess it must have been the police who upended the litterbins onto the floor to rummage through their contents, turning drawers and cupboards upside down, but I know the apartment was never all that tidy in the first place. The floors are greasy, the plates and dishes unwashed, encrusted with food and cigarette butts. The sheets are soiled and smelly. I wander round like a ghost.

On the walls hang posters of Luca's successes, the live shows of *The Waiter* and *Lunch from Hell*. He'd kept the name of the show. He was welcome to it. In the bathroom there's also an old handbill for *Luca & Sammy, cheesy & hammy*. I wasn't expecting that. On the photo we're both smiling, I'm cross-eyed and my brows are furrowed. How young I was, how young we both were.

I don't know what Bastoni thinks I'm going to see, but nothing of particular interest leaps to my eye, no "significant leads" as they say in detective stories. I look, and I do not understand; I am trying to keep my thoughts calm.

The only place that is relatively neat and tidy is the little studio that looks out over the Via Washington, with the daylight brightening it up through the dusty windows. The police have done their work here too, but they've left the sheets of paper on the desk and the computer all in one piece and switched on, with the screensaver churning over its brilliant patterns of light.

The papers are Luca's work. They're sketches for gags, bits of script, all printed out and hand-corrected. His regular handwriting has become scrawled and illegible, the sheets are covered with stains and cigarette burns. I start to read, impelled by curiosity. They're all variants on the English Waiter theme – a bit of a rehash: not very funny. Here and there, something interesting crops up, but for the most part it looks like the work of a dilettante, a loser, someone who hardly understands his own mother tongue.

I move the computer mouse, and the screensaver dissolves: I see the desktop decorated with Luca's face, repeated dozens of times over.

"You had a bit of an ego problem, old pal," I say these words aloud, and the sound almost frightens me. The apartment is silent, and the walls insulate it from the neighbours. But Bastoni said they complained about the quarrels between Luca and Caterina; they must have been yelling pretty loud.

In the computer there's a good deal of material. Not just scripts, but photos and videos too. I don't look at these, and use the mouse to click on the most recent folders. Luca arranged the folders by period, and, depressingly, there aren't many from the last two years. No stage photos, few complete scripts. Just odds and ends, incoherent fragments. I open and close the folders quickly, and pause only when I reach the folder from last month. Here there's just one piece. An almost complete script, as I discover with some surprise. I read it all through, and if it weren't for the situation, I'd almost find it funny. It's in Luca's more effective style, but with a black edge to it. No more Waiter, but rather a character very similar to the Italian comic actor Beppe Grillo – satirical gags about the government, ecology and world hunger. He didn't have time to use them.

It's starting to get dark, and I can't take any more in. I leave the apartment, treading lightly. The elderly neighbour is still on the landing, or maybe he came out when he heard the key turning in the lock.

"You haven't picked anything up," he says, pointing to my empty hands.

"I didn't find what I'd come for. I need Caterina to give me more details of where to look."

The old fellow nods. It's easy to see he wants to talk, and I give him a chance, bearing in mind my role as a private dick. The *poor fellow*, the *poor lady* – the old guy expresses his compassion for the living and the dead with all the courtesy of a bygone age, but it's clear that he thinks that Caterina is guilty and that Luca is a shit. "You know Signor Luca didn't always come home?" he says eventually. "He used to say he was on tour, but I'm pretty sure he . . . well, that he was a bit of a lady's man."

I nod without saying anything. Bastoni had already mentioned Luca's infidelities to me. He put it around a bit – and this could be a possible motive for murder. Caterina had put up with it for as long as she could, then she'd topped him. The Caterina of once upon a time wouldn't have done so; she'd just have changed the lock on the door. As for the Caterina of now – who knows?

I say goodbye to the old guy. I know where I need to go now; it's on my to-do list, but I don't really feel up to it. To get myself in the mood, I go to one of my favourite places, the kosher ice-cream parlour in Via Ravizza, in the heart of the Jewish district. Kosher ice cream is different from ours: if it has milk in it, they leave out eggs, the wafer is like unleavened bread, and the chocolate is crushed water ice. I really like it, and I also like the idea of eating it among people who wear skullcaps on their heads and speak in a Milanese dialect. It makes me feel a man of the world. The ice cream doesn't actually help me relax, so I jump into the car and go back to the Trade Fair zone, to a street I used to visit quite a lot, once upon a time.

The main entrance hasn't changed, and even the sign on the doorbell – a kangaroo with sunglasses, surrounded by the words *Champagne Agency* – is still the same.

I ring the bell and go up to the office on the second floor. Two hundred square yards of creative confusion, posters and photos on all the walls, young secretaries, telephones ringing. All exactly the same as the last time I saw it, apart from the faces. I don't recognize a single one.

The secretary, an attractive brunette of about twenty with a ring in her nose, asks me what I want and reacts rather officiously to my request to see the manager.

"Without an appointment, it's really rather difficult. If you leave your name with me, I can . . ."

"Sammy!" the exclamation comes from right behind me. Then someone flings her arms round me and forcibly hugs me.

"Hi there, Rosa!" I say.

Rosa is in her forties, a dumpy figure who hardly comes up to my chest – and I'm no giant. "Let's have a look at you, young fellow!"

"You seem in good shape."

She shakes her head. "Don't tell lies. The years are passing, and at my age every year counts twice over. Don't tell me you're coming back into the biz?"

"No, I just need to talk to the boss."

Her expression becomes sad. "You've heard about Luca, I take it?"

"Yes."

"I know you'd stopped seeing each other, but . . ."

"I'm really sorry about it, believe me." I point to the girl with the nose piercing. "Can you get me past the doorkeeper?"

"Of course I can."

And she does indeed succeed. Marcello receives me standing behind his desk with the plastic kangaroo on it. He too hasn't changed much – he still looks the same as when he told me: "I think you're going to have to find another agent."

The momentary embarrassment lasts until the ritual hug. By the time we're sitting down opposite one another, it seems as if we're back in the good old days. He offers me a glass of champagne from his private fridge, I tell him I've stopped drinking, and his smile broadens. He's blond and wears his hair long: he looks younger than his fifty years. He dresses with elegance, formally, perhaps to set himself apart from his clients, who are generally slobs.

"You know about Luca, I suppose?"

"Yes. That's why I'm here." I explain to him about the solicitor. Perhaps a real detective would lie, but this strikes me as being a waste of time and energy. And I need a hand. Marcello expresses his incredulity at my new role, but after switching off his mobile that never stops ringing he has no hesitation about talking to me.

"I don't know what I can tell you that you don't know already."

"Were you still his agent?"

"Yes, to some extent. I hadn't got him any new contracts for at least a year. No need for me to tell you why."

"Was he in such a bad way?"

"Worse." Marcello fiddles with a fountain pen. In front of him rises a pile of contracts and scripts. "You know how, once you acquire a reputation for unreliability, it's difficult . . ." He interrupts himself in embarrassment. "He couldn't remain on stage for more than ten minutes. The RAI contract, well, they tore it up when he didn't turn up for rehearsals three times in succession." He tells me of how the performances became less and less frequent, and the scenes of rage that alarmed everyone in the office. "For his last performances, he didn't even use the agency. Walk-on parts, odd minor roles."

"Do you know where? And how?"

"Wait."

Marcello calls in the girl who looks after live performances and introduces her to me. She has red hair and round glasses. She gives me a short list of the places where Luca performed over the last few months. Unbelievable.

For a comic actor there are three levels. The first is the top class – national TV, theatre, cinema and business conventions; then the second division, with occasional appearances on video and in well-known cabarets, then the third division, comprising clubs out in the sticks where the audience never tops fifty or so, max. Before he died, Luca was gravitating towards the fourth division. The only venues left were church clubs and the street. I take a few notes, struck by the similar way Luca's professional life and mine had ended – except for the fact that I never got to the top and that I fell much, much more quickly.

"But was he working with anyone in the last few months?" I ask Marcello and the redhead.

Marcello shakes his head. "I didn't see him either, you know. If it hadn't been for the home video rights, we'd probably not even have been in touch by telephone."

The redhead raises a finger. "He did do one thing with Gringo, so I was told."

"Gringo? He's still alive?" I ask.

"More or less," the girl replies. "I found out by chance a month or so ago. But if you want to talk to Gringo, I can't say I know where you'll find him."

"Thanks anyway."

The girl goes back to her paperwork.

"Let's have a meal together one evening soon, okay?" says Marcello as he bids me goodbye.

"Are you going to make me an offer I can't refuse?"

"Who knows? Eating and drinking stimulate the brain cells. Might get loads of new ideas."

"Why not?"

He promises to ring, and he almost seems sincere.

It's seven in the evening. I call by at the Crocodile, where they've rather given me up for lost. Mauro has found the notes I left him for expenses, and he's making all the arrangements. I'm starting to think that the owner of a club is only ever needed for public relations. I order a *mortadella* sandwich, listen to the cashier's report and the lamentations of a newly hired waitress (her shifts are too long, and she doesn't want to clean the loos), then I say goodbye to the merry throng and go out.

It's stopped raining. The Milan traffic is almost tolerable, if you know the best way to navigate round the streets. I stick on the dashboard the list of clubs that Luca played over the last months and start at the nearest, practically a workingmen's club. I talk to the manager, have a Coke and leave. By two in the morning my stomach is gurgling because of all the fizzy drinks I've consumed, and I'm pissed off at all the time I've wasted. I've only managed to pick up useless gossip and descriptions of crap performances. Luca did anything and everything, quite shamelessly, including presenting *Dear Fido*, an animal lovers' show at the Teatro dell'Uva in Lodi. One of the managers even gave me the flyer, which he read out: "You'll be wagging your tails at the songs, dances and quiet times for reflection IN DEFENCE OF ANIMALS. With the Blue Angels Children's Charity Chorus."

According to the manager, they'd had to wake Luca up between one number and the next, and he'd behaved like a pig to the audience. I felt obliged to buy a charity video for the Angels.

At two a.m. I call by to pick up Lisa. She's just tidying up behind the counter. Bruto is at the door waiting to leave.

"Listen, why don't you ever come on to your waitresses, eh?"

"I never pick any that are pretty."

For a moment he turns serious. "Is everything okay? You've been in the papers a lot recently. They're using old photos."

"I won't let them take any new ones. I can run faster than the paparazzi. Yes, everything's okay, thanks for asking."

He nods at Lisa, who's putting on her coat. "Don't do anything I wouldn't do, my dear Lovelace."

I'm not even listening to him as I slip my arm under Lisa's. We make a lovely couple under the streetlights of Milan.

We walk to her place – she doesn't live any great distance away. We go in quietly, as her son is asleep. And we keep quiet after that too, so as not to wake him up. Usually I'm not much good the first time. I come from too well-brought-up a family to be a real playboy, someone who can have a different girl every night. I'm at my best in the long term, like a diesel engine; to begin with I keep something back, trying to work out if I'm being too brutal, too delicate, too technical, too selfish and wondering if this is going to be the last time since she'll never want to see me again. But I've obviously been beating my brains out all day long, and with Lisa I simply let myself go, and I'm reasonably satisfied with the result, when she leans her head, in the usual way, on my hairy, sweaty chest and allows me to stroke her hair. She must be satisfied too, since for a while she doesn't mention that genius, her son, and when she does get round to the subject it's already six a.m., and I have to go. When I do so I bear the traces of her perfume on me, and I'm floating on air until I embark on the next round of my travels down Desolation Row.

10

I continue doing the rounds for another couple of days, without getting very far: just the usual catalogue of woes. The only good thing is that Lisa and I are still sleeping together, even if I always have to disappear before her son wakes up. The Crocodile, somehow or other, manages to keep going without me. On Thursday Mauro manages to track down Gringo. The phone call reaches my mobile while I'm checking out the umpteenth club on my list, late in the afternoon. This time I'm in Sesto San Giovanni, a suburb of Milan that was awarded the Gold Medal of the Resistance. Luca has been playing to the Old Partisans' Association, with jokes about the concentration camps, in the worst possible taste. He risks being lynched, but none of the old folks who hang out in the Association seems to me capable of any elaborate act of vengeance. However, I take notes – you never know if Bastoni might be able to get something useful out of them. I get onto the solicitor during a break in my peregrinations. No news from the jail, apart from the fact that Caterina isn't eating. If she continues to refuse, they'll have to feed her with a stomach tube, like fattening a goose.

Gringo has a clown gig at the opening of the new Rhododendron shopping centre, out on the ring road, a kind of pink steel-and-glass lump with a three-hundred-foot-high flower at the entrance. The locals protested, saying it ruined the landscape, but they must have lost their battle. When I arrive, the show is practically over, and I thank the Lord. I really don't know what can possibly drive a seventy-year-old man to dress up as Michael Jackson, but it must be something worse than mere hunger. On a stage that is half-hidden from the crowd of shoppers, Gringo sings "Thriller" in cod American, wearing a pair of lamé trousers that have seen better days, and with a frilly shirt that was once white. His face seems covered with shoe blacking, in the best racist iconography of the last century – definitely darker than the present skin colour of the real Michael Jackson. Gringo is out of breath by the time he finishes his song, then fires off some gag that was already old in Adam's day. Nobody laughs, and the guy who must be the manager takes the microphone off him before everyone can make a dash to the exits.

I join Gringo at the foot of the stage, as he is removing the blacking from his face with a handkerchief. He stinks alarmingly of wine, and to begin with he doesn't recognize me. I have to tell him my name ten times over, then Luca's. At this point he starts to cry.

I try to console him and he flings his arms round me, getting my shirt all dirty. I'm torn between pity and a strong desire to murder him and put an end to his sufferings. Eventually I decide to drag him to the indoor bar, decorated with yellow flowers like my aunt's bedspread. We manage to find a table free, I sit him down and bring him a double brandy. He swallows it down as if it were fresh water, drooling a little. I bring him another one, and at this point Gringo is in good enough shape to talk. The difficult thing now is to stop him. He goes on and on about Luca, how nice he was, how good he was onstage, a natural talent.

"And he'd promised me he'd take me on for his new show. I must be jinxed. I had a real chance, and then he goes and gets murdered. By that whore."

He starts crying again, but I try to stop him. "What show?"

"The new one. He'd got the script all done, now he just needed to get a new agent. That bloody fool Marcello wouldn't take him on any more. But Luca would have made it all right. He'd have got back on telly. Me too. I was going to play the stooge. Instead, sweet fuck all. All because of that whore."

"I don't know if it really was Caterina, Gringo."

"Course it was her. I saw Luca a week ago. He was totally pissed off. He was saying that whore wanted to screw him. And screw him she did. We should have been performing together today." A great big tear trickles down his nose.

A week ago. Just before Luca was bumped off. "Screw him how?" He doesn't reply. I shake him. "Screw him how?"

Gringo pushes my hand away. "What's it got to do with you? She bumped him off. Like a dog. Poor Luca." This time, he's started to cry for real. I can't take any more and I leave him there like a living health warning against alcohol abuse. Then I have second thoughts and go back. I slip a fifty-euro note into his breast pocket. "Don't spend it all on drink, okay?"

He stares at me vacantly. It doesn't make me feel any better. Luckily, Lisa phones just as I'm getting into the car and tearing up a flyer advertising Rhododendron Two at Orzi Nuovi.

"You haven't forgotten about this evening, have you?"

"This evening?"

"It's Thursday! And you know what that means?"

"Gnocchi for supper?" The icy chill of her response reaches me even through the mobile. "Only joking. It's your son at the Culture and Entertainment Centre, right?"

"Well done! That way I can introduce him to you, and you can give him some useful tips."

"I don't know if I'm still up to giving anyone any tips about showbiz."

"Don't be modest. You know, I'd like you to be his manager."

God really has it in for me at the moment. But if this is Lisa's only drawback, I can reconcile myself to my fate. "We'll talk about it. Without getting too excited, okay?"

We agree to meet up there. I drive to the Crocodile. Mauro pretends he doesn't recognize me until I threaten to kill him.

"How was Gringo?" he asks.

"Beat it."

I go into the backroom to reflect, among the vats of beer and crates of drinks, where I always feel better. I haven't learned any more about Luca, except about how low he'd fallen. And the only person who's given me any information is an old guy whose brain has turned to mush and who's convinced that Caterina's the guilty one. She'd screwed Luca in some rather ill-defined way. But how, and why? I feel frustrated and, as ever when I feel like this, I regret having stopped drinking. For about one second.

I take a clean shirt out of my wardrobe, change into it and slip out like a thief in the night.

11

Lisa is waiting for me at the door of the Centre with her little prodigy. There he is, Alberto, all in his Sunday best, with jacket and tie. There are loads of people coming in mainly men and women of a certain age, but also the occasional youngster. The new acts are obviously drawing in the punters.

Lisa leans towards Alberto. "Have you seen who's come?"

Alberto proffers me his hand, and I step forward to shake it, but he pulls it back and gestures with his thumb. "You need to go via my secretary!"

Lisa laughs aloud. "He's good, isn't he?"

I could die laughing. "I'm Sammy."

Alberto gazes at me seriously. "I know. Mum told me. I've got a book at home with your gags."

"A collector's item. Do you like them?"

"Some, yes – but if you don't mind my saying so, in my view you laid on the swear words a bit thick. Swear words are a cheap trick."

I don't know what to say. He's got a point. "All right – just you make sure you don't say any then."

"Of course." His mother tries to adjust his tie, and he pulls away in annoyance. "Leave it out, Mum. You know I don't like anyone touching me in public."

She laughs again. "You're right. Sorry." Then she turns to me. "Come on then, Sammy. Give him some advice."

Alberto looks at me with a great deal of interest. I sigh inwardly. "Well then, Alberto. This is a piece of advice that Walter Chiari gave me. You know who he was, don't you?"

"Of course. He used to tell jokes."

"Rather a summary description, but basically true. Anyway, what he told me was this: if you're getting big laughs from people, drag it out a bit; if you see you're not getting many laughs, speed up, and don't be afraid of dropping your pants."

"That it?"

If his mother hadn't been here, I'd give him a kick up the backside, but I can't. "No. I'll tell you a trick of my own. Focus on one member of the public, the one who seems to be giving you the fewest laughs, the one who's just glaring at you, okay?"

"Then?"

"Then concentrate entirely on him. Think of him as an enemy that you have to win over. Pay attention to his reactions and try to catch him out. Perform for him. You'll see that when he starts to laugh, you'll have the whole audience eating out of your hand. It worked for me."

He thinks it over. "Thanks," he says finally. "But I can't use it this evening, since everybody here likes me."

"It's true!" interrupts Lisa. "Alberto is the star of the show." The boy nods. "Tell him the good news, Alberto."

He lifts his chin. "I'm doing *Anything For A Laugh*."

Lisa hugs him. Alberto pulls away. "Isn't he great, Sammy? His first professional contract. He'll be a guest for ten shows. He'll have his own spot!"

"Congratulations," I say.

"Thanks." Alberto smoothes down the collar of his jacket. "Now you'll have to excuse me, but I need to get ready before the show."

Alberto strides off through the main door, and I'm left with Lisa. "Can I kiss you or will it embarrass you?"

"Better not. Alberto doesn't know about us, he thinks you're an old friend." She lights up a cigarette. "I'm so excited . . . They're paying him, you know?"

"Now that *is* good news."

I feel her gaze scrutinizing me. "You don't seem convinced."

"I'm just being careful," I say with some caution. "Aren't you frightened he might be running before he can walk? He still needs to grow, play around, go to school . . . If he starts appearing on television, his ordinary life will go down the can."

"And whoever said that it's better to have an ordinary life? Take me for instance. It'll never be much fun just being a waitress."

"Come on – I give you a few laughs."

She softens. "You do. But it's not enough. Alberto can study with a private tutor, if he needs to." She squeezes my hand. "Sammy, it's a great opportunity for him. He'll be able to make his way through life and do what he's always wanted to do. He won't have to do a shitty job just to earn peanuts, like me. Will you help him?"

"It seems to me that he's doing just great by himself."

"Don't get taken in by his poses. He's really good, but he's just a kid. He's scared. Me too. This morning the television people sent me a contract, I don't know a thing about any of that."

"I remember it vaguely . . . Let me have a look at it."

"We can go back to my place later. I'll cook a meal for you, and you can read the contract." She smiles. "And Alberto will be going to bed early. He gets really bushed doing these shows."

"It's an alluring prospect. Can I possibly turn it down?"

She looks round, then gives me a quick kiss.

"Seems like I can't," I conclude. "Okay, let's go in. I want to see him in action."

*

The Centre has an auditorium as big as a sports hall, with benches arranged at the foot of a stage constructed out of metal tubes. The benches are almost all full, there must be about a hundred people there. Not bad – in my day I've done a show with far fewer people, and I wasn't a twelve-year-old kid.

Lisa and I sit a certain distance away from the stage, so as not to crowd in on Alberto. He isn't the first to go on. The acts are introduced by a young man with a red jacket and an accent from Emilia Romagna – he does quite a good job of taking off the TV presenters. I sit back and enjoy, in succession, two young gals of seventeen dressed as telly hostesses, who jiggle about on a desk and dance with roller skates on their feet. They are followed by a

271

seventy-year-old who tells children's jokes, a three-hundred-pound tub of lard who blows raspberries with his armpits in time to the music, three boys pretending to be gay and a girl who relates her misfortunes in love. She's too cute to get many laughs – an old showbiz rule – but the audience applaud the acts warmly, hers as well as everyone else's. The acts are playing to a home crowd, it's evident.

Lisa nudges me. "Here he comes." Her expression becomes attentive; she concentrates totally.

The presenter in the red jacket jumps onto the stage, waves the girl off and then clears his throat. "And here's the moment we've all been waiting for. Our youngest performer: ALBERTO!"

The presenter comes off, and Alberto comes onstage to a round of applause that shakes the rafters. He's wearing a cheeky expression on his face. He plants himself in the middle of the stage, legs astraddle, and the lighting operator directs the spotlight full on him.

The boy pretends to look round. "I've drawn up a contract with the manager," he says. "If any of you dares not to laugh, we're dropping laxatives in your beer."

Gales of laughter all round. I look at Lisa. I realize that, all of a sudden, nobody exists for her right now apart from her son. I see her repeating Alberto's words under her breath, barely moving her lips.

"He's doing great," I say.

But she doesn't move. She continues to mime Alberto's words without taking her eyes off him; her body is tense and stiff.

Her son seems more relaxed than she is. He's not afraid of the audience, and he doesn't start floundering; he carries on with a few moderately funny jokes, all standard cabaret gags, fluently delivered. As he speaks, he gesticulates, without ever going too far away from the mike – a trick that some of my ex-colleagues have still to learn. Then he stops, and raises a hand to ask for silence. "And now," he says, "let's move on to more serious matters."

Almost without drawing breath, he fires off, one after another, a series of jokes about current affairs. Precise, sharp, absolutely hilarious jokes. Everybody roars fit to burst. They're all holding their sides with laughter. All except me.

I'm staring at him in horror.

It's really difficult to go to Lisa's after the show while trying to keep a normal expression. She seems not to notice, full of enthusiasm as she is for her son – who is tired and sweaty. I mechanically congratulate him.

At home Lisa tells me to make myself at home in the dining room, while she lights the stove to heat up what she prepared before going out.

"I thought we'd do this first," she says from the kitchen.

"Of course." My stomach is tied in knots.

Alberto joins us at the table. He's wearing a pair of pyjamas that still make him look more like a kid than like a little prodigy.

"Did you really like it?"

"A lot," I lie. "But by the way, how'd it happen they invited you to do *Anything for a Laugh*?"

He smiles. "It was Mum's doing. She made a video of my latest repertoire, and then I made heaps of copies and sent them round. Isn't that true, Mum?"

Lisa comes back with a baking tin full of *gnocchi alla romana*. "Of course. You have to keep plugging away if you're going to make it. Isn't that what I'm always telling you?"

"Always," confirms Alberto.

"And you were good this evening. Even though you did do the joke about the cars without pausing in the middle."

"The audience was laughing . . ."

"Never mind. What do I always tell you?"

"You have to get the timing spot-on."

"That's right! Anyway, this evening I'll give you eight and a half out of ten."

"Aw, come on, Mum, at least nine . . ."

"No, sorry!"

I'm sweating, even though it's not all that warm. "But did you make up your repertoire all by yourself?"

Alberto seems a little embarrassed. "Is it all right if I tell him you help me, Mum?"

"Of course." Lisa gazes at me.

I flinch from her gaze. "You're good, really good. Practically a professional."

"You can see I've learned something by working in a club." She hugs her son. "Now let's eat. But first . . ." She picks up a bottle of wine and uncorks it, then pours out an inch or so for her son, cuts it with water, and then serves both him and me. "Let's have a toast to Alberto's future success."

"I'd love to, but I don't drink any more – remember?"

"Wait. I'll get something for you." She goes back into the kitchen and gets a little bottle of Coke. She pours some out into a clean glass for me. "It's gone a bit flat."

"Never mind."

We raise our glasses. "To Alberto." We drink.

"Good, now let's get those *gnocchi* inside us." She serves me a scoopful, I stare at them without any appetite. "Not hungry?"

"I've been a bit stressed out these last few days." I pick up my fork. "I've b-been . . . been so veeeeery busy . . ."

All of a sudden my tongue isn't working at all well. I feel it getting heavier and heavier and sticking to my palate. I try to move it.

"It's soooo ss-trane . . ." My voice echoes in my own ears.

"Feeling a bit tired?" asks Lisa.

"Veeeeery . . ." The sounds and voices around me have become muffled. And Lisa's face is now a grey oval shape. For a moment I seem to be standing on a stage, with the audience in the distance, murmuring in disapproval, jeering. I close my eyes and return to the present. "I don't feel . . . too good. It's as if I'd d-druuuu . . ."

"Drunk? It's Lexotan," says Lisa. "Quick-acting stuff. Alberto, go to your room."

"But Mum . . ."

"Into your room and don't answer back! Now!"

Outside my field of vision, Alberto gets up and walks towards his room. "Mum, you promised . . ."

"Into your room!" Lisa's voice has changed into what sounds like a roar. I try to clutch at the tablecloth to drag myself to my feet, but the only result is that I pull the dishes and glasses down onto the floor. They fall in slow motion. The sound of the smashing glass melds into that of distant applause.

I come back to the present. "Wwww-why?"

"You know why." Lisa is observing me from a fraction of an inch away. "How did you manage to find out?"

"The gags . . ." I've lost all sensation in my legs. "They were . . . Luca's gags. The new . . . show . . ."

"And how did you find out?"

"At Luca's place . . . I saw them on the comp . . . the computer . . . You did him in . . . It was you . . . Not Caterina . . . Gringo . . ."

"I made a mistake. I was stupid. I realized as much at the Centre. The way you were staring at him." She gets up. "I'm really sorry. We'd have made a good couple. You'd have been the perfect manager for my son. You know how much he needs a father. Instead, you've ruined everything." I hear her rummaging around in the kitchen drawer. I make an effort to pull myself up but fall back to the ground. I crawl along. The invisible auditorium is filled with murmurs, I think I can see the lens of a television camera pointing at me. I try to adjust my cook's hat, but I don't have it on.

I'm on the floor.

"Please, Sammy, don't make everything difficult for me."

Lisa is a shadow standing over me. She's holding something; I move. A terrible pain on my shoulder.

"Don't move! Don't move!" shouts Lisa. She places a foot on my back to keep me in place, but the pain has roused me a little. I roll over, Lisa loses her balance and falls. I advance on all fours towards the door, grasp the handle, wrench it open.

Another blow on my back. But I've now managed to get my head outside. I clutch the doorpost, and push myself towards the stairs. I can't even see them as I roll towards the landing. Lisa is standing at the door, shouting. Someone pokes their head out of their door. I carry on crawling and roll down another flight of stairs. I hurt all over, but the pain is distant. I carry on crawling on all fours along the pavement. Hands pick me up. I vaguely hope they aren't Lisa's. I lose consciousness.

Or I die.

13.

I didn't die, I just broke three ribs and a shoulder bone. From my hospital bed I follow the developments in the affair. In Lisa's wine

SANDRONE DAZIERI

cellar they found traces of Luca's body. He was left there until she had a free evening and could take him to the wood.

Can you commit murder to ensure your son gets a television spot?

Of course. I bet she's not the first to have done so.

I'm out of hospital in time for Luca's funeral. There are lots of showbiz people there, actors, singers, presenters and hostesses, real ones this time. There are also journalists, but Marcello has managed to get the police to keep them at a distance. They try to interview me; with a swipe of my good arm I send a mike hurtling past the crush barriers. The journalist isn't best pleased; God knows what he'll write in tomorrow's paper. Not that I'm all that bothered.

I walk behind the hearse next to Marcello. "They tell me you managed to stay awake despite having a whole little bottleful of sleeping pills inside you," he says.

"That's the advantage of having once been a boozer. You learn how to keep standing no matter what happens. But I only ever felt that way once before. Guess when."

"I give up."

We are walking alongside Caterina, who is holding the arm of a solicitor. Bastoni winks at me – an odd gesture at a funeral. But Caterina doesn't seem to recognize me. It's better that way, I wouldn't know what to say to her. Not yet.

"At the RAI rehearsals, for the show with Luca. The time I bombed so badly. The same sensation. Identical. In fact, I relived bits of it while I was trying not to get killed."

"That's pretty strange."

We walk along in silence for a while as we enter the cemetery. Luca's going to be cremated. Properly cremated, I mean.

"By the way, Marcello. We're on sacred ground here, you can't tell a lie. Did Luca want to do the show with me, or had he already decided to go it alone? Because this would explain a whole lot of things. For instance, a bottle of whisky in my dressing room, with sleeping pills dissolved in it."

Marcello stares into the distance. "What difference would it make now?"

"You're right. It wouldn't."

276

"Anyway," says Marcello, "there are plenty of people asking me about you. I've got half an idea to get you back on stage."

"Drop it."

"It's my work. I'm an agent: I grasp opportunities whenever I can. And you're in good enough shape, seeing that you were hit with a rolling pin."

"It was a steak mallet, one of those with cast-iron handles. I used to play a cook, or had you forgotten?"

"D'you think I'd forget that? Anyway, if you want my opinion, you could really make a fresh start."

"Just drop it, I said."

"Let's have dinner together one of these days. I'll make you an offer you can't refuse."

"Want to bet?"

We've reached the crematorium. The cortège stops, the bier is placed in the narrow aperture. I have only one good hand, so I can't join in: I just stand there watching as Luca receives his last round of applause.

Curtain.

The Guest of Honour

Giorgio Faletti

So there I was, sitting like a pig in clover, ensconced in a comfortable office armchair, and in front of me stood Mario Manni, editor of *Talent Scout* and the rightful owner of both office and several other comfortable armchairs, staring at me like someone who's seen the man who saw the man who threw the stone into the pond.

"I just know it's one of your usual con tricks."

"No way. When have you ever seen me con you?"

"Always."

I knew Mario, and I knew he never missed a chance to make a witty reply, especially when one was served up to him on a silver platter, like now.

But if he thought I was going to sit there applauding, he had another thing coming.

I got up.

"Okay, I can see you're not interested in following up this story. So . . ."

"No, hang on. What the hell happened to your sense of humour? Did you sell it off? How much did they give you for it?"

I sat down again.

"Much less than you're going to give me when I bring you the photos and the interview. Exclusive."

Mario took off his glasses and pinched the bridge of his nose with the thumb and forefinger of his right hand.

"I see." He looked blearily up at me like a short-sighted trout. "You're saying you know where Walter Celi is . . ."

I put on my most brazen expression and stated unequivocally that it was I who had thrown the stone into the pond.

"I'm not just *saying* I know where Walter Celi is. I *know* where Walter Celi is."

On Mario's face there appeared, as if from the heavens, an angelic expression.

"Oh yeah? Where?"

I couldn't help laughing. So I laughed.

"I wouldn't even tell my mother, if she were still alive. So don't imagine I'm going to tell *you*. I know perfectly well that Lanzani, in the room next door, has grown elephant ears so he can hear everything we're saying. Do you think I haven't noticed you left the intercom on? If I tell you, that great hysterical fairy will have dashed off before I've even taken my coat off the hook."

Mario's angelical expression was overshadowed by incredulity. *Et tu, Brute* . . .

"But what do you mean? I . . ."

The door flew open, and Benito Lanzani burst into the office.

"Falchi! Fuck you!"

"Cheers, old pal! I can see even *you* remember your Sunday school lessons – you know, that bit in the Gospels: *do unto others as you would have them do unto you* . . . Do you manage to turn the other bumcheek too?"

He was on the verge of a hissy fit.

"You are one fucking dickhead, and I . . ."

I interrupted him with seraphic calm. I sat astraddle the armrest of the chair and started to count off the alternatives on the fingers of a limp-wristed hand.

"Well now, you can't thump me, 'cos that's what men do, and you can't scratch my eyes out, 'cos that's what women do. So all you can do, honey, is hate me, hate me, hate me!"

For a moment I had the impression Lanzani was going to fling himself at me, and perhaps, for a moment, he had the same idea.

"Hey, you two, that's enough!"

Manni banged on the top of his desk. He turned to me.

"You, stop it. And you . . ."

He turned his blazing eyes on Lanzani.

"Get out of my fucking hair, you idiot."

The poor sap had a flicker of pride. He looked like a Nero who's just sung his party piece only to be greeted by his centurions with a chorus of jeers and raspberries. He stalked off, almost slamming the door behind him. He'd probably go and set fire to Rome.

Mario Manni turned to me as if nothing had happened, as if I hadn't caught him red-handed.

"How much do you want?"

"A hundred thousand."

"What? You're crazy!"

I examined my fingernails.

"You can bet that if I go and offer my services to *Gossip*, they'll give me the hundred thousand. Do you know what news like this would do for circulation? Let alone the fact that you can bring it out bit-by-bit, like they did with Ducruet and Princess Stephanie of Monaco, or Clinton and Lewinsky. The material I can give you will keep you going for a good couple of months."

I was bang on target. His eyes were signalling "sunk battleship".

"I can't give you a hundred thousand for something of this kind."

I returned to an examination of my fingernails. I really must remember to give my manicurist a bigger tip. She'd done a nice job.

"All right. I tell you what we'll do . . ."

"What's that?"

"Give me fifty per cent of the increase in turnover the scoop will bring in."

He looked daggers at me, like Scrooge McDuck.

"Let's go with the hundred thousand."

He didn't seem best pleased at my smile of triumph.

"I hate you."

"You too? You been spending a bit too much time with Lanzani?"

"Fuck off. I'll get a contract drawn up for you by admin, and I'll fax it over to you. You send me back a signed copy. The boss is going to have a heart attack . . ."

I got up.

"The boss is going to get a heart attack when he sees the bonus you rake in. You get a percentage, don't you?"

Sunk aircraft carrier. He turned purple, and I headed for the door before I could witness a cardiac arrest.

His voice stopped me on the threshold.

"Falchi . . ."

I turned round.

GIORGIO FALETTI

"Yes?"

"How the hell have you managed to find out where Walter Celi is?"

I shrugged.

"Oh, you know, the usual gifts that turn a good journalist into a great journalist. A vivid imagination, powers of deduction, a sharp eye . . ."

I delicately closed the door behind me as he erupted in an explosion of bile.

The minute I stepped outside the office I saw Lanzani. He was standing at the desk of one of the editors, talking to her as he leaned on her computer monitor. There was pure poison in his gaze.

I crossed the spacious room with its glass doors to various offices. Everyone stopped and stared at me. I slowly walked up to Lanzani, who watched me with increasing anxiety. His pants probably contained, not two hairy balls, but a snapshot of two hairy balls stuck on with a drawing pin.

I came up to him and gazed right into his eyes.

"Benito, there's something I've never told you . . ."

There was a slight tremble in his eyes.

"What's that?"

He didn't have any time to react. I suddenly grabbed his face in my hands and pulled him towards me. I violently pressed my lips to his.

I said my line with all the intensity of the Actor's Studio.

"I've always loved you."

I turned on my heel and left, while a roar of laughter raised the roof.

Curtain.

*

Apart from showing a sharp eye, it had been a bit of sharp practice too.

There wasn't a journalist, real or assumed, in the whole of Italy who wouldn't have given a slice of his backside (Lanzani would have given his whole backside and a bit more too) just to find out what had become of Walter Celi.

And I was the only one who knew.

Walter Celi had been a television star. Perhaps it would be better to say that, for a certain period, Walter Celi had been Mr Television in person.

And he had become so as fast as Benito Lanzani manages to pick up and take home a nice young guy he's just picked up at Stazione Termini.

(Please don't tell him I said so. Not Lanzani, I mean: the nice young guy.)

At a time when there was a massive expansion in the amount of material available on television, and a war to the death between the two main groups, RAI and Mediaset and a third group that was always lying in wait, ready to explode into action at any minute, everyone was frantically looking for new ideas, either for programmes or for personalities to present them. At this juncture, Walter had swooped down from the heavens like the Hale-Bop comet, something that you get to see only once every 2,000 years.

He had begun quite by chance, after languishing for years as a tour organizer in little villages. It had started with a broadcast for kids, a daily slot before the evening's TV news on one of the Mediaset channels.

His success had been stupendous. The man seemed to incarnate all the gifts that make a successful artist. He could talk, he could make people laugh, he could sing and dance, he was an extremely handsome young fellow, and the women liked him. Outside the studios there was a permanent army of young girls who literally tore out each other's hair when they saw him. Indeed, I had more than once thought it would be profitable to set up a kiosk selling wigs at just that spot.

Whatever clothes he wore, whatever car he drove, whatever product he advertised, was, within half an hour, the latest trend, and sales went through the roof.

In a word, Walter Celi had *charisma*.

His agent had cobbled together a contract giving him exclusive rights for five years. It was like a player's contract with Juventus plus one with Milan put together, and the Mediaset bosses smarted at its overgenerous terms for months. The smart faded away once the first audit figures came in; after that, it was the sponsors who were itching to get in on the act.

Then: disaster.

He was hosting *It's Saturday!*, a programme broadcast live every Saturday evening (of course) on a Mediaset channel (ditto), and the programme was breaking all previous records for audience share. So he and the producers had been asked to go beyond the ten programmes originally planned, since the broadcast was continuing to grow week by week.

The sponsors were fighting for a piece of the action, the journalists were fighting for a piece of the action, the guests were fighting for a piece of the action, and the producers, who already had a piece of the action, were rubbing their hands like Boy Scouts rubbing sticks of wood together to make fire.

In the ninth programme, there was a real A-list of celebrities lined up as guests of honour. A rock star who was the pop idol of all pubescent girls (his latest CD wasn't doing all that well, but this was something best left unsaid), the complete cast of an American film with the gorgeous gal and handsome hunk *du jour*, as well as Vicky Merlino, the Italian soubrette who (well, just look at *her!*) had first got half of Italy drooling senselessly over her and was now having the same impact in the States before finally getting to Hollywood where she was at present making a film.

On the evening of the show Walter had done his spiel introducing Vicky before she had emerged onstage, shimmering her way down the flight of stairs to an orchestral accompaniment. It was a suitably glamorous entrance for a Hollywood star, with that hint of irony that never goes amiss – though I don't think she quite managed to grasp this aspect in all its ambiguity.

Anyway, the lovely lady had sauntered over to Walter, had greeted him, embraced him, kissed him – and then, in a movement so natural that it appeared rehearsed, she had collapsed, fallen to the floor and died.

Dropped dead. Just like that.

At first everyone had imagined she'd just fainted from exhaustion, and even as Walter was leaning over her he'd come up with a joke, something of the "Gosh, I never knew you fancied me *that* much!" variety; but the truth had soon emerged when it was realized that her heart had stopped beating.

The viewers at home were horror-stricken, but not so horror-stricken as to prevent the figures from reaching almost ninety per cent, hitting an unprecedented peak before, in flagrant contradiction of the law that the show must go on, the show was taken off the air.

The post-mortem had established that death had occurred from natural causes, a cardio-circulatory blockage due to a congenital malformation that Vicky didn't know (or had never said) she had.

The journalists, habitual vultures like myself, had feasted on the funeral, if you'll pardon my black humour. The newspaper kiosks blared their full-page headlines at every street corner, and the TV news programmes could talk of nothing else, even though nobody at all could lay the least little blame on anyone else.

A few days later, Walter Celi vanished.

It wasn't that he just disappeared for a break or took time off to think things over. Nothing of that kind. I mean he'd really vanished, disappeared, as in a puff of smoke, into thin air.

His agent, his friends, his current fiancée (Walter's parents were no longer alive) and the Mediaset bosses were all sitting around waiting for him to show that he was still around, even if he only phoned.

They'd been sitting there waiting for four years as the spiders spun their webs . . . But as for any telephone call: nix. Nobody in the whole wide world knew where he was.

Nobody, that is, except me.

*

When I came out of the elevator onto the landing of my pad (a bijou penthouse with rooftop view, cost an arm and a leg, *molto bello*) my niece Sara was sitting on the doorstep.

"Hi there, handsome!"

"Hi there, gorgeous! What you doing here?"

"I was waiting for you."

"You don't say. It's not as if you'd be waiting for the next metro train here . . ."

"The concierge wouldn't give me the key."

"Ah. This Christmas I must remember to give her a nice fresh *panettone* and not one I picked up cheap from the year before."

She got up so that I could open the door and followed me in. Sara was the daughter of my brother Claudio, she was eighteen years old and as beautiful as her mother, as tall and slim as her father and as cunning as Ulysses' niece. I hope you get the picture.

As she closed the door, the fax started spouting the sheets of paper with the contract that Manni was sending me. As I sifted through them, Sara looked innocently around.

"What have you done with my slides?"

"What slides?"

Sara turned to me and forced me to lower the sheets of paper I was holding in front of my eyes.

"Riccardo, don't play dumb with me. You think I'm going to swallow your stupid little stories?"

When she called me "Riccardo" instead of "Uncle", it was a bad sign. I could easily understand Manni's state of mind. At that very moment, somebody was sinking *my* battleship. And, damn it all, the person doing so was a young girl of eighteen, my own flesh and blood, a chip off the old block.

Thank God she was my niece and not my daughter . . .

In actual fact, Sara was the epicentre of the huge stroke of luck that I mentioned above, a piece of damn good luck equivalent to winning the Lottery in a week when there was a double roll-over.

A couple of evenings earlier, I'd been to dinner at my brother's place, something which I did at least once a week. Sara had only just got back from a holiday in Guadeloupe and I had settled down without a murmur of protest, and indeed with a certain enjoyment, to watch as she showed us her slides. The three of us – *viz* my brother, my sister-in-law, and I – had sat ourselves down on the sofa while Sara, standing in front of us, made the images skim before our eyes with a click on the control.

Click! white beach with palm trees, *click!* picturesque street market with friends busy haggling, *click!* Sarah topless and admiring whistles from present company, *click!* a trip in a boat *click!* . . . As the images sped past, something had attracted my attention. I'd asked her to go back, and I'd gone up to the wall for a closer look at the slide. My heart was pounding. In my avid, vulture-like imagination I could already see, stretched out on the desert sands, the lifeless figure of the managing director of a certain weekly scandal rag, deceased thanks to the hefty transfusion of money I was going to take from him, if what I was seeing was true.

In the background of the photo there was a handsome guy disguised in a thick beard, a pair of sunglasses and a baseball cap. Walter Celi.

Sara returned to the attack.

"You got me to lend you the slides. You gave me some feeble excuse or other, leakier than the Titanic after it hit the iceberg."

Still, not bad for a young girl. She even had the divine gift of a sense of humour. God knows where she'd got it from. If I'd been in my brother's shoes, I'd have asked for a DNA test.

Yes indeed, I'd got her to lend me the slides with an excuse that, well, was rather . . . The minute I was back home I'd slipped the one that most interested me into my scanner. The computer screen had immediately filled with the image, and I'd blown it up it and homed in on the suspicious section. There was no way of being absolutely certain, given the way he was hiding behind his beard, glasses and cap; but certain I was. I'd interviewed Walter Celi before, in the swimming pool of a hotel in Rimini, and I'd noticed a strawberry birthmark with an irregular lozenge shape just above his wrist.

And there it was again, the very same birthmark, with a reddish gleam on the suntanned skin of the figure in the slide. I had kissed the man on the computer screen (Lanzani does the same but without the computer screen) and I'd seen, in my vulture's mind, the body of my bank manager lying in his office as huge cheques made out to me fluttered about on every side.

"Well, don't you think that artistic interest and a certain affection can easily . . . ?"

She interrupted me with a wave of her hand and sat in the armchair in front of the computer.

"Uncle . . ."

When she went back to calling me "Uncle" after calling me "Riccardo", it was an even worse sign.

"You're a nice guy. You're even quite good-looking. There are quite a few of my girl friends who'd forge ID papers just to be here where I am, but their mothers swear to them that you're one of the biggest sons of bitches that have ever slimed their way into this city (no offence to grandma)."

"Sara, I'm appalled at the kind of language a young lady like yourself . . ."

"The young lady like myself has been on the pill for the past three years and doesn't have the slightest intention of being taken for a ride by an old fox like you, even if you *are* my uncle. Well?"

Heaving a trumpet-blast of a sigh that would have brought down the walls of Jericho, I told her everything. As I did so, I went into the kitchen to get a couple of Cokes from the fridge.

As I filled the glasses, her voice reached me from the other room.

"How much are they giving you for the job?"

"Thirty thousand."

"The contract here says a hundred."

Shit. Sara wasn't just Ulysses' niece: she was Ulysses in person. And I was a ninny. I'd left the sheets of paper from the fax machine lying on the desk, right under the Sherlock-Holmesian eyes of my niece.

Sara appeared on the threshold of the little kitchen.

"How do you think you're going to find him? That photo doesn't mean a thing. He might just have been passing through."

I shrugged and handed her a glass of Coke.

"Well, in any case it's a lead. Once I'm there I can play it by ear. I'll show the photo round. There's bound to be someone who saw him and spoke to him . . ."

I took a sip.

"If it's of any interest, I know where he is."

A fine spray of Coke issued from my mouth and covered the white furnishings of the kitchen with a pattern of leopard spots.

"What? You know where he is?"

"Of course."

"Where?"

"How much?"

"How much what?"

"How much will you give me?"

"You mean to tell me you want money before you'll give me information that . . . ?"

288

"Information that will bring you a sweet hundred thousand, my dear Riccardo."

When she went back to calling me "Riccardo" again after calling me "Uncle", it meant I was well and truly screwed, whether as Riccardo or as Uncle.

"How much do you want, you snake in the grass?"

"A reasonable figure would be, let's say, thirty per cent."

"You're crazy. Five."

"Twenty-five."

"There's one thing you're forgetting. I could easily find him all by myself."

"You'd never find him. You can take my word for that."

I don't know why, but I believed her.

"Okay. Ten per cent."

She threw back her head and laughed. She was adorable. She was a bloody fool. I couldn't decide whether to hug her or throttle her. But in her eyes she had the spark, the bright spark that makes human beings different from the beasts of the field. Had it in spades.

"Fifteen. Not a penny less."

"All right. Where is he?"

She laughed again. This time I just wanted to throttle her.

"There's no need for me to tell you. I'm coming too."

"Oh no."

"Oh yes. It's a condition *sine qua non*."

Ah, Manni, Manni, if only you were here, what a deep feeling of satisfaction you'd have. He who lives by the sword . . .

"Let me know when we're going."

She picked up the shoulder bag she'd thrown down on an armchair, slung it over her shoulder and opened the door.

"All expenses paid, of course. By you."

She was just about to leave when I blocked her exit.

"Sara, there's one thing I'd like to know."

"What's that?"

As I asked, I could hear Manni's voice ringing in my ears.

"How the hell have you managed to find out where Walter Celi is?"

She looked at me smugly.

"Simple. I fucked him."

She went out, leaving me firmly convinced of one thing.

Thank God she was my niece and not my daughter.

*

When I turned off the shower I stood for a moment dripping and savouring my bliss.

I have a strong dislike of aeroplanes. Oh, heavens above, nothing excessive: let's just say that even the sight of a drawing of an aeroplane makes me feel unwell. Eight hours sitting on the equivalent of a bed of nails with my ears tuned to the tiniest little variation in engine sound had left me with two mountain torrents gushing from my armpits. When the plane had landed at Point-à-Pitre, Guadeloupe, I had the distinct sensation that I'd sweated out at least a couple of salmon amid the torrents.

I wrapped myself in my bathrobe and, still dripping, went out onto the balcony to enjoy the Caribbean evening. No sooner did I step outside than the humidity enveloped me like a sheet of cellophane, and I was greeted by an intimidating chorus of frogs. I'd reserved two rooms at the Hôtel Méridien, and I realized that this concert was costing me as much as a Cream reunion gig, with the difference that here there was no possibility of getting up and going away.

Apart from the soundtrack, there was no cause for complaint: people hereabouts did rather well when it came to the view. There it lay in front of me, a real picture postcard, perfect in every glowing colour. Palm trees, vegetation and the enveloping warmth, as humid as a sigh of desire and sensuality. There was a beach of white sand and, in the background, the sky and the sea constantly swapping places on the horizon.

Despite being a fully paid-up, card-carrying vulture, I couldn't manage to evade the thought that there are certain places where you're better off staying in your bedroom protected by the "Do Not Disturb" notice. Perhaps it's a narrow-minded way of looking at things, but are we sure it's worth going to all that trouble just to earn a fortnight's holiday somewhere the locals can look down on you just because they have the privilege of actually living there?

Sara, without knocking, came in through the communicating door between our two bedrooms and interrupted my train of thought.

"Are you ready?"

I left the balcony and came back into the room. When she saw that I was still in my bathrobe she made a gesture of impatience.

"Still not dressed? I'm raring to go!"

I looked at her in surprise.

"Ah, Baroness, are you here again? Never could I have imagined that you might leave your home town of Oxford right in the middle of the polo season . . ."

My niece looked at me with an air of insufferable smugness.

"Very well. As soon as my learned friend has dressed his eminent self in appropriate apparel, would it be too much to ask him to accompany the Baroness as she stuffs her face with the products of the local cuisine?"

There was no gainsaying it: my niece was a girl with a marvellous brain and, in these rather curious circumstances, she looked really beautiful. She would make a wonderful woman if someone, her uncle for instance, didn't murder her first.

I continued to harp on the same theme.

"Would it be asking too much if I were to ask Lady Ballbreaker for a little privacy while I get dressed?"

Sara gave a snort that made the lampshade swing and went back into her room, slamming the door behind her. When I was alone, I took off the bathrobe and, still smiling, sprayed myself with a little deodorant and a little eau de toilette.

I opened my suitcase and slipped on a white T-shirt and a pair of blue cotton shorts. On my feet I placed a smart pair of gleaming white Superga loafers, which would within a quarter of an hour be transformed into a potentially lethal weapon.

I looked at myself in the mirror. Not bad.

The same thought flashed across Sara's face when she saw me. She pursed her lips together and uttered a whistle.

"Riccardo, have I ever told you that quite a few of my girl friends . . . ?"

"You have indeed, but, although I've heard of these girl friends, I've yet to see a single one of them."

"You're an old pig."

I put my arm over her shoulders and drew her towards me, as if I were a close friend.

"Actually, to tell you the truth, I don't feel the least bit old."

We could laugh and joke affectionately like this because maybe we *were* the same age, at least in our own minds. In the corridor we crossed a woman in her thirties, suntanned, quite attractive, dressed in clothes that were all too obviously made in the USA. I could see from the way she stared at us and the expression on her face that she imagined us as a brilliant thirty-year-old man on holiday with his teenage "niece". At the first opportunity I would explain to her that the niece was a niece without inverted commas and that I wasn't actually a dirty old man but was quite ready to become one – with her, if only I could join her in her room. Unfortunately, right now I had other things on my mind.

Per ardua ad astra.

We emerged unscathed from the embarrassed silence that every elevator includes as an optional extra and emerged into the entrance hall of the hotel. We prudently followed the arrow luring us to the "Restaurant" and – such is the miracle of organized tours – did indeed find ourselves in the open-air restaurant.

The decor must have been designed by the same architect who had laid out the Earthly Paradise, since it seemed to consist entirely of plants. I absolutely must remember not to order any apples, I thought.

Various waiters, white, black and of suitable gradations in between, were circulating with an air of efficiency and immaculate jackets between the tables.

A maître d' with a small neat moustache, who resembled Hercule Poirot, took us in charge and showed us to a table. As we were ordering, I discovered that Sara's French was much better than mine, so I chickened out of my struggle with the menu and left things to her.

"Local cuisine?"

"Absolutely."

From the respectful glance she darted at me, I realized that I had gained brownie points in my niece's eyes. Neither of us belonged to that category of Italians who expect to be able to eat spaghetti under every latitude and who go round the world's restaurants gazing at the fare with an expression of disgust on their faces.

Sara chattered away to the maître d' with worrying fluency and entrusted me with the task of looking after the wine. I chose a New Zealand white, a nice though little-known label, which earned me the esteem and the satisfied smirk of complicity that a maître d' usually reserves for connoisseurs.

We waited for our food to arrive while sipping our wine, with its subtle notes of citrus fruit, and observing the people sitting at the tables. We passed remarks on them in a low voice, laughing loudly, feeling silly and not caring the least little bit.

My niece lifted her eyes from her glass and saw that I was observing her with peculiar intensity.

"What is it?"

"Nothing. I was just thinking about you . . ."

"And what were you thinking about me?"

"If one day I decide to have a daughter, I think I'll put her into production with a photo of you right in front of my eyes."

She blushed slightly and lowered her eyes to her glass. This somewhat awkward moment passed when two waiters came over, one white of skin and the other black, one pushing a trolley with our food. They set before us a metal container with a round lid and, unlike in chess where white moves first, they simultaneously, like well-trained ballet dancers, lifted the lid and displayed to us the treasure within: an elaborate dish with a rice and banana base.

On my mental clapometer I awarded them seven out of ten for the ceremony and, once I had tasted it, a much higher mark to the food itself.

We devoured our food in famished silence. Uncle Vacuum Cleaner and his niece hoovered up the contents of the dish with an impressive speed and prepared for the next act in the drama, announced in advance by the two waiters with the trolley. I realized with something of a start that Sara had ordered enough food to end world famine. I started to dart glances at the door into the kitchen in the same way General Custer kept looking towards the hill from which the Indians would soon be arriving.

Towards the end of the meal, I observed with ill-concealed admiration as my niece attacked, with two spoons, an ice cream that was as elaborately and brightly coloured as the national flag of some African country – an ice cream in the face of which I had been obliged to lay down my arms.

All at once I wasn't quite so sure I wanted a daughter like this . . .

"Congratulations . . ."

Sara looked up, and I was granted my own quick flash of innocent blue sky.

"What for?"

"To be quite honest, I'd rather pay for your studies than for your meals. You've just eaten your way through a whole MBA at Stanford. Now I know why your father has to slog his guts out morning, noon and night . . ."

Sara chuckled, though this didn't prevent her from demolishing the ice cream as if it were a personal enemy of hers.

"My father indulges in habits that are much more expensive than my liking for food. My mother too. Haven't you ever heard that neglected girls, starved of affection . . ."

"Don't even think of palming off that story about your parents' expensive hobbies on me, young lady. You've inherited a congenital propensity for bingeing that is unparalleled in our family."

And indeed, few people could have been as closely bound as were the three who made up the kernel of my affections, and this was the reason why I saw them so often. Indeed, my fondness for them was somewhat tinged with envy, even though I would never have confessed as much, not even to the Spanish Inquisition.

A huge cup of American coffee arrived to signal a ceasefire, and I then lit up an enormous cigar that Poirot the maître d' had recommended and heaved a sigh of satisfaction.

This is the life . . .

I exhaled a puff of smoke that, in the motionless air, formed a perfect circle. A good omen. Before it could disperse, I put my finger right through it and made a wish. It was a happy man who, with a secure future ahead of him, turned to his young niece and said, in friendly tones:

"So when you . . . yes, well, anyway, when you met Walter Celi, you didn't recognize him?"

"When I slept with him, you mean? What's the matter, Riccardo, are you too ashamed to call a spade a spade?"

Sara transfixed me with a gimlet stare that bored into my head and made me feel utterly stupid.

"Not in the least. It's just that I find it hard to view you as a man-eater . . ."

Sara leaned back in her chair and allowed her gaze to drift round the restaurant.

"Actually, I'm not. This is a special, a very special case . . ."

She paused and then changed tack to answer my question.

"When it all happened, Walter's success I mean, four years ago, I was fourteen and obsessed with foreign pop music . . ."

I remembered very clearly her intense teenage passion for an American rock band, and I nodded. She'd filled her bedroom with posters and practically driven her father and myself crazy begging us to let her go to their concert when they came to Italy. Then the band had split up, and Sara had shed floods of tears . . . but the family had heaved a huge collective sigh of relief.

Sara continued her narrative; she herself seemed abashed by her girlish passions.

"I didn't bother much about what was on Italian TV. I have to admit that I only learned who the person in the photo was when you told me."

"So you mean you hadn't realized that . . ."

"Precisely. I hadn't realized that the guy in question was Walter Celi when I . . . well . . . got to make his acquaintance, here in Guadeloupe."

I cursed myself. I was no good at pretending. Sara had earned herself a holiday, free, gratis and for nothing – plus a significant percentage of my scoop. And I'd walked straight into it. I felt the blood rising slowly to my face from the tight knot of embarrassment deep in my belly. I decided to adopt a different attitude. Sara guessed as much from my changed tone of voice.

"Okay. Where is he?"

"Where's who?"

Was I mistaken, or had the innocence suddenly disappeared from the flash of blue sky in her eyes?

"You know perfectly well who I'm talking about. Where is he?"

The subsequent moment of silence seemed to last a century. Sara looked down and suddenly the sky turned black.

"I don't know."

I calmly leaned back in my chair.

"You know, the food, the wine and the journey must have played a nasty trick on me. For a minute there I thought I'd heard the words *I don't know*."

If it's true that attack is the best form of defence, Sara interpreted this strategy in the way most advantageous to her. She looked up at me and the sky was again visible in her eyes – but this time a storm was brewing.

"You heard me perfectly well. I don't know where Walter Celi is – damn him!"

Suddenly the storm broke, and the rain fell as Sara burst into tears. Her head fell onto her arms on the table, and she sat there sobbing. The few customers still left in the restaurant couldn't take their eyes off us.

I managed to twist my lips into a smile that would have made a Geiger counter start ticking for all its worth. I placed a hand on her shoulder and leaned towards her.

"Hey, listen, young lady, if you're going to go on like this it might be better to do so in private before some cop launches an investigation into the two of us . . ."

Sara again granted me the gift of her face. She dried her eyes (she wasn't wearing make-up) with the table napkin. Tears, rice and bananas. And explanations. There was no diversionary tactic, whether of laughter or of tears, that was going to allow my niece to evade her responsibilities: this young lady had been telling lies.

God might forgive, but I wouldn't. Or so I thought.

"Can we talk about this with all the seriousness that such a moment of high drama requires? Apart from your display of emotion, which I find perfectly-judged from the tactical point of view, there still remains the minor problem that I feel, ever so slightly, that you've been screwing with me."

She sniffed and, as if by miracle, a Kleenex appeared. Women are incredible: young and old, they always have a paper hankie with them, even when they're in the nude. Perhaps human evolution created the belly button so that women will have somewhere to slip their Kleenex.

Sara interrupted my train of thought.

"I really didn't want to take you for a ride . . ."

She paused for effect. Unfortunately her attempt failed miserably, smashing as it did into the wall of my increasing mood of bloody-mindedness. Sara realized this and decided to lay on the pathos with a trowel.

"It so happens, whatever you may think, that Walter Celi was the first man in my life. I'd decided that when it happened, it would be with someone who counted – and that's how it turned out."

"Meaning?"

"Meaning that I fell in love with him at first sight . . ."

My hair stood on end like Elvis Presley's quiff. But this was a scene from *Gone With The Wind*, and I had no intention of singing *Love Me Tender*.

"Listen, young lady . . ."

She looked at me as if she realized that, if I was calling her "young lady" after calling her "Sara", there was trouble brewing.

"You're not getting me to travel five thousand miles in a damn aeroplane only to palm me off with a love-at-first-sight story. Don't you think that, whether this is a farce or a tragedy, I might just deserve a few more specific details right now? Are you telling me that he galloped up on a white horse, plucked the flower of your virginity and then vanished into thin air? Are you telling me that all the time you were with him, he never told you who he was, where he was living, when he was there and what he was doing there?"

In spite of myself, the tone of my voice had risen a few decibels too many. Hercule Poirot and several waiters were staring apprehensively in our direction, and the other customers looked on disapprovingly. Sara snuffled, and the Kleenex reappeared.

"We met in the street market, ten minutes after the photo was taken. You have to believe me, I'm not some stupid little girl . . ."

"No," I interrupted her. "You're just a little girl. I'm the stupid one here."

Sara's voice was so heartbroken that she'd have made the Little Match Girl sound arrogant in comparison.

"No, Uncle, when I heard his voice I realized that something totally special was happening – the stranger I was talking to, just because he happened to be there, had already become someone important for me. And suddenly, instead of hearing a voice saying 'wait', I heard a voice saying 'now', and that's when what happened happened . . ."

I found a range of succulent but rather unedifying retorts springing to my lips. I chewed them over for a while. But then I swallowed hard. After all, Sara had made a choice and this deserved respect, whether it was the right choice or the wrong one. My silence drove her to pursue her story, and it was an uphill climb.

"I more or less dropped my friends, and he rented a cottage right by the sea. We only went out . . ."

This was a moment of justifiable embarrassment. Lowered gaze. Kleenex screwed into a ball. The unmistakable presence of divine justice.

"We only went out to eat or to swim. I don't think I've ever been so happy in all my life. Everything I'd ever read or heard about love seemed to me utterly banal in comparison with what I was feeling . . ."

She immediately corrected herself.

"With what we were feeling . . . He stayed for just under a month, and it just flew by. In a flash. The evening before I left Luca . . ."

"Luca?"

"He'd told me to call him Luca Moro . . ."

"Well, it's better than Seymour Butts, I suppose . . ."

Sara didn't pick up the joke and carried on.

"The evening before I left, Luc . . . I mean Walter . . . wanted to stay in, just the two of us. We'd cooked a special meal for ourselves. He took the motorbike we'd hired and went out to get some champagne and . . ."

"And?" I prodded.

"And from that moment on I never saw him again. I stayed there all by myself for hours on end, wondering what had happened. The house was quite a way from the centre of town, and I was afraid of walking all that distance by myself in the darkness. Then I went to sleep, and the next morning I hitchhiked in and joined my friends at the airport. When the plane took off, I felt as if my heart were being torn to shreds. From then on, I've done nothing but try to work out how to get back here. Then . . ."

She paused. I couldn't help but feel a sense of tenderness towards her. I could imagine her all alone, afraid, working her way through a whole consignment of Kleenex with her trembling fingers and her floods of tears. But, at the same time, I was furious – and this was obvious.

"Then your damn fool of an uncle turned up and gave you a perfectly good excuse for travelling – served up on a silver platter"

Perhaps my words sounded a little bitter.

"And hasn't it occurred to you that behaviour like that is just typical of a man who's found a pretty girl to have a bit of fun with before he leaves her in the lurch?" I added.

I immediately hated myself for these words, but I simultaneously hated the bastard who had caused me to say them and had made my niece cry. And I was sure that it wasn't the first time this had happened to Sara. Perhaps I was being boring and overprotective, but I'd have happily set a bear-trap for him and watched as it snapped shut on his balls. I'd have released him sooner or later, of course. I'm not the vengeful type.

Sara looked up. I had never in all my life seen bluer eyes than hers, as they were shining now, washed by her tears.

"No. That's not the way it is. I just feel it . . ."

Ah well, if everyone were as half-deaf as people in love, the sales figures of hearing aids would rival the turnover of the Medellín drugs cartel.

But I didn't say so. Sara's voice turned into a whisper.

"Then there's something else that's happened. It rather complicates matters . . ."

"What's that?"

"I'm expecting a baby."

Touché. My Adam's apple suddenly started bouncing up and down like a basketball in the hands of Shaquille O'Neal.

"What do you mean, a baby?" I stammered.

Sara took advantage of the point she had just scored to recoup a little of the poise that I had completely lost.

Her next words gave the *coup de grâce* to a man already dead.

"You know those little things that grizzle and wear nappies and sooner or later say 'mummy' and 'daddy'? Well, one of those."

My tongue could have been quietly served up as a veal cutlet *alla Milanese*, and the satisfied customer would have tucked into it with relish.

"And who's told you that you're expecting a baby?"

Sara opened her eyes again and looked at me the way you look at a man who's just disembarked from a spaceship after being abducted by aliens.

"A certain gentleman called the 'gynaecologist', and before that another gentleman called 'Predictor'. Is the opinion of these two experts enough for you?"

I stared down at the floor as if I were looking for the fragments of the flowerpot that had just fallen onto my head. For a while I said nothing. My shorts clung stiffly to my sweaty legs. My niece had the ability to make a man feel like a total saphead.

She gazed at me and, even though she had found her voice again, there was a trace of bewilderment and a flicker of fear in her eyes. After all, she was still just an eighteen-year-old girl.

"What are we going to do now?"

I rose from the table and smoothed down my shorts.

"Now we're going to get some sleep. I feel like a sausage sizzling in its pan, and my brain just won't cooperate in these conditions. Tomorrow morning we can think again."

We went up to our rooms in silence, as if we had done the whole journey in the elevator. We came to a halt in front of her room. I saw how despondent she was looking, and I gave her a hug. She wasn't as tall as me, and the way she leaned her head on my shoulder made me melt with tenderness.

"Come on, everything's going to be all right, just you see."

"Thanks, Uncle."

I pushed her gently away and looked her straight in the eyes. This time it was my turn to leave Oxford.

"'Thanks, Uncle' – oh yeah! This is going to cost you your modest but guaranteed percentage!"

She finally smiled. A tremor of relief was starting to gleam in her worried eyes.

"Frankly, my dear, I don't give a damn. Good night."

300

She shut the door behind her and left me alone in the corridor. I went into my room and, as I was getting undressed, I could hear her in the next room getting ready to go to bed. Through the thin walls, I could hear her talking to somebody. I realized she was on the phone to her parents, telling them that we'd arrived safe and sound and everything was fine and so on and so forth. God only knows what my brother and my sister-in-law, a kind and considerate mother and father, would have said if they'd know they were going to become a kind and considerate grandma and grandpa . . . I got undressed too and climbed into bed. The chorus of frogs, strangely enough, had fallen silent. No doubt the fee paid for the concert didn't include encores. I put out the light and lay in the dark listening to the hum of the air conditioning in the same frame of mind as that with which I had listened to the roar of the aeroplane engines. What Sara had told me continued to bounce around against the walls of my brain like a ping-pong ball.

Still, now that I knew my niece better, I couldn't help but ask myself one thing.

Was the ping-pong ball the news that she had been taking the pill, or the news that she was expecting a baby?

*

"Well?"

As I sat at the wheel of the hired Peugeot, I looked disconsolately at my niece next to me in the passenger seat. It was as hot as hell, in spite of the air conditioning in the car, and we both felt grimy and sweaty. And frustrated. And goddammit.

"Nothing. They haven't seen him here either. I even showed his photo to the geckos."

We were in the car park of the Coconut Golf Club, a kind of mega-structure Ceausescu would have been proud of, with eighteen holes, yes, eighteen, and a clubhouse that must have been run by Jean-Luc Picard in person. Our dusty, clapped-out old banger looked like Cinderella's carriage at five minutes past midnight.

We're on a hiding to nothing, I thought.

We'd scoured the whole island, up and down and side to side, and we hadn't been able to get the spider out of his hole. We hadn't even found the hole, actually. The morning after our arrival we'd started off from the market in which the photo had been taken and from there had embarked on an odyssey that would have made Marco Polo grow pale with envy. The agency from which Walter had rented the cottage hadn't been much help. They'd been paid in advance and hadn't been able to tell us a thing. Sara didn't know where the motorbike had been hired from, and in any case, in a place where, as the signs announced, it was possible to "rent a bike" almost anywhere, it would have been a fool's errand to track down the hire agent.

We'd visited the places in which she and Walter had been together and then pretty much everywhere else: hotels, travel agents, accommodation agents, ports, airports, shops, nightclubs, bars, restaurants and chemists'. We'd interrogated men black and white, women, children, homosexuals, whores, scuba-diving instructors bobbing in the waves, dogs, cats, horses and even the odd statue or two. Just to make absolutely sure, I had brought with me, as well as the photos of his bearded self, some old photos of Walter Celi in his clean-shaven guise.

Nothing. Nix. Nobody knew him. Nobody had ever seen him. The answer was always the same. A shake of the head and a "*Non, Monsieur, jamais vu*" that was now engraved on me like a tattoo. I'd also managed to pick up a couple of *fuck off*s in Creole but, since I had understood only their general and not their particular import, they hadn't hurt so much.

Our disappointment was evident even though there wasn't much to be expected from a situation of this kind, when we thought it over. Swept away by the euphoria of my scoop, I too hadn't considered the difficulties of finding someone in a tourist spot to which, every day, an alarming number of new faces throng. I had taken it for granted, in a rather hit-and-miss way, that the fugitive had been living on the island, or at least would have been there long enough to leave a few traces, but this was obviously not so.

He'd probably just been passing through, he probably lived somewhere else entirely and spent his life drifting like a nomad across the world. Probably . . .

Fuck off. This time in my own language.

Sara and I looked at each other. The brilliant sun outside the car windows cast a long shadow of disappointment across our faces. She looked tired.

"How are you feeling?"

There was obviously a note of apprehension in my voice that made her suddenly angry.

"You couldn't by any chance be suffering from male anxieties over a pregnant woman, could you? I'm feeling absolutely fine. How the hell do you expect me to feel? It's just that all this is a real pain in the butt. And it's so freaking hot . . ."

I didn't take advantage of my great experience in the matter to explain to Sara that a pain in the butt is unlikely to leave you sitting comfortably at the best of times. It didn't seem the right time to lay it on with a trowel. Anyway, she was the one most affected. I could throw money around and draw on my prestige as a twopenny-halfpenny journalist, but it was her life that was on the line, as the newly emerging facts had made clear.

As I drove off, since the car was where we happened to be, I brought up the question that I had been burning to ask for several days.

"Have you decided yet what you're going to do about the baby?"

Sara stared straight ahead of her at the street as I entered and then left a township by the name of Capesterre-Bel-le-Eau, which was actually much smaller than the road sign indicating its name, and turned into the road that led to Trois Rivières, past an incessant procession of palms, dust and tropical vegetation.

"I don't know. I can't stop thinking about it, and I can't make my mind up. I don't think of myself as a ninny – in fact I'm a pretty practical person, generally speaking – but this time I really don't know which way to turn . . ."

As she spoke, she started to wring her hands, and for the first time I saw her for what she really was: a lost, frightened girl. The full responsibility rested on her shoulders, and she alone, nobody else, could press the button that would change her life. The only thing I could do was reassure her that she could always count on my support. So this is what I did.

She looked at me as if she were seeing me for the first time.

"There's nobody like you, Riccardo. You're much nicer than

you make yourself out to be and maybe nicer than you actually think. When we set off on the trail of this story, I was looking for somebody on your behalf, to help you do your job – but after everything I've told you, I know that you're looking for him on *my* behalf. I can't thank you enough."

This session of psychoanalysis was taking a turn I didn't like. I refused to allow my niece to shrink me and fillet me like a tuna fish and dissect me with a bread stick, like in the ads. I made the car do a slalom-type swerve and shook us out of that moment of shared emotion.

"I've just had an idea."

"Namely?"

"We're in the Caribbean. We've got sun, sea and coconuts. Why don't we take an afternoon off? Driving around like this, we're getting about as suntanned as lorry drivers. I tell you what we can do . . ."

I stopped the car at a sort of lay-by. Or rather, the spot in question became a lay-by as soon as I had decided that it was one. The road ran along the sea, and to our left lay a beach that was to a quite shameless degree filled with white sand, next to a blue sea, not to mention the equally blue sky. I opened the door on my side of the car, walked round the car and went to open hers.

"We're going to have a nice little swim in this picture-postcard place, and until tomorrow, as the pinball machines say, *game over!*"

Sara climbed out of the car and, without uttering a word, slipped off the T-shirt she was wearing, to display the upper part of a swimming costume and a smile that said *silence indicates consent.* We walked over the road and made our way across the beach that was overlooked by a long line of palm trees, listening to the sand crunching under our feet like face powder. We deposited our few clothes in a little heap next to the water's edge and dived into the sea. We stayed there, playing about in the warm, crystal-clear waves like two kids, laughing, splashing each other, and swimming side by side with long, slow strokes. Half an hour later I dragged myself out of the water, panting. Too many cigarettes, too many nights of partying and rock 'n' roll and not enough sport – in the final analysis I couldn't keep up any longer. I collapsed on the beach, in the shade of a palm tree, and gratefully relaxed on the warm, crumbling sand. Sara stayed out swimming, and I lay down on my side, parallel to the water's edge. I watched her for a while. All of a sudden, I heard a muffled thud behind me. I looked round and spotted a big coconut lying on the ground where, a minute before, there had been nothing. In my mind's eye I could clearly see the headlines: "Famous Columnist Is Killed in Guadeloupe by a Coconut". I had a vision of my funeral with all of my friends there. They'd never stop laughing. I got up and moved over to the place where we had left our clothes. Just then, Sara started to come in out of the water and headed towards the clothes too. We reached the pile at the same moment, and I had an opportunity to admire her in all her beauty. Maybe I was biased, but still . . .

In any case, Walter Celi had thought exactly the same, and we would have living proof of the fact a few months later. Nine, to be exact.

"This is just fantastic!" said Sara as she leaned her head to one side, wringing the water out of her long hair. A few drops of water fell onto the beach, and the sand drank them in thirstily.

"Sure is. It's just a pity we can't . . ."

Sara suddenly heaved a sigh, raised her eyes heavenwards, and, with a movement that seemed too fluid to be natural, her knees folded beneath her. I just managed to catch her before she fell to the ground. She went limp in my arms, leaving me to wrestle with a doubt worthy of Hamlet: what does a man do when he finds himself alone on a Caribbean beach with a young woman who's pregnant and has just fainted?

*

"And how is she now?"

My sister-in-law's voice sounded a little shrill, perhaps due to the fact she was speaking on the phone, perhaps because she was worried.

"She's perfectly okay. She just felt weak due to the heat and the sun, that's all. The doctor who saw her said that everything's just fine, she's in great shape. He's keeping her in hospital overnight just as a precaution . . ."

"Who's with her now?"

"For God's sake, Marzia, she's not the Lady of the Camellias. Your daughter's already kicked up a rumpus because she wants to leave, and whoever's with her now, unless it's the Devil in person, must be having a hell of a time."

"But the place is at least clean, I hope?"

"Of course it's clean. The day they need to hospitalise me, I'll ask to be brought here. It looks more like a florist's than a hospital. There are more bougainvilleas than syringes."

My sister-in-law seemed reassured.

"All right. It's a good thing you're there, Riccardo. I'll ring off now, keep me informed and if I need to fly out there, just tell me."

"No, there's no need for you to come all this way. I'll phone you tomorrow. Ciao."

"Ciao."

I hung up the phone and snorted. In this whole business, the most onerous task by far had been this telephone call. I paid the cashier behind the bar (an almost toothless, hairless gent) for my drink and phone call and went out. He continued to pick his nose, each nostril in turn, gazing meditatively at the fan hanging from the ceiling, praying that Our Lady of This Part of The World might miraculously get it working again. I crossed the road where, instead of *fiat lux, lux non fuit*, and went through the gate of the hospital to which I had taken Sara. I walked down the entrance path, leaving on my left the car park where I'd put the car, and entered the cool, well-lit main hall, immediately enjoying the benefits of the air conditioning.

After Sara's fainting fit, I'd been filled with an overwhelming panic that would have made a meeting with Freddie Kruger a picnic in comparison. I'd tried to bring her round by splashing her with a little seawater, but it had been no use. I'd made sure she was breathing as she should be and carried her to my car, reclining the seat so that she could lie out full length but with her head slightly raised. I'd hit the gas and headed for Basse-Terre, a big centre some twelve miles away, where I hoped to find something resembling an emergency ward. On my way in, I broke every rule (except the "no parking" rule) in Guadeloupe's Highway Code, which in any case could probably fit onto a single page, given the way everyone drives hereabouts. At a certain moment, Sara had started to return to the land of the living, simultaneously allowing me to do the same.

This time, I breathed a sigh of relief that could have shattered the windscreen.

"You okay?"

"More or less . . . What happened?"

"What happened was that you fainted. And I almost died of panic."

She propped herself up on one elbow and stretched her head round to look at the road. She was a little pale, but, all things considered, she looked pretty normal.

"If it's of any interest to you, the same thought is going through my head right now. Could you slow down?"

I'd lessened the pressure of my foot on the accelerator. Almost immediately, the huge cloud of dust the car was kicking up diminished by half. We entered the town at a more or less normal speed, and I followed the signs to the nearest hospital. Sara protested.

"I'm not going into any hospital round here, not even if I'm dead."

With the frown of an adult for a wilful child, I silenced her.

"But that's exactly where we are going. I promise you that if we don't get a medic but a witch doctor with a bone through his nose, we'll leave. But up until then, you'll do as I say."

As I argued and she protested, we suddenly found ourselves outside a small hospital that seemed to have been built more by a stage designer than an architect. I wouldn't have been at all surprised if the nurses had all at once emerged in an all-singing, all-dancing group like in the musicals. It was an elegant, low building in a V-shape, built with a nod to local architectural styles, with plenty of wood and bamboo. There was a central building where the emergency ward was located, together with Reception; on either side there were two wings for the in-patients' rooms. Everywhere was spotlessly clean, and it was all surrounded by a tropical garden that would have made a professional botanist go green with envy.

We'd both been reassured by this sight, and our first impressions had been corroborated by the extreme efficiency demonstrated by the staff. The doctor who had a look at Sara was an American with blondish copper-coloured hair – someone I could have easily imagined in a football team. He'd calmed my fears about Sara's fainting fit, but when I told him she was pregnant, he expressed his firm desire, or rather ordered, that my niece spend at least one night in hospital.

Sara had grumbled a bit about this, but she was probably so favourably impressed by the quality of the place that the idea of spending the night there didn't cause her so much worry. A nurse with a uniform whiter than white, with the dazzling whiteness you see only in washing-powder ads, led us down the long corridor to a room that was not at all bad, at least not for a hospital room. I waited while Sara got into bed and left her there by herself while I went in search of a telephone – the one in the hospital was out of order. I made the ritual phone call to my brother and my sister-in-law and now I was heading back to Sara's room.

Stop!

I smiled at the secretary sitting at Reception and crossed the main hall to the corridor on my left. I walked all the way down it and absent-mindedly, without entering, walked into the last door on the right. Even now I'm glad I did so. I immediately realized that I'd got the wrong room. Wrapped in my own thoughts, I'd taken the corridor that led to the rooms for male patients – perhaps I was confused by the fact that we'd first come in from the other side.

A fraction of a second after entering the room, my heart soared like a man on a flying trapeze. I couldn't believe my eyes and my incredible good luck.

Lying in bed, with his leg in plaster, was Walter Celi.

*

"And you went to all this trouble to find me?"

I bristled.

"Oh, I went to all this trouble . . . ? Do you have any idea of the mess you left behind you in Italy when you disappeared? Even now there are people who'd hand their own mothers in to the Gestapo just to know what became of you. And then you come here under an assumed name, meet a girl, et cetera, et cetera, and then pop off again. You do a better disappearing act than David Copperfield."

Walter was still lying in bed, and Sara was sitting on a chair next to him. They were holding hands. They looked suntanned, crumpled and happy. Straight after accidentally entering the wrong room without knowing that it was actually the right one, I'd left a laconic *sorry!* floating in the air behind me, dashed to Sara's room, swept her up without a word and dragged her to a blissful *well-well-just-look-who-it-is!* Well, the two had stared at each other in disbelief and then hugged with a joy that I would never have imagined. Especially from him – there were tears in his eyes and probably music in his ears. Sara was wearing the same expression as Bernadette when she saw her vision of the Madonna at Lourdes. I quietly left the room, feeling that my presence wasn't needed and my absence discreetly desired. I returned the following morning, but I don't think they even noticed.

But now, perhaps, I deserved something of an explanation.

Walter stared at me with the dark gaze I remembered, the one that had set the TV cameras alight and given the viewers the impression he was sitting in their own living room with them. Four years had gone by, and he'd put on a few pounds in weight, but he didn't look any the worse for it, and his charisma was still intact.

"I've already explained everything to Sara. I got run over by a car the last night she was here, when I went off on my motorbike to get the wine. The next morning, I woke up here, with my leg in traction . . ."

Sara was radiant and eager to explain everything all at once. She interrupted him, "He doesn't live here, which is why we couldn't find any trace of him . . ."

"I've got a house in Marie-Galante, the island off Guadeloupe. I almost never travel anywhere and if I do, I try not to go more than twice to the same place. I use a light aircraft that I pilot myself. There are plenty of small islands within easy reach in just a couple of hours by plane, so it's not difficult to get around without being noticed. There's a semi-private landing field here, next to Lamentin, a kind of control tower with a pretty bumpy clay landing strip where it's possible to stop and fill up without too many questions being asked. And I usually leave big tips so people are happy to pretend they don't know me . . ."

That was why nobody had been able to help us, either at the airport or anywhere else. Our hero moved from place to place under his own steam, and I could have kicked myself for forgetting that he was the proud possessor of a pilot's licence. I'd seen more than one photo of him looking like the Red Baron in times gone by. But I managed not to feel too stupid – after all, perhaps without realizing it, Walter had sown the seeds of doubt in my mind. From his words I surmised a hunted, hidden life, which he probably took for granted, but which I could barely imagine.

"When I met Sara . . ."

Walter turned and smiled to her. It was if a light had been turned on in a mirror. My niece returned his smile with eyes shining like a car's headlights on full-beam. The silence that fell between them was more eloquent than any speech.

And yet there was still one thing that I wanted to know.

Why?

Walter looked at me the way a knot of tangled hair looks at a comb. He knew that I'd have asked this question sooner or later. He knew that, sooner or later, someone would have turned up to ask him, and he'd have to give an answer. He feared this moment and probably, at the same time, desired it. No plane on earth is fast enough to whisk you away from your inner demons. He started to speak like a man getting a huge weight off his mind.

"Well, you remember, four years ago, the kind of life I was leading . . ."

I nodded.

"I was in a real mess. You can't imagine. Not that I didn't enjoy it; I'd been working for ages and every satisfaction was welcome, however much time and energy it consumed. Each time that I felt pissed off at having to sign autographs day in day out, I told myself that I'd be much more pissed off if nobody was asking for my autograph at all. Basically, it was thanks to the public that I drove around in a BMW and kept a Ferrari in the garage – so I felt I owed my public something in return. Then I started that series . . ."

He hoisted himself into a more comfortable position in bed, and Sara helped him arrange the cushion. After that, Walter raised his eyes to the ceiling: but there was something vacant in his gaze.

"Everything was going just hunky-dory, we were full of enthusiasm, it was marvellous – we were a fantastic success. Then along came that episode, the one Vicky was supposed to take part in . . ."

He paused for so long I started to get gooseflesh. A fly buzzing round the room suddenly fell silent. It was probably keen to hear the story too.

"The rehearsals started three days before the live broadcast. Usually we got together on Tuesdays to discuss the treatment, on Wednesdays there was the writers' meeting, and on Thursdays they started rehearsing the songs and dances. The rehearsals with the guests happened on Fridays, or, if there were any problems getting them there, during the dress rehearsal on Saturday afternoon . . ."

I lit a cigarette and listened in fascination to the sound of his voice. I wasn't in the least bit surprised that he'd been such a success. It was a pleasure just listening to him, irrespective of what he was saying. He'd have been just as enthralling if he'd been reading from the proverbial phone book.

"It was on the Thursday, as I remember, that I saw the man for the first time. He was standing a little to one side, always somewhat apart from the centre of activity, as if he was there visiting or accompanying somebody. I didn't pay much attention to him, to tell you the truth, since a TV studio is always total mayhem. This one, given our success, was a real hive of activity – journalists, stage managers, press agents and what have you . . . anyone and everyone was there. What did attract my attention, more than his strange clothes, was his lollipop . . ."

I looked at him, intrigued. Sara's face wore pretty much the same expression as I imagine mine did.

"The lollipop?"

Walter didn't seem to have heard and carried on with his story as if he were really talking to himself.

"He was wearing a dark suit made of some strange fabric that seemed to reflect the light in an odd way, as if the colours were floating on the surface and then fading back into it. He had a yellow shirt and a red bow tie, if I remember rightly, and a waistcoat with a flower motif – the flowers looked real, as if picked out in relief on it . . ."

It seemed as if his memory were stirring up new details, as if the fact of speaking about these things had brought to light particulars that he hadn't noticed at the time.

"And he always one of those round lollipops in his mouth, the Chupa Chups sort that Kojak liked – you know the ones. You could see the little stick emerging from the corner of his mouth and the swelling in his cheek. He was gazing all around him, with a curious, innocent air, as if he'd never seen any of this before. Then Vicky arrived, and I didn't pay him any more attention – wherever that girl went, she brought chaos in her wake. She was an absolute pain in the balls, poor dear, because she knew she had no artistic talent whatsoever, apart from her physical endowments. She couldn't dance, she couldn't sing, she couldn't act – but she was one of the most beautiful women I've ever seen . . ."

He glanced at Sara and squeezed her hand with a gesture that obviously meant "present company excepted". Then he went on:

"She made up for her deficiencies by sheer force of will and by rehearsing obsessively. We were supposed to be doing a thing together, a kind of medley of songs from the shows – this was after an interview in which she'd be talking about her experiences in Hollywood. She drove the writers and producers just crazy, since – like all insecure people – she needed continual reassurance. Her PA, poor man, was for ever on the verge of a heart attack but, somehow or other, it all seemed to work. Ever since she'd arrived, the whole studio had filled up with people who'd found one excuse or another to come and gawp. They were mainly men, so I wasn't all that astonished to see this guy with the lollipop wandering round too. He stood there, quite a small man with chubby cheeks, his hands behind his back and the little stick of his lolly jutting out of his mouth, just watching. That was all. Watching."

Walter was finally putting into words something he'd been carrying round inside himself for a long, long time. And it was like a huge weight he was lifting from off his heart. Sara tenderly stroked his hair.

"On Friday we all went off to have dinner, once we were through with the rehearsals. There were the producers, my agent, the director, Vicky and her PA and myself. We went to . . ."

He mentioned the name of a restaurant that I knew very well. It wasn't all that wonderful, but, thanks to one of those strange alchemical processes, it had become fashionable in the showbiz world, and there were plenty of people there prepared to pay exorbitant prices just to have dinner sitting next to the stars of TV and cinema. Such is the way of the world.

"All eyes were on us – and especially on her. The men devoured her with their eyes. The women could have burned her alive. You know how it is . . ."

I knew all right.

"The manager led us into a small separate room that he'd reserved for us, and as we followed him I noticed, at a table on the right, in a corner next to the door, sitting all by himself, the little guy with the dark jacket. It was difficult not to notice that yellow shirt and that absurd red bow tie. I remember that he'd placed an unwrapped lollipop on the tablecloth next to his plate. As we sat down, I asked Gorla, the producer, who the devil this guy could be.

"'What guy?' he replied.

"'That little guy with the dark jacket who keeps wandering round the studios with a lollipop stuck in his mouth.'

"Vicky came to my aid.

"'You mean a guy with a yellow shirt and a red bow tie? The one sitting over there?'

"'That's the one. You've noticed him too?'

"'Of course. He's not exactly inconspicuous.'

"The conversation carried on along the same lines, until eventually Gorla got up and went into the other room to see who we were talking about with his own eyes. When he came back, he said that there was nobody at all sitting at the table we'd indicated . . ."

I didn't have any idea why, but at this point I started to feel a distinct sense of unease. All of a sudden I wasn't at all sure I wanted to know how the story was going to end. But Walter carried on as if anxious to finish it. He was now on the home stretch, galloping down the final furlongs.

"It didn't go any further – after all, it wasn't all that important. Then came the broadcast, and you know how that turned out. The sensation I felt when I realized Vicky was dead was, in order of importance, the second most dreadful thing I've ever experienced in my whole life."

Walter paused. The hairs on the back of my arms were standing bolt upright like hundreds of toy soldiers on parade. But I couldn't help asking, "And what was the first?"

Walter looked into my eyes, and I didn't like what I saw in his gaze. I didn't like it one little bit.

"That night, when I went home, I was devastated. Everyone had been so shocked and cut up when they took Vicky's body away. It shakes you up, seeing a person like her, so full of life and beauty, being carried off on a stretcher covered by a white sheet. It shakes you up, seeing a man with a yellow shirt and a lollipop stuck in his mouth watching the ambulance door close with just the same curiosity he'd shown for the dance rehearsals . . ."

There was a tremor of dread in Walter's narrative, and this dread was now starting to transmit itself to us too. The air conditioning must have suddenly started to kick in full blast, since I suddenly felt a cold shiver run down my back.

"I usually videoed all my broadcasts, like everyone else. Usually I watched the programme the next day so I could take pleasure in the things I'd done well and improve on the things I'd done not quite so well. Instead, that evening, the minute I got home, I don't know why, I went over to the TV and watched the recording of the programme straight away. I fast-forwarded the tape until the moment when I was introducing Vicky. The orchestra struck up the signature tune, she emerged from the wings and started to come down the stairs. And just a step or so behind her, following her like a shadow, was *the man in the dark jacket and yellow shirt.*"

By now the hair was standing up all over my body, like quills upon the fretful porpentine. Sara gave Walter's hand an extra squeeze. I saw that her eyes were filled with tears. Walter's voice was trembling slightly, as if he wanted to bring his narrative to a close but couldn't.

"I saw the poor girl walking down the stairs to a big round of applause, I saw her coming up to where I was waiting for her in the middle of the stage and, just after we'd said hello to one another, I saw the man behind her lift his hand and touch her temple . . ."

His voice broke, and there was a brief, timeless moment of silence.

"Vicky slid to the ground and died. In the recording I saw the moment when I was leaning over her while the studio director came on, but now the only thing that interested me was the man with the dark jacket. As Vicky lay there, and we started flapping over her, I saw him take a lollipop out of his pocket, calmly unwrap it, pop it in his mouth and quietly leave the studio.

He stopped to draw breath.

"I don't know how I managed to stay sane . . ."

Sara and I looked at him. I think our expressions must have given away what we were feeling. The room felt icy cold. Walter interpreted our bewilderment as scepticism.

"You're free not to believe me – I really don't care one way or the other. I know what I saw, and that's enough for me. I immediately called my agent, made him get out of bed and come over to my apartment. I was screaming at him – I was in a state of total panic, maybe I even had a panic attack, I don't know. The fact remains that when he arrived he told me I looked like a madman. I practically forced him to sit in the armchair, and I made him watch the recording of the broadcast. When we arrived at the crucial moment, I found myself standing there in front of Marati, my agent, who was staring at me as if I really was off my head. In the recording that I'd just shown him the man with the lollipop had vanished. I was there, Vicky was there, and so was everyone else, but there was no trace of the man I'd seen before . . ."

Walter removed his hand from Sara's embrace to reach for a bottle of water on the bedside table. He took a long swig from it. This left us time to take in what we had just heard.

There was one question I was burning to ask. It was all so incredible, but if I were to formulate this question, it would more or less imply that I believed his story. And I did.

"And the man with the lollipop . . . did you ever see him again?"

Walter stretched out in his bed and seemed reassured: a burden shared is a burden halved, or so they say.

"No, I never saw him again. But once was enough. Even now I still dream of him, every now and again, and I'd prefer not to. Especially because, out of all the people there, I know this for certain: *only Vicky and I had seen him.*"

He paused for a moment to let the significance of what he had said sink in. Then he continued.

"That's why I disappeared. The next day, I went to a lawyer friend of mine and signed a proxy so he could sell everything I owned. I closed my bank accounts and transferred all my money to a numbered account in Barbados that I'd opened via a bank in Monte Carlo. Thanks to an organization that helps anyone who wishes to disappear to get away without leaving any traces behind, I managed to obtain ID papers, a new name and a place to live. The rest you know. But there's only one thing I'm completely sure about. For as long as I live I'm never setting foot in a television studio again."

Silence hovered in the room, just above the floor, like a cloud of dry ice. The only sound was the hum of the air conditioning. Sara got up off her seat, went over and gave Walter a hug. The two held each other for a while in silence. And this silence was, again, a form of speech from which I was excluded.

I went over to the window and stood gazing out. Suddenly the bougainvilleas no longer seemed so colourful, and the leaves of the plants no longer looked so green. There was the sun and there was a patch of sky, up above, beyond the edge of the roof, but all of a sudden they'd lost any allure.

I didn't know what to think. In spite of myself, I found myself remembering, with a bitter smile, Li'l Abner, when he said that there's nothing more confusing than confusion.

My prevailing impression was that, well, I'd been the one to take the lid off the can. Now I'd have to swallow the worms.

*

Opening the door to my apartment, I was almost surprised to see that everything was just as I'd left it. However, the cleaning lady had taken advantage of my absence to inflict a major blow on my habitual disorder. I'd need a whole week to find where I'd put things, but basically I wasn't too unhappy to be entering an apartment that, for once, seemed as if a real human being lived there.

Sara had stayed on in Guadeloupe with Walter Celi. They'd soon moved into the house in Marie-Galante.

Together.

Perhaps true love doesn't exist, but the love between these two seemed to me an adequate substitute that would stand them in good stead for quite a while. Then, life being what it is, we have to take risks. It's not possible to put on a condom, as you can on other occasions. In any case, when you're on a motorbike and your head starts itching, it's no use scratching your helmet.

Before leaving, I'd gone to the airport to pick up my brother and my sister-in-law, who'd arrived as soon as they could after they'd spoken to Sara by phone. Marzia had broken into lamentations at the news of the forthcoming baby, and my brother had kept a stern silence, but – as happens in films – justice had eventually triumphed, and they'd all kissed and made up.

Amen to that.

*

I left my suitcase in the corridor and breathed in the smells of home for a while. Through the half-open window came the noise of the Rome traffic, and there was something reassuring about the sight of the dome of St Peter's. I went over to my computer and switched on the screen to pick up the messages from the fax plugged into the modem.

There were a few messages from wannabe girlfriends, an urgent little inquiry from Manni who hadn't heard from me for a while, a colleague who needed an address, the secretary of an agency urgently inquiring after an invoice and a couple of friends asking whatever had become of Riccardo Falchi.

I lit a cigarette and flung myself into an armchair. The last question was one that had been going round in my own thoughts too. Perhaps the question I'd come up against in my hotel room in Guadeloupe needed an immediate reply, perhaps I smoked too many cigarettes, perhaps I was getting old, perhaps . . .

I sat there thinking and smoking and finally decided that it was time to do it. I got up and went into my room, where there sat in splendour – apart from the bed, which was the real star exhibit – a forty-inch cinema-style Grundig TV set. I went to sort through my video cassettes until I found what I was looking for. I knew what it was. I'd set it up to record that programme and then I'd just put it in with the other videos without even watching it. I was sure I'd never taped over it.

Sitting on my bed, I stared at the video I was holding as if it were some object of unknown provenance. And as I stared at it, my eyes glazed over and reality was replaced by memory. I thought back to that evening, I saw it as if through the lens of a movie camera – I saw my hand locking the car door, my walk to the main studio entrance; I saw the people I'd greeted as I turned into the corridor, I saw the doors of the dressing rooms with the names of their occupants, and the open doors of the dresser and the make-up girl.

And then I saw *him*.

As I entered the studio where the show was just about to start, right at the entrance, I'd crossed the path of that odd man with the dark jacket and the little stick jutting out of the corner of his mouth and his cheek swollen by the round lollipop. There'd been that momentary hesitation that always happens when one person is coming out of a door while someone else is trying to enter. We'd stood there for a moment, before slipping past each other, he on the right and I on the left. The colour of his shirt and that waistcoat with its design of flowers that seemed picked out in relief were just a brief flicker in my memory. His eyes were in front of me, just as sharp as the first and only time our gazes had met, close enough for me clearly to distinguish his pupils, in which the colour was not immobile but seemed to be permanently changing. It was like leaning, for a moment, over the edge of a well, in which the water reflecting the moon was not a flat mirror, but moved as if being drawn into the eddy of a whirlpool. Only now did I understand the strange sensation that strange, chubby-faced little guy had caused me to feel. And then I was in a hurry, in a wretched hurry to get there, to see what I wanted to see, hear what I wanted to hear and find out what I wanted to find out. There's always a reason for the things that happen. You can pretend that's not the case, and come and go and sleep and think you're living, or hide your head under the sheet until someone or something comes along to show you that it's all in vain.

But I didn't put the video on. At that moment, it would have been absolutely superfluous. I thought of Walter Celi, I thought of Vicky Merlino and of myself, as I rose to my feet and went into the living room to pour myself a large glass of something strong. Three people united by the chains of causality and perhaps by the unhealthy curiosity to find out what that lollipop had tasted of. It had probably not been any coincidence that I, I myself and nobody else, had managed to find out where Walter was hiding. This was the mystery I needed to solve, even if I didn't know where to start looking. But I had time, perhaps too much time, to do so, even though I had no desire for the task.

There would be other days and other nights, and my acquaintances would inevitably start asking what had happened to me, what had become of the person they'd known, the one who could laugh and joke even when faced by the Devil in person. There would be no point at all in showing them the video. I was sure that, if other people watched it, the man with the lollipop and the dark jacket who was there for me would not be there for them.

And the answer to all these questions could only be the same.

Now I was afraid.

About the Authors

Niccolò Ammaniti was born in Rome. His novels *I'm Not Scared* and *Steal You Away* were international bestsellers, translated in forty-four countries.

Andrea Camilleri was born in Sicily and began his career as a stage director in 1942. He is a leading figure in the Mediterranean Noir movement. His well-loved Inspector Montalbano series includes *The Shape of Water* and *The Voice of the Violin*.

Massimo Carlotto, born in Padua and living in Cagliari, has published *The Goodbye Kiss* and *Death's Dark Abyss,* among others, in the UK and the US.

Sandrone Dazieri is from Cremona. This is the first time his work is available in English. His novel *La cura del gorilla* is being made into a film.

Diego De Silva was born in Naples. Following the success of *Certi bambini* (2001), he has concentrated on crime writing as a means of social critique. *I Want to Watch*, his first novel to be translated in English, came out in 2007.

Giancarlo De Cataldo is an appeals court judge in Rome and the author of the novel *Romanzo Criminale*, which was made into a much-acclaimed film in 2005.

Giorgio Faletti, actor, songwriter and author of the thriller *Io uccido*, which sold over a million copies, lives in the Asti region in northern Italy.

Marcello Fois was born in Nuoro, Sardinia, and won the Italo Calvino Prize in 1992. His novels *The Advocate* and *Blood from the Skies* were recently published and widely reviewed in Anglophone countries.

Carlo Lucarelli, born in Parma and living near Imola, is the author of eleven noir novels. His first to be translated into English, *Almost Blue*, was shortlisted for the CWA Gold Dagger prize.

Antonio Manzini is a young Roman author. 'You Are My Treasure Chest', written with Niccolò Ammaniti, is his first published work.